THE GUEST BOOK

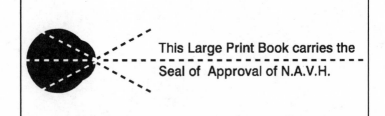

This Large Print Book carries the
Seal of Approval of N.A.V.H.

WITHDRAWN

The Guest Book

Sarah Blake

THORNDIKE PRESS
A part of Gale, a Cengage Company

A Cengage Company

Farmington Hills, Mich • San Francisco • New York • Waterville, Maine
Meriden, Conn • Mason, Ohio • Chicago

LIBRARY OF CONGRESS CIP DATA ON FILE.
CATALOGUING IN PUBLICATION FOR THIS BOOK
IS AVAILABLE FROM THE LIBRARY OF CONGRESS

ISBN-13: 978-1-4328-6639-6 (hardcover alk. paper)

Published in 2019 by arrangement with Macmillan Publishing Group, LLC/Flatiron Books

Printed in the United States of America
1 2 3 4 5 6 7 23 22 21 20 19

For Eli and Gus

And in memory of my brother,
T. Whitney Blake, 1962–2017

People are trapped in history and history is trapped in them.

— JAMES BALDWIN

Surely it was time someone invented a new plot.

— VIRGINIA WOOLF

"It's the usual story," the man at the tiller reflected, regarding the beautiful derelict on the hill. "At the end of old money there is real estate."

There were three of them in the boat that Saturday in June. They had set out from Rockland, Maine, on a day's sail into the bay, and tacking into a cove of one of the many granite islands eight or nine miles offshore had come face-to-face with the great white house before them, some sea captain's pride, sitting squarely on top of a long lawn leading down to a boathouse and dock.

The house needed paint. The lawn needed cutting. The boathouse roofline sagged and the shingles slipped. Empty of boats, the dock in front of them had been patched and patched again.

It was magnificent.

"I'm waiting for it to go up for sale," the host of the weekend went on. "Low-hanging fruit."

9

"Whose is it?" the man sitting beside him asked.

"One of those families who used to run the world." The host stretched his legs, pressing his bare feet against the boat's hull. "WASPs."

"WASPs?" The other chuckled. "Do they even exist anymore except in their own heads?"

The host smiled. He had just made a fortune in health care.

"What happened?" the man beside him asked.

"The usual, I'd suspect. Drinking, apathy, dullards in the gene pool."

"What's their name?"

"Don't know." He jimmied the boom. "Milton? The Miltons?"

"Milton?" The third man, the man in the bow, who had been staring up at the house all this while, turned around. "As in Milton Higginson, the bankers?"

"Sounds right," answered the host, pulling the mainsail in so the wind caught, sending them on an angle out of the cove and back into the channel, running with the wind along the coastline of the island. The sailors fell into a companionable silence, punctuated by the host's "Ready about" and "Hard to lee," calling them to shift their weight from one side of the Herreshoff to the other, leaving room for the boom to sail unchecked over their heads.

"It's one of those tragic families," he said as they reached the end of the island's granite spine. "They say somebody drowned there."

"Where?"

"Just there, off those rocks." He pointed to a mound of white granite boulders humped high above the waterline, backed by a ridge of spruce rising into the sky.

There was nothing to see.

"Ready about," the man at the tiller said. And they tacked away.

THE ANCHORESS

ONE

The fall had turned to winter and then back again without conviction, November's chill taken up and dropped like a woman never wearing the right coat until finally December laughed and took hold. Then the ice on the black pathways through the park fixed an unreflecting gaze upward month after month, the cold unwavering through what should have been spring, so that even in April, in the Bowery in New York City, the braziers still glowed on street corners, and a man trying to warm his hands could watch the firelight picked up and carried in the windows above his head and imagine the glow traveling all the way along the avenues, square by square above the streets, all the way uptown and into the warm apartments of those who, pausing on the threshold to turn off the light, left their rooms and descended in woolens and furs, grumbling about the cold — *good god, when will it end?* — until it turned without fanfare one morning in May, and spring let loose at last. All over the city, children were released from their winter coats and out into the greening arms of Central Park. *So here we all are again,* thought Kitty Milton, stepping into the taxicab on the way to meet her mother at the Philharmonic.

It was 1935.

She wore a soft cloche hat that belled below her ears, casting her eyes into shadow and making more pronounced the soft white of her chin tipped forward a little upon her long neck. Her coat swung easily around her knees, her upright figure swathed in a foamy green silk dress, the woolen coat just a shade darker.

The taxi pulled away from the curb toward Central Park, and through the window spring unfurled above her head in the elm trees, and down along the walkways the forsythia shouted its yellow news. She leaned her head upon the leather.

Life is wide, girls, Miss Scrivener had bid them all, years ago. *Cross it with your arms open.* And standing before the schoolgirls ranged in rows, all six feet of her — an old maid, her fiancé killed in the Great War — their teacher had thrown out her arms.

And Kitty hadn't known whether to laugh or cry.

Well, wide it was, Kitty thought now, spring begun and nothing ahead but possibility.

16

Ogden would be home soon from abroad; the ground had been broken on their house in Oyster Bay. She was thirty. It was '35. Neddy was five, Moss was three, and baby Joan had just turned one. Her head filled with the delicious math of *life* — the word flushed up onto her cheeks and into her eyes, broadening into a smile as the taxi moved up Fifth Avenue.

She caught the driver's eye in the mirror and knew she ought to turn her head away so he didn't see her, smiling like an idiot, but she held his gaze instead. He winked. She smiled back and slid down on the seat, closing her eyes as the taxi plunged into the tunnel moving east to west, underneath the playgrounds in the park where her children were playing with a concentrated fury against the end of the morning, the arrival of lunchtime, crawling around the great bronze statue of a beloved Scottish poet, perching like little sparrows on the giant knee, climbing (if they were lucky, if their nurse wasn't watching) all the way up to his massive sloping shoulder.

But the Milton boys were not lucky that way; the Milton boys' nurse told them to get down, right now, get down immediately and come here.

Moss, the younger, who did not like when grown-ups looked at him with that distant, frowning attention that signaled more attention coming after, coming closer, slid off the

17

statue, too quickly, and landed on one bare knee. "Ow," he mouthed, and lowered his cheek to the hot, scuffed skin. "Ouch."

But his brother had paid no attention to Nurse below him, their baby sister, Joan, on her big hip; Neddy kept climbing, creeping to the top of the statue's head, and was — what was he doing?

"Edward." Nurse moved quickly forward. "Edward! Get down. This instant."

The boy was going to fall.

He had planted both feet, one on either side of the great head, the shaggy bronze hair covering the two ears, a foot on either shoulder, and was carefully, slowly, pushing himself up to stand, aloft.

The boy was going to break his neck.

"Edward," Nurse said, very quietly now.

The other children stopped their crawling, frozen where they were on the statue, watching the boy above them who had climbed so high. Now he was the only thing moving upon the bronze.

"Edward."

Slowly, carefully, Neddy raised himself, pushing off the poet's head, wavering just an instant, then catching steady, and stood all the way up. Steady and up so high. Compact, perfect, he stood on the statue's shoulders, a small being in short pants and a cardigan, now regarding the world of upturned, worried faces below him.

"Moss," he squawked. "Lookit."

And Moss tilted his head and saw up through the folds of the statue's jacket, the great thick hands, up past another boy clinging to the open page of that enormous book, Neddy far above, standing, grinning, and crowing.

If he'd held out his hand and said *Come, fly!* Moss would have flown. For when your brother calls *come,* you step forward, you take his hand and go. How can you not? It was always him in the front, going first.

His head tipped, his cheek still on his knee, Moss grinned up at his brother.

Neddy nodded and lightly, easily, bent again and slid from the top of the bronze lump, clambering all the way down, arriving with a little bounce as he dropped to the pebbled ground.

"Your father," Nurse promised, "will hear of this. This is going on the list."

She unlocked the brake on the pram and pushed the boy's shoulder roughly. "The list, Edward. You hear me?"

Neddy nodded. And started marching forward.

Moss stole his hand into his brother's. Both boys kept step, ahead of the pram, their little backs straight as soldiers. Smiling.

There would be no list, they knew. It was only Mother at home. Father was in Berlin.

Indeed, Ogden Milton had just turned off the busy Tiergartenstrasse, thick with its double-decker buses, the determined low-slung black Mercedes entering the wooded park at the center of the city and merging onto Bellevue Allee, which stretched through the Tiergarten in a quiet and solemn line to the spot where he was bound. Almost immediately, the city vanished behind him. He walked beneath the thick alley of lindens in bloom overhead, gathering him immediately in that scent he had tried but never managed to describe to Kitty. Through the black trees along his left, one of the park's vast meadows rolled all its green way to a distant, flashing lake. And everywhere out in the sunlight and air, in pairs and groups, on bicycles or on foot, there were Berliners turning their faces toward the long lovely end of the day, as they had done since the time of the kaisers.

With the easy grace of a man whose winning stroke was a sweeping crosscut from the back court, Milton made his way through the park, his lineage hanging lightly on his well-formed limbs, the habit of knowing just what to do in any given moment having been passed down from generation to generation. Descended as he was from one of the families to arrive just after the *Mayflower* (*Aristocrats,*

Ogden, not refugees, as his mother, Harriet, once corrected him), Ogden had been raised with every advantage and told so. There had been a Milton in the first class of Harvard College in 1642 and a Milton in every subsequent class for which there was a young man to offer. A Milton Library was tucked under the wings of the Widener.

With his open American face, his frank American voice, one might think to oneself, *There walks a good man. A noble man.* He appeared dashing and splendid. He had the place and the power to make good, to do good. And he did so. He believed one could do right. He had been raised to expect that one could. His was the last generation for whom those givens remained as undisturbed as a silk purse.

The third in a line of Miltons at the helm of Milton Higginson, a bank begun in 1850 that sat squarely at the center of the fortunes of his country and now, increasingly, of Germany's, this Ogden Milton had taken over the firm quite young, steering at first cautiously, then more and more easily before the wind into the broad, lucrative waters of the 1920s, advancing into Europe with the schoolboy's grin that would never leave him even as an old man, an infectious grin that seemed to say *Isn't this marvelous. Isn't this something.* Meaning life. Meaning luck. Meaning his world.

The Miltons had excellent liquor and an adequate cook, and it was around their table that the men who did not have a visible hand in Washington, but who in the shadows remained most useful to the president, gathered. Families like the Miltons had always pulled the levers of the country in quiet, without considering that quiet to be anything strange, passing down that expectation to their sons early on — in the schools, the churches, the places along the sunlit rocks of the East Coast where all of them summered, from Campobello to Kennebunk to Oyster Bay. Franklin Delano Roosevelt, after all, was one of them.

This was Ogden's second trip to Germany in the past nine months, certain, as he was, that good men, fair play, and the open sluices of capital pouring into the right coffers would combat the madmen and fools. It was why he had invested heavily in this country. It was why he was now walking toward the party he could see ahead of him spread upon the lawn that edged the roses at the end of the broad walkway.

"You must come," Bernhard Walser had remarked that morning after the two men had signed the papers, the notary had left, and the ink was drying between them on the oaken desk in the enormous green damask offices of Walser Steel, overlooking the river Spree. "It was Gertrude's favorite spot in all the city."

Walser turned his head toward the high open windows as if he'd heard her, as if his wife, dead for years, might any moment be coming along the pavement.

"She would have been fifty-seven today," he mused now.

Milton reached for his pipe and tobacco, touched as always by the older man across from him. Bremen aristocrat, veteran of the Great War, chairman of the Walser Steel Company, in possession of one of the finest antiquarian libraries in Europe, and yet still a man who had wooed his wife, a famous English beauty — and a Jew — by reciting Goethe in a twilight garden in Mayfair. Walser was a man who wore his many jackets easily. A singular man one couldn't pin down, Ogden thought, tamping the tobacco in the bowl. Bigger than his britches.

No. Bigger than his cloth. The kind of man Ogden aspired to be.

Fifteen years ago, Ogden had walked out of the gates of Harvard Yard with the men in the class of 1920 and found his father leaning against a new Model T with a smile on his face. *Go on over to Europe, for a look-see,* he'd said. *Invest,* he'd said. *Find the right men and the good ideas and put our money there.* They had shipped the black car over, and through the summer months the lanky American had motored through England, down

23

into France, and then to Germany, arriving in Berlin in the last golden days of autumn, the tremendous heady chaos of the Weimar Republic palpable in the narrow streets and cobbled squares and under the tiny lights embedded in the twining vines above men and women gathering in the open air of city biergartens. Refugees had poured in from the east after the war, and the new breath of strangers, perfumed with yeast and salt, honey and garlic, blew through the city. Talk was plentiful, passions were high, but neither would fill a stomach.

These people needed jobs. And no one had seen what this meant for the country with more clarity or insight, thought Ogden Milton now, as he had at the time, than Bernhard Walser.

So it had been with a clear conscience that Walser had quietly broken the Versailles treaty very early on and, with the help of investors like Ogden, built back Walser Steel through the twenties, incensed by what he saw as a French and British move to keep Germany out of competition, disguised as a false pacifism. True peace was only guaranteed by jobs. The machinery needed to build a strong economy was the machinery of peace, no matter what that machinery made: faucets, hairpins, or, as the Walser Gruppe had begun to do, the wings for planes.

"You must come," Walser said again, returning his attention to the man before him now. "Elsa will be there. And some others you may know."

Walser looked at him a moment.

"But you have not seen Elsa this trip, I think?"

"No." Ogden rose. "I haven't."

Walser pushed across the desk a thick yellow envelope, emblazoned on the front with the Walser Gruppe letterhead, over which was stamped the Nazi seal.

Ogden took the envelope and smiled. "There we go, then," he said.

Walser nodded. "There we go."

Elsa Hoffman pulled the door shut and turned around on the stoop, depositing her key in the basket on her arm. There was no one on the street. No one loitering, watching. No one walking past the house. She turned right, toward the shops on Friedrichstrasse, her heels clicking down Linienstrasse, the sun reaching its long arm onto her shoulder and resting there.

"It is the prelude," Gerhard whispered into her hair at night, the two of them lying under the open window, the night breeze on their bodies, his leg thrown over her, his hand cupping her face. "These are the days of *tempo rubato,* the tempo off, but we can't see where the beat was stolen, we can't see the changes." Gerhard pulled the single sheet across them.

"Wagner knew it — when you steal time from the ear, the body yearns for the order back, inside our chests beats the need to stop this, to resolve — the need to close the open chord."

"Like this." She lifted her head from the pillow and kissed him.

"Like that. Or like this." He pulled her close.

No one followed. She walked steadily, having grown more and more practiced at evading attention. At first the work was only to be carrying notes for Gerhard to the others in the group. Then it became a bit more complicated, though still it seemed like playing, like childhood games. That first time, Gerhard's brother Franz pulled her aside in the line for the champagne at the Philharmonie and asked if she might sit in the café outside the Hotel Adlon and take a coffee.

She had looked up at him and nodded. *"Und dann?"*

"Und —" He leaned to kiss her cheek in farewell, his hand on her waist and then sliding into her pocket. "Stand, and pay, and leave this money on the table," he whispered, pulling away.

Today she was to meet the S-Bahn at Friedrichstrasse at eleven and simply watch that a man and a woman were not followed.

"And who are the man and the woman?" she had asked.

"You do not know. You should never know."

She was to wait at the bottom of the stairs and follow the couple holding hands, the woman laughing up into the man's eyes. Like any couple.

"How will I know it is the right couple?"

"She will stumble on the stairs, and he will hold her tighter so she doesn't fall."

It was a play.

Elsa went into the butcher shop first, nodding from the back of the store at Herr Plaut, then to the grocer and the baker. Meat, eggs, potatoes, bread.

Above the street the cathedral tower rose, and the three-quarter bells sounded as they did every hour. As they did every morning at this time, she knew, because she was out every morning, just like this, walking, the basket over her arm. The fear, that was the difference. *This is happening. This is no game. You could be hurt. You could be arrested and taken away. For looking wrong. For catching the wrong person's eye on the train.*

If anyone watches you, let them see nothing.

The earlier train hurtled along on the tracks overhead at Friedrichstrasse and the silhouettes of the waiting people on the distant platform burst free and moved like the figures on a music box.

She shifted her basket.

Meat, eggs, potatoes, bread. Now stamps to

write letters. The newsstand at the bottom of the U-Bahn station stairs.

"Morgen." She nodded at Herr Josten.

Distantly, she heard the second train approaching. *Ja. Sehr schön,* beautiful, she answered Josten, opening her change purse for the coins. The rails above her head hummed.

"Bitte?"

"Your father," Josten asked. "He is well?"

"Ach ja, danke." She smiled, handing him the coins.

The train pulled into the station on the tracks above.

She forced herself not to turn and look, to take the three stamps Josten held for her, to slide them into her change purse, to nod and thank him, smiling, just as she did every morning, turning away at last, and glancing up at the train only as one would check a blue sky suddenly crossed by clouds.

A couple descended the U-Bahn stairs hand in hand.

The picnic made a pretty picture upon the lawn beside the circle of roses that ringed the alabaster statue of bare-breasted Venus bending over her flowers, at its center. The stark white uniforms of the Reichswehr punctuated the otherwise indistinguishable men in dark suits, and there were two women in summer hats so wide they floated like birds in the evening air that hung delicious and lingered around them all. Ogden heard Elsa's laughter like a ribbon on the breeze before he picked her out in the crowd in a yellow dress the color of sunflowers and summer, quick, small, and urgent.

He slowed. For there she was long ago, in the box at the Stadttheater, sitting with her father, her dark head turned away from him that first night, her brown hair piled high. Ogden saw that, and saw the lapis blue velvet drapes in the box, the chipped gold of her chair pressed against the curve of her bare back. And Ogden, practical to his core, but impressionable, and in Europe for the first time, believed in the truth of serendipity. He was twenty-two. Elsa Walser was older, and German. All this flashed through him in the moments before Elsa had turned and seen the awkward American at the back of their box.

"Entschuldigung," he'd managed. Excuse me.

Her father had introduced them, he had slid into the empty seat beside her, and the three of them faced the stage, where the first violinist had just taken his seat to the left of the conductor, and the hall fell silent. And when the man had touched his bow to the string, touched and then drawn the bow across, holding that long first note, Ogden had understood that every life had at its center a beginning that was not birth, a moment when the catch on the lock in one's life opens, and out it comes, starting forward.

And the memory of Elsa opening the door to him at Linienstrasse 32 the next morning flooded up as it did each time he saw her after an absence. If there are places that hold us, keeping us in them, surely too there are people, he felt, people who work like mirrors for the selves we have forgotten. The young Ogden stood on the stoop below Elsa Walser that day, stock-still, stuck and dumbstruck, staring back at the woman in the doorway, unsure whether to look or look away. In that instant, he imagined himself in love with her.

"Ach," Elsa had teased him. "The American. But he does not move."

The Mouse, she was nicknamed by the circle of friends she brought him into, though Elsa was not shy or retiring, not mousy at all. "I am" — she leaned over and tapped his shoulder at the end of a long late table littered with ashtrays and napkins — "how do you say? Undercover." And smiled.

"Milton!" Elsa called now, catching sight of him, her eyes resting on him even as she continued speaking to the woman beside her.

He waved.

And as he walked forward into her gaze, the gap between what he'd imagined and what was the truth appeared as it always did whenever they met. At first, he was a figure of curiosity to her, and then, fairly quickly, a figure of gentle fun: a man of property, an old man at twenty-two she teased. She had marked him as an American through and through — appealing and fundamentally uninteresting. She had married Gerhard Hoffman, the man on the stage that night Ogden first saw her, the principal violin for the Berliner Philharmonie, a genius. And like her father, she had married a Jew. Now they had a little boy. Ogden could never have been the man she needed. He would have always fallen just shy, just short. Though short of what, and why, still continued to elude him, and — if he were honest — to irritate, albeit softly, like a hole worn into his sock. He knew himself to be more than what she saw.

"Here is Milton," Elsa explained in her perfect, accented English as he arrived. "We pretend we do not know his Christian name."

The heavy German *r* tolled beneath her words. He leaned to kiss her on both cheeks, smelling the lilac in her hair.

"Ach, so?" One of the women in the little group around Elsa extended her hand from beneath her hat, ready to smile, unsure of her own English.

"I do have a name, as it happens," he replied cheerfully. "The Walsers refuse to speak it."

"My father likes to claim he's had a Milton at his table." Elsa had turned from him. "He

31

is a great reader of *Paradises Lost.*"

"One," Ogden retorted mildly, "is enough, I should think."

She smiled back at him, resting her hand on the soldier standing beside her, so inordinately proud of his uniform it seemed he would not bend for fear of creasing it.

"Private Müller —" she introduced him, and the man's arm shot up in the air with the greeting Ogden still found impossible to take seriously, but was everywhere, even here in the open air of a spring evening in the park. He had heard from Bill Moffat at the embassy that there had been American tourists beaten for not responding with the required gusto.

"And Colonel Rutzbahr," she continued, pointing to another man who had wandered into their group, this one genial, bowing, fluid. The stiff and the smooth — Ogden held his smile in check — a perfectly German pair.

"Heil Hitler!" He nodded, turning back to Elsa. "Where is your husband tonight?"

"He will be along," Elsa answered. "He had to meet someone."

"*Ach,* always the Someones for Gerhard Hoffman." Colonel Rudi Pützgraff appeared beside Elsa with a champagne bottle and glasses.

At her husband's name on the man's lips, a light shut off in Elsa's face as if a hand pulled closed a door at the end of a hall.

"Our national treasure," the colonel said as he pressed a glass into Ogden's hand, "is kept quite busy."

Ogden nodded his thanks.

"It is good to see you here, Herr Milton," Pützgraff remarked, tucking the champagne bottle under one arm and reaching for his cigarette case. "I gather you are to be congratulated."

"Am I?"

"American money and Nazi industry." Pützgraff offered the cigarettes. "You and Herr Walser."

Elsa slid one of the cigarettes free.

"German industry." Ogden shook his head at the case.

"But they are the same," Pützgraff replied. *"Natürlich."*

Ogden didn't answer.

"Your husband will play the Wagner on the twenty-fourth?" Pützgraff asked Elsa, leaning toward her cigarette with his lighter. She drew in the flame.

"Of course." Elsa exhaled, her eyes on him. "That is the program."

Pützgraff straightened. "He does not like Wagner?"

Elsa turned her smile up to him. "But I said no such thing, Colonel."

Ogden glanced at her. She was holding herself at attention, like a sentry in a box.

"Prost." He raised his glass to draw the

man's gaze.

"Prost!" Pützgraff tipped his glass toward him and moved away.

The golden light caught on the lower branches of the lindens across the park, softening at the edges. Two rowboats on the lake raced across the flat, darkening water. In the growing dusk, the brilliant white statues glowed in a line beneath the trees. One of the uniforms and Elsa's friend, the hatted woman, wandered together slowly toward another fountain.

Dropping to the blanket on the ground, Elsa patted the spot beside her for Ogden to sit as well.

"Where is Willy?" he asked, lowering himself down.

"At home." Her face softened. "In bed."

"Poor fellow. My boys hate to be put to bed before sunset."

"Ah, but sunset lasts much longer here."

It was true. Even now, verging on nine in the evening, there was little sense of the end of the day. Twilight hovered in the grass and in the crushed petals of the roses, but the sky above stretched a sweet and endless blue.

Pützgraff strolled round the group with the champagne, dropping into conversations and moving along. Ogden was aware of Elsa beside him watching the man as well. A little farther along the pathway, he caught sight of her father deep in conversation with a German economist who had trained in Wisconsin. Beside them stood the director of the Reichsbank, an old friend of Walser's and, to Ogden's mind, a reasonable man. Ogden raised his hand in greeting; Walser nodded and held up his glass.

"You have signed the papers," Elsa said quietly. "That is good. That will be good for Father."

He glanced at her. She was looking past where her father stood now, talking to the economist.

"Have you traveled outside the city on this trip?" she asked.

"No."

She nodded and inhaled.

"Take a bicycle ride in any direction, on nearly any road, and you will see it all — plain as day."

"What will I see?"

"Training fields, airstrips, Brownshirts in the woods. We are all Nazis now."

"Elsa —"

"You don't believe me."

"Believe that all Nazis are the same?" He shook his head. "There are too many good men, too many with too much to lose to let the thugs rule."

"But which is which?" She turned to him. "How can you tell? How can any of us tell?"

He held her gaze.

"It started so slowly, Milton. Coming

toward us like a river shifting from its banks, one centimeter at a time. One lie, then the next. Lies so big there had to be a reason to tell them, there had to be some purpose, maybe even some truth — Goebbels is not an unintelligent man —"

She spoke without seeming to care if he heard, thinking aloud in the dusk. "Perhaps a communist truly *did* set off the fire in the Reichstag, though it made little sense. Perhaps there was a *reason* so many people were arrested that night, in Berlin alone. Perhaps there was a danger no one could see yet." Her voice caught. "But now has come the slow awakening — this will not pass. This will not stop."

She looked at him. "But it must be stopped."

She was admirable, Ogden felt, but untempered. Too quick to jump to dangerous conclusions.

"Elsa —"

"They are beginning another phase," she said quietly. "Gerhard is certain they will demand he step down by the end of this year. They are talking of passing 'laws.' "

"But he is first chair." Ogden frowned. "He is one of the primary draws of the Philharmonie."

She flicked her cigarette into the grass before them.

"There are thousands of jobs for the taking

now. Jobs that belonged to Jews, even Jews like Gerhard. Thousands. So it is Christmas morning here in Germany," she said, shaking her head, "and here is Papa Deutschland. Papa with the Christmas goose, Papa with presents —

"And no one asks *Where did the presents come from, Papa? Whose tree did you rob?* Because Papa hasn't robbed anyone. Only Jews. Those jobs — those houses — those belonged to Germans all along. And all Papa needs to do is join the Party. Then it is Christmas morning, everywhere. That's all."

He masked his impatience. "The Nazis are nothing but thugs. It cannot last."

"Milton." She shook her head and turned away. "You are not listening."

"I am listening very hard."

"We have been . . . purloined," she said. "In plain sight."

He cast a brief, considering gaze at her.

"Frau Hoffman! Herr Milton! Meine Freunde," Colonel Pützgraff called. *"Ein Foto! Kommen Sie hierher.* On the blanket, there —" He pointed to where Elsa and Ogden sat. Good-naturedly, the others began to move toward the blanket as Pützgraff busied himself.

"We need you," Elsa said to him swift and low beside him.

"We?"

"Gerhard." She nodded. "The others."

37

"Elsa —" he protested. "What can I do?"

"*Ach.*" She turned her face from him. "Still the man with the courage of his conventions."

Ogden pulled away from her, pricked.

"Closer." Pützgraff frowned playfully. "Much closer."

Ogden drew his knees up and wrapped his arms around them.

"You should not condescend, Elsa." He stared straight into Pützgraff's camera. "It does not become you."

"*Eins, zwei —*" the colonel counted.

"Become me?" A thick, unhappy laugh burst from Elsa in the moment the flash went off.

"*Sehr gut!*" Pützgraff raised his fist in satisfaction.

Kitty had crossed out of Central Park at Seventy-second Street and was walking steadily east toward the river. It had been a lovely afternoon. The Philharmonic had played the Mendelssohn, and Kitty and her mother had run into Mrs. William Phipps and then, unexpectedly, into the Wilmerdings. She had put her mother in a cab and decided to walk the rest of the way home. She stopped on the corner to wait for the light.

Across the street, protected by its green awning and polished brass railings, stood One Sutton Place, one of the many unremarkable granite squares on the Upper East Side whose address did all the work, as nothing about its unadorned face suggested the wealth inside. This had been entirely purposeful. When the building went up in 1887, there was a general sense among its first occupants (all of whose apartments commanded corner views of the East River) that the thick-shouldered, rather showy mansions of arrivistes such as Frick and Rockefeller on Madison and Fifth did not bear repeating.

And certainly had not been repeated here, Kitty mused, delighted by the old building, stolid as an uncle. Delighted by it all. By everything. By the light. By the day. She raised her eyes and counted up fourteen stories to where the windows of their apartment stretched.

Even now — seven years after Ogden had bent without a word and picked her up in his arms on the day they arrived back home from their wedding trip, carrying her, wrinkled traveling suit and all, straight toward the double brass doors out front, straight over the threshold and to the elevator, where he leaned her against the satin-covered wall waiting for the elevator to open, and kissed her — even now, she had the short, sharp sensation sometimes here, on the street outside where they lived, that she was playing at house. She had tripped along the pathway set down for her life, footsteps light on the flagstones — there went Kitty Milton, arms full of flowers for the front hall, there again at lunch, and again later beside her husband, her arm snugged under his elbow, the three children born every two years in perfect, healthy succession, proof if anyone was ticking off the boxes (as she knew they were; she had grown up beneath the myriad eyes of dowagers and gossips who occupied the stiff-backed chairs in front rooms and back gardens between East Twelfth and East Twenty-eighth streets) that Kitty Houghton had gotten it right.

When she had vowed to love, honor, and obey, she'd never have guessed how easy Ogden would make it. Or how much she would want to. How she wanted what he wanted. She moved through the world with a natural reserve. The longing to speak out, crack open, start up suddenly did not run in her. Cool, calm, observant, she knew it was these very things that had drawn Og to her. And yet, when he had come to her on their wedding night and slid his hand down her bare arm, her body rose under him as if another girl had lain there coiled and waiting. She shivered now with the memory.

And the thought of the children in their baths up there, the drinks set out on the bar in case anyone dropped in, the single place setting at the long table ready for her dinner, the bed turned down at the end of the evening and the curtains drawn, gave her a happy jolt. Her rooms were full. She was not playing at all.

The light changed and she stepped off the curb and toward two little girls walking toward her in their crisp dresses, faces forward, holding on to either side of the pram in which a new baby lay. "Up you go," the nanny breathed, raising the front wheels to take the curb. Wordless, the little girls climbed up onto the curb, still holding on to the pram as on to the straps of a rope tow.

"Do we have to go to the park?" the biggest one asked as Kitty passed.

"Yes, Miss Lowenstein, you do."

Jews, Kitty noted, making her way toward the dark green awning that shaded the well-polished door, straightening her back without thinking. Little Jewish girls. And up here, on the Upper East Side.

"Hello, Johnny." She inclined her head toward the doorman with a smile.

"Mrs. Milton." He nodded, holding open the door for her, Neddy's stuffed bear in his arms.

"Oh lord, they've done it again?" She smiled, taking the battered bear from the doorman's hands. "It's a game, you realize," she said. "You only encourage them."

"Keeps me busy." Johnny's eyes danced. "Out of trouble."

"Is that so?" She cocked an eyebrow by way of her thanks. Beneath the uniform — any

41

uniform — men all just wanted to play ball.

I must speak to Neddy, however, she promised herself, making her way across the black-and-white tile to the elevator doors. He oughtn't to presume on Johnny's good humor. Johnny had a job to do, and it didn't include retrieving the stuffed bear that Neddy had tossed from the open window, fourteen stories up, to see if Bear could fly.

She smiled. Neddy, who wouldn't sit still, Neddy, whose hand she had to keep a tight hold on — he had a tendency to go off and explore. No one had prepared her for boys and their impulsive wandering, setting off this way and that, a creature on some scent, following their noses into trouble. Little ferrets.

She waited as the machinery of the lift hummed its way downward and bounced lightly before the grate was pulled and then the door slid across.

"Hello, Frank," Kitty said to the elevator man as she walked into the lift.

"Mrs. Milton." Frank glanced at her and pushed the grate across.

They rode in silence up the fourteen flights, both pairs of eyes watching the light on the dial as the elevator rose through the numbers. At her floor, Frank spun the gear, slowing the elevator until it stopped just at the lip of the threshold. He pulled the gate back and waited.

"Thank you," she said, catching sight of

herself in the mirror hung in the center of the tiny elevator hall. She had a flush on her cheeks, and the pleasure of the afternoon still shone in her eyes.

The light was on in the library. To the right the early-evening sun lit up a swath of the living room, out of whose windows Kitty glimpsed the bright green spring waving in the treetops. She slipped out of her coat and reached for a hanger in the cedar closet, tucking the wooden shoulders into the cloth and hanging it back upon the rod, where it hung now beside Ogden's. *Mr. and Mrs. Milton.* She smiled at the cloth couple, touching the sleeve of his coat, and then leaned and buried her face in its neck, possessed by this wild, irrepressible love of the coat and her coat and the hall and — *Oh, I am ridiculous.* She smiled. Absurd. But the sense of joy that had begun that afternoon in the taxi and had carried through the music in the hall, back out into the park, that sheer abundant light in her heart as she had walked home, open windows, *oh,* she wanted to burst out of her body, she realized, pulling herself out of the closet and shutting the door on her coat beside his.

Ogden, she thought, *come home.*

The afternoon her cousin Dunc Houghton had first brought Og, newly returned from Germany, to one of her grandmother's interminable soirées — one moment there she was, Kitty Houghton, standing next to her sister, Evelyn, just inside Granny's library door, bored and perfumed, but ready and on hand to be the girls at yet another musical evening, and the next moment, there she was, quite simply, not.

She was something else entirely. Standing there with Evelyn, she'd heard the commotion in the hall behind her as the street door was thrown open and men's laughter clattered over the yellow silk settee and the two Queen Anne chairs — *Hello, Barker, hello, sirs, may I take your hats* — and crash-banged right into the front room, where Granny's guests were busy finding chairs.

Go and see what that is! her grandmother's face had commanded Kitty silently. And Kitty had slid round the door, emerging into the hall just as Dunc crowed, "See, Ogden. This is what I'm talking about —"

Dunc was pointing to the John Singer Sargent portrait of her grandmother hung (*too high,* the little curator from the museum had sniped when he had stopped by one evening) above the entrance to the library behind her, but the man next to him was not looking at the painting.

"I do see," he said.

She blushed.

"Oh yes." Dunc turned to his friend and clapped his hands appreciatively. "Yes, my

44

cousin Kitty. The flower of an altogether different age."

The young man had crossed the rug between them and taken her hand in his. "I'm Ogden," he'd said.

One of the Pierpont Place Miltons, he was a catch in anyone's book, though he was quite a bit older and had traveled, and there had been whispers of a woman somewhere. But the man in front of her had blue eyes and a lean face ending in a grin that seemed to her right then, her hand in his, to shine on her alone. He had experience. Very well. She hadn't been frightened in the least. She was not her mother. A man's life stretched into all corners, ran like water where it was tipped. The past was, simply, past. He had come to her with his arms wide and his heart full, and they had begun.

All her life Kitty had moved hand to hand forward, lightly holding on the line strung between signposts for a woman's life. As a girl, it had been firmly set down that one ought never speak until one was spoken to, and when one did, one ought not speak of anything that might provoke or worry. One referred to the limb of the table, not the leg, the white meat on the chicken, not the breast. Good manners were the foundations of civilization. One knew precisely with whom one sat in a room based entirely on how well they behaved, and in what manner. Forks and knives were placed at the four-twenty on one's plate when one was finished eating. One ought to walk straight and keep one's hands to oneself when one spoke, lest one be taken for an Italian or a Jew. A woman was meant to tend a child, a garden, or a conversation. A woman ought to know how to mind the temperature in a room, adding a little heat in a well-timed question, or cool a warm temper with the suggestion of another drink, a bowl of nuts, and a smile.

What Kitty had learned at Miss Porter's School — handed down from Sarah Porter through the spinsters teaching there, themselves the sisters of the Yale men who handed down the great words, *Truth. Verity. Honor* — was that your brothers and your husbands and your sons will lead, and you will tend. You will watch and suggest, guide and protect. You will carry the torch forward, and all to the good.

There was the world. And one fixed an eye keenly on it. One learned its history; one understood the causes of its wars. One debated and, gradually, a picture emerged of mankind over centuries; one understood the difference between what was good and what was right. One understood that men could be led to evil, against the judgment of their better selves. Debauchery. Poverty of spirit. This was the explanation for so many unfortunate ills — slavery, for instance. This was the reason. Men, individual men, were not at fault. They had to be taught. Led. Shown by example what was best. Unfairness, unkindness could be addressed. Quietly. Patiently. Without a lot of noisy attention.

Noise was for the poorly bred.

If one worried, if one were afraid, if one doubted — one kept it to oneself. One looked for the good, and one found it. The woman found it, the woman pointed it out, and the man tucked it in his pocket, heartened. These were the rules.

She could hear the children in their bath and Nurse's steady scolding, like a drum beneath the children's patter. She shouldn't bother them, she thought. She should let them be.

But a squeal and then the delighted laughter of Neddy drew her back, and she turned the knob on the bathroom door.

"Mummy!" Moss cried.

Two wet heads turned to her, standing on the threshold.

"You've got Bear," Neddy crowed.

"I do." Kitty stopped herself from smiling. "But we must have a talk —"

"Indeed, we must." Nurse turned on her stool, her face quite terrible. "I've told the boys I would report their behavior today."

Behind her, Neddy grinned and held his nose, sliding under the water. Moss stared.

"Very well," Kitty said, knowing she was

47

meant to be stern, knowing she was meant to speak. But here were her two boys in the bath, their hair wet and their faces shining — Neddy rose back up out of the water, with his yellow car that he took everywhere in his hand. "Plonk," he said, running it along the rim of the tub. It was too sweet, too delicious.

"We'll have a talk after the bath," she promised Nurse. "Send them down to my room when they are out." And she turned from the steaming room to hide her smile.

Oh, she thought again, hurrying down the hall. *Here it is. Again.* Life.

The wide bed with its white bedspread tucked precisely beneath the two pillows appeared wider in the late sun. The windows were shut against the evening and she set the bear down on the window seat and shoved one of the windows all the way up, wanting all the air in, the city in, the sound of traffic and far below the click of someone's heels on the pavement. The smell of heat reached all the way up to her, with the deep dark of spring.

She turned, stripping her wrists of her charm bracelet and her gold watch, slipping out of her flats, and walked into the bathroom, the green tile cool beneath her stockinged feet, and opened the china knobs in the sink. A hard cold gushed out of the tap. Startled, she pulled her hands out and caught sight of the grimace on her face in the mirror. The woman looking back smoothed her frown and studied herself. She had the Houghton lines, the Houghton nose, the high cheekbones above a curved mouth that now smiled back at the glass and at the generations.

"Born a Houghton and married a Milton," her father had crowed appreciatively, raising his glass at their wedding. "Kitty has exchanged one 'ton' for another!" Then, chuckling to the room around them, he finished — "And she's shown the great good sense to remain in the same weight class!" And the long bare arms of Kitty's bridesmaids lifting their champagne glasses lazily upward in the toast had reminded Kitty of swans at twilight, swimming effortlessly, beautifully curved and silent.

"These are the best years of your life." Mrs. Phipps leaned across the white tablecloth to her, putting a hand on Kitty's for her attention. "You don't know it, but it's true."

Kitty had flushed, nodding at her mother's friend, knowing she ought to thank her, knowing it was meant well. But old women were thieves. They wanted to steal possibility, put one in one's place and snatch the time they had lost back into their own baskets. Even here, on her wedding night.

Well, she had declared to herself that night, she wouldn't do it. No matter how wise she grew, she promised, curving her lips into a smile for Mrs. Phipps, she'd never tell a girl like her *at the end of every meadow there is a gate.*

She buried her hands and then her face in the thick towel and then, lowering it, saw in the mirror that Neddy and Moss, freshly bathed and now in their wrappers and slippers, their hair combed, had come silently into the room behind her, where they had found Bear and had climbed onto the window seat.

Her heart stuttered.

The window was pushed high above their heads. There was nothing at all between them and the air.

"Get down, boys," she said into the mirror.

They hadn't heard. Moss was on his knees, perched against the sill. Neddy was standing above him and leaning out, leaning out way too far, about to launch Bear over the sill.

Kitty spun round, moving to get to him. "Neddy!"

Startled, the little boy turned. And Kitty saw that she would never get to him in time. There would be nothing to save him from the open sky.

And then he simply fell.

TWO

She comes again in her clean white Keds and stands at the foot of the bed, waiting. They are on the Island, in the pink room, in the Big House. In the rooms around them, the others lie sleeping, everyone sleeping in the thick sea-dark.

Evie, she says, *we must go. We must get there before it is gone.*

It's a dream, Evie tells herself in the dream.

Evie. Her mother stands, waiting.

I am sleeping, Evie says, lying in the bed that was not her bed in the room that was not her room, but the room they all slept in as girls. *I don't want to go.*

Evie —

And when Evie rises, her mother turns, her shoulders set, her step quick along the hall and down the stairs, determined. *Goodbye, Granny K,* Evie says to the door where her grandmother slept. *Goodbye. Goodbye, Aunt Evelyn. We must go.*

They move out of the house across the lawn

and up the small hill to the graveyard where the Miltons lie, the little humps of granite, the names —

Ogden. Kitty. Evelyn. Moss.

Joan.

Whose is this? Joan points at this last one, the new one, hers.

We thought you'd died, Mum.

Joan looks down at the stone.

Died, she whispers.

Died? She turns around. *But not here, Evie. I told you. Not —*

Here.

Evie Milton woke, the word bolting out of her throat, its afterclap hanging in the air. She lay there in her own bed until the pieces of the dream fell back into their places, the walls around her became her own walls in the dark bedroom in the apartment she shared with her husband and their son on the lower end of Manhattan in New York City, in the present, now. It was another morning. The city was awake. Her pulse slowed. Mum was dead. Had been dead for months.

Paul was in Berlin. Seth was sleeping down the hall. *The king was in his chamber, the queen was in the parlor, and they —* Evie squinted at the ceiling, trying to remember the words of the song — *all fall down.* But

Paul was coming home. She smiled. Paul was coming home, tonight.

A siren's high G wound its way up Sixth Avenue, and the city symphony that played through the hours — the sustained murmur of cars, syncopated by chatter, people walking beneath the windows, talking, and then at times the sharp rap of someone's laughter — soothed. The world went on without her, the outside world clattered ahead, and she was a girl again, awake in her bed, amid the grown-up voices echoing up the stairwell in the Big House on the Island, her cousin Min asleep next to her in the dark.

Evie shoved the covers aside and swung her feet onto the floor, pushing back her hair and sitting up, still in the grip of the dream.

What was it?

Fogged in, there was something slipping away just past the ridge of dark trees, just there and hovering; she could nearly see what it was there in the fog past the ridge, tiptoeing around, as if not wanting to bother, not wanting to mention, as if the past had grown suddenly kind. What was it that hovered on the outside of her brain, what was it?

She needed Paul. She needed him to help her parse it all. He would know what it meant. He'd make sense of the quiet.

Her phone pinged on the bureau.

Walser, Paul had texted. *Ring any bells?*

The dance? she typed back, teasing.

The name, he returned.

Nope, she wrote, and stared at the screen. *Come home,* she thought. *Fly safely,* she texted.

The morning sun stretched along the hall, the closed doors ranging one after the other like holes punched in a margin — her study, Paul's study, the bathroom, Seth's bedroom — all the long way to the kitchen and living room at the end, overlooking Bleecker Street. Along the inner wall, the cherry red bookshelves they had built in Berkeley and moved from apartment to apartment, from job to job, ranged now floor to ceiling along the length of the hall. Shelved alphabetically and in sections, the spines of their books told one history of their lives: in color and girth, and in the margins of those books Evie could trace her trek from girl to scholar.

"You know we live in a library, right?" Seth had grumbled the other night. "Nothing but books, books, books."

"And dirty socks," she retorted.

"Mom." He was firm. "Someone's got to keep it real."

She headed toward the bathroom.

"Mom?" Seth called.

Evie pushed open the door to his room.

"Do I have to wake up yet?" The voice from the middle of the blankets in the middle of the bed was still half-asleep.

Evie smiled into the dark, the shades pulled

down tight against the city outside.

"Ten minutes," she said, moving to the end of his bed, her eyes on her fifteen-year-old, her boy, his arms wrapped around his pillow, utterly still.

"Mom?"

She drew in her breath, realizing she was standing exactly as her mother had in the dream.

"Ten minutes," she said again, making for the door and pulling it quickly shut behind her.

Evie had spent her life keeping her mother at arm's length. The folded in, the silent woman at the center of her parents' more silent house, was not her, would never, she had vowed, be her. Something had happened to her mother, something that had knocked Joan off her feet, something that fuzzed her. Because Joan Milton — unlike her sister, Evelyn, unlike their mother, Kitty — had been smudged somehow. Clouded. Obscured.

So when the dream began in this month Paul had been away, and kept coming morning after morning, the dream with its insistent, urgent, *vital* woman taking Evie by the hand and leading her out of the Big House on Crockett's Island to the new grave, and pointing — what could she do?

She followed.

She was an historian; the past was her butter and bread. But, she thought as she made her way to the bathroom and turned on the taps, nothing had readied her for the gentle persistent feeling growing stronger through this month, a steady rain in the back of her mind, that there was something she was missing, that she had failed somehow, that there had been a turn, back there in the road of her life, a trailhead, an opening she'd barreled right past. Somewhere back there had been the right route, the way through, and she'd missed it.

She raised her eyes now to the woman staring back at her from the bathroom mirror, looking like her grandmother, Kitty Milton.

There was something she was supposed to remember. Something she was not meant to forget.

THREE

It took nearly two weeks to get back home, though Ogden had booked the first free berth. They had delayed the funeral, waiting for his return. The great stone church packed with old New York ranged pew after pew, united in its sorrow, singing the hymns Kitty's mother had chosen, to console. There was the Christian soldier, the lamb meek and mild, and the quick afflicted. There were the rows of mourners, the hats, the wool of the hats giving off the steam from the May rain they'd all come in from. Damp. Warm.

Ogden sat beside Kitty, staring straight ahead of him, seeing nothing. Moss and Joan had been kept at home, and Neddy — whom he carried on his shoulders, whom he played tag with in the park, the little boy who slapped at his hand and ran away laughing, crying out *I got you* — lay there in the oaken coffin in front where Ogden and the ushers had set him down.

How?

The boat had docked very late the night before last, and it was past midnight when Ogden had let himself in. He made his way quietly down the long hall of the apartment toward their bedroom, past the two lamps glowing on the lowboy, and pushed open the door. It was pitch-dark inside, where usually there was a small night-light in case the children needed to wake them, and he put his hand out, feeling his way toward the bed, inching forward blindly and stumbling against it, nearly falling. Carefully, he laid his hand down where he imagined her arm to be to wake her. But there was nothing, no one there. The bedspread was on the pillow. He snapped on the light. She was not in their room, the bed made up, tucked tight. He wandered back through the empty darkened apartment, library, living room, dining room with its enormous table — where was she? And wandering into the kitchen he saw a light on in the back hall, in one of the maid's rooms. And that's where he found her, curled tight, her hands in front of her face as if she were hiding in sleep.

"Kitty," he whispered, his hand on her shoulder. "Kitty." He pried her hands softly apart.

She opened her eyes and stared at him above her.

"It's Ogden." His voice broke. "It's me."

"Ogden?" she asked. And that was all she said.

So the single word that had tolled in his head all the way across the ocean, all the way here, never sounded; he couldn't ask her how.

Time and quiet, everyone counseled, would help. Best not to mention it. Best not to dwell on it, his mother had said. It was a terrible accident. It must have been hot. Windows were open all the time. And time would heal. Some things were better off left unsaid. Though the truth was, he couldn't bring himself to say his boy's name. If he said the word Neddy, his heart might fall out of his mouth.

He reached for her hand, and she let him take it, treading and retreading back and forth in her head as she had every day, returning to the room and to that last moment when Neddy was still there, still standing on the window seat with Bear in his arms, when she might have crossed the ten feet between them and snatched him back from death, instead of standing frozen in the doorway while he fell beyond help, her mind refusing the picture of him falling in his bathrobe and slippers out there — *out there?* — and still alive. Those were the moments she couldn't bear. When he was still alive. Had he cried for her? She hoped his mind had shut down on itself, she hoped the brain closed its own curtains.

Ogden's hand tightened on hers. They were to stand again. The minister raised his hand in blessing. They stood.

Frozen, she had stood there in the doorway after he fell. Surely the empty spot where Neddy had been was wrong. Surely what she was seeing wasn't right, surely someone would stop him, someone would catch him, someone would come, bring him back to her, close the window, and —

"Mummy?"

Moss was sitting on the window seat, staring at her.

At last, she had moved. Crossed the ten feet of carpet to snatch Moss, wrap him in her arms, turning from the window to the bed, where she sank down, her heart beating again. The world beating again, beating in her body with its *no, no, no,* and Moss's face buried against her chest, clinging to her neck as Kitty wrapped her arms around him and closed her eyes, rocking. And she would not let go. She would never let him go.

So he was in her arms when the nurse came into the room. In her arms when the terrible men with the stretcher came. Still in her arms, nearly asleep, when she rose from the bed at last to meet her mother and father out in the hall.

"Have you got Neddy?" Moss asked, turning his head to look at his grandparents.

"Neddy," his grandmother said, leaning

60

over her grandson, "has fallen ill. He has gone to the hospital."

And Kitty dropped, sank to the floor before her father could grab her, like a bird, straight down, a bird shot from the sky, poor bird, before her father could catch her, with her son still clinging to her neck, fallen.

"Where is Neddy, Mum?" Moss asked in the days that followed. "When is he coming back from the hospital?"

Kitty couldn't answer.

"He'll forget." Her mother was gentle. "Children forget. It is best for him to forget. The truth is unspeakable."

"But Moss was there," Kitty said. "He saw Neddy fall."

"Where is Neddy?" Moss asked every night.

And on the third night, Kitty pulled him into her lap and was going to tell him, was going to say, *You remember what happened, you remember, darling, don't you?* But his body was so small and so trusting against her, and so *Neddy flew* was what she'd said.

"Neddy flew?" Moss looked at her.

She nodded. "Neddy flew to heaven."

Moss rested against her, thinking. "With Bear?"

Kitty gathered him closer. "Yes," she whispered into his hair. "With Bear."

"Let us pray." The minister had finished speaking.

Our Father, the voices around them said,

61

who art in heaven.

And Kitty tried to do what she had not yet done. Tried to do, but failed. Under the surface of the others, here in the chapel, she tried again to imagine Neddy all the way down until the end. She was determined to think him all the way down, to carry him in her mind's eye all the way to the ground. To carry him with her. So he was not alone when he died. But her mind, her tired mind, picked swiftly back from the sight her mind put there that she did not want to see. Instead, she imagined Johnny had caught him as he fell and brought him back to her, and she had taken Neddy in her arms and taken Moss by the hand and she had put her two boys to bed as she always did. She had kissed Neddy good night, she had tucked him in, she had straightened his covers, she had looked at him as he turned sleepily onto his side, his head on his hands. And then she had done the same with Moss and snapped off the light, closing the door on the two of them, her hatchlings, her boys in the big room, the city honking far below.

"My dear," Mrs. Withers said, and drew her into a powdery embrace.

Kitty allowed herself to be pulled in, to be held, and to be put back. Mrs. Withers searched her face. "It will get better," she whispered.

Kitty nodded and smiled. How she hated

them all.

And Mrs. Withers turned to Ogden, standing beside Kitty in a receiving line as if it were their wedding, and Kitty stood and smiled and took the wishes for her, and understood that if she gave in to the tears in front of others, there would be no way back. Her father was right. There should be no waterworks. Better to construct a ladder inside, better to set each foot upon the wooden rungs to climb up and away from the empty, terrible hole. Better to cling to the ladder and pull oneself up, up, and away from the image that she couldn't see, but couldn't leave. Neddy on the ground between the legs of strangers, and all alone.

In the days afterward, Ogden went back to the office and Kitty went to church, though there was nothing to pray for. There were no words for what happened. She had found a tiny little church off Lexington Avenue, with a battered door and one single round window above it. She went to church to sit in the cave of stone, filled with voices of strangers. Murmurs coming through the air, bowling in the ceiling and sifting down with the speckled greens and blues, the deep dark red of the stained glass at the end of the nave. She sat in the hard wooden pew and waited for the hymns. And when the singing started, she could weep. She went to church to open her mouth and feel her heart again, constricted, struggling, banging against her throat, the tears there in the place of words, her voice struggling out in the vast air, stopped by grief. And the parishioners grew used to the tall woman coming in each morning, coming in from another part of the city. And let her be. So she sat alone, day after day, singing but not making a sound, her tears streaming down her cheeks, her throat, below the collar of her dress.

Time would heal, she was told. Time will bear your sorrow away.

Instead, there Neddy lay, a permanent grief, and it was she who was borne away, her sorrow worming through her brain, a slow unwinding body burrowing a tunnel into which she could stumble at any moment. A windy hole inside her, from which the view was pitiless and unfathomable.

Ogden was no help. There was no help. She had left the window open. She had opened the window.

FOUR

Like voices humming along a telegraph wire, Evie thought. That was how to teach the past. One could rest one's hand upon it, feel the vibrato, one could close one's eyes, lean low and listen hard. If one was paying attention, one could hear the voices underneath the past. And *that* was Time.

She stopped at the corner of Waverly and University Place in New York City. Around her the university students streamed across, hurrying to classes in the squat buildings that framed Washington Square Park. In ballet flats and a sky blue sleeveless dress that set off her shock of silver hair, Professor Milton's lean figure was a place on which to rest one's eyes in the midst of all that motion. *Queenly,* her younger colleagues described her as when they thought she was out of hearing, and she knew it was as much to dismiss her as to signal their respect.

A medievalist by training, the history of women's lives her concentration, Professor

Evelyn Milton had come out of the starting gate twenty-five years ago with *The Anchoress: Foundational Trope of the Patriarchy from the Middle Ages to the Present,* arguing that although the bedrock of every Western hierarchy rested upon a silent woman — seen quite literally in the case of the thirteenth-century anchoresses, the nuns walled into a cell at the side of an abbey to pray out the duration of their lives — that silence was the source of both the Church's power and the nuns'. The anchoress was the power, the glory, and the victim all at once. It was the 1990s. Rereading a woman's silence was all the rage. The book had won her prizes, a job, and eventually tenure, landing her at the foot of Manhattan in the Department of History at NYU.

Nowadays, however, Evie heard the word *trope* and wanted to run for the hills. And furthermore, no matter how powerful an anchoress was in theory, in the end, there she was — still a woman who had buried herself in a stone room, alive.

Metaphor, Evie thought as she stepped off the curb as the light changed, was for the young. Or, at any rate, for the younger than she.

Evie pulled open the double-paned doors to the history department, passing out of the hot bright day into the cool of the marbled lobby, and shoved her dark glasses onto the top of her head, nodding on the way to the elevator to a pair of students whose names she couldn't retrieve.

The door slid shut and the elevator rose through the numbers on the brass board, flaring and extinguishing like momentary stars. She stood quite straight and watched them go, then dropped her eyes to the polished brass of the elevator door, realizing with a shock that the silver-haired woman reflected there was her.

She kept forgetting. It was *her.*

She crossed her arms at the reflection. *Never mind,* she thought as she stared back. *It's elegant.* A fist in the air. No more pretending. She was over fifty, after all, married for twenty-five years, and with a teenage son. And, anyway, she had never banked on her body to get attention, even when she had had a body to speak of. Her husband, Paul, had wanted her and she had wanted him and that had been that.

"You know, there's a name for us," her oldest friend, Honey Schermerhorn, had remarked last week.

"Oh?" Evie said. "What's that?"

"The In-Betweens."

"In between what?"

"Good question." Honey considered. "Girls and hags?"

"Oh, for god's sake."

But that's just it, she thought now. There was no good name for this spot. Evie, who had shot like an arrow from school into life, who had never wavered, who had seen clear right from the start where she wanted to get to, had lately found herself more and more in the brambles. Somehow, here she was, no longer certain where she was going. Or even if she wanted to get there.

The jobs had been won, the beds made, the dishes washed, the children sprouted. The wheel had stopped, and now what? Where, for instance, was the story of a middle-aged orphan with the gray streak in her hair, the historian who had rustled thirteenth-century women's lives out of fugitive pages, who believed more than most that there was no such thing as the certainty of a plot in the story of a life, in fact who taught this to students year in and year out, and yet who found herself lately longing, above all else, for just that? Longing, against reason, for some kind of clear direction, for the promise of a pattern. For the *relief* — she pulled against the shoulder strap of her satchel — the unbearable relief of an omniscient narrator.

Adolescence, she reflected, pushing open the classroom door with a kind of savage glee, had *nothing* on this.

The rows of students quieted and looked up.

It was the second class of the summer semester, Introduction to Medieval History, and the unspoken rules of the game had not yet been determined. What Professor Milton might be looking for remained to be seen. She nodded at them and slid out her laptop, appearing stately, in possession of answers, and clearly unfazed by quiet. She pulled a small book out of her satchel, folded it in her arms, and looked at them.

"If you worked at the World Trade Center, and you were told to go back to your desk in the second tower after the first tower had been hit, would you?"

The class went utterly still.

"What would you have done? It is the thing I ask myself over and over. Would you have gotten up from your desk and started walking down the stairs? That panicky feeling, *what to do, what to do,* meeting head-on with a supervisor saying go back to your desks, go back and wait for the firemen to come. That's the procedure —" She paused. "Would you have kept walking? Or would you have turned around and gone back to your desk?"

She looked at them.

"If a Jew came to you in 1939 and asked to be hidden, would you?"

She nodded at the students ranged in the first row. "Would you risk your life, your family's life, to free someone enslaved?"

They were all listening now.

"If we can imagine the answers to those questions, then we are beginning the semester right."

She paused.

"I'd have gone back to my desk," she said quietly. "I'd have been the good one, the obedient one."

She looked at them. "Who are you? Each one of you?"

They stared back at her. One boy looked down.

Good, she thought, letting the words hang a few moments in the air. Then she put on her glasses and opened the book.

" 'Long after the bricklayer vanished behind the wall he was building around me, I could hear the scraping of his trowel. He was careful. Devoted. And throughout the hours of my enclosure, I heard the setting down of bricks, one upon the next, the mortar slapped on and then smoothed, slapped and then smoothed, and even as I prayed, even as the light dimmed, then lessened, then vanished, the clay and the mortar grew in my mind's eye. Grew to God.' "

She paused and looked up. "This is the account of Marie, anchoress of Saint Leraux, written in 1341," she said, and continued on.

" 'And I could not keep myself from picturing the wall he built, the wall he built around me, as though I were standing on the outside and looking in. The bricks like notes — soldier, sailor, rowlock, and shiner — the wall would sound the song he made from clay and lime and water. And the beating heart at the

70

center of his song, behind his wall, sang in silence with the bricks. My heart sang to God.' "

She closed the book.

"That," remarked a boy sitting in the middle of the room, "is sick."

Male or female, it didn't matter; there was always this student in every class, self-appointed provocateur who imagined himself fearless, unafraid to poke at the classroom orthodoxy to ask questions, to nudge aside the hand that was feeding them. Evie recognized it; she welcomed it. She had been that boy long ago, skeptical, insightful — and wanting to paint her name across the classroom sky.

"Sick?" Evie took off her glasses and considered the boy. "As in excellent? Or as in horrible?"

"Horrible." He grimaced. "Why would anyone let themselves be bricked into a room at the side of a church for their whole life?"

"Faith," she replied firmly, "and power."

The skepticism in the room was palpable.

"Let me ask you something." Evie put down the reading. "What does a firsthand account like this make you want to do?"

The same boy grinned. "Get her out of there."

"Go on," Evie said. "How?"

"Guns," he answered. "Love. Or money."

"Or email," another boy, emboldened,

71

cracked. "If she had wireless."

The room laughed. Evie walked to the single window in the classroom and wound the lever, opening it. Then she turned around, still waiting, the students saw, for an answer.

"How about writing her history?" Evie asked calmly. "How about history?"

They watched her.

"When I was not much older than yourselves, a librarian handed me this anchoress's prayer book," she said. "It was small, quite worn, the leather cover gone gray from age. The pages were soft, and the words upon them still quite sharp. But on one page, a word had disappeared into the margin."

"What word?" someone asked.

"God," she answered.

Even the boy paid attention now.

"How had it?" Evie asked. "And why? Why would a word on the side of the page disappear when all the others had remained?"

They waited.

"I sat there, in the library of the coldest town in England, holding her prayer book, staring at the page, and a picture of this anchoress, this twenty-year-old girl bricked in her cell, began to grow in my mind.

"And suddenly, I understood," Evie said. "Julianne had rubbed the word away — touching it, like a beat on a drum. Every time she came to the line of prayer. *God, God, God.* She had come to life. She was alive, *there.*"

Evie crossed her arms over her chest.

"But," the boy protested, "how do you know she did that?"

The grin on Professor Milton's face was electrifying. No matter how savvy students thought themselves, when they first truly understood the complications of backward looking, they arrived here at this gate. If they were good, that is. If they were really thinking. She crossed the room to stand by his chair.

"What's the difference between history and fiction?"

"Facts."

"Facts." She nodded at him. "Very nice."

The boy looked up, saw she was sincere, and then looked away, flushing.

Evie walked back to her chair and clicked for the image she had waiting there. On the screen hung over the blackboard, two moss-covered headstones, each with the name CROCKETT written in bold, leaned in a grassy plot.

Here lies Louisa, aged 31,
Died August 31, 1840 and her two children,
Stillborn

Henry, b 1846, d 1863
Gettysburg, Pennsylvania.
Far from home.

"Look," Evie instructed. "What are the facts here?" She was gentle around the word, delicate, as though it had gone off slightly.

"Well," said a girl who had spoken on the first day of class, "all of it. Everything there happened."

"Okay," Evie agreed. "Good. Now, where does the history start?"

Everyone looked at the gravestones again.

"Gettysburg," a boy with a Medusa's mop of curls answered.

His neighbor shook her head. "Far from home."

Evie crossed her arms. "Do you see?"

One by one, they looked at her. She was smiling.

"Here is a sixteen- or seventeen-year-old boy named Henry, who died at Gettysburg, far from home." She ticked off the list. "Those are the facts. But you" — she nodded at the boy with the curls — "will write a history of the battle, and it would be tremendous and enveloping, I'm sure." She was deadly earnest. He almost believed he *would* write this history; she was not playing around.

"And you" — she shifted to the girl — "might write the history of that era's displacement, of this movement of boys from North to South, and the effect it had on the late nineteenth century in America. It would show us just what 'far from home' entailed. What constitutes *home,* for instance? Fascinating."

"Not just the *boys*," observed a girl sitting to Evie's left, whose woven braids were coiled high on her head and bound in a scarf. "There would have been the freed slaves wandering about. And what could *home*" — the girl's scorn was palpable — "mean to them? You'd have to take that into account."

"Exactly." Professor Milton turned to her. "You are just right. Another history."

She crossed her arms and appealed to them.

"Wars, plagues, names upon tombs tell us only what happened. But *history* lies in the cracks between. In the inexplicable, invisible turns — when someone puts a hand down, pushes open one particular gate, and steps through. A man saying no instead of yes, two hands grasped on a dark street. A twenty-year-old nun in her cell, eyes closed, praying, touching the word *God* in a book we recover, over and over and over, so that what we have left is the trace of her devotion. In the erasing of that word" — she paused — "is a person. *That* is history."

There among the stares of the boys and girls regarding her with a familiar mix of disbelief and incomprehension was dotted a face or two returning her gaze, studying her with a vague frown, a curious worried apprehension that signaled they knew precisely what she said. Knew, without any idea yet what they knew.

She folded her arms and leaned against the

classroom wall.

"Below the pattern, the great sweeping pages, the wars drummed out and fought, are the questions: What if? What happened? *How?* Beware the vast magisterial history unrolling a carpet across time: this followed by this, leading inevitably to that. The march of history, the teleology. Nothing is inevitable; everything is tangential, particular — *human.*"

They were all listening.

"History is in us. Our history lives in us. Lean low and listen, that's your job. Not *that* they had lived," she pushed on. "But *how.*"

She smiled at them, walking them forward, hoping they'd come.

"Heroes are the people who are bigger than their times. Most of us" — she smiled at them — "are not. History is sometimes made by heroes, but it is also *always* made by us. We, the people, who stumble around, who block or help the hero out of loyalty, stubbornness, faith, or fear. Those who wall up — and those who break through walls. The people at the edge of the photographs. The people watching. The crowd. *You.*"

They were all listening.

"So know yourselves first," she finished. "*Then* look back and account."

The room was still one single instant, then relaxed. No matter how long she had taught, she loved this moment. The class had begun in earnest. She had pushed open the door.

She nodded at them. "See you Wednesday."

In the quiet after the students had packed up and left, her eye fell on the Crockett Island graves still projected on the wall at the front of the classroom. She had taken the picture in a dense fog, and the cut letters of the graves were thrown into relief by the dull air and the sharp, bright grass on the ground, the familiar gray humps leaning toward each other, like a brother and sister telling secrets, side by side with the Milton granite, the stones her mother turned away from, every morning, in the dream.

Evie shivered.

Know yourself? she thought. *Ha.*

What was not pictured was the lichen-covered railing that ringed the tiny graveyard, under which Evie and her cousins had slid to play among the graves. Nor the path from the graves toward the Big House through the fields, where she had hidden as a girl, where she had sat smoking with her cousins as a teen, where the twenty-year-old had lain in the night, kissing boys from other islands, laughing at the thistles catching her long hair — one of the Miltons of Crockett's Island, the four hundred acres of spruce that covered one square mile from granite shoreline to granite shoreline, plunging straight down to the sea, the place that held them, the place that belonged to no one else.

What was not pictured was her grand-mother Kitty Milton, sitting on the green bench outside the Big House surveying the lawn before her, or her aunt Evelyn on the granite steps at the front of the house, or her mother, Joan, standing between these two, saying —

Evie.

What? Evie thought impatiently. The image of the three of them, silent and facing her, facing down the lawn, rose so clearly in her mind just then it had the force of a specific memory, as if she had stumbled on the reason for the silence that had seemed to live between them like a vow, like a gauntlet thrown down. As if something might happen in that moment. As if something *had* happened if Evie could only see it.

Patient as a safecracker, Evie had worked her whole career to coax lives out of diaries, recipes, the epitaphs upon gravestones, taking tiny, inexplicable moments to sketch a fuller portrait of an age, concentrating on the girls at the side of the page, the women who were not heroines, the ones without a plot. That she was one of the best at it was commonly recognized in the field. But these three. Evie could detail the slow turn of her mother's head, her aunt's impatient hands snapping peas or packing picnics, her grand-mother's grace getting in and out of a boat; still she could not have told any casual acquaintance what drove any of these three women, save for the Island.

(*Nothing,* her grandmother used to say, *is simple. Unless you are a hero, a coward, or simply simpleminded.*)

"Oh, for pity's sake." Evie closed the laptop, and the graves and the Island disappeared.

Here she was, standing in her classroom, longing like one of her students for the certainty of a single moment as told by the old histories. That there was a kernel at the bottom of every life, the beginning of every event — the gunshot, Archduke Ferdinand falls, world war — a cause. A seed nestled in the heart from which a life sprouted and could be explained.

But that was fiction, a fantasy. She knew silence often flew in between families and roosted. Slow, inexplicable angers grew without roots. Nothing special, no story. What the study of history had taught her, clearly, after years and years, was that she might pull up the single moments from the darkness where they lay centuries old, she might point to a spot in time, a line in a diary, the particular shredding of a blue ribbon used to tie a shoe, she might string these together and say, *Here is what happened.*

And history would sit back on her heels and laugh and laugh.

FIVE

Soundless, the year wheeled round on its colors. Summer spun down green to gold to gray, then rested, rested white at the bottom of the year, rocking the dark of winter; rocking, then rolling slowly, wheeling up again through a dun brown, a mouse gray, until one day the green whisper, the lightest green, soft and growing into the next day, then the next until suddenly, impossibly, it was spring again. Above the newspapers printed out and slapped down onto the doormats, above the posters on the streets, the lindens bloomed and horse chestnuts gathered their spiky conkers, hard green ornaments hanging from the great black boughs above Berlin. Hitler marched into the Rhineland, Franco marched on Madrid, and Mussolini bombed Ethiopia, showering it in a poisonous rain, claiming it for Italy.

It was the end of April 1936.

"Yes, I will," Elsa answered her father, going down the three steps ahead of him while he locked the front door. It was a cold spring day, and the sunlight slanting along the iron gratings held no warmth. She dipped her chin into her scarf.

Across the way, Frau Müller stood in her narrow window, her hand upon the curtain. The woman did not hide the fact that she was watching Elsa and her father on the stoop.

Elsa raised her hand in a wave.

The old lady didn't move. Bernhard Walser slowly descended the steps to stand beside Elsa in front of their house.

"Frau Müller," he called. *"Guten Morgen."*

The woman nodded and bowed, and drew the curtain shut.

"There." Walser took Elsa's arm in his and firmly steered her away. "She must not have seen you wave."

Elsa squeezed her father. "She saw me."

He didn't answer.

"She taught me how to bake crullers," Elsa reminded him, reaching up to kiss him goodbye. "Every Saturday."

"She is misguided, poor lady."

"Tschüss, Papa," Elsa whispered, and walked swiftly away down Tucholskystrasse. *Poor Papa,* she thought, glancing at the windows in the houses above and then looking away. A man used to being in charge, a captain of the ship, her father believed in the ship. He believed in the people on the ship,

81

believed they could steer clear of what was wrong. That was the evil these days laid bare, surely — this sustained, precious belief that everyone could see it all clearly, the hope that someone would come to stop it, that there would be people who could stop it, doomed them instead. She crossed over the street and joined the crowds on Friedrichstrasse. The only people who could stop it were themselves.

The excitement of resistance two years ago, when it had seemed certain the Führer's inordinate excesses, his purges, his *insanities* would yield a revolt among his own ranks and knock him out of power, had been flattened into quietude by the steady, unsleeping machinery of the Reich operating in plain sight.

At the U-Bahn station, the glass sheath above the stairs glittered in the cold. Clumps of workers rose into the light.

Gerhard waited in front of the BrotHaus, and she waved and smiled as if they were only two lovers meeting. He smiled back and uncrossed his arms, walking toward her. She could see that today's lookout was a child, or little more than a child. It was a girl, school age, in a blue serge cap.

He pulled her into his arms, then turned her round, and the two of them started walking in the direction of Wilhelmstrasse, her husband keeping his arm around her shoulder, holding her close. They walked slowly, hips touching, without speaking — as if they were on their way to a nice lunch, and then perhaps to a dark room and a bed.

If the Jews are the *syphilis of European peoples,* Herr Goebbels, then very well, Gerhard had promised, we will make you sick. We will dirty your walls with the truth. In coal black or chalk white, a single phrase had appeared all over the city in the past month, written by the members of Gerhard's group, day after day. Big enough to catch attention, to be seen passing by, proliferating on the sides of freshly painted buildings, black needles pricking at the Nazi balloon. Black marks on the white walls all around the Nazi stadium — a white sepulchre of the insanity — the waking beast rising into the skyline in the west of the city. And though each night the words were painted over, each day the group would write them again.

At the end of the short block, Gerhard leaned her against a wall, protected from sight by the corner of another building. She raised her face to his and wrapped her arms around his neck and pulled him to her. He pressed himself against her and kissed her. And — for that moment — Elsa could forget what they were doing, she could die here in his arms, it wouldn't matter, she felt, it was the full sum. He slid his hand around her back, and she arched a little so he had room to write with the bit of chalk, or the piece of coal, depending on the color of the wall.

Gerhard wrote the words, pressing close into her, writing and kissing all the time, gently, intently, his hands as steady as when he pulled the long slow note from the strings with his bow. If anyone passed, they'd see a couple kissing, the woman's shoulders against the wall, her body arching, her hips pressed into the man. They wouldn't see the gap left by the curve of her back in which the man could write —

Das Nazi-Paradies ist eine Lüge.

The Nazi Paradise is a lie.

"Getan?" Elsa whispered.

He nodded and took her hand. They walked away without looking back at the words.

The men knocked later that evening just as they were sitting down to the soup. Her father rose and went to the door. "You will wait," he said to the men standing there. And though it was clear they did not like it, the men had nodded and remained in the hall. Elsa could see through to where they stood waiting from her seat at the table. One of them had not removed his hat. This frightened her the most. He did not care where he was, whose house he was in. Gerhard had not looked up. He ate without making a sound. Her father poured a glass of wine. Gerhard met her eyes. *Eat,* his eyes said.

Beside her, Willy was concentrating on lifting his spoon to his mouth without spilling. He was very proud to be sitting there with his father and his grandfather. At age six, he had just earned the privilege to sit at the table. She looked down. She picked up her spoon. The spring light had begun its unraveling outside in the lindens.

When he had finished, Gerhard wiped his mouth, pushed back from the table, and stood. Her father looked up at him and nodded. Gerhard came around the table, leaned down, and kissed the top of Willy's head. "Bye-bye, my boy," he said softly.

"Bye-bye, Papa," Willy said, still concentrating. She put down her spoon and turned in her chair, rising, but her husband's hands gripped her shoulders, and she sat back down.

"Elsa," he said very low, and she raised her face, her eyes holding his.

"Yes," she said as his mouth met hers and she closed her eyes. *My love.*

He lifted his kiss, then his hands, and went through the dining room door. He pulled his coat from the closet, his hat from the rack, and his violin case from off the lowboy where it sat. She had not seen him pack the violin. But there it had been, waiting. She gave a violent shudder and had to pull her hands down off the table and under the cloth, so Willy could not see her shaking.

"Elsa," her father said.

She stilled.

"Where is Papa going?" Willy asked.

She turned to him, her little boy.

"To the symphony," she answered as the front door closed.

Six

In New York, it was another Wednesday night, and Ogden Milton was sitting in one of the wing chairs at the edge of the reading room at the Harvard Club, where he'd stopped in for a drink and the evening paper, filled that night with the outright disregard for borders, for the rule of law. Hitler's and Mussolini's expansions were going on in plain sight. *Pay attention,* the headlines exhorted. But in the streetcars, in the byways, along the breadlines of this country, the question on men's lips was *What of it?* The idea that the country ought to prepare for war in a time of peace seemed nothing but a cheap and dangerous patriotism. Americans wanted none of it. They were weary, they were wary, and Europe was weak. It had gotten itself into the Great War, found itself unable to pay its own debts. Why the hell should America? More neutrality legislation was called for. GIVE US BREAD, the billboards cried along the highways, NOT

BULLETS. Europe was a tinderbox, best left alone.

"Did you see the article in there about shoes?" Harry Lowell threw himself into the empty chair beside Ogden.

"I didn't," Ogden answered, lowering the *Times* and repressing a sigh. They had known each other since boarding school and gone on to Harvard together. "Hello, Lowell."

"Eighty million pairs produced nowadays, where there were twenty million before 1913. Peasants are not walking on straw, Milton."

Caught up in the heady enthusiasms of the decade, Harry Lowell had published pamphlet after pamphlet praising the great Communist experiment: A feudal nation transformed under Stalin! Peasants eating! Children clothed! A great society! Good-looking in that loose, unfocused way that catches the eye in passing but doesn't hold, the kind of man Ogden had grown up with and now steered clear of. A man of prodigious — and empty, Ogden felt — talk.

"The frontier for a better world," Harry continued, "must stake itself in the necessary undoing of the moneymaking classes."

On the polished mahogany wall behind Harry's head, the trophies of the club's members hung — Teddy Roosevelt's buffalo casting a shadow over the massive fireplace.

"The undoing?" Ogden returned mildly. "Look where you are sitting, Lowell."

Harry didn't turn around. He had played defensive end on the Groton football team, and as far as Ogden was concerned, Lowell had always had the sweating passions of a stevedore, incapable of nuance or complexity. The high-storied windows looked placidly out over the teeming city.

"When we are cast out" — Lowell refused to be diverted — "it ought to come as no surprise."

"I don't intend to be cast out," Ogden retorted, "by anyone. And especially not by an idea. I'll put my bid on the work of good men. Every time. Men who know what they are about, men who can see better than the rest and know how to act on it."

"Ha." Harry was dry. "Nobility, thy name is Milton."

"As usual," Ogden said, looking at him, "you've gotten it completely wrong."

"Have I?"

Ogden leaned back in his chair and didn't answer.

"Listen," Harry drawled. "I've had wind of something you may be interested in."

"What's that?"

"One of the islands up by us is for sale. Crockett's Island. I thought you might like to come up and see it," Harry said. "Bring Kitty. You can come stay with us on the Point, afterward."

"Well, thank you, Harry." Ogden was

89

thoughtful. "Thank you very much, indeed."

"Old man Crockett wants fifteen hundred for the house, the barn, and four hundred acres, and —"

"And?"

"Well, Lindbergh is also interested in the place. Though from what I've gathered" — he paused — "Lindy is hung up in Europe through the end of the summer."

Ogden whistled.

"I thought you might like to come take a look-see first." Harry grinned. "Get the jump on him."

Ogden gave a long, slow smile at the man sitting across from him. Nothing would give him greater satisfaction than to pull the rug out from under Lindbergh. Watching Lindy with growing alarm as he had been lately, it was clear to Ogden that bravery notwithstanding, Charles Lindbergh was a team player only until he was handed the ball. And then he simply had to run with it. The sort of man who could not hand it off, as he ought to, the sort of man who would risk the game to score a point. The wrong sort. Lindbergh was undoing all of Ogden's own careful work to keep the pot from boiling over, over there.

"Lindbergh ought to know better," Ogden said. "What the hell does he think he's doing other than lighting a match under the burner in Berlin?"

"Agreed," Harry answered, looking at

Ogden curiously.

One of the club waiters appeared. Did they want a drink?

They shook their heads.

"Along those lines," Harry said, "Father tells me Walser's sending his manuscript collection over here to exhibit at Harvard."

For a brief time that first summer in 1920, Harry and Ogden had both found themselves guests of the Walser household on Linienstrasse, Harry doing business for his own father. Ogden had half forgotten the connection. He nodded. "I'd heard that. It's generous of him."

Harry shook his head. "Nazi showmanship. An expression of the power of the Reich."

"He doesn't need to share it with the world."

Harry snorted. "Herr Walser is not concerned with the world. He is a man of property, first and foremost. I'll bet he is sending it over here to keep it safe."

"He's a businessman," said Ogden carefully.

"Meaning?"

"Business has its own politics."

Harry snorted. "That's the state of affairs in a nutshell, isn't it?"

"He's a good man," Ogden said evenly, looking at Harry. "He's built a great company."

"Good returns, Milton?" Harry tented his

fingers and sank further into the chair.

"Very," Ogden answered.

"And his workers?" Harry pushed.

"His workers have bread and steady jobs. Walser is one of the ones we can count on."

"To keep Germany out of the hands of the Communists."

"To keep Germany stable." Ogden didn't hide his impatience.

"Germany is the most stable nation on the globe," Harry observed dryly. "That's what beatings in the streets and arrests will buy you. Order."

"Walser's a good man," Ogden repeated.

"And a Nazi," Harry observed crisply.

"He is in the Nazi Party. I draw the distinction."

"Semantics, Milton." Harry shook his head impatiently. "Now is the time to pull out all capital and show the Nazis —"

"Show them what, Harry?" Ogden faced him. "If we divest now, we risk setting off the tinderbox."

"Yes" — Harry was heated — "and then Hitler will fall."

Ogden shook his head. "Hitler *will* fall, and German capital will survive the Nazis."

"So you won't pull out?" Harry pushed. "You stay in, Milton, and you're one of them. Can't you see —"

"Of course I see," Ogden broke in calmly. "But I am my own man, and more to the point, it's not the right thing to do. The world does not want another Panic. We can't afford it."

"The world?" Harry rose to his feet. "You are speaking for the world now, Milton?"

Ogden looked back at him. "We see it differently, Harry. But we want the same things."

Harry stared down.

"We see it differently," Ogden said again.

Harry put on his hat. "So long, Milton."

"Harry." Ogden nodded.

He watched the other man make his way slowly from the immense sleepy room and out the door.

As a child, his father had taken him up the Erie Canal to see that great feat of ingenuity and engineering, and the lifting and lowering of the locks, the approach of the lock keeper, who turned the waters off and then on again, the running alongside the narrow barge as the waters filled and filled, and then with the wheel's turn, the great crashing release of current had thrilled Ogden and stuck with him all through his childhood, into his twenties, when he grew to understand the water in the lock was the central principle he could live by. He liked to think of himself as the lock keeper — a steady man who believed in the water's flow, who understood the value of keeping sluices open. This credo, more than any other, was handed down from Milton to Milton through the years. Miltons were men of character and capital. The world — he addressed Harry Lowell in his head — needed more of these, not fewer. Good men and capital invested wisely grew thick and ran strong, sustained by open channels and in the hands of those who knew what to do with them.

He stood and headed for the door.

A slight crowd had gathered on the sidewalk across the street as Ogden walked slowly down the broad stairs of the club and onto the pavement outside. And as he approached, he saw a man at its center standing on a milk crate, shouting. Heavyset, hoarse, his arms sunburned up to the elbow, his face weary, the man shouted out what appeared to be the same single question. "For what, at last, would you give up your life?" Men and women streamed around him, though it didn't matter. Standing his ground, the man hurled that question like a ball into the mitt of the world. He did not care that it was not returned. He threw it over and over, insistent.

"For what, at last, would you give up your life?"

Ogden Milton slowed. The question seemed to have been hauled up out of the heat and into the air for his attention.

"For Europe?" the man cried.

Ogden stopped and searched the faces around him, listening intently as if there were something hidden beneath the words. The man beside Ogden was nodding his head, his arms crossed upon his chest, his hands jammed in his armpits, rocking back and forth on his heels.

People could not stand so much uncertainty, Ogden thought, watching the speaker start to weaken in the heat. It led to leaps of passion. Idylls. Impossible dreams that a system could save you, that the great cataclysm they were in could be solved by shifting governments. Quixotic. The man was quite likely another Communist.

And there floated Harry Lowell, a balloon of conscience. Ogden stepped back out of the crowd and continued walking, leaving the shouting man and the watchful faces behind. Harry had always been a mischief-maker, the boy at school who liked to set fires to see who'd put them out.

Yet Harry's anger back there in the club had called to mind Elsa's white face turned to him on that blanket in Berlin last year. Ogden straightened his shoulders.

They were wrong. That was all there was to it. He came to a stop at the corner.

The light changed, and as Ogden crossed, a woman hurried out of the awninged portico ahead of him, her heels tapping away on the pavement, calling Kitty to mind.

He stopped.

Possessed of a long, straight nose and a strong chin set atop a slender neck, when she had first turned her head upon that neck to look at him, he could not look away. "Arresting," his mother had pronounced Kitty. And that was that. And Kitty had gone from the tall girl with a smile like a breeze in summer to the elegant, upright woman who could still make him catch his breath as she waved at him in a crowd.

Despite the last year, despite the resolute expression with which she now turned to him every morning when he left her at the breakfast table and the distant, abstracted face every evening when he returned, pushing open the door into their apartment, she remained for him his moon. The center of every room. All that was good, and right, glowed eternal in her. Cool, undiminished, his wife possessed an idea of order unchanged by the heat of fashion or enthusiasms, or passions engendered by a momentary ideal. Slim and determined, she could draw anyone out, make anyone feel right at ease — be they a child, a Midwesterner, or a Sikh. This last he had heard her boast, with the snap in her brown eyes that was hers alone, and as he knew for a fact she'd never laid eyes on a Sikh, it had delighted him to no end.

She had not had that snap in her eyes for months.

People had remarked upon how resilient, how resourceful, what a model the Miltons had been in the face of their sorrow. And on the surface they were right. It seemed Kitty had picked herself right up and thrown herself back into their life. She sent out invitations, filled the apartment with flowers, and turned, gracious and smiling, to her guests with that long, cool gaze that somehow warmed and welcomed and promised nothing but a good evening ahead.

He had watched her at the other end of their table, guiding her dinner partner toward some confidence, the slight smile that was only hers aimed at the man beside her. He had listened to her turn a conversation back away from dangerous shoals, he had smiled as she had smiled at some idiocy or a joke, and he had almost been convinced of her return. But he had come upon her too often sitting still, lost to the world, intent on returning to that day and going over it once more. She had grown opaque, tending her grief like a nun in a cell, the white walls a solace, the white walls her face.

Some things are better off left unsaid, his mother counseled. So he'd let Kitty be.

But despite himself, despite his mother's words, he was impatient. What could he have done? What could any of them have done? It had been a year. He needed Kitty to return, take up the reins in her hands, climb back onto the box, and set the carriage going. He wanted Kitty back. All of her. He wanted her to look at him again. Only him. Not the empty place beside him where she put their little boy.

He wanted her laughing up at him, into his face, as she had that one brilliant fall afternoon, years ago, turning to him in his great-aunt's orchard and laughing, saying, *I love apples, I could make myself sick eating them all, I wish I could stop at only one apple, I wish* — and he had stopped her wish and kissed her. The day had been glorious, golden and russet, and everything lay ahead of them. It was the day that beat in his chest as steady and as unchanging as his heart. An ordinary day, but the day where he knew himself irrevocably bound to her.

A gull lifted from the lamppost on the corner. Lifted and stroked the air, and then wheeled slowly overhead, past him and down Fifth Avenue to the bottom of the city, where the waters led outward to the sea. Ogden turned all the way round to follow it, his throat closing in sorrow. Down and away, he watched the sea bird's patient, silent glide.

For what, at last, would you give up your life?

He cleared his throat, following the bird's white body.

For her.

SEVEN

Out in the hall the commotion of changing classes bowled up into the arched stone ceiling of the history department. Evie made her way down the white-tiled length, leaning into the oak door of her office with her shoulder as she unlocked it, sliding in and swiftly pulling the door closed. Professor Milton was not in.

The noise shut off abruptly. Inside her office reigned the unruly clutter of a curious mind. Four bookcases groaned, the books ranging side to side, and up and down, a patchwork of color and graphics that extended one entire wall. The massive desk Evie had rescued from the law school renovation next door extended the length of a second wall. Two comfortable chairs made up a conversation corner, sitting seat to seat. On a low bench between them was an electric kettle and three mugs, all of them chipped, all of them made years ago by Seth in middle school. A clothesline stretched from the top of the window frame across the room to the opposite corner. Scraps of paper, a piece of tinsel, several photographs, and a leather glove now hung from the wooden clothespins, the map of Professor Milton's mind strung up like that, making her more formidable to her students, rather than less.

She tossed her keys on her desk, laid her satchel down, and went to stand beneath the line, staring up at the photograph she had found of Granny K and Pops when she was cleaning out her mother's apartment.

Handsome, tanned, Kitty and Ogden Milton stood ramrod straight and smiling into the camera on the afternoon in 1936 when they had chartered a yawl, sailed out into Penobscot Bay, and bought Crockett's Island. The mast of the boat rising behind him, her grandfather's broadcloth shirt rolled up at the elbows showed the ropy muscles of his forearms and the good thin watch upon his wrist. Her grandmother stood in the curve of his arm, her cardigan buttoned at the neck and draped over her shoulders. She was thirty-one years old. Nothing had touched them. That the skein of old money and power would snag upon the 1970s and unravel would have been inconceivable to these two, Evie thought with the historian's eye. The white-shoe bankers of Milton Higginson, the investment bank her great-great-grandfather began, had floundered in the free-for-all after limits on commission fees were lifted and finally sold themselves to the hungry and enormous Merrill Lynch. But there in the thirties, the two of them stared down at Evie like hosts at a good party. Like life was a good party. Before old money ran out of its money. When *summer* was a verb.

The photograph had nothing to do with anything she was working on, and yet it comforted her. The two up there were so certain, so clear, their life so — unquestioned. It reminded her of her mother, and of summer nights when she was a child, crouched in the bow of the *Katherine,* her grandfather at the helm bringing them all back from a party at one of the other islands, her mother, her aunt, and all her cousins, and the lights of the Big House shimmering across the water seemed to promise nothing but still water ahead, all her life. Light and water and clear sailing.

And it was exactly this kind of picture that drove her husband, Paul, nuts. Here stood the blue bloods, their faces turned with blind assurance to a leeward breeze, hands resting steady on the tiller, nobility at the helm, no matter that they had sailed us into Vietnam, interned American citizens, and, he'd observe, turned a blind eye to the Jews when they could have done something.

Since the afternoon in the photograph, four generations of her family had eaten round the table on Crockett's Island, clinked the same glasses, fallen between the same sheets, and heard the foghorn night after night. "The land before time," Paul called it with the distance he had always put between that life and theirs, two professors living in university housing at the foot of Manhattan with their teenage son. "Can't you see what that place is?" he'd ask her over the years. "Of course I do," she'd answer. "It's laughable, yes, but it's also beautiful, and full to the brim with —" "Miltons," he'd finish dryly. "I'm more Jewish up there than in a synagogue." "We don't see the same place," she'd answer. "No," he'd say, "we don't. I don't like sailing, I don't drink Scotch, and I could care less what the market is doing." He had gone up to the Island less and less over the years, begging off to do research in summer libraries.

Never mind. Evie folded her arms, addressing Paul in her head. *You'll probably win in the end.* There was no way of knowing how long she and her cousins could hold on to it. Before he'd left for Berlin, she and Paul had discussed selling the share she'd inherited and using the money for their life — their real life, as he would say. Though in the past few days it was growing harder to imagine *actually* selling it, harder to imagine who she'd be without it.

"Are you in?" The door to Evie's office had opened.

Evie turned around, not sorry for the distraction. Her colleague Hazel Graves stood in the doorway, her arms crossed over the enormous mound of her belly, in the eighth month of a pregnancy that had taken over her body like an occupying army.

"Hey." Evie smiled. "What's up?"

Hazel hesitated in the doorway. "I had a thought I wanted to run by you."

She sounded a little nervous.

"I'm flattered."

"You may not be, once you've heard it."

Though she was ten years older than Hazel, had championed Hazel's hire and mentored her through the first two years of teaching, theirs had grown into a rich collegiality of equals that had only stumbled a few times over the course of the past ten years, the two women finding in each other a close and attentive ear.

Lately, however, if Evie was honest, Hazel seemed to have the persistent ability to remind her that though her work was considered groundbreaking, even foundational, both ground and foundation were places buried in the dark, and that she, Hazel Graves — younger, black, brilliant, and now pregnant — clearly held the torch.

"Sounds ominous," Evie remarked dryly. "Come on in."

She pointed Hazel to one of the comfortable chairs and sat back down at her desk.

Hazel moved heavily out of the doorway and paused under the clothesline, distracted by the photograph of Kitty and Ogden.

"That wasn't there last week. What's this?"

"The Twilight of the WASPs," Evie answered without thinking.

"Polo shirts and jodhpurs and all that?"

It never failed. Bring up WASPs, and everyone went at it with great hilarity, the one group Americans could comfortably laugh at, about whom nobody really knew. Unless, of course, one *was* one. Evie considered her colleague.

"Polo shirts have nothing to do with WASPs."

"No?" Hazel pressed.

"No," Evie said firmly, "that's Ralph Lauren."

Hazel nodded, unconvinced.

"Who are they?"

"My grandparents."

"They look happy." Hazel studied the image. "When was this?"

"Nineteen thirty-six," Evie answered with a wry smile. "The day they went sailing, took a picnic to an island off the coast of Maine, and bought it."

Hazel turned around. "An island?"

"He bought it to keep her happy. That's what we'd always heard."

"How nice for her." Hazel was arch.

"One could do things like that in the thirties."

"If one were wealthy and white. That was the middle of the Depression," Hazel retorted.

There was an edge now in Hazel's voice. Evie looked at her.

"Fair enough."

Hazel turned her eyes back up to the image. "And did it?'

"Did it what?'

"Did the island keep her happy?"

Evie thought about this. *Happy* was not a word she'd assign to her grandmother Kitty Milton. Then again, neither was *sad,* or *angry,* or any number of adjectives that might ruffle the surface of a pond. *Satisfactory,* she could hear Granny K pronounce, pleased. All of a piece.

"It kept her," she said.

Hazel nodded, still staring at Kitty and Ogden.

"All these people inside us," she said softly. "No wonder this country is fucked."

Evie stiffened. "What does *that* mean?"

"You've got these two in you who can sail away and buy an island while the Klan is on the rise and seventeen million people are out of a job —"

"Well, they weren't Bourbons, for god's sake," Evie interrupted.

"They don't need to be, do they?" Hazel was quiet, her hands on the small of her back.

Evie had to fight the urge to pull the photograph off the line and out of her reach.

"And you?" Evie was wary. "Who's inside you?"

"The invisibles." Hazel turned around. "All the ones these two wouldn't see."

Evie looked at her for a long moment. "And never the twain shall meet?"

Hazel didn't smile.

"Not always," she answered. "What's over is *always* under. And you never know, do you, when it will pop up?"

Evie shook her head. "You can't reduce it like that. You have no idea who these 'people' are —"

"Can't?" Hazel turned around. The two women regarded each other.

They had stumbled into the gully that opened between them every so often. White. Black. Evie exhaled.

"Okay, Hazel. What did you want to run by me?"

"It can wait."

"No," Evie prodded, wanting to pull them out of this uneasy quiet. "Go on."

"Okay." Hazel nodded, and started in.

"For the Festschrift." She made her way over to one of the chairs. "In honor of her twenty-five years, I was going to revise your *Anchoress* slightly."

"Oh?"

"Slightly." Hazel hit the note again, light but determined.

"Go on."

"Your reading of silence, that is."

Evie waited.

"What if power comes not — as you proposed then — in the anchoress's silence, but in her choice of a husband?"

"How's that?"

"Take the vow of the anchoress literally. When she becomes the bride of Christ, she marries — up," Hazel suggested. "Way up."

The idea sliced through the last twenty years of feminist theory, returning as it did to marriage as a source of power. Avant-garde and retroactive in one stroke. Elegant. It was all about whom you married.

Looking at Hazel just then called to mind a plant in summer, thrusting her exuberant branches into the garden with that vegetable abandon — alive, I am alive, and growing. It made Evie tired.

"*Revise* me?" Evie raised her eyebrow. "That's more like burying me."

"No, no. Don't you see? It's an homage. It's an extension of your thinking." Hazel shook her head, alight with her idea, smiling at Evie and expansive now. "It's just that the more I thought about it, the idea of a woman gaining power through keeping quiet seemed so —"

Hazel stopped, frowning as she tried for the right word.

"Quaint?" Evie offered.

"Wishful. Too neat, actually," Hazel finished firmly.

"Perhaps." Evie leaned back and crossed her arms. "But we all know power is passed on in all the unspoken rules of the game, passed on by the rule keepers. How one ought to behave, who belongs in the club —"

"Such as?"

Evie cocked an eye at Hazel, pointing up at the photograph.

"Enter every room with a smile, my grandmother taught us. *Speak to everyone, regardless of their place, as another human being, a reasonable person — so as to create an atmosphere of goodwill around you."*

"That's just manners —"

"Yes. And manners were *the sign.*"

"Of?"

"Good breeding. Ill breeding."

"Ill breeding?" Hazel raised her eyebrow.

"When one has money, one ought never talk about it, and one ought to think about it as little as possible," Evie recited, sure of her footing but not entirely sure of her point. What was she arguing? she wondered. "One doesn't mention Money or one's Good Fortune. Or Bad Fortune. One's Place in the world. One doesn't speak of oneself, draw attention. One

doesn't want to seem to be flaunting one's fortune in the face of the less fortunate. One doesn't want to make others feel ashamed, or remind them of what they don't have."

"And so one can cover it up."

The edge was back in Hazel's voice.

Evie frowned. "Say more."

"The truth. The gap. The code that holds the whole structure. You pretend it's all equal. You hide it under manners. You all are involved in a vast conspiracy, a cover-up. Silence protects a white woman's story and —"

"And condemns her," Evie pushed back.

"Only if she chooses."

"Come on, Hazel," Evie snapped. "Is it a cover-up simply not to speak of it, every time? *All* the time? Honestly, I am not certain it was ever that simple, and it certainly isn't now."

Hazel's eyes widened. "Are you serious, Evie? You know it is. You've spent your career pointing this kind of silence out."

It was true. *If you see something.* Evie had hung one of Homeland Security's anti-terrorism posters on her clothesline, years ago. *Say something.*

"Perhaps," Evie answered, not wanting to give Hazel an inch. She watched as Hazel pushed herself out of her chair, making for the door, having done due diligence by way of her senior colleague. *It's about power, idiot,*

Evie reminded herself; she had just been told she was going to be revised.

Evie listened to Hazel's footsteps echoing down the marble hallway. For an instant, she could almost retrieve the feeling of being heavily pregnant and yet still so light, ready to charge, sword in hand. At thirty-eight she too had been ready to shape the future in her own image. Ready to take on the field with that kind of urgency, fueled by the belief that you and you alone saw it clearly. Hazel reminded Evie of the sweet weight of that clarity, that sureness.

That thievery — she grimaced — called revision. A truck backed up outside her office, the steady *beep beep beep* a percussive to her thoughts. Evie lifted her face and stared up again at her grandmother in the photograph on the line.

Never mind. Kitty's voice rose in Evie's head. *Never mind all that.*

Eight

They were an attractive group, thought the harbormaster's wife, watching from the doorway of the ferry office when the Ogden Miltons and the Duncan Houghtons descended early one morning at the end of June on the public landing in Rockland, Maine, having ridden the overnight train from Manhattan. The men hoisted the weekend's bags upon their shoulders and disappeared down the gangway toward the boat, leaving the wives to unbend after the long night's ride. The two women divided neatly into tall and short, slender and plump, fair and dark. Mrs. Winslow noted the high-waisted, wide-legged trousers that were all the fashion in the magazines and decided the short one looked like a pirate, the other, like a pirate queen.

That one appraised the clear sky, the steep shingled roof of the ferry ticket office, and then gazed down on the dock where the *Sheila* was tied up, the bronze fastenings shining against the wooden deck, an American flag snapping in the wind off the stern. And everywhere, the smell of the sea.

"God knows what's in that." Kitty shook her head at Priss, who had turned to her, holding up a canvas bag, zippered and bulging. "Probably lunch. Let Dunc take it."

Priss nodded and put it back down.

"Anyway, you oughtn't lift anything," Kitty observed dryly. "In your condition."

"I do love that part," Priss admitted, sinking into one of the old dock chairs, "though I'm growing fat as a pig."

And so she was. Kitty smiled at her old classmate, now married to her cousin. Beef consommé and saltines had never been enough for Priss, and certainly were off the menu now that she was finally and safely pregnant at last.

" 'Reach for a Lucky instead of a sweet'?" Kitty suggested.

Priss chortled. "I don't need to slenderize; that's the beauty of it all. Though I wouldn't mind a cigarette right about now."

She pulled the book she had been reading onto her lap and opened it.

Kitty nodded. The woman in the ferry office had gone back into the little watchhouse at the end of the landing. Her dog thumped its tail in the sun outside. Kitty's attention wandered back to their husbands down on the dock.

Ogden was inspecting every inch of the

yawl, rubbing it down as one would a horse, nodding in agreement to something Dunc called from the bow. What nuts they were, she thought, idly watching. So serious about knots and lines and hooks. Everything in order. Everything in its place. As if any of it mattered.

No. She halted. *No, I mustn't.*

"I don't care what you say." Priss sighed luxuriously and closed her book, her finger lodging her place. "I love a good secret."

Kitty blinked and struggled to return. It was a conversation the two had begun sometime after midnight on the train from Manhattan, sitting up and sleepless in the tiny unlit compartment, the dark world outside sliding by. Sprawled on the opposite side of the compartment, Ogden and Dunc lay, hats over their faces, arms folded across their chests, passed out cold.

"Not if it isn't told," she observed.

"*Especially* if it isn't told. Precisely because it isn't told."

"But that doesn't make any sense. If it isn't told, then you don't know there's a secret."

"Yes." Priss smiled. "But it festers. Deliciously."

"Festers?"

"Oh, don't be such a snob." Priss rolled her eyes. "Yes, festers. Yes to the Dark, to the Deep, to Red *festering* Life."

In spite of herself, Kitty smiled. Dunc and

Priss went to parties in Greenwich Village, where the neckties were red, the ashtrays overflowed, and the conversation roamed hot and furious on topics from Moscow to Montauk. The two of them did not just dip their toes in life, they dove. And sometimes Kitty envied them.

"You realize, don't you," she said, "that you've begun to speak in capital letters. It's a contagion —"

"It's honest," Priss demurred, arching her back. "We are living in a time of capitals. You ought to try it."

"I might just," Kitty tossed back lightly, "you wait and see."

Priss snorted. She had known her since boarding school. Kitty Milton would never join the throngs gathering in back gardens in the Village after five, drinking gin and lime and battling hourly over the End of Civilization, the Beginning of Truth, the emergence at last of the Forgotten, the Downtrodden, the Masses, though the anger flashing on the streets anywhere you looked this summer was evidence that History's bright sword was flaming now, cutting swaths through the sheaves of the mystifying past.

"Honestly, though, do you tell Ogden everything?" she asked, turning her gaze down onto Dunc and Ogden.

"Of course," replied Kitty without blinking.

"Too bad," Priss reflected, turning away,

"because I'm willing to bet that a good marriage relies on secrets."

"Oh, for god's sake, Priss!"

Priss chuckled.

"Secrets are the stuff of books," Kitty pronounced.

"Good books." Priss slid the book into her bag.

"Not if they rely on secrets to keep the story humming. Life doesn't work that way."

"Oh, well — *life*," Priss snorted.

"Yes," Kitty affirmed. "Real people don't have secrets, because real people can't keep them."

What a liar I am. Kitty flushed, sliding her hand down into the pocket of her trousers to feel for the little yellow toy car she had carried with her since Neddy had died.

On the dock below, Ogden had taken the end of a line and was running it along his tongue, wetting it so it would thread easily through the bronze eye straps along the boom. And his care, his absorbed attention, made her sad.

They had carried on all through the year in quiet, the name *Neddy* unspoken between them. She'd grown used to his eyes flickering over her and past in the quick investigating way he had developed, checking on her, reading her as if he could tell what was in her heart simply by the cast of her head or the tip of her shoulders.

And when he'd appeared in the doorway of the nursery, weeks ago, the train tickets in hand, and asked her, hesitantly, wouldn't she like to take a trip, a little voyage without the children, his voice gruff, his eyes fixed on her, she had heard, clear as if he'd said it aloud, *Come back.*

"Darling, it's perfect." She leaned forward now, calling from the top of the gangway. "It's all just perfect."

"Lord love a duck, Kitty's right," Priss drawled. "Is it safe to board yet?"

Kitty started down the gangway to the dock. That hadn't been what she had meant at all, and she didn't want Og to think so. Kitty hadn't meant *hurry up, let's go.* She stepped off the end of the gangway and onto the wooden dock, the day's warmth just starting on the boards. She didn't want him to misunderstand. Especially now. She meant to make the most of this weekend. She meant to try.

She looked up and saw her husband smiling at her.

"Come on." Ogden reached his hand to her across the gunwale, and her heart stirred. He'd understood. In three steps Kitty had taken his hand and climbed over into the cockpit of the boat. He gave her arm a little squeeze.

"Hang on, you two," Priss said. "Let me take a picture."

Kitty and Ogden turned and smiled for Priss, standing still. Out of the corner of her eye, Kitty watched the woman in the ticket office light a cigarette and toss the match in the harbor as she looked on.

"Got it," said Priss, and lowered the camera back onto her chest, her eyes on her husband, who stood on the bow, his hands on his hips.

"Say there —" she called out merrily to him. "Are you planning on leaving the dynasty behind on the dock?"

Dunc Houghton straightened and turned around. Kitty shaded her eyes, watching the expression on his face soften. Rangy and dark haired, his dear bony face as familiar to Kitty as her own, he had become a Somebody in the New Deal, working in a dusty regulating office in charge of an obscure but vital agency somewhere in Manhattan and doing what a Houghton had always done — pitching in. He leaped off the bow and onto the dock beside his pregnant wife and grabbed the bag at her feet, took her elbow, and piloted her up and onto the bow deck.

And then they were off. Ogden at the tiller, Kitty beside him, and Dunc and Priss up in the bow, their backs against the mast as Ogden tacked his way carefully through the harbor pocked with the great boats of summer families not yet arrived. Cabot, Lowell, Hallowell, the boats bobbed at moorings painted with the names of Old Boston. Clearing this thicket, Ogden made straight out past the breakwater, pointing the *Sheila*'s prow out into Penobscot Bay, where a low line of islands lay just visible on the horizon ahead. The waves slapped soft against the hull as the *Sheila* cut the water, bouncing a little in search of the wind.

The day was glorious. They were to sail through to lunchtime and make a picnic at one of those islands ahead of them before arriving at Harry Lowell's summer place for the weekend. The plan seemed to have been conceived in one of the sudden bursts of enthusiasm Ogden was given to, and which Kitty had learned to give *in* to, though the Lowells were tiresome. They had an overly high opinion of themselves, as if the air they inhaled was purer, their morals unimpugned, the very blood that ran through Boston veins, bluer. Mrs. Lowell had been a Saltonstall, and she dropped the names of her forbears every twenty feet, like the buoys now marking the channel out of Rockland Harbor.

It was absurd, Kitty thought. Especially now, when it was men like Ogden, the New York bankers, who had steered the country through the Crash, and the collapse, and into the New Deal. They had all been spared because of that farsightedness. That clarity. Everyone agreed. Ogden had seen above the fray, past the mess — into the future. He always did. She studied him from the curve

118

of the cockpit.

Ogden lounged on the tiller, his shirt rolled up to his elbows, his long legs stretched along the cockpit, crossed at the ankle, his body falling into easy, perfectly rendered lines, as though he had been put together by an excellent draftsman. There was a suppressed excitement about him, a jauntiness that made her smile. He was up to something. She pushed herself forward into the prow of the cockpit, the smile still on her lips. He was up to something good.

"Darling, the jib," Ogden said, his eye on the sail.

She turned to grab the end of the line, pulling the smaller flat sail tight till it caught air. The *Sheila* shot ahead into the waves. Kitty lightly cleated the jib line and sat back down, lifting one trousered leg up on the bench across the cockpit to balance herself.

There wasn't a bird above or a boat on the horizon. The sea around them was as vast and open as a meadow.

On the bow, Dunc's fingers crept up to rest just underneath Priss's collar, and the soft blue cambric of her shirt set off his lean tan. He was famous for these small gestures of attention, always had been. And her whole life, Kitty had been a little in love with her own cousin because of this. She slid back down on the seat, closing her eyes, her long neck arched toward the sun.

"Can we please, please not talk about Germany?" Priss's voice drifted back. Dunc answered something Kitty couldn't hear.

"Because," Priss said, "it's all the way over there, and we're all the way over here. And you can't do anything about it this minute."

Kitty opened her eyes.

"Or Roosevelt," Kitty added, sitting up. "I don't want to hear about the wealth tax, the president, *or* the bank this weekend."

"Anyway, whatever's going to happen will happen," Priss said.

"At the bank?" Kitty asked.

"In Europe," answered Priss.

"Not if I can help it," Dunc murmured.

Kitty frowned. Her cousin always ran a little hot, leaping forward to take the reins as though life were a runaway coach and he the only one who could save it. It was admirable, even noble, but she thought he took things too far for his own good.

"Heard you hired Weinberg," Dunc said. "That true?"

"True," Ogden replied.

"Sol Weinberg?" Priss said lazily.

"Yup."

"What's he like?" Priss asked.

"He's a Jew," Kitty observed.

"A brilliant Jew," affirmed Ogden. "As good as they come."

"He was at Princeton, wasn't he? With Dick Sherman? Class of 'twenty-five?" Dunc asked.

"Yup." Ogden trimmed the sail. The prow of the boat dipped and rose.

"I hear he's after Susie Bancroft," Priss continued.

"That won't fly," Kitty remarked. "Her mother would never even invite someone like him to a dance."

"Someone like him?" Dunc repeated.

"Don't be exasperating, Dunc," she said. "You know what I mean."

Duncan turned around and draped his long legs into the cockpit, facing Ogden and Kitty now. "If he does all right, dots his *i*'s and all that, will you bring him into the firm as a principal?"

"Absolutely." Ogden nodded. "A good man is a good man."

Kitty pushed her hair off her forehead, considering her husband. *Do business with anyone,* her father would say, *but only sail with a gentleman.* Their world was quite clear about where that left Sol Weinberg. No matter what Ogden said, no matter what his enthusiasms, *a good man* would not help Susie Bancroft if she married Sol; she'd always be the girl who married a Jew. That's how it was. Men never seemed to look directly at a thing like that. They wanted to slide around, make adjustments. Talk. And then women had to live the life they had made.

The sail filled.

"But that's all just words," Kitty said firmly. "You know it doesn't really figure in. That's not the way of the world. You wouldn't ask Jo's boy to step in and run a company." Jo was Granny Houghton's gardener.

"Not without training," Dunc said.

"Even with training." Kitty shook her head. "Solly Weinberg, for instance," she appealed to Ogden, "no matter what you say about him, will never get the girl because he always behaves as though he's up against some kind of door."

"He *is* up against a door," remarked Dunc.

"That may be, but without the right girl a man like that will never get through. It's not fair, but it's just how it is. It's all in whom you marry."

"Just how it is," Ogden repeated, his eyes resting on her.

For a brief second, Kitty thought she'd overplayed her hand.

"He's part of the change ahead," he said.

"Change for what?" she pushed.

"New fields."

She shook her head.

Ogden raised his eyebrows.

She could see it all so clearly. The talk of what was best didn't leave her cold; she understood the need. Still, it was just talk. Just chatter. What *was* needed was to hold tight to what was best, what had been proven best. And to make sure everyone saw it. Saw these men and how good they were, how right. These were the men who had their hands on the tiller and knew what to do. They always had.

"Listen, you and Dunc are the very finest there is. We don't need new men. We need more of you."

On the bow, Priss raised her hand in a silent mock salute.

But Kitty knew she was right. Men had to be guarded from their enthusiasms. Women had to hold the chalice high, sometimes hold it up out of men's reach so they didn't break it in fits.

"You ought to speak to Harry Lowell about that." Dunc smiled at her. "He was positively gleeful at the club the other night. Did you hear him, Og? The moneymaking classes having seen their end, and all that."

Odgen nodded.

"How very pink," Priss observed.

"Though it'll never be level," Dunc put in. "And Lowell, of all people, knows it."

"The club," Kitty murmured inconsequentially. "I didn't think the Lowells ever left Boston."

"Sure they do," Dunc said cheerfully. "They like to get out of town every so often and see New York."

"The Harvard Club is hardly New York."

"Why do you think the entrance is fifty steps from the doors of Grand Central?"

Ogden grinned, pulling the jib sheet tight, and pushed the tiller close to his body.

Kitty laughed.

"There." She squinted, smiling, through the sun at him. "You've broken my rule."

"What's that?" he answered, his voice light.

"No talk about work or the world, and here you are. First thing."

"It's not respectful," Priss chimed in. "It's not kind."

"Dearest, marital politics are never kind," Dunc advised.

"Oh you," Priss drawled at her husband. "You think you can get off with a quip?"

"I do." Dunc's voice dug down, rich and low below his slow smile. "As you know, I'm a quipper."

He was staring at Priss, his love for her right there for anyone to see, and she reached up and touched his face, and the look between them bolted through the air and struck Kitty to the core. She turned to find Ogden, and there he was watching her.

"Listen to you." Ogden cocked his head. "You sound like Mother with all that talk about rules."

"I'm not a bit like your mother," she said, and smiled, holding her hand up off her face to shield the slant of the sun. "I'm a realist."

"What in heaven's name are we talking about here?" Priss asked.

"Nothing," answered Kitty, her eyes on

Ogden. "Are we, darling?"

Ogden pushed the tiller away, the flash of a smile starting over his face, and he shook his head, his hand loose on the tiller, his head tipped to check the mainsail. Her heart stuttered up in her chest. It was as if she'd stumbled out of the woods of the past year and found him. *Here we are. Oh, here we are. Ogden.* She raised her arms above her head and stretched, overtaken by this startling, brooding happiness, catching Ogden's eye and smiled.

He winked. And she felt it right in her middle. She winked back and pushed herself up on the seat, her heart surging forward with the bow of the boat reaching through the blue chop toward the gray and green humps ahead, slowly now distinguishing themselves into the separate islands.

"Where are we headed?" she asked.

"Just here." He pointed generally to the names marked on the chart. He had anchored it on the wooden bench of the Herreshoff with the aluminum tin of sandwiches and the bottle of gin, and between them she read: *Vinalhaven. Swans Island. Crockett's Island. North Haven.*

She nodded and rested her elbows on the gunwale. The waves slapped against the boat.

"Ready about." Ogden eased the tiller and let the sail out, running before the wind so it carried them on a long run forward, fast and forward into the lee of the islands, past the first stony point of Vinalhaven, the largest of them. An osprey nest, heavy in the tallest tree, tilted to the right, seeming to Kitty like a stick figure doffing his hat.

The boat shivered as they shifted and stalled. Ogden tacked again, and then the wind caught and slowly they slid forward on the angle, arrowing toward the center of the Narrows, the watery passage marked on the chart as a fairly shallow way through. Ogden pulled the sails in tight, and Dunc reached for the oar stowed under the gunwale, clambering up to the bow to push off if they got into trouble on the rocks.

They nosed forward easily now toward what looked like one unbroken stretch of land until suddenly the Narrows opened and an island sprung free of the low line, uncoiling, its long, rocky beach curving toward the four in the boat. Great chunks of granite made natural causeways down to the sea from the forest hanging at the water's edge. Along the curve, thousands of smaller granite stones covered the beach with a pebbled hide. And dead ahead, at the end of a cove, a narrow dock extended out from a shingled boathouse.

Ogden gave a low whistle. "Take a look at that."

In one tack, he nosed the boat easily down the lee and into the dock.

Dunc leaped from the bow, holding the

126

boat while Og released the line for the mainsail. The sail came shuddering down in folds around the boom, the sound like bird wings beating water. Priss uncleated the jib line so the jib sail lowered too. And then it was quiet. After the motion, after the wind on the bay, it was as if they had fallen off the world.

Nailed to one of the pilings in front of them a hand-lettered sign read:

FOR SALE — R. CROCKETT

Behind the boathouse, a grassy slope led up to a large white house perched high on top of a hill, its two chimneys rising from the steep black roof like the cutouts of castles against the summer sky. Unexpected and grand, the house had the serene solidity of having clearly occupied that hill, this lawn for at least one hundred years.

"But what would anyone do with a place like this?" Priss asked.

"Own it," Ogden answered promptly.

"Own it?" Kitty glanced at him, startled.

"Why not?" He smiled at her broadly.

"All the way up here? Everyone's miles away."

"They'd come to us." He leaped out of the boat, tying the line to the iron ring on the dock.

"It's all part of the plan," Dunc advised

127

her, a conspirator's smile on his lips.

"Plan?" She searched Ogden's face. "What plan? Ogden, what *are* you up to?"

He held out his hand for her to come.

"We can't just go up there," she said. "We can't just go in."

"Sure we can," Ogden urged. "Come on."

"But what about the people who live here?"

"We'll introduce ourselves," he said gaily. "Come on."

Slowly, Kitty took his hand and stepped over the gunwale and onto the dock. Priss and Dunc slid down from the bow, and the four of them walked up the gangway to the pier. Inside the boathouse, lobster buoys hung from pegs beside coiled tackle lines and lanterns, smelling of wet wood and salt and the sharp bite of kerosene in barrels, clear evidence that someone was using the place. Wooden oars leaned against the wall above an old rowboat turned on its side. The sound of their feet on the old wooden planks repeated the slap of the water on the rocks below.

They emerged through the open doorway onto the green lawn stretching up to that house at the top. The slate roof cut the blue sky. Eight windows stared down, flanked by dark green shutters. A lilac grew to the side of the door, where granite blocks were set for the front stoop. It was simple and ample, a dream of a kingdom. All of a piece. All of a place.

"Do you think there's electricity?" Dunc mused.

"Or hot water for a bath?" Priss addressed Kitty, slipping her hand into Dunc's and pulling him forward. The two of them wandered up the hill with the boiled eggs, the tin of sandwiches, the thermos of coffee, and the bottle of gin slung from Dunc's shoulder in the canvas bag.

Kitty and Ogden remained at the bottom of the lawn in the shadow of the boathouse. To the left of the house and up a small hill a granite obelisk and the rounded tops of four gravestones rose. A family of graves. She had a short, sudden shock of looking ahead into the years to come, here. The house on the hill, the spruce line behind it, these wide verdant fields whose grasses waved like girls at a fair.

And Neddy was dead. Her eyes clouded. Neddy would always be dead.

Ogden wrapped his arms around her from behind, and she leaned against him and felt his breath in her hair.

"It's yours if you want it."

"If *I* want it?" She glanced up at him. There was salt caught in the corner of his eyes, which shone sharp blue just then. He had gotten some color in the sail over this morning.

"I want this place," he said quietly. "I want this house to be ours. And everyone sailing by would know it stood for us. It would mean something. They'd see it and think, there's the Milton place. Kitty and Ogden Milton. The Miltons of Crockett's Island."

He looked back down into her face, willing her to shift off all the sorrow and quiet of the last year, willing her forward toward the flank of granite beach, the spruce trees and this light.

"Come on." He squeezed and pulled her up the lawn with him. And she felt the shock of seeing forward, how many times they would walk up the hill to that house with their children, and perhaps their children's children. Ogden's dream in place. Ogden's dream right here. And Kitty walked toward the house on the hill, a spot in time she would return to like a stone in her pocket she could reach for and rub, over and over in the years to come.

NINE

Evie turned down Bleecker Street, heading home, the thick force of the afternoon recalling all the Junes she had lived through on this street, just this way, the damp heat suddenly dropped like a curtain to walk through — spring done, summer here. And, as it always did, the city's summer heat conjured its opposite: the path into the woods on the Island, the fog covering the meadow between the Big House and the barn, the steady call of the foghorn in the bay. All her life that contrast had underscored her summers, the cool patch underfoot. Always, shining there at the end of the heat, at the end of the grime and heavy city nights there'd be the promise of Maine. At the end of the summer there'd be the Island.

With a pang, she fingered the strap of her satchel on her shoulder, Hazel's words rankling.

The Big House needed a new roof. The dock needed new floats. The barn was sinking into the field, foundationless. In the thirty years since her grandparents had died, the place had limped along — beautiful, thread-bare, and inexorable in its need, Joan and Evelyn waging a fierce and inscrutable battle over change or improvements of any kind — Joan resisting Evelyn and winning in the end, surviving her sister by a year. But now that she had died, the Island and its upkeep had passed down to Evie and her four cousins, only one of whom had had the wherewithal to go into a profession that made any money. So Crockett's Island floated up there in Penobscot Bay, curled like a question, or a fist, depending on how you saw it.

They were caught like flies in amber in the place where time had stopped. There was the tarnished silver ice bucket inscribed with Evelyn's initials, September 1959, a wedding present. There were the buoy doorstops. The furniture her grandparents had bought in the thirties recovered, repaired — though even that had last been done sometime in the early seventies — but never replaced. The Island collected and then contained their summer days. Seth's rock collection lined up on the windowsill in the upstairs yellow bedroom, adding to Evie's cousin Henry's, which had, in turn, marched beside their uncle Moss's. Children there rowed boats, climbed trees, picked mussels, ending every summer day cleaned up and carrying the ice in the silver bucket, the Goldfish crackers, and the Scotch, down to the dock at six, where they'd stand ranged along the splintering wooden boards looking down at the white bodies of the flashing fish, while the grown-ups behind them drank as the sun fell into the sea. The Miltons of Crockett's Island.

It was an absurdity. An affectation. Unreal. And yet summer wasn't summer without it. The year could not turn without time on the Island.

At the end of the block ahead of her, the shade of the trees in the tiny triangle park had tipped into evening and the promise of the cool to come. Three black men sat on the single bench, legs stretched out, shirts hanging loose around their sweating chests. One of them smoked and watched her approach, watching without any interest, without any movement toward her — a white woman in her middle age, neither young nor pretty, simply walking.

She stared at him through her dark glasses, walking toward him down the block, and after a little bit, he looked away. She had seen him before, sitting there, and she had that sense — as she often did in the city — of the many layers of all of them, familiar strangers, sliding along the surface of each other's lives, visible and invisible, like fish in a clear pond. The door to her building clicked open and she passed into the cool marble silence, the

133

sounds of the city muffled as the street door swung shut behind her. Years ago, when she and Paul had first moved into the apartment, she'd lie through the long, airless midsummer nights with the windows flung wide open for a breeze, hovering between sleep and waking, the voices of the people in the park outside coming to her like radio broadcasts from another world, comforting and incomprehensible — human noises in the dark.

She pushed open the front door into the long hall that tunneled the length of the apartment to her grandmother's oval gilt mirror hanging squarely at the end. Far down the hall she heard the clicking of Seth's keyboard.

The typing stopped. "Mom?"

"Hey, love," Evie answered automatically, staring at a letter marked Special Delivery that lay on the mat under her feet.

After a minute, the typing started up again.

She picked it up. It was on expensive stationery, and the handwriting — *handwriting!* — in indigo ink. *Miss Evelyn Ludlow Milton.* For an instant, her own name looked to her like someone else's, which of course it was. It was her aunt's name and her great-aunt's, and her great-great-aunt's. With a slight dread, she turned the envelope over and ripped it open. Addressed to herself and her four cousins, it read: *You are respectfully reminded of the meeting arranged in the offices of Sherman, Troup, and DeForest on Friday, June 29.*

It was six months to the day her mother had died. And it was next Monday. They were being gathered to discuss what was next. She slid out of her shoes, pulling her satchel over her head, and threw her keys onto the table, where they clattered off the old wood before sliding down onto the carpet with a *thunk*. And what *was* next? She doubted she and Paul could afford it, and if they had to pay for it, she was pretty sure Paul would want out. And then what? It wasn't just the Island, it was all of them — it was Mum.

Wandering down the hallway with the letter in hand, the woman walking toward her in the mirror looked exactly like Granny K. Her eye rested on the Polaroid tucked in the frame of the mirror; she reached and slid it free.

There on a sunny afternoon stood Moss, Joan, and Evelyn Milton in front of the Big House on Crockett's Island.

Moss stood slightly to one side, his short dark hair blown loose, his right fist raised in a salute of some kind, a grin on his face that seemed to be the end of a joke someone must just have told. He looked to be somewhere in his twenties. He wore a madras jacket over an untucked white shirt, cupped a cigarette in his left hand, and looked straight at the camera, as if daring it.

Beside him, long limbed, in their twenties, their brown hair cut attractively short, Joan and Evelyn Milton stared serenely into their future, their arms wrapped lightly around each other's waist, the familiar line of windows at the front of the house framing their heads. In narrow shorts and button-down sleeveless blouses, fine boned and easy, they stood beside each other, clearly linked. Sisters. The Milton girls. The girls who were raised to say yes. Yes to their parents, yes to a world of parties and dances and green hopes at the far end of the lawn.

Mum.

Evie looked into Joan's smile — into that laughing, open *trust* in all that was ahead. Evie had never seen this expression on her mother's face. Not ever. The woman she knew had been nothing at all like this girl.

Of silence, her mother had been the master, entering rooms as carefully as if each one held a bomb, hesitating on the threshold, moving quietly inside a conversation, quietly out. And Evie had spent most of her teenage years in a state of barely suppressed fury, ready to erupt at the simplest provocation, living a heady mix of righteousness and outrage, determined to explode every bomb she could. She vowed to be nothing like her mother. Her life had been wrong, somehow, a life lived in the slipped track, as though the right reel of film had never caught on the teeth of the projector and the life she and her father lived was just off — almost right. Evie couldn't say why she felt this; her mother and father dressed the way everyone else did, ate the same food, Evie had gone to the same schools. It was as if her parents had inherited their days rather than chosen them, made do with what they had, and so they peopled the rooms rather than lived in them, ghosting their own lives.

But here, the tilt of her mother's chin, the open smile, showed a young woman straining forward, delighted. Fresh. A woman alive and expectant as a summer morning. The kind of character some novels of a certain type began with. Bright, alert, emerging onto the white stoop of a lovely house at the start of a day. *What a lark! What a plunge!*

What happened?

Written on the bottom of the picture in her mother's careful print was the date, *August 22, 1959, the morning of* — punctuated with two exclamation points.

Of what, Mum? Evie had asked.

Oh? Her mother's face was vague. *I can't remember.*

It was nobody's birthday or anniversary. As far as Evie had ever been able to figure, it was nothing remarkable at all. A summer day at the end of the fifties on the Island.

But it had been this very photograph her mother asked for in the winter as she lay dying. It had been her sister whom Joan had called for, though Evelyn had died a year before — and died in a punishing silence, refusing to speak to Joan at the end. Evie had never known the sisters to have had a breach. But in her last days it was as though Evelyn had been possessed by a spite that seemed to gather her high-handedness into one furious ball, against which Joan had batted on her own deathbed, calling for her sister over and over as she died. And the sorrow that that had caused, the inexplicable meanness of it all, erupted in moments like this when Evie would find herself studying the two of them gazing serenely toward their future.

"Mom?"

"What?"

"Never mind." Her son's voice drifted back into his room. "I found them."

She slipped the Polaroid back into the frame.

She hadn't seen her cousins since the funeral. Mum's will had gone through probate. By now the cousins were meant to have a plan. Instead, they had fallen into a shared paralysis undercut by an unspoken but persistent campaign on the part of her cousin Henry, the eldest of "the Evelyns," as they were called, to assert his natural right — natural, as he saw it — to run the Island, because his mother had always taken charge. Aunt E had run the roost. Evie could weigh in, but Evie was not an Evelyn, she was "a Joan." There were four of them and one of her, and after all, Henry would point out over and over, Aunt Joan had been lovely, but for most of her life she had never taken charge up there. And though she never liked to agree with anything her cousin Henry said, he was right. Her mother had never insisted on anything except that nothing change.

Never, that is, until the week before she died, when Evie had come into her mother's room and found her sitting up in bed with this photograph in her hand.

"I want to be buried on Crockett's," Joan said, and turned to look at her daughter.

"All right," Evie answered, her voice sticking in her throat. It was the first time either of them had talked directly about the fact that her mother was dying.

"At the edge of the picnic grounds."

Evie put down the tray on the bed.

"And the stone should say 'Here.' "

" 'Here'?" Evie was bewildered. "Not 'Joan Milton —' "

" *'Here,'* " her mother repeated. "One word."

"Okay," Evie managed. "Why?"

Joan had turned on her pillow and looked at her daughter intently, considering her — as if, Evie realized, she couldn't be sure of her.

"But I told you that. I told you that already."

What had she told her? Evie wondered. When?

"Promise me, Evie."

"I do," Evie said. "I will, Mum."

"Evelyn won't like it," she said.

"Aunt Evelyn is dead, Mum," Evie said gently.

And Joan had nodded, leaned the photograph up against the lamp on her bedside table, folded her hands across the faded silk coverlet over her chest, and closed her eyes.

It had seemed easy just then to say, *I do, I will.* It had seemed simple, and easy, and right. But nothing at all now was simple, or easy, or right.

"Mom?"

"Lordy!" She was sharper than she meant. "Seth, could you come out here and talk to me, instead of yelling the entire length of Bleecker Street?"

Her son emerged from the doorway of his room, six feet tall, the knapsack with his name stitched on it that he had had since fifth grade slung over one broad shoulder, and she smiled. He smiled back, the fifteen-year-old in full possession of his beauty and his charm, the boy still shining through the man's body.

"I've got to go to the library."

She nodded. "Do you have money?"

"Yup," he said. "Later."

She leaned back in her chair.

"As in, see you," he said.

"I am familiar with the phrase."

"Okay." He slid around the door. "And it's not the entire length of Bleecker, anyway."

"Wait," she called after him, smiling. "I'll drive you."

He backed up and peeked his head in with a surprised grin on his face that was all Paul's. "You will?"

She nodded. "Hold up."

He took the flights of stairs at a run, his sneakers making that single, sharp, high-pitch shriek against the linoleum that always reminded her of gym class and whistles.

"Hey, Mom, do you know what Dr. Conklin told us yesterday?" He waited for her at the bottom.

"What."

"All the major questions have been answered in physics," Seth said cheerfully, and pulled open the front door.

She looked at him. "That's horrible."

"It's progress."

"What does that mean for physics?"

"It means I don't need to take it, right? I mean, seriously, why would I take physics when it's all over?"

"Hardly all over."

"It is, though, Mom." He grinned. "And

anyway, I can use the free period for homework. And then I'd have more time to study Russian, and then I'd be able to say I speak two really hard languages."

And then, she thought, looking at him. The car was parked haphazardly at the end of the block, evidence of her distraction. *And then* — stretching out into a vast, leafy life. First one thing, then the next. She slid behind the wheel. Every day something will happen, something new will come. And then, and then. She remembered this urgent push toward the next thing and the next. She pulled into traffic, joining the line that snaked toward the corner. It was all going forward toward some unknown, wonderful end.

The light turned green and Evie waited, her hand on the gear stick, for an older woman to cross. A woman in a skirt and jacket, her groceries clutched in one hand. Evie wasn't paying attention at first; she was calculating when she could nudge forward and make the turn without scaring the woman or being rude. In the passenger seat, Seth stared ahead. The woman stepped off the curb, her eyes on the walk sign, crossing very slowly, determined to make it in the one go of the light, determined to keep moving forward though Evie could see the effort it cost her. In her living room, Evie imagined, there might be a chair, a stopping point, to take a little rest. Whereas Minetta Lane, all thirty feet of it, was a vast distance to be crossed before the light turned again.

"So brave," Evie murmured.

Seth glanced at her.

"It takes so much courage to keep getting up and going into the world when you are old or sick."

"I know, Mom."

"I'm serious."

"I know, Mom," Seth said again gently. "You've said."

Evie's eyes filled. "I have?" And sitting there, waiting, her boy beside her, it came to her that this woman in front of her was moving the way her mother moved in the last year of her life, before they'd understood it was cancer that had twined around her bones and was pulling her backward, slowing her down.

He nodded. The car behind them honked. The woman was almost at the halfway point, though not yet. *Go,* Evie heard herself whisper. *Go on.* It was unbearable. How old was she? Maybe not old. Maybe just sick. And where was her family? The car behind honked again.

"Mom!"

Evie had opened her door and was out on the street, moving toward the woman and reaching a hand to take her groceries, without thinking, without paying attention to the driver behind her, leaning on his horn now.

The woman was much older than Evie had

thought, and stopped, her gaze drawn to Evie. The driver called out his window. "Hey!"

"Can I take those for you?" Evie pointed to the bags.

The woman looked down and handed them to Evie without a word. If she could have, Evie would have picked the woman up too and carried her the rest of the way, nearly frantic with wanting to move her, to get her to safety.

"Let me help." She offered her arm.

And slowly, the woman took it. And Evie turned toward her and they walked the last ten feet, slowly, the bag of groceries in one hand. She took in the fact that her car door was wide open in the street, that Seth was turned in his seat looking at the driver in the car behind, who was shouting something. She saw and heard and concentrated on getting this woman across.

They made it up onto the curb. "Thank you, dear." The woman pointed to her groceries. "Very nice of you."

Evie nodded and hurried back to the car. She had never once done anything like that for her own mother, never. She slid into the driver's seat, slammed the door, and put the car in gear, driving away, forward, passing the woman on the curb, now waiting to cross Sixth Avenue.

"Mom?"

"It's all right, Seth," Evie said. And then she simply started to cry. He sat stiffly beside her. They pulled through the traffic up Sixth Avenue, in the stream of cars heading north, in silence. Her mother dead but not yet buried. Her son looking straight ahead, the tears sliding down her cheeks.

"Oh," she sniffed. The woman had been nothing at all like her mother, not in shape or size. Nothing, except for that nearly childlike concentration as she crossed the street, the will to get where she was going, no matter what. Nobody warned you about this stuff. Nobody said, *Watch out for the echoes. Watch out for the ghosts.*

"Mom," Seth said. "It's okay."

She nodded and tried to smile. At the library entrance, Seth slid out of the car, bounded up the stone stairs, and turned quickly to find her before she drove away. Their eyes met through the window, and he waved.

She nodded again at him and did smile. And watched as he climbed the rest of the stairs, yanked open the heavy doors, and disappeared inside. The wind rustled through the leaves in the two old maples that stood like sentinels on either side.

Six months ago there were leaves still hanging on in winter, different leaves on the same trees. Her mother's cancer had been vicious and implacable. An enemy with too much

firepower sent in to topple such a soft target.
Never mind.

"She'll sleep more and more, and then one day she'll just stop drinking, and that's when you know she's decided to die."

Evie had nodded at the hospice nurse, not wanting to be rude, but it seemed to her an absurd bit of wishfulness that the dying would come to terms with death so neatly. Out the window, the afternoon was closing down and the winter dark rising in the park across the way while her mother grew pale and paler inside, the sheets pulled straight around her in long white lawns. Snow on snow, so quietly — as she had gone about everything in her life, until her last morning, when she had woken up, her eyes wide with fright.

"Evie," she'd whispered, "am I dying? I dreamed I was dying."

"It's all right, Mum," Evie had said, looking straight at her. "You're right here."

No matter how well you take care of the dying, no matter if you sit beside them every minute, every day — in the end they must go, and you stay. And you wave them off. You lie.

TEN

The house needed paint. The shutters needed slats. The granite slabs that stood in for front steps were fuzzed with moss. But the bees droned in the lilac by the front door, and shafts of irises gone to seed waved in clumps along the low line beneath the windows.

Ogden rapped upon the wood and then leaned toward the door to listen.

"Come on," he said, and pushed down the latch, and they followed him into the empty front hallway.

"Hello!" Ogden called. Kitty put her hand on the banister of the painted gray staircase that stretched steeply up to the second floor. "Mr. Crockett?"

No one answered. Whoever had lived here had left long ago. In the front sitting room the wallpaper tattered over the windows and dead flies spotted the sills. Four heavy wooden chairs occupied each corner, the stuffing leaking, stalwarts in decline. A braided rug wound its circle in the middle in faded grays and greens. They walked through into the dining room, where a long oaken table stood at its center. No chairs surrounded it, no rug supported it; the massive table seemed to Kitty abandoned. Out the side windows the timothy grasses waved high from the wide field. There was a door to a back hall, a door to the front hall, a door to what looked like a pantry, and then another door off its hinges that showed the bottom of a flight of back stairs.

"It smells like a barn," Priss said.

Despite it all, Kitty couldn't get the image of Goldilocks out of her head. It was so clearly someone's house. So clearly had held a family, many families, in its rooms. Where were the Crocketts? The light coming in through the windows patterned long squares on the painted floor. She walked through into the pantry, where there were dishes stacked on three open shelves, and farther into a dark kitchen, where a tiny window at the back had lost its glass. The hump of a great rock loomed through the window like the shoulder of a white whale.

The others' voices scattered throughout the house, first Ogden's, then Dunc's. Kitty wandered over to the narrow stairs to the second floor, resting her hand on the worn knob of the banister before climbing. The rooms above were furnished with beds whose mattresses sagged and split, cane chairs, and china washstands, the white curtains torn. The sink was crusted with dirt, and brown water spat out of the tap when she turned it. Spat and stopped. It had been a long while since someone had slept in the house. Still, the hard, clear light of the midday sun through the side windows along the floorboards had a peace in it. The house waiting. She stopped in the middle of one of the bedrooms and imagined a newly painted bedstead in the corner, fresh curtains hanging in the window, and a bedside table tucked next to the bed.

She reached and tied the curtain sash and came slowly down the back stairs into the kitchen and out the door over to the flat rock behind the house, where Priss and Dunc had arranged themselves, Priss leaning against Dunc's knees, her legs stretched out and crossed at the ankles. Ogden came around the other side of the house carrying the bag with the bottle and the tin of sandwiches.

"No water inside?" Dunc asked.

"It'll have to be gin for the babe, I'm afraid." Ogden set the bag down, pulling out the bottle and the four silver shot glasses.

"Oh well." Priss took the one he filled. "Just a smidge."

They ate their sandwiches under the shadow of the house in quiet. The crickets played their tune. And the heat and the gin made them all sleepy. Kitty lay down in the grass.

Ogden's hand closed on her foot. She opened her eyes, rolled onto her elbow, and smiled at him. He squeezed her foot. She sat up. "Let's take a walk," she said. "Come on, you two."

"You go on," Priss answered drowsily. "I'm going to take a little snooze."

"Right." Ogden was on his feet and pulled Kitty to hers, keeping hold of her hand as they set off away from the house toward the crowd of trees that bordered the field at the edge of the lawn.

The graveyard they had seen from the boathouse lay just up a rise on the way to the woods, and they stopped outside the iron railing that ringed the four Crockett graves. Someone, Kitty noted, had recently mowed around the headstones. *Rufus, Ship-Builder,* and his brother *Increase, Captain and Farmer,* were buried at the front of the tiny yard. And then, just behind the brothers, were two others:

Here lies Louisa, aged 31,
Died August 31, 1840 and her two children,
Stillborn

and

Henry, b 1846, d 1863

150

They stood a minute, and then Kitty reached for Ogden's hand and they turned away and through the field. A narrow path appeared, and they entered the cool interior woods, sunlight catching on the green branches. He pulled her closer, wrapping his arm around her shoulder so they walked side by side, stepping over the moss-covered roots spread like tendons across the path.

Deeper in they went, away from the house, from Dunc and Priss and the world. The moss was so deep it swallowed their footfalls, and though they walked on granite boulders, they made not a sound. For now, it seemed to Kitty that the two of them walked right out of the picture, into a thick, deep dark, so when Ogden paused a moment in the middle of the path, she was nearly breathless with wanting to shut her eyes and have him kiss her right there. Stop time.

She put her hand on his chest, and Ogden pulled it up to his mouth and kissed her fingers. And with the other hand he pulled her close to him, against him, and she smelled the gin on his breath and smiled under his lips.

He buried his face in her neck as he stirred against her. She smiled languidly and let herself be kissed. He grew more insistent,

151

holding her tighter.

She smiled. "Ogden."

"Come on," he said huskily, pulling her forward. She saw the trees thinning ahead and the light of the afternoon bouncing off the water. And there the path stopped. They stood hand in hand at the edge of a flat clearing that sloped down to an apron of granite. It was a turning tide, and the water sucked softly at the rock. One could still slip in and out of the sea easily from those giant rocks, though the black rim of mussels was starting to show.

He drew her back a few steps into the partial bower of the forest's edge, a pine screen.

"Let's make a little island baby."

"Here?" She was smiling.

He ringed her waist with both hands, pulling her against him. "Here," he said, and then slowly drew her blouse free of her slacks, and she lifted her arms, letting him draw the cotton over her head. "Kitty," he said. And she nodded under his lips and his hands, as he unsnapped her bra, her skin alive in the air. She unbuttoned her slacks and let them fall so she stood against him, her eyes closed.

"Kitty," he whispered, sliding her panties down and gathering her in. All the longing of the morning rushed through her, and she shut her eyes and went with him.

■ ■ ■ ■

One by one her senses returned. The breeze moved across their bodies, carrying the smell of the sea. They lay together side by side, his hand resting on her hip, lazing in the dappled sun. They had left the dock in Rockland and sailed somehow here, where the world pushed away, and had returned to each other.

An osprey called and the wind pulled through the tops of trees above where they lay. Ogden's heart thumped against hers.

She opened her eyes and saw he was watching her.

"Hello, darling," he said quietly.

She touched his face.

"Promise me," he whispered, "promise you'll never leave like that again."

Her eyes filled.

"Here is the beginning," he whispered, tucking her hair behind her ear. "Our beginning."

"Of what?"

"Our lives." He smiled down at her. "All of it. All that is good. We'll buy this island and begin. Again." And gathering her close, murmuring into her hair, he began painting pictures in the air. Moss and Joan would learn to sail and pick mussels for their supper. They would dream of this place all winter long, he murmured, this would be their nugget of gold, what they buried inside them, what made them Miltons. And when they arrived again at the start of every summer, when they tumbled off the boat and stood here and saw this house and the dock, and that obelisk in the graveyard — all exactly as they'd left it — they would have cheated Time. Just a little bit. Over and over.

"Hush." She cast a glance upward. "You can't cheat Time."

"Life" — he touched her face — "cheats Time."

She turned her head. Through the trees, the grassy clearing unrolled green to the great rocks. He was calling her forward, taking her by the hand away from the last year. Away from Neddy. And she must choose. Forward or back; it was very clear. Not which way, but that she must.

A chunk of her heart dropped down and lodged. She turned back and stared up at Og.

He leaned and kissed her arm, then rolled and reached for his trousers, pulling them on swiftly and standing up. Sunlight blared above his head, blacking out his face.

"Come on," he said, smiling down at her.

Nodding, she sat up. The air chilled her skin, and pointing to her tossed blouse, she kneeled and found her trousers. Beside them, Neddy's car had slid from the pocket and settled there in the moss, a yellow spot in the green. A finch on a bough. A child alighting.

He dropped down beside her. For a moment the mother and father were still. Then, gently, he bent forward and took the car, reached for her hand, and turned it over, placing the car in the cup of her palm, closing her fingers around the yellow metal.

The tears rising in her throat, she slid the car back into the pocket of her slacks and reached for her blouse, buttoning in silence. Then she stood too and pulled on her slacks, zipping them to the top of her waist.

"Ready?" he asked.

She looked up at him and nodded. He wiped the tears off her cheek with his thumb. And then the two of them turned from the water and moved back inland through the trees hand in hand, emerging from the woods into the suddenly blinding sun, where they stood for a minute. There was nobody about. The topmost eave of the house cut a black angle against the sky, and it seemed to Kitty they had been away for years.

Ogden squeezed her hand. The kitchen door stood open, and they went inside, Ogden pulling the handle shut behind him, already caring, already owning. They wandered back through the pantry, the dining room, and into the front hall that was blue, Kitty now saw, a china blue.

"But who on earth is that?"

At the end of the lawn, Priss and Dunc were standing by the boathouse talking to a woman in a narrow skirt and yellow cardigan.

Ogden stopped behind her.

She looked up.

"Ogden?"

With one swift motion he pushed open the screen door and passed through. The door slapped in its wooden frame.

Dunc pointed, and Priss and the other woman turned around. Ogden took the steps of the house two at a time, starting down the lawn.

The woman was slight, her small face shining out of a mass of black curls. She raised one hand to shield herself from the sun, her eyes on Ogden.

From behind her, a small, exuberant boy dashed out from the door of the boathouse into the silence, laughing, and pulled on his mother's hand. Then he catapulted past her up the lawn, throwing himself on the grass and rolling back down, his arms crossed over his chest, his delighted cries rising and lowering in tufts of sound.

Kitty reached for the branch of the lilac that grew there by the door, her gaze faltering at the sight of the quick, small body, the joy barreling down in the sunlight.

"Mama!" the boy cried, lying at his mother's feet.

But the woman didn't look down at him. Her eyes had never left Ogden walking toward her, his hand outstretched. She stepped forward.

Kitty watched as Ogden stiffened, hesitating an instant, and saw that this woman was a shadow on the lawn somehow, wanting something, a shadow stretching across Ogden even as he started forward again and took the woman's hand, pulling her forward, his head bending toward hers as he leaned to kiss her cheek. There was a concentrated coil in his body, Kitty recognized. They knew each other, and quite well.

Oh. Kitty looked past them toward the water at high tide, lapping the white rocks in the cove, and stood frozen in the doorway of the house. *Begin again,* he had whispered to her not half an hour ago. She shuddered.

Harry Lowell emerged from the boathouse with a picnic basket, lazy and watchful as a man who is playing his hand.

"Hullo, Milton."

She couldn't hear what Ogden said.

The boy had picked himself up and started running again, his legs pumping in short pants, his arms spread, flying in a Fair Isle sweater through the blue air away from his mother, flying now up the hill toward Kitty.

No, she thought. *No, no. Get away.*

But he was running headlong, laughing, released. Upward, forward, making a low, steady noise in his throat Kitty recognized. A plane. A car. A train. Look at me.

He stopped dead and stared up at her, the

157

tall woman in the doorway of the old house.

He had the same crop of wild black curls as the woman down there. The collar of his shirt was half-pinned under the neck of his green woolen sweater.

"Ich bin Willy."

He was smaller and darker than Neddy had been. Not as tall. Though the same waiting expression. The same abandon —

"Und" — he turned around and pointed — *"das ist Mama."*

Kitty stared down at him. She couldn't speak.

The boy wheeled round and ran away again, down the hill back toward Ogden and the woman. And the hungry longing on Ogden's face as he watched the boy run toward him hit Kitty with the force of a blow.

She couldn't bear that the boy was not Neddy. She couldn't bear that boy running over the grass, where Neddy should have been. She slid her hand into the pocket of her trousers and felt for Neddy's car.

"Kitty," Og called to her. "Come and meet Elsa."

ELEVEN

A little older than Kitty, perhaps a little older than Ogden, Elsa was not beautiful, Kitty decided. She was not tall. She had curly hair and a fluid, vibrant face, full of silent exclamation, her thoughtful dark brown eyes anchoring a smiling mouth. She would miss nothing, Kitty saw. She had taken Kitty's hand when they first met with a frank appraisal.

"You are just as they described." Elsa smiled at her.

"Who is 'they'?"

"Milton," Elsa answered, glancing at Ogden, "and Harry."

"Elsa is an old friend," Ogden remarked. "I do business with her father."

"When did you arrive?" asked Kitty.

"Last week," replied Elsa, watching Ogden drawing Kitty tight against him.

"And will you be here long?"

"Not long."

"How long?" asked Kitty.

"Until I have completed my father's business," she said, lifting her eyes to follow a fish hawk crossing the open sky.

"I hadn't expected to see her," Ogden answered Dunc, later that afternoon, as the four of them sailed away from the dock. Elsa and Harry and the boy had gone on ahead. "I'd forgotten Harry knew her."

He seemed to have completely recovered himself; the moment of shock Kitty had felt in the doorway might never have happened. Kitty watched him, the line for the mainsail tight in his hand. And yet she saw he had been shaken. It was not sexual, not romantic, but something else. This woman hovered somewhere in her husband's heart.

"Go on," Priss prompted Ogden in the boat. "Why is she here on her own?"

Ogden drew the tiller in close, leaning low below the boom to watch the water line.

"She's married to a Jew. I'd guess it has to do with her husband —" Dunc said.

"He's been arrested," Ogden said.

"Hang on." Dunc turned all the way around to stare at Ogden. "Bernhard Walser belongs to the Party. He's the head of German Steel."

Ogden pulled his pipe from his shirt pocket, tapping it against the hull. "That's right."

The sail was luffing.

Kitty kept her eyes on Ogden, who worked the tiller back and forth to catch the breeze.

"You'd think Hoffman would have been protected." Dunc's worry was audible.

"So that little boy is a Jew?" Priss asked.

Ogden nodded. "Fully."

"Fully?" Priss looked at him. "Elsa's a Jew?"

"Her mother was a Jew. But Walser is an Aryan," Ogden explained. "With money. And clout. So she is protected."

"It won't be enough, Ogden," Dunc answered. "Elsa is a *Mischling.*"

"Let's hope it won't get that dark." Ogden put the stem of the pipe in his mouth and looked at Dunc, clearly troubled.

"Where is Hoffman now?"

"Sachsenhausen," Ogden answered.

"What is that?" Kitty frowned.

"A detention center. Just outside Berlin."

Dunc held Ogden's gaze, a pained expression on his face. "It won't be enough, Ogden," he repeated.

Kitty frowned. Her cousin had a taste, approaching a hunger, for tragedy. He always had.

"See that, Dunc. You always see black, when brown will do."

"Damn right." He gave Kitty a slight smile. "Though in this case, I'd take the black over the brown."

"Ready about," Ogden called, and pointed them close to the wind, moving them swiftly along the chop, the roof of Lowell Cottage appearing through the trees at the end of its

161

point, surrounded by others of North Haven's summer colony.

By the time they emerged onto the great veranda of Lowell Cottage, having freshened up and changed, it was evening. The foghorn in the bay had started calling, and the first tendrils of an evening mist snagged upon the spruce tops. Harry was mixing drinks with his father, Harry Sr., a jovial, solicitous man with a broad face beamed by eyebrows that winged up and away from his open, interested attention. Elsa was nowhere to be seen.

"What can I get you in a glass?" Mr. Lowell cried.

"Vermouth." Kitty smiled. "On the rocks."

"Ogden?" Mr. Lowell asked.

"Something brown" — Ogden had taken Kitty by the hand — "and lots of it."

"A man after my own heart." Mr. Lowell turned to the drinks cart cheerfully.

They fell into a loose semicircle, the women placed in rattan chairs, the men standing, all of them facing the sea. The sun lowered farther down, a cooling breeze picking up the sleeve of Priss's dress, lifting and replacing it like a thoughtful suitor. Beside her, Dunc rested his hand on the back of her chair. The broad expanse of the bay lay before them, the mainland in distant view.

Famously as expansive and eclectic as the facade of the house around him, Harry

162

Lowell Sr. was credited with singlehandedly having procured for the Harvard Library one of the six extant copies of the Gutenberg Bible, the first folios of Shakespeare's histories, and just lately, a pristine copy of the first printing of Burton's *Anatomy of Melancholy.* Having now scored the coup of the Walser collection for the summer exhibition, the man was irrepressible. It was to him, Kitty learned, that Elsa had been charged with bringing her father's library, the reason for her visit among them just then, the old man explained, handing Kitty her vermouth.

Kitty raised her eyebrows. That was not the reason Elsa was here. Even she could see that.

"Her father's library?"

"Oh yes, good lord, the Walser collection is one of the finest collections of illuminated manuscripts in Germany. I'd heard of it, of course, but never seen it. The Nazis are very canny to produce a show alongside the Summer Games. Puts to rest some of the stories about the brutishness."

"And wouldn't the Germans want to show it off closer to home?"

"Showing it is the way to keep it safe," said Ogden.

"And to share it with the world," Mr. Lowell added generously. "Ah, there you are, Mrs. Hoffman — and Willy."

"Elsa," Harry greeted her as she drew onto the veranda, leading Willy by the hand.

The boy had had his bath and was wrapped in a blue cotton robe with matching calfskin slippers. The smoothed hair, the faint scent of soap his body carried, the glow from the heat and the scrubbing was so familiar, Kitty had to look away. Elsa sank into an empty chair, pulling him onto her lap and drawing all their attention, like the low flames of a fire.

It was unorthodox. Unheard of. Children did not belong at the cocktail hour.

"How uncomfortable," Mrs. Lowell remarked.

"Most comfortable spot on the porch, I'd say, Mother." Harry put a drink in Elsa's hand. She smiled up at him, taking the glass.

"But surely he'd rather be in a bed upstairs," Mrs. Lowell pressed forward generally. "It must be time."

"It is time," Elsa agreed, turning her gaze to the older woman. "But he is too frightened."

"I beg your pardon?"

"Ever since his papa's arrest," Elsa said as she leaned back in the chair, "he cannot fall asleep on his own."

"My dear."

"See that." Mr. Lowell shook his head. "I'd get the hell out of there if I were a Jew —"

"A Jew, dear!"

"You would not get the hell out, Father, and you know it. You'd stay and fight."

"I'd like to think so," Mr. Lowell answered. "I'd like to think I'd do the right thing."

"What's right" — Dunc spoke for the first time — "is to pressure Hull to open the quota for the Jews, right here."

"Damn right," Harry agreed.

"It won't work." Ogden shook his head. "Less than five percent of this country wants to raise the quotas."

"But these are refugees, not immigrants."

"These are Jews."

"Not all."

"Most," said Ogden. "And ninety percent of the Communists in this country are Jews."

"But not ninety percent of Jews are Communist," Harry retorted.

Ogden shook his head. "I know that. You know that. But it doesn't matter, don't you see? It's what people believe."

Willy had settled more deeply into his mother, sitting there beneath the language he couldn't speak, his dark eyes following the voices as balls in a game, his head against his mother's shoulder, his slippers hanging down, off his feet.

"And why *should* these poor people face more unfriendliness?" Mrs. Lowell rang out.

Incredulous, Harry turned. "Unfriendliness?"

"Well, I know, dear, I'm just saying they should go where they are wanted. It's not fair to anyone, the Jews least of all."

"I'm with Harry." Dunc took a great swallow and set his glass down. "What I know is when business decides to do something — when something is good for business — it gets done. I'm just one of the poor slobs in government. You" — he fixed his attention on Ogden — "are not."

"No matter what business might want, or decide, that's where we are in this country," Ogden said evenly. "We are *not* hospitable. FDR knows this. He won't push."

"Then you must push him," said Elsa.

The ice fell in Kitty's glass, registering the quiet.

"No one pushes Roosevelt." Mr. Lowell lumbered to his feet. "That man marches to his own tune."

"And what do you think your president would need in order to change his tune?" Elsa asked, glancing at Ogden.

"A sense of peril," Dunc mused. "For the ordinary American."

"There is no need. This madness will settle in good time." Mr. Lowell dropped ice into his glass and turned around. "There are too many good men in charge. Your father is one. I've always liked him."

"Hitler is toying with the world, Mr. Lowell." Elsa shook her head. "With one hand he negotiates peace; with the other he sets us on the path toward war. We all see it. Right before us. He is a magician of the finest order." Her voice caught. "And we do not look away. Instead, we draw closer; surely what we see cannot be believed. Surely our eyes deceive us."

"How can that be?" Dunc asked.

"We *want* to be deceived. There is bread again. There are jobs." Her voice softened as Willy reached his arms behind his head and brought Elsa's cheek down to his. She let it rest there, her voice dropping as she finished. "That is his genius."

"Hitler's genius," Harry concluded, "is to have marched into the Rhineland, all the while proclaiming himself a man of peace."

"Though war *was* averted," Ogden remarked.

"Yes," agreed Elsa, her eyes on him. "And now all steel factories in the Ruhr are in his hands."

Ogden held her gaze.

"No one wants war," he said after a moment.

Elsa set her glass carefully down. "Then we are lost."

Abruptly, Ogden moved out of the circle toward the back of the porch, joining Mr. Lowell at the drinks cart.

"I can't understand why there isn't some protest." Mr. Lowell frowned. "There are many ways to protest," Elsa answered, her eyes on Ogden, his back to them all.

Ogden did not turn around, but it seemed

to Kitty the cord between them tightened. What was she telling him?

"*I am not a dictator,* the Fuhrer has proclaimed," Elsa remarked. "*I have only simplified democracy.*"

"Brilliant." Dunc exhaled beside Kitty.

"He is brilliant," Elsa agreed. "And that is the trouble. Too many see only the thug. They do not see the genius. So it happens swiftly, without stopping. In a matter of months. Right under your noses."

"Good lord," said Mrs. Lowell spiritedly. "You can't be suggesting that could happen here."

"Forgive me, Mrs. Lowell." Elsa turned to her with a small smile. "But it is a mistake to think news happens somewhere else. To others. The news is always about you. You must simply fit yourself in it. You must see how — you must be vigilant."

"Mrs. Hoffman, we have laws to protect the weak." Mrs. Lowell was determined to do battle.

"Protect." Elsa stopped a minute, looking at the older woman. And when she spoke again, she was soft. "Who protects those Negroes pulled from jails and hanged in trees?"

She might as well have thrown a bomb, Kitty thought. There was a shocked, sudden silence. It was a horrible image, *unmention-*

able — and now here in front of them all.

"But that's different, that's completely different," Mr. Lowell protested.

"Is it?" Harry asked.

"Don't be provoking," Mrs. Lowell said with dignity. "You know that it is."

"Never mind that," Mr. Lowell broke in. "Surely, Mrs. Hoffman, someone of your stature, your father's stature, shouldn't worry —"

"No." Elsa's smile was sad. "My father does not worry. He believes in the good of people."

"And that is good, surely?" Mr. Lowell pressed.

"These days, goodness is frightened, Mr. Lowell."

Ogden turned around at last, listening intently.

"There is so much talking," Elsa said. "So much talking. And no one *acts.*"

Impatience flashed across Ogden's face. And watching him, it occurred to Kitty for the first time that Ogden did not *like* Elsa. A dizzy relief coursed through her. It was too much. This woman was too much, holding her boy and talking of war. It was clear Ogden thought so as well.

"And every day it grows more simple," Elsa went on, quietly. "It has all become quite simple. Everywhere there are single, lonely acts of heroism or cowardice."

"There cannot be an in-between?" Kitty

asked, shifting her gaze to Elsa. "Something in the middle?"

"The middle?" Elsa turned her full attention on Kitty with barely disguised scorn.

"You ought to leave, my dear. Why not leave?" Mr. Lowell leaned forward before Elsa could finish.

"We cannot leave Germany to the Nazis."

Harry moved out of the shadows and leaned against the curve of the veranda's arch.

"*Now* is the time," Elsa said. "At the height of the preparation for the Olympics — the anti-Juden signs are being pulled off the streets, erased from around the stadium — we must prove his falsehood, we must —"

"We?" Restless and uneasy, Kitty set her vermouth on the wooden floor.

Elsa looked at her, nodding. "You must act."

"Act." Kitty pushed up out of her chair impatiently and moved out of the ring of chairs toward the low balcony of the veranda wall. The sun hovered, trembling, just above the flat water. This woman sitting there, the boy in her lap like an ember, a coal of such intensity and purpose, it threatened the talk, the porch, this hour meant to be only the hour before dinner.

Willy's slipper slid off his foot, and Elsa leaned and put it back on without looking, without a word. That boy should go up. The boy should be in bed. He was clearly so tired.

And so little. Kitty forced herself to look away.

"It is no secret that Hitler plans to *arm* the country," Elsa continued. "But do you understand he's been doing it for years now? Father's factory has been making triggers for the howitzers."

She had everyone's attention now.

"And the stock?" Ogden folded his arms.

"In Düsseldorf."

"The muzzle?"

"Essen."

Something was being decided, Kitty felt it, right on the surface between them.

"But how is that possible?" Dunc asked, incredulous.

"Heydrich had a warning system," said Elsa, looking at Ogden. "When the French inspectors are expected, we send hairpins and faucets down the line."

"Go on," Ogden said.

"It is worse." She leaned forward toward him. "Last month the factory began forging small propellers that will move by the plane's speed to make horrible sounds."

"And what is that?"

She paused, searching for the words. "Every Stuka bomber flying over England will scream —"

"England?" Priss broke in.

"England," Elsa maintained. "Then Russia."

"Is there proof?" Ogden asked.

Very slowly, Elsa nodded at him.

Ogden grimaced and looked off.

"Hear that? I'd like to get my hands on proof like that," vowed Harry. "That would get this war started, get this show on the road. That's what's right —"

"What is right," Kitty said as she launched forcefully from the edge of the veranda, "is to stop talking and look at the sky. Just look," she insisted, catching the frown on Dunc's face and wanting to close it up and pack it away quickly, stuff it like a handkerchief into his pocket. "Look where you are."

Past the veranda, at the edge of the lawn, a shock of gold swept across the darkened blue of the evening sea, reaching to the rocks at the edge of the lawn as the sun hovered before its final drop. The granite shimmered.

She could feel Og's eyes on her, and she turned and looked at him over her shoulder and gave him a brilliant smile. She didn't understand the battle he seemed to be waging, but she would fight it — with him. Elsa was asking something of him that he couldn't give, that he was at odds with himself to give. And Kitty would stand beside him. She had come back to him. She was here, now.

He nodded at her, clearly moved.

"Kitty's right," he said, drawing toward her from the shadows of the porch.

"Kitty is not *right*," Priss observed good-humoredly, standing up and stretching. "But Kitty has just done what she does best, pointed out the good, thank god, and the beautiful. Never mind the rest for now."

"Hear, hear," said Dunc, raising his glass. "To the good and the beautiful," he said, and finished his drink in a swallow, setting his glass on the low table and pulling Priss by the hand to go and sit facing the sunset on the broad steps of the veranda off to the side.

No one spoke. The sun lowered slowly into the black below. In an instant it was gone. The sun vanished into the sea, but trailing such a hot curtain of color, it seemed the sky hung pink fire, hot and rich, baroque as a cathedral's inner dome.

And Kitty glanced back to see that Elsa had put her hand on Willy's head and was speaking in a low murmur against his cheek.

Slowly, the little boy's arms loosened as he fell off to sleep in his mother's lap. How she longed to have the weight of a child against her chest. How Kitty longed to hold him.

"It's time to crack the lobsters, Harry," said Mrs. Lowell, rising from her chair and moving toward the dining room. "Cook is waving at me from the hallway."

Mr. Lowell began to gather glasses and set them upon the cart. Behind him the dining room sprang slowly into light as Mrs. Lowell made her way around the long, wide table, lighting candles. The maid came in with an enormous steaming bowl and set it on one end of the table. Another followed with cut-glass bowls filled with melted butter. Tomato aspic shivered in a jelly dish. The wooden ceiling arched above the table, a tongue-and-grooved dome, as if the room sat on the top deck of a schooner. A great mirror at the back only amplified the effect of space around the table.

"Harry?" Mrs. Lowell called through the open doors.

Harry pushed himself reluctantly off the veranda wall.

"I'll help," Ogden offered, following him inside.

Wordless, Elsa and Kitty remained where they were. Kitty could just make out the heavier shadows of Priss and Dunc leaning against each other at the darkened edge of the veranda.

A heaping platter of steamed red lobsters was carried out by one of the maids and set on a side table, and Harry and Ogden put on the aprons another maid held, Harry turning at something Ogden said, with a smile of agreement. The two men were perfectly highlighted in the frame of the French doors. Harry donned the cooking mitts and began to rip the tails from the bodies. Ogden took up a hammer and started to crack the claws.

"This place becomes Milton," Elsa mused. "I didn't see that until now."

Kitty sat down on the low veranda wall. The place did become Ogden, though she didn't like Elsa's easy familiarity.

A man with a lantern crossed from the back of the house and down the dark lawn toward the hedge and through it. Kitty watched the small light flash between the trees as he descended the path to the dock. She was aware of Elsa watching as well, behind her. The light was carried all the way out onto what must have been the end of the dock. A spark and then the flare of a second light rose above the dark shimmer of water. Then the first light turned and walked back along the dock, leaving the second lantern burning at the end.

"How quiet peace is," Elsa said softly.

The man reappeared at the end of the garden and passed along the pathway to the back of the house. The lantern at the end of the dock remained.

The shadows on the porch darkened another notch as Elsa shifted the sleeping boy higher on her lap, so he was curled close against her chest.

"Do you believe there is one story for each of us, one alone that we must follow?" Elsa asked.

"Fate, you mean?" Kitty turned to her.

"If you like."

"No," Kitty replied. "I do not. It is too cruel."

Elsa looked at her, and then, as if deciding something, sat back in her chair. "Good," she whispered. "That is good."

Kitty glanced at her.

"God, then?" Elsa went on. "Some great eye above who watches? Who watches over us all?"

Kitty shook her head. "I cannot," she admitted.

Elsa looked up at her with sympathy. "Because of your child."

"My child?" Kitty stiffened.

Elsa nodded. "There is no one watching. No protecting hand. No one watching. There is only us. We know that, don't we?"

No, Kitty thought mutinously. Not at all. And what did she mean, *we*? There was no *we* with this woman who had been pushing and pushing, needling Ogden to do something he didn't want to — with her little boy in her arms.

Elsa was still looking at her, considering her. "And yet, this whole evening, you haven't taken your eyes off Milton or me. What is it you think you see?"

"That you are dangerous," Kitty answered, raising her head.

It was not what she expected to say. It was not at all what Elsa, apparently, expected to hear, because a low, unhappy laugh of recognition burst from her. A laugh that nonetheless made Kitty feel ashamed.

"Dangerous? *I* am not dangerous. I'm not . . . anything at all."

Kitty flushed in the dark.

"Lobsters on." Mrs. Lowell had come to the threshold of the veranda. "Come in, everyone."

Priss and Dunc unfolded and moved from the shadows where they'd been sitting toward the lighted doorway.

"Coming in?" asked Priss.

"In a minute," Kitty answered, trying to compose herself, turning her back on Elsa.

"Kitty? Mrs. Hoffman?"

"Coming," Kitty called back. Though she did not move.

Behind her, the wicker creaked as Elsa sat forward.

"I have seen how you've watched Willy."

Kitty drew in her breath. For there was Neddie turning on his pillow in his little bed, sleepy. There was Neddie, *Good night, Mama.* There he was asleep in her arms.

"Take him, Kitty," Elsa said, low and fast, bowling the three words into the quiet.

"I beg your pardon?" Kitty turned.

"Take him." Elsa reached across Willy and put her hand on Kitty's arm, her face white. "Keep him. Can you keep him from the war?"

The war? Kitty was speechless, standing before Elsa. "There is no war," she heard herself answer.

"The war that is coming, the war that will

take us all," Elsa insisted. "He is the same as yours."

The same? Kitty stiffened. Neddy was blond and tall, with a smile he tossed at the world like a coin, everything this boy was not, this one who was dark and slight — and a Jew.

"But he is not the same. He is not at all the same."

The two women stared at each other.

"Where would he sleep?" Kitty asked.

"Where would he sleep?" Elsa repeated, bewildered.

Kitty flushed. "Ogden and I wouldn't know what to do with him. Surely you'd want him to be with people who knew better how to raise a —"

"Oh." Elsa gave a shudder of comprehension. *"That's* it." She hugged her boy toward her, as if Kitty could hurt him, as if *she* were hurtful.

And all the stupidity of the last year rose in Kitty, all the replies to all the people who had imagined they understood, all that she had folded and boxed and shoved away rather than taken out and waved, shaken free in front of them — rose in Kitty now as she faced this woman who dared to imagine she knew *anything* at all about her.

"That's not it. Nothing is *it,*" Kitty retorted. "How dare you turn me into that. You don't know what you ask."

"How dare I?" Elsa rose slowly, with Willy heavy in her arms. "I dare everything. I dare it all — all." Her voice trembled. "While you go around buying islands, kingdoms in the sea."

"Kitty?" Ogden stood in the doorway.

"For god's sake, it's not so simple." Kitty was fierce.

"But it is." Elsa looked at her, her voice catching. "It's *very* simple. It always is. And the right hand pretends it does not see what the left hand does."

Then she turned and without a word walked past Ogden into the house, leaving Kitty standing there on the dark veranda, shaking.

And in the morning Elsa and Willy were gone.

TWELVE

The Miltons had the big white house painted, had the spruce trees that marred a view to the water cleared, planted geraniums and daisies in the old sheep's corral, and arrived the following summer with Moss and Joan and the new baby, Evelyn — *our baby of the rocks,* as they thought of her — followed by their nurse, and Jessie, the cook. Moss darted like a sparrow straight off the boat onto the dock, running, laughing up the hill, released onto that wide green, and Joan not far behind him. It was more beautiful than Kitty remembered. The broad white rocks, the dark woods whose trees hung with a light green moss the color of a witch's hair. Everywhere was magic for the children. Ogden had been right.

They passed through the boathouse and onto the lawn, walking slowly up the hill, Ogden pushing the loaded wheelbarrow. And as Kitty approached the house again, there in her mind's eye were Priss and Dunc, standing in the shadow of the great roof as they were last year, Dunc laughing, holding Priss tight against him. And when she reached the house herself and stood on the granite steps, turning round, there was Elsa at the bottom of the lawn, and Willy rolling down the hill, his laughter catching.

It would always be that first day here, Kitty realized with a start. Every arrival, every year would have them in it. The island would hold them all.

"Mum!" Moss came round the side of the house with a rock the shape of an arrow. "Mum!" he cried. "Mum, look!" And there was her boy. She smiled at him.

They painted the walls white and the floors gray, kept what furniture of the Crocketts' was usable; they slept on new mattresses and sat in old chairs, and ate that first summer off a set of china they had found stacked in the attic under the wide rafters. Kitty planted rhubarb and lettuces between the granite ledges behind the house, and *What a marvel* friends from the city cried as they walked up the lawn. *What a knack you have.*

Not at all, Kitty would demur, standing in the doorway, pleased.

Mornings, the sea air stole through the open windows with the first light, hovering along the beadboard in the bathroom, upon the scrubbed linoleum on the kitchen floor, pulling the Miltons awake, the first sound that greeted them the single foghorn's note far off in the bay. And the summer days proceeded as if by sorcery. Lobsters were delivered into wooden crates tied to the dock every evening, and bacon onto the dock every morning with the milk. The Miltons woke and descended to the smell of eggs and toast, sharp coffee, and went out immediately into the sun if there was sun. They sailed. They climbed along the great rocks, found picnic spots. Swam in the cove. Knitted. Rowed across the narrow Thoroughfare to walk. And at twilight, they gathered again at the dock, or down on the rocks at the picnic grounds, and drank bourbon and vermouth, and cracked nuts. Darkness didn't fall up there, it took its time, it ceded glory to daylight, which lingered, longing to stay.

They became the Miltons of Crockett's Island. It set them apart, it marked them. In the living rooms of Manhattan, on the tennis courts of Long Island, the island, *their* island, clung round Kitty and Ogden Milton with an enhancing glow. And though the city claimed them every winter — the dinners, the dances, nights at the theater, Ogden leaving every morning and returning, school shoes, school, the boy and the girls descending in the elevator — one of them could come round a corner in January and a shaft of light through the library window on the green sofa recalled the dark, deep green of the woods. The Island sounding through their city life like the beat of a drum. The Island like a bell.

So the days rose up, stretched wide, and unrolled into years. June after June, the house was opened by Crockett's daughter, Polly Ames; the white organdy curtains starched and returned to flank the windows, the flies swept from the windowsills, the window glass wiped of the salt blown up from the sea's winter rages, and Mrs. Milton's guest book sent from the city, unwrapped, and placed on the table in the front room, ready for the new year: 1938. Crockett's lobstering gear stored in the boathouse rafters gave way to white sails wrapped around mahogany booms. A deeper well was dug. 1939. The curtains blew in and out on the breeze and the fog drifted across the lawn, and when the Milton children tumbled off the boat each summer, they saw again the obelisk of Crockett's gravestone, the crooked ridge of spruce, the fish hawk's nest cradled in the top of the tallest tree, as it always was.

And when Kitty turned on the threshold each September, pulling shut the door against winter in the house — the unimagined winter — there was the tug in her heart: *Will we return?*

(Her eye fell upon Ogden's khaki cap hung on its peg after yesterday's sail. Should she put it away?

It hung there, the long brown bill of the visor like the beak of a duck. She turned. Left

183

on its hook it was a promise — a sail always in the offing. Tomorrow. The next day. Or the next.)

And in the house, the children grew. Here they ate breakfast in the fresh mornings, bare feet kicking at the wooden legs of the chairs. The oven baked and went cold, the dishes were washed and rinsed and stacked in the drainer. Someone in the front bedroom upstairs might shout, and the pair in the front sitting room trying to read grumbled and poked at the old stove. The house held their place. Here was the spot at the turn of the stair where Evelyn tripped that morning and gave herself a nasty bump. (But no one heard her — they were all outside — though she cried and cried. And after a little while she had pulled herself up on the banisters, wiped her nose, and went on slowly down to the bottom.) The stair remembered, the stair remained, so that as she grew, Evelyn hurried past the spot as if it could hurt her, without remembering why.

There was the summer Moss built a shack of driftwood and ropes, directing the girls to gather mosses and shells for the windows, and Joan's chimes hung from a lobster pot washed up and flickered in the breeze, the shells clacking. At night in July, in the dead middle of summer, every window pushed open through the short hours of the dark,

Joan and Evelyn lay in the twin four-poster beds asleep and awake — it was so hot — the dark undersung by the moan, the endless lonely note of the foghorn. And then, in the quiet right after, the sea pulling back over the pebbles of the shore. Rocks and sound. Sleep. Joan turned again in her bed.

There was the war going on, over there. Mrs. Ames's boy was over there.

Across the Narrows there was a boy named Fenno Weld. He came with his parents. He'd row over, and the three Miltons would look up and he'd be standing, waiting. *Hello, Weld,* Moss would say. *What's doing?*

There was nothing to do and not enough time to do nothing in. Day after day. Joan made a map of her father's paths and the four children named the great broad central path down the middle of the Island the Broads. The round-the-Island loop was named Circle Puck.

Why Puck? fumed Evelyn, already the one of the three who always asked why, though perhaps it was just a sturdy insistence on the literal, the steadying demands of what was real. *Why not?* Moss answered, paying her no attention.

Why not? Why not take the boat out at midnight to the center of the Narrows, lay there with your head in the triangle bow seat and watch the night sky heave itself down in great billows, shooting stars dropping and racing, the black electric with motion. Why not paint a pale blue binder of rocks along the picnic grounds. *Why not?* thought Joan.

After the war, after the rationing, Ogden brought a generator from the mainland and installed it in one of the chicken hutches on the granite ledge behind the house. And then that year, and the next, there were parties. Then there was light pocking the summer air. Moss brought college boys, and there were girls with short hair and bare legs who talked Plato and played tennis and threw cardigans around their sunburnt shoulders and went down to the dock where there were drinks every night at six. And there was singing. There were square dances in the barn up the hill from the Big House, there were charades in the front room lasting late into the summer nights, and friends clapped through the screen door into the darkness, turned out into starlight, the sound of low engines and women called one to the other across the night water. There were moonlight rows out to the middle of the Narrows, there were morning swims, and fogbound, drifting sails.

Summer nights along the Thoroughfare, the Big House shone light from all eight windows facing front, and one could see it from Vinalhaven, if you were on a boat and coming around the point. Those lights shimmered on the dark and, stretching out, seemed to promise nothing but still water ahead. Nothing but light and water and clear sailing all the way across the broad blue of the fifties. Though looking back, everything lay just under the surface, just under the skin.

There, Mrs. Ames thought, taking the first of Mrs. Milton's summer packages wrapped in brown paper and tied firmly with knotted cord from Frank Warren in the post office. Mrs. Milton's guest book. She placed it in the basket of the curtains ironed and ready to be rowed out to Crockett's. It was still cold. She pulled the sheets off the horsehair sofa, the three stuffed chairs, eaten, she saw, by mice, and moved to the dining room, where the chairs were pushed in tight against the broad table, at attention. "At ease," she muttered to them. Years ago, her son had come home with a piece of France in his leg. He'd been running, he'd said, running in the dark and the rain one night, that's what he remembered, he said, the rain, and he was going to make it to the edge of the field, to the barn they were all making for, and he was nearly there, nearly there, when the barn exploded into the air, the beams javelining out at all angles, laying waste to the boys around him. He'd never run again. At ease, he tried to tease her back then. My boy. She laid the dark green leather volume stamped with the new year on the table in the front room by Mrs. Milton's Morris chair and shut the door. My poor boy.

It was the first of June, 1959.

A Cappella

THIRTEEN

"Here," Joan Milton prodded, "right here."

Fenno Weld glanced at her, dubious.

"Go on," she said, coming to a halt at the edge of the Sheep Meadow in Central Park. "Test me."

The day had been a scorcher. In the park, the heat smelled of grass, and through the shade and the trees' slow shifting — in the flash of silver Buicks, a blue Pontiac on the avenue — the city appeared to her distant as a bright river.

He fastened his attention on a point past her shoulder, too uncomfortable to look directly at her.

"Cunt," he began.

"Cunt," she repeated, keeping her voice even, toeing the pavement of the path.

"Cock." He grew bolder.

"Cock," she said.

"Slick," he countered, dropping his eyes to rest on hers.

"Slick," she managed, feeling the hot flush

rising in her cheeks. "*Damn* it," she chuckled.

Fenno's expression softened, curious. "You balked at *slick*? Why?"

She shook her head and crossed her arms.

"Why?" he pressed.

She shrugged.

"You're blushing," he said, studying her.

"Am I?" She raised her face. "That's no good."

"Exactly my point, though." He was earnest. "Adjectives are the triggers. Pull that trigger and it shoots, it hits you in the heart. But *Cunt. Cock. Prick. Clit.* Just words. Just bullets. Nothing."

"Filthy bullets," she pointed out.

"Filthy bullets," Fenno agreed. "But only because someone has led us to think so. Lawrence called the obscenity watchers 'censor morons.'"

"He also thought a woman who was not a bit of a harlot was a dry stick," Joan observed, "which seems a bit much."

He nodded, a little deflated.

"Go on." She raised her cheek. "I've got to get home."

Fenno leaned over and kissed her on the cheek. He smelled of cigarettes and aftershave.

"So long," he said.

She wrinkled her nose at him as he pulled away, nodding her goodbye, then stood a minute watching him go off. Tall and loose-hipped, he walked as though he had never quite taken possession of his body, as though he had rented it. His voice was very deep. She remembered the summer it had changed. He hated attention, and that voice mixed with his dark curls could bring a room to a halt. He'd spent most of that summer in a furious silence.

She turned away toward the edge of the park. Fenno Weld was right in every way, which made him wrong. He was, she reflected, eager — too ready to step up, to step in and offer help, an arm, a cigarette, a drink, too attentive. She recognized this trait in most of the boys she'd grown up with, knew that they simply didn't have a choice — Moss had been raised to do the same.

Though Moss had something else, she thought. Something hidden, some secret place he seemed to go to and visit and emerge from, slightly changed. It was his appeal. He promised the same world they all lived in, seen anew. One never knew for certain what he'd make of anything.

Poor old Moss, she thought reflexively, crossing out of the trees, *the jig is up for him.*

It was the beginning of the last real summer, "the end of the beginning," as her father was fond of quoting Churchill. The fall would touch off the new part, the next part for all of them: Evelyn was getting married, Moss was going to start work for Dad at the firm, and she had finally convinced her parents to let her take the job she had stumbled into.

The traffic ran swiftly down the avenue as light after light turned green. She walked quickly, keeping in the shade.

"It's just typing," Joan had replied when her father had asked. "But it keeps me busy."

"Why on earth would you want to type all day?"

"Pin money." She'd smiled up at him opaquely.

"I cannot make sense of the feminine mind." Ogden Milton had regarded her. "No amount of school appears to give a girl reasoning."

But she had carefully and clearly been able to argue her case, and he had come around, a fact which she totted up on her side of the ledger of quiet triumphs for 1959. Just yesterday, she had signed the papers for an apartment in a brownstone on East Eighty-first, one block from the Metropolitan. The key lay at the bottom of her pocketbook, and nothing gave her more satisfaction than that little piece of metal. She could close a door and lock it. It was all hers.

Twenty-five years old, in a wide skirt and a narrow cotton blouse belted at a slim waist, she could have been any one of a number of girls who had come out at the Plaza, gone to college at one of the Seven Sisters, and now came in and out of the city for some fun. But

194

she wasn't. She had gone to Farmington like her mother, Kitty Milton, sung the school songs, worn the white dress, and tossed her daisy bouquet into the air, just as her mother had done — and her mother before that. But Joan Milton was not her mother, nor her grandmother. She was determined about that. Life stretched wide before her, and she meant it to be interesting. She meant to do something *purposeful* in the world, since she couldn't marry.

Her steps slowed as she slid that thought away and pulled out the next. It couldn't be helped. She couldn't have children because of her condition. She was barren, the doctors agreed. And so she needn't choose. The choice had been made by her body, her incorrigible body. A man expected a wife and children to put in a house. And she couldn't. That was that. It was unfair to ask any man to give that up. So she wouldn't marry.

But she could love. And she could work. There was nothing to stop her from either of those. She tipped her chin at the light, her heels clicking through the sun.

Men seldom make passes at a girl who surpasses, the song went, but Joan didn't worry about that. She had learned how to type at boarding school, how to make hollandaise, and how to pack a linen skirt so it didn't wrinkle. Two of these had been useful, but the third had been the ticket to the party.

Fast and efficient, Joan could type like no one else, the words streaming through her like music. When Isobel Day had heard a little publishing house was looking for someone, Joan had gone in for the job, and now here she was at the center of a firestorm, typing for Barney Rosset, the man who had defied the U.S. Postal Service and the Comstock Laws and brought the uncut version of *Lady Chatterley's Lover* to press, and then to market, where all copies were promptly seized. The fate of the novel rested now in the hands of a United States District Court judge, and the ruling was due to come down next month.

She had told no one where she actually worked. All eyes were on Evelyn and her September wedding under the wide white tent in Oyster Bay. And that suited Joan fine, because D. H. Lawrence was just the beginning for Rosset. He had his sights on Henry Miller, on William S. Burroughs, on all the sham boundaries the world had put up, as he said, and that he was determined to rip down. What was obscene about a man and woman coupling? What was dirty about the longing to touch another human being? This was the talk in the tiny crowded office where four men sat, manuscripts stacked on every flat surface, magazines on the floor, desks askew, and smoked and picked up phones and slammed them down and drove their days with an urgency, a power, like nothing she'd ever seen.

She stopped at the corner. Though she had blushed up there in the park just now with Fenno, it wasn't a game. When he'd hired her, Mr. Rosset told her he thought perhaps she might be useful somehow — a young woman of impeccable pedigree, he'd said, a *Mayflower* girl, an original Pilgrim. The backbone of the kingdom. *We might stage a reading,* he said. *If we can get you to say the words, and show that they are made obscene simply by our hypocrisy, that could make it into the papers — of course we'd get a few marquee names to do it too.* She had nodded and slid behind the desk he pointed her to, put her pocketbook at her feet, and pulled the type-writer toward her, keeping to herself the fact that she was neither an original Pilgrim nor a particularly good public speaker. *But never mind,* she thought. Never mind all that — she was here on this boat, this boat with its four argumentative crewmen, riding the surge straight through the sluice gates.

"I'm rereading," she'd said, looking up at Mr. Rosset this morning. He had picked up her copy off the desk, opening it to where she'd left her bookmark, and nodding at the spot — closed it again.

"Is it *arousing*?"

She eyed her boss. He sat down on the edge

of her desk and crossed his arms. "Arousing" was the charge against them in court.

"That's a dare," she responded.

"Yes."

"No takers," she said.

Grinning, he opened the book again to the first page and read the sentence aloud to the office. " 'Ours is essentially a tragic age, so we refuse to take it tragically.' " Then he flipped the book shut.

"What's the key word there?"

"Tragic," she answered without hesitation.

He studied her.

"Nope," he said. *"Refuse."*

At Pennsylvania station, she pulled open the great brass doors and stopped at the top of the marble stairs, surveying the cavern below. The day's heat that hung above the pavement and in the doorways outside, wilting the lilac boughs in the florist buckets, the newspapers folded upon the stands, drawing close in here, wilting the men still streaming out of the railway cars, their sweatbands dark upon the hats they couldn't cast off until they reached the cool of a bar, or a spot on a park bench under suburban elms at the end of the long day. Voices rose in drifts to where she stood, and though it was the end of the workday, the people below her still rushed around, bent on some purpose, and only the air and heat and marble acre of the station stood between them and what they were bound to do.

IF I HAVE ONLY ONE LIFE — the girl in the Clairol advertisement winked at her from the wall across the station — LET ME LIVE IT AS A BLONDE.

Joan winked back, her dark hair waving around the pale flower of her face. She crossed her arms and leaned her hip against the balustrade, idly following the figure of a man in a seersucker suit cutting a straight path through a crowd clustered around the information booth. He walked easily forward, going somewhere. A burst of laughter from the crowd he passed through fluttered up to her there under the vast dome of the station, and Joan had the sudden uncanny image of herself as one of the overlooking angels painted into the corners of cathedral ceilings. She uncrossed her arms and leaned forward.

Slim, with the sculpted shoulders of a good athlete, she could pitch a softball and bat like hell. She was an excellent archer, Oyster Bay's winning shot. And though she was not immediately pretty — that was, everyone agreed, her sister's terrain — it was moments like this when she drew the eye.

The man in the seersucker suit was standing completely still in front of the newsstand. She considered him. The seersucker, the short crop of dark hair, the calm suggested an Ivy man, groomed but not impeccable. A large man, she noted as he moved again into the crowd, who wore his height easily, joyfully, almost, it seemed to her — as though he relished taking all that room.

"Very nice." Evelyn pinched her arm. "But he's not your stew."

"Hello." Joan turned around and smiled at her sister.

Though three years Joan's junior, Evelyn generally sought the upper hand, and Joan generally gave it. The sisters shared the same high cheekbones and small round chin, the same dark eyes under soft brown bangs, but Evelyn's features were sharper, more defined, as though the master's hand had understood its lines and drawn them firmly in.

Now the two of them turned twin sets of dark brown eyes, appraising the man below, like cats perched atop a dresser.

"He doesn't look like he can carry a racquet or a tune."

"Maybe he doesn't want to," Joan replied.

"Maybe so. How dull," Evelyn said. "Did you get to ask Fenno today?"

"Ask him what?" Joan's smile faded.

"If he'll play his ukulele at my party in August?"

"Damn," Joan said, and shook her head, "I completely forgot. But he's up there every summer. I'm sure he will." Out of the corner of her eye, she saw the man put the paper down and turn around.

Evelyn snorted.

"No." Joan turned toward her, irritated. "Don't get any ideas. I hardly saw him to speak to. I sat on my own and listened to Mr. Ginsberg read his poem. Fenno was far in the front, organizing the whole thing. Anyway, I don't *like* him that way, Evelyn, and you know it. I wish he'd get the picture."

Evelyn raised her eyebrows. "You're going to have to do more than wish."

Joan groaned and looked back down without thinking; the man below was now staring up at the sisters perched against the marble balcony.

And Joan, who was accustomed to the shift in attention as natural as rain crossing the faces of those who stood when she and her sister entered a room, who took her hand and nodded, who looked at her and then slid their attention to Evelyn, saw — with a little jolt — that this man was not looking at her sister; he was looking at her. He was staring. And for a moment, she couldn't move.

"Lord." Evelyn nudged her. "Doesn't he think he's the nuts."

Paying no attention to her sister, Joan leaned a little forward in an elaborate and playful bow. She saw the surprise and then the smile, but his laughter vanished soundlessly into the stone air around him. He pulled his hat from his head and held it high. Not doffing it, or bowing, simply holding it up like a balloon. Laughing too, Joan stepped back from the balcony's edge, turning toward her sister, the fun of it all on her lips, about to say something about the man, about a man staring, about how nice seersucker suits are in the summer, when the seizure split her — as it did every time — straight down the middle, quick enough to knock her to the ground before she could cry out.

The waves crashed into Joan and she pushed back, jerking against the tide of air that shook at her, trying to call to Evelyn, trying to pull her arms into her chest to beat off the tossing air. She felt her body hit the marble floor, heard it thump at the same time as the breath was knocked out of her, and saw all in one glimpse the fear on her sister's face. It was black and white and gray all around, and silent. As though the sound had been switched off in the world but for the thick beat of blood in her head. She was drowning with her eyes open, and Evelyn remained on the surface above her, her mouth opening, calling. Something grabbed her mouth and yanked it open, put something cold between her lips. She shook in the waves, shook and shook and twisted help-lessly, her eyes on Evelyn up above her, so far up there. *Don't fall in, Evelyn,* Joan opened her mouth to say. Spots of light glittered high up, higher than Evelyn poking and winking at the black surface of the world, *like shook foil,* the phrase swam up and passed by. Joan shivered. The air tensed. *Joan* —

And Evelyn reached through the air that was like water, and Joan heard her this time, the sound came first and her sister's voice pulled her, like a rope, slowly back up, bit by bit. *Joanie. Joan.*

The fit eased. Up she came, back to the surface of time, just before it shook her, back into the heat and the afternoon, and onto the floor of Penn Station, where she lay gasping, back in her own body, the waves pushed off, as though spat back onto dry land. She closed her eyes.

"Get away," Evelyn hissed above her at the little knot of the curious who had stopped to watch. "Please," she was saying. "It's all over. It's none of your business. Leave us alone."

"Do you need an ambulance?" a man asked.

Joan's breathing slowed. She could feel again the floor, separate from herself, her toes in her shoes, her fingers curled in the fabric of her skirt.

"Is she all right?" the same man asked.

"She's fine now."

"That's not the first time," he said quietly. "Is it?"

"It's the heat, that's all."

"Are *you* all right?"

"I'm fine," Evelyn snapped. "Please —"

Joan opened her eyes on the man in the seersucker suit and her sister staring at each other across her chest.

"Evelyn?"

"I'm right here." Her sister patted her arm. "Don't worry, Joanie."

Joan closed her eyes again and waited for the swell of nausea to pass through her. The floor was warm, and then she realized with a start that it was because the man's hand had covered hers, holding it calmly under the folds of her skirt. She opened her eyes.

"Can you sit up?" he asked.

Joan turned her head toward the voice and settled her gaze on his chin and then up farther into a pair of deep blue eyes. He waited for her attention to get to his face. She stared up at him, still disoriented. Up this close he was even more attractive, and his eyes had green shot through the blue. His hand remained on hers.

"Are you a doctor?" Evelyn asked him.

"Not a chance." A smile cracked open his rather serious face. "Leonard Levy. Len."

Joan stirred, and he pulled away his hand.

"Sit up, Joanie," Evelyn pleaded. "The floor is filthy."

Joan pushed herself up to sitting. She couldn't look at Len Levy. He was a man with a name now. And she was a girl with the shakes. A condition. She flushed.

"Don't breathe a word to Mum," she said to her sister.

"Agreed." Evelyn nodded.

"She doesn't know?" Len asked.

"She does." Evelyn's eyes rested on her sister thoughtfully before turning to the man and unfurling her famous smile to stop him asking any more. "But she doesn't like scenes."

Joan curled her legs underneath her and pushed herself to standing, not taking his hand up. She felt confused and funny on her feet. And the three of them stood a minute, awkward and stuck like partygoers at the end of the party waiting for a cab. There was a brief silence, and then he raised his hat to the sisters just as Joan put her hand out to thank him. He looked at her, and he took it in his, and without thinking she stepped forward and gave him a quick darting kiss on the lips.

She stepped back and risked a glance. "Thank you," she said.

He did not seem to know what to say. He dropped her hand and nodded.

And then he was off back down the wide cold steps into the crowd grown dense and loud as it veered closer to rush hour.

"What was *that*?" Evelyn asked.

Joan watched him move through the vaulted room. "My thank-you."

"I'll say."

He had kissed her back. Joan shivered and refastened the buttons on her cardigan down to the last three, not looking at Evelyn. And his lips had been warm. "Well, he is a Somebody, you can tell."

"By the suit?"

"By his bearing." Joan smiled up at her sister, teasing, *His noble and erect carriage.*

"By way of Ellis Island, I'll bet. An Italian, or a Jew."

"Agreed," Joan said. "Nobility under the bushel."

"*Definitely* under a bushel." Evelyn wrinkled her nose.

"Don't be a snob, Evelyn." Joan cocked her eyebrow. "It's unbecoming."

Their mother's phrase made them both smile, easing them back into their regular life. But it raised Kitty between them.

"Oughtn't you go and see Dr. Southworth, Joanie?" Evelyn ventured.

Joan shook her head firmly. "There's no need."

"That was the second one in as many months."

"You shouldn't worry." Joan tipped her head at her sister. "I'm not."

But her sister was right, she ought to go to the doctor — if she was having the fits again, she ought to change her dose. Though it had happened only twice, and both times Evelyn had been there, and both times it had passed over her quickly. If it happened in Mr. Rosset's office, or in her apartment alone, or crossing the street, she didn't like to think about.

Never mind. These were the cards she had been dealt. She'd manage. And without any more help. There were limits. More of the pill would only make her weak; it already made her feel woolly-headed and numb. She slid her pocketbook up to her elbow and looked at her sister.

"All right?" Evelyn asked.

"As rain." Joan nodded and drew her hand through Evelyn's bare arm.

The Milton girls walked slowly down the stairs and into the crowd, toward the train for Oyster Bay. And Joan wondered, as they went, which direction Len Levy had taken, and wondered where he was going, and last of all, wondered if he pitied her. She tossed her dark head and squeezed Evelyn's arm. She hoped to hell he didn't pity her.

But pity was the farthest thing from Len Levy's mind just then, walking away from the sisters through the crowd. The surprise of the girl's lips on his lingered, and when she'd stepped away, she'd looked as startled, as lovely, as any girl he'd ever seen. It got him, all right, the look she gave him, sweet and somehow — daring. He felt it in his groin. As though she had a secret for him and him alone. *Accident,* his father had always said, *is not accidental.*

Len turned down the marble hallway heading for Seventh Avenue. Some girls did and some girls didn't have any idea what they had. And that girl sure as hell didn't. Her sister, however, knew exactly what she was about, and knew exactly how to let you know it. And typically, she hadn't bothered to introduce herself after the thank-you. But then, their kind never did. She was one of these girls who tucked their white-gloved hands under the arms of men named Hunnicutt or Pierce and wandered through life, gracious and polite, beaming as all get-out. As though all the world were a glorious party. As if that glory would never die. And though a Levy may be invited to the party — even if he behaved — his would never be an arm they slipped their hand beneath.

So what. There it was.

Raised outside Chicago, Len had been taught to see the limit as well the horizon of a Midwestern sky, and it served him in good stead. Now he pushed open the glass doors of the station into New York, which *was* the world.

The midsection of the island recalled his heartland city, the broad and regular avenues lending a predictable pattern to the streets, dissected only by the diagonal, irregular slash of Broadway. For fifty blocks, you could rely on the park remaining to your right as you went south, the green tops waving in summer at the ends of blocks, the stark branches holding the white sky up above the gray buildings in winter. Then on past the park into the city's grid, where still you could imagine yourself in charge, the world pivoting evenly on its bearings, twenty blocks to a mile, a light at the end of every block, the buildings climbing straight to the horizon over your head. You could walk this way for nearly one hundred blocks, and then it all ran to a happy hell in the Village.

He had stepped off the train from Chicago ten years ago headed for Columbia University and wanting everything. And knowing that whatever that was, it was right here. All of it. He spent four years at the rough-and-tumble Ivy, where good old boys rubbed shoulders with the Jewish sons of Brooklyn and argued the world into shape. Argued and prowled through the streets of New York, in search of their fortunes. In search of their future. Impatient. Eager to get it all started.

Graduating with honors in 1953, he had gone to Korea with some idea of honor, some idea of paying back the country that had taken in his mother and father, fleeing Germany. Instead, he stood in the humid KP lines waiting for meals and saw nothing there except the others like him, released for the duration from the forward engine of their lives, who — bored, tired, and fearful — saw nothing at all, until the morning his division was hit from nowhere and he had found himself in a pocket of air beneath the kitchen rubble, looking stupidly across the three feet at the guy he'd just passed the coffeepot to, dead.

When he came back he was quits with whatever debt he thought he'd owed. He'd paid his dues. He came back, roaring. He got a summer job at a brokerage firm where a college classmate worked, only meaning to get his feet wet, but discovered himself to be a natural at numbers, and more important, at getting himself through a door and into the next room. The summer had led to a year, at the end of which he found himself at Harvard Business School.

"I see exactly who you are," his advisor had chuckled over lunch. "I see exactly where you are going."

"Where is that, sir?"

"Right to the top, I'd wager. Though the question remains, Levy — do you want to be a lamb among lions, or a lion among lambs?"

"Sir?"

"Choose, Levy. Choose where you land."

Len understood. Seek the softest target and take your best shot. When he'd graduated from Harvard a month ago, he turned down the Rothschilds, choosing instead to work at Milton Higginson and Co., a white-shoe firm with a pedigree on its masthead stretching back to the *Mayflower* and a reputation for quiet and solid investments, without advertisement of any kind. *If you don't know about us,* the joke went around the halls at the firm, *then you don't need us.* But Len had every intention for them to know all about him, and soon. Len intended to be the lion.

A girl on the opposite corner paused, her foot hovering on the curb. A taxicab slid past, pushing the yellow light into red, the cabbie leaning on his horn like a scold, forcing her back onto the curb, flushing. Len watched her hand brush her hair into place and thought again of the girl in Penn Station, the toss of that dark head and the salute before she had collapsed. He'd started off at a run, pushing through people coming down the stairs. And then, when she was lying there, so still on the floor, watched over by her sister. Why had he taken her hand? For those few minutes, he had felt her fingers resting under his, like a bird he'd caught. For those few minutes, he'd wanted nothing more.

The light changed back to green, and Len stepped off the curb and into the throng on Broadway, whose asphalt line planed all the way to the tip of Manhattan, down into the Village, where he was headed, where the lights were coming on in the cafés and bars, though it was not yet dark and the light in the sky still burned.

On the corner of Hudson and Bank Street, the Italian grocer pulled the guard down over his shopwindow and the metal banged his good night on the pavement. The heat of the day still draped a light wool over the streets, and girls in their summer dresses flickered in and out of doorways, under men's arms, or tilted away, teasing — so that the men wanted to reach out and touch them, as if they were in a story. And it was a story, a story of a summer evening and the city that roared above the small pockets into which anyone could stumble and find quiet and a cold beer.

Moss Milton was sitting where he always did at the back of the White Horse Tavern, watching the table of writers through the haze of smoke. The loose federation of men, leaning one toward another, speaking what he was too far from to overhear, leaning in, and then away, syncopated the smoke; their bursts of tight talk and laughter, a pattern. Moss watched them as if he were invisible, indeed was invisible, just another young man in horn-rimmed glasses, clean-cut, his thick black hair parted on the side.

If he could get all this into a song. This smoke and the talk on a summer evening, the dark wood of the tavern walls rising around the hot, flushed faces. Men with their sleeves rolled above the elbow, one of them punching his point out with a cigarette. Fellowship. One voice, pure and lovely, a single tenor in the air, then another joining, the two weaving, then one. A third voice, higher by a third, in and out flashing like a bird through the trees of the other two. Then a fourth. A cappella. Men coming together and moving apart lightly, but sure-footed and strong — everything possible, everything flying on the wings of a song. If a song could manage all this, could catch you so that you stopped where you were to listen, and then, listening, could hear the strands being woven, twined and tuned until that silver lane — the ten chords where all the voices, all the notes combined — opened out for one bar, for two, for a wide mile of sound riding forward on those bars, then everything really might be as possible as it seemed to Moss these days. These days the country seemed poised, holding its breath, like a diver at the top of a dive. It would be a song for America — for this moment, right now — and he could almost hear the notes in his head.

Almost. The two-beat word sounded. He shut his eyes and tossed the last inch of the whiskey down. Too late. Almost.

He had money and an old name. He had everything one is supposed to have to launch forward in the world made of frame houses and evening trains from the city and dry martinis before dinner and the well-turned curls of perfumed wives. He had suits cut from good cloth. And he was unforgivably wild with protest. His future lay before him like a brick cell appearing — solid, ineluctable — in the middle of what had up until then been an open meadow. It was the last summer, the last true summer, for him. In the fall would come the end of all this singing. There was no way around it that he could see.

The rim of the chair met him as he leaned his long frame back and crossed his arms. For the past few months, he had been going along cheerfully enough, putting on the suit when it was asked for, meeting his father at Milton Higginson for lunch once a week, all the while certain that something would give — something had to give — one of his songs would get picked up, published, or better, one of these guys he knew down here at one of the joints would play one of his tunes. Though tonight, that seemed more and more like a dream, and he was a fool for dreaming.

The picture in front of him shifted almost audibly as a slight brunette nudged her way into the group at the table. The men at the end hailed her, one of them turned and grabbed the back of an empty chair, shoving it toward her, the legs grating on the tile. She smiled at him, teased another one, and sank into the chair, talking all the while, her bright, high tones crossing over the top of the talk to Moss, like froth on the roll of waves.

He'd read her pieces in the *Voice,* and they were not froth at all, her sentences arrowed clean and clear. Moss thought she'd come in once or twice with Mailer, who wasn't sitting at the center of the table as he often was. And Moss was glad. Men like Norman Mailer changed the contours of a song and flattened the middle parts, the sustaining notes that traveled down the track, carrying the pattern forward.

Moss got to his feet and wandered through the press of hot drinkers, forward toward the bar on the wave of voices and laughter. There was no birdsong as beautiful as this, he decided, wondering in the same moment whether he could get it down in a score. He lifted his glass and nodded to the bartender, *one more.* Birdsong and laughter. The one not the other. The one not a reflection or a repetition. The skein. And there, outlined against the evening outside, a girl hesitated at the threshold of the tavern considering where to alight. A heron, he thought, watching her. On the rocks at the end of Crockett's Island. A high treble. Like his sister Joanie, he thought.

Behind the girl, just off the sidewalk, a slight Negro man was pointing one of the new Polaroid cameras at the long table of dockworkers ringing several pitchers of beer, set outside the bar. His white shirt was brilliant in the twilight. But the men at the table didn't see him; they were pulled tight into the table, making fun of another man, one of their own, who sat, elbows on the table, grinning, nodding — going along, but coiled,

Moss could see. It was a game of chicken. Would he crack, or would they stop? Moss drank. The goading went on. The man kept smiling from where he sat.

Moss watched, the moment building to its crescendo, thinking without thinking how he would score this — *legato and piano* — step by step. The light in the sky shifted slowly down.

The black man waited with his camera, still unnoticed by the group. Moss frowned. He was familiar somehow, though Moss couldn't think how.

Suddenly — game over — the cornered worker rose to his feet, roaring, pushed to the end of the teasing at last, and the others sprang up also, smiling, crowing, bloodlusty, ready to fight, loving the fight, erupting — and one of these caught sight of the black man and pointed at him, the anger turned.

The camera went off with a flash. The whole table's attention shifted, and now there was angry shouting as two of the men pushed back their chairs and stood.

Moss put down his drink.

The black man lowered his camera.

No one moved. Was he daring the men?

His eyes on the table, the photographer pulled the picture from off its roller in the waiting quiet.

Jesus, Moss thought.

"Sit down," said the big man who had

started it all, as he sat back down at the table.

"Sit down," he said to the two still on their feet.

Moss watched as the black man stepped off the curb, walking backward, keeping his eye on the group, moving away, and then — as no one followed — turned his back on them, his wrist shaking dry the picture in his hand.

Reg Pauling walked away smiling, seeing nothing, the adrenaline surging through him, carrying him past his feet, his shaking hands, the relieved laughter; he could have gotten himself hurt, he knew it, and the fear had held him, grabbed him, and let him go. Right now the blood in him was so strong, he could have run laughing all the way down to the tip of the island. He'd gotten it back there. He'd gotten it down in film — whatever it was, that moment inside these workers' heads when they saw him. He'd gotten the look. He'd caught the shift in the one man's eyes when he'd seen Reg and seen *Negro* and put him away, closed the box and pushed it back in its line, the handler inside his head coming forward.

The moment Reg wanted to capture, wanted the man to see — to see himself seeing. The American moment.

Shut up, man. Reg snorted, catching himself.

Who was he kidding? If people came to see

this kind of thing at all, it was usually at the end of a fist or a stick.

JUST GO! the billboard rising above the Christopher Street subway station urged him. JUST GO! To the beach, to the mountains, into the hot, lit city — a dark-haired boy and a blond girl in the back seat of the new blue Plymouth mirrored the good-looking man and his blond wife in front, smiling and pointing toward the imagined road before them. Anywhere was possible in a car like that. A family of four could drive across the new interstate highways, staying along the way in the new Holiday Inn, eating at the new Howard Johnson's restaurants, tossing a Frisbee back and forth on the freshly asphalted parking lots. They ate fruit cups, steak and french fries with peas, a roll and butter, followed by apple pie à la mode washed down with coffee. On fresh mornings in the newly minted suburbs they drove through, neighbors called to each other across the hedges by their first names, and girls went downtown with their hair in curlers and a kerchief. If you were white.

Reg stalled in front of the image stretched above his head, used to this kind of chatter, this near constant magpie in his head, pecking. That breezy, inclusive belief that anyone could get in their car and *just go* was the fundamental American lie, and catching sight of it was the reason he'd come back home after three years in Europe. The grades of difference, these shades of meaning, only hit if one were in one's own language. One's own country. For the colors of *this* country — Reg shoved his hands deep in his pockets — are laid down in American English. Black and white. And seeing it like this, stretched baldly across the avenue, gave him a peculiar satisfaction, as if he'd caught the country once again with its pants down, and he grinned as he turned from the billboard and started walking.

Small but well proportioned, Reg Pauling favored white oxford shirts and navy blue ties no matter the occasion, and leaned forward at the waist when he listened, giving him a courtliness he couldn't shake, and then stopped trying to, as he realized both whites and blacks turned toward him because of it. There were advantages in not speaking until one is spoken to, developing an ear and a patience for listening to what was not being said. As a writer it was an essential tool. As a black man it allowed him to look everyone squarely in the eye.

A man and his girl walked toward him, loosely joined. Reg's hands lifted to the camera that hung around his neck, though he saw what was coming would be too quick to catch. The eyes of the girl darted toward him, then away, as though the sidewalk in front of her were empty of anything but air, but the man kept his eyes on Reg as they drew even, straightening his shoulders when he passed as though he could flick Reg off him like a bug.

See that, thought Reg, wheeling around and framing the two of them, the girl's heels clicking down the pavement.

Every American writer must leave America to find America in him, Jimmy Baldwin had told Reg four years ago, waving him off, telling him not to come home until he had something to say. So he'd gone away. He'd gone away Reginald Pauling, Harvard class of 1953, son of a doctor from Chicago's South Side, and worked his way across a postwar Europe where playgrounds had risen on bomb sites in Berlin, and the gaps in a block of buildings still marked the murderous skyfall over London. He sent back vignettes, portraits of life after the war for *Ebony,* for *Jet,* and three short pieces for Norman Mailer's gig, *The Village Voice.* He chronicled the giddy, dizzying effect of American cash, even now, ten years after the Marshall Plan had run its course. There was meat again. Apartments rising. Like a child restored to health after the wasting effects of a fever, Europe was flushed and laughing, running forward.

The first time a white man had passed him on the street in Berlin, his gaze glancing over him without heat, Reg had stopped right where he was, turned around, and watched the man walking away until he was out of sight. Then a woman. And again. People passed with quick, curious attention, but the fear he saw on the shuttered faces of the Germans had nothing to do with him. He wasn't a Jew. He wasn't a German. He was free of that history. So he was free.

And he was miserable. Though he couldn't square why.

With his Italian, and some German, he could buy his dinner in the market, his coffee in the bar, he fell into talk at tables late into the night, walked the streets of Europe easily and widely. An American. Unreadable man. A book without a cover, an animal without markings taken in with the anonymous glance he'd never felt before back home.

Three months ago, he'd been standing next to an American couple on the *terrazza* of a famous expat who threw party after party into the Florentine evenings. The slender woman in the white linen shift and the man in the bright blue shirt and ruddy tan of his class had taken to him, Reg observed, once they heard the magic, improbable word *Harvard,* and, meaning to be friendly, thinking this the way to show their true colors — the way that people intent on harm advance with their palms up — began telling him what it was like to be a Negro.

"Well, you've *struggled* so," the wife said,

regarding him. "Struggle has been the way up, I'd guess."

"The way toward being an individual," her husband corrected her.

A flush sprang into the hollows of her cheekbones. "If you like," she'd allowed.

They were only in Italy for a year. On sabbatical. And the freedom, the immense freedom of walking out of their apartment — anonymous, he said; *invisible,* she'd added — and simply closing the door had been terrific. No demands. No expectations.

"I wish it could go on and on."

Standing there, nodding at her beneath the twining vines, in the perfect umbered dusk, Reg had understood simply and precisely the difference between those who were running toward something and those who were running away. He had been free without history. But there was no freedom without history. *That* was America in him.

So he'd come home. He had walked off the plane at Idlewild on a late spring evening in April and — hanging on to the leather strap of the city bus, his typewriter between his feet — he bent at the waist to catch glimpses of the skyline as it drew nearer and nearer, and started grinning at New York. He'd followed his stories back to the city where he had sent them. Len Levy, his oldest friend, had a fifth-floor walk-up in Greenwich Village, and when an ad appeared that first week for a copy editor at Houghton Mifflin — the publisher of *The American Heritage Dictionary* — he'd answered it, gotten it, and gone to work. It was a good steady salary, and his days were full of words.

With his first month's salary, he'd bought a camera.

The slight breeze coming off the Hudson River to the west, the wet damp in the midst of heat carried with it the memory of summer nights in childhood. On the right, he drew even with the triangle park, the coming dark hanging there in the deep summer green of the leaves, three white men sitting on the bench below the tree, old men, the likes of whom peopled every city square, men who sat in silence, past working, past family, who sat and watched and remarked. He felt the shove of their stare between his shoulder blades, *move along.* He nodded. And not a word. Not a word need be said.

One's own country? Even silence here was colored.

The sprinkler was on in the children's playground, and the smell of water in the hot air carried all the summer nights in Chicago where he'd run through water, just like these Italian boys and girls, hair plastered to their skulls, shrieking as they ran back and forth through the wet, their skin dripping, cooling, pushing the heat back.

"Buonasera," he said politely to the mother

who had turned to stare at him, and walked into the swarm of children without pausing, shielding his camera through the wet, and out the other side, the water sliding down his cheeks and from the top of his head into his collar, the air immediately cooler as he continued down the avenue, smiling to himself and feeling the damp on the shoulders of his summer jacket.

At the corner of Bleecker and Tenth, Reg climbed the steps to the door of the apartment building and slid in his key, holding the handle to jimmy the old lock. In the dim cool of the hallway inside, the sounds of children playing in the tiny inner courtyard mixed with the clarinet in 4B and the smell of fish frying. It was hot, and he took the stairs slow.

He and Len shared a tiny apartment at the top. The place was as spartan as an army barrack, but through a door just outside their apartment were the stairs to the roof. There was no deck or railing, just a flat tarpaper expanse, and no one else in the building ever seemed to use it, so they got used to thinking it was theirs. Up there they watched the lights of their adopted city rise in a ridge against the night sky, northward to Midtown, or dwindling down westward in the direction of their childhood to the dark river, across the green fields of New Jersey, across Pennsylvania and the flat expanse of Ohio to Chicago, where the two men had met as boys in a grammar school marked equally for its teachers as for the sometime brilliance of its pupils. Levy had been seated next to Pauling that year, as the M's, the N's, and the O's had all been placed in the other third-grade classroom.

Their friendship was as unthinking and as familiar as the coins in their pockets, each of them knowing without seeing by heft and size just how much they had. They had found each other that first day, the P and the L in 1939. Together they could believe the world was theirs for the taking, if they concentrated with both eyes open. Not half-shut, as it seemed his father's were. *Stay smart,* his father said, *stay low* — you'll get there.

But where? Reg had gone through Abernathy High on the South Side of Chicago, sailed through the classes with Len alongside, and graduated fourth in his class. *Where will you get,* he wanted to ask his father, *if here is all there is?*

He had never asked, and his father had never answered, but when Emmett Till's body had floated onto the national news, that poor wrecked child's body — a black boy from Chicago who had wandered into the wrong set of eyes — Reg knew *there* is what his father would have answered. This far and no farther.

Fuck *them,* Len had telegrammed Reg.

Fuck *that.* It had always been clear to Len that but for an accident in geography and time, the two of them would have been dead or in chains. Reg was used to this simple clarity and relied on it. They had been friends so long Reg did not think of himself without Len. Every day of his life since that first day when they had met and taken stock of each other with the rapid assessment of children — friend, not friend — Len had been right there, the face Reg had looked for to check himself. Reg was black and Len was white, but together they were neither. Or rather, together they were both. They were each other's shield. And Reg knew, without having to say it, that Len saw what he saw, Len went through with Reg, alongside Reg, the hurts, the slights, the silences. Len *saw* him. The loneliest four years of Reg's life had been the four years at Harvard, which he referred to as "the Exile."

The apartment was empty and still, all the windows pushed wide open to catch any breeze from the river. There was a tiny kitchenette, a living room, and a separate bedroom they outfitted with two beds, each pushed squarely against the opposite walls.

He took the Polaroid from the White Horse out of his pocket and pinned it next to the others on the living room wall. Shedding his jacket and rolling up the sleeves of his shirt, Reg went to the icebox and pulled out a cold beer and held it to his forehead. Then he rolled it along the back of his neck and slowly down each forearm before opening the beer and taking a swallow. He went into the bedroom to change out of his shirt and tie.

The yearly letter from the Lowells leaned against the bottom of the mirror on his dresser. He took it and went to sit on the bed, pulling off his shoes, tossing one and then the other across the five feet between the beds. They hit and bounced off the side of Len's to lie on the ground.

Right where they would trip him. Reg grinned with satisfaction.

He unbuttoned his shirt, picked up the envelope, and ripped it open. The familiar card in his hand covered with Mrs. Harold Lowell's careful blue script tilted just to the right asked him again, as it had every year since 1953, to please consider coming to visit them on North Haven. *We would be,* she encouraged him, *so pleased if you would accept.*

He took off his shirt, stood, and opened the closet door, the motion stirring its own breeze. The Lowells had taken an interest in him long ago, when he had first arrived at Harvard College in 1949, a Higginson Scholar. Mrs. Lowell had found him pressed up against a wall at the back of the Lowell House Opening Day Cocktails and, holding her hand out, had introduced herself as Sally Lowell.

"Reg Pauling," he had said, taking her hand and shaking it.

"Good." She looked straight at him. "You have a nice solid grip. You'll be fine."

"Good to know." He'd nodded back at her with a stiff smile.

The heat of the day still shimmered in the black tar when he emerged from the stairs onto the roof. Len stood at the far end, looking south toward the tip of Manhattan. His familiar heft always worked on Reg as a kind of landmark: wherever they were, there he was, larger than most, the place in any room where Reg could fasten his eyes.

"It's like crossing the goddamned Sahara up here."

"Hey." Len turned around, greeting him. Reg came to stand at the end of the roof.

The river stretched silver in front of them. It was dinnertime, and the clatter of dishes escaped through the open windows to the two men. There was the barest hint of a breeze. The city below them burned bright and hot, and the steady noise reached up to them standing above it, like the pulse of a heart buried somewhere unseen. The single line of a jet plane crossed above.

"How are you?" Len asked after a while.

Reg nodded. "You?"

Len pointed to his friend's chin. "I was

thinking about how soft it is right there. On a girl. Soft and hard."

"Jesus H. Christ."

Len smiled. "I met a girl today."

"Uh-*huh.*" Reg glanced at him. "And what did she look like?"

"She was a girl in a sleeveless blouse with a big pocketbook, and a sister."

"And?"

"And she tipped her chin at me."

Reg chuckled. "You're sunk, man."

"Yeah?" Len grinned, flicking his cigarette off the roof. "Maybe so."

Fourteen

Evie parked the car three blocks from their apartment and started walking home. Paul should have landed and cleared customs by now. If he'd made good time, he'd be home.

Early in her freshman year, and swept up in the feminist winds of the late 1970s, Evie had decided to take Milton, her mother's maiden name, for her own, over the objections of both her mother and grandmother. "How very hurtful," Kitty Milton had said, frowning, "to your father." "He won't mind," Evie insisted. And indeed, when she'd told him finally, the look he gave her was nearly approving, as if it were apt somehow to have her own name. Anyway, it had nothing at all to do with her own father. It was a blow at the patriarchy: she would be Eve Milton, full stop. She had not counted on the fact that a name like that would draw ironic comments from classmates and professors on the first day of every class throughout her years of undergraduate and graduate course work, except in the discussion section for African American Poetics led by a graduate instructor, Paul Schlesinger, whom — perhaps because of his silence, or his stare, or both — she fell in love with and married.

"He's watching you," a girl in that class had said matter-of-factly during finals week. "He's been watching you all semester."

"No, he hasn't." Evie had smiled. But she knew he had.

A specialist in James Baldwin and the poetics of race, Paul's inner life was spent in books, and she used to imagine them stacked in his head like ladders along a wall, leading to high windows. He had read everything, it seemed, and had an idea about everything he had read. More, he could spin the web between what he had read and what had happened in the supermarket, or what he had heard on the radio. Dylan, the Dreyfus Affair, the troubadour poets, "A Season in Hell," it didn't matter. One pressed on him, and his thoughts sprang open in sentences that climbed easily into paragraphs. The world was all there. Generous with his students and unsparingly honest about his own weaknesses, he was, it was generally agreed, a great teacher, a marvel.

Two days after the grades were filed, he had called the phone in the hallway of her dorm. "It's that grad student," the girl who answered had mouthed, handing her the receiver. And in the silence on the phone for those seconds before he spoke, Evie decided.

"Hullo, Evie," he began.

"Yes," she said, "whatever it is. Yes."

They came together cleanly, swiftly, as if they'd each been waiting for the other to appear. They understood each other, knew each other without discussion, though he was a Jew from the outer boroughs, he'd tease, and she was from one of those families who'd bought Manhattan for shells. *Not true,* she'd protest, smiling. But true enough. Theirs was a table others wanted to sit at, and did, long and late into the night. Their coupling was proof positive of the heady democracy of the land of ideas, and proof too (she thought) of how far she had sprung from home.

When Evie first told her parents Paul's name, her mother had blinked.

"Schlesinger?" she repeated quickly. "He's Jewish?"

"Yes, Mum."

Joan had chuckled, her eyes on her daughter, a deep helpless chuckle that rose up and circled in the air between them, though Joan put her hand over her mouth, but it was too much; she dropped her hand, helpless in the wave of laughter that poured out of her.

"For god's sake, Mum. It's not a joke," Evie said stiffly. "You couldn't be more insulting if you tried."

"No." Joan opened her eyes, trying to still

the laughter. "No, of course it's not a joke. It's not at all a joke." She paused. "I just never saw this coming."

"Well, welcome to the twentieth century," Evie returned acidly. "We're all in it together."

"I don't care how many degrees you rack up," a friend of her father's had said, waving his fork at her at a dinner party, "how much money you make, or how many chances you take to make good — none of that matters. It all comes down to getting the right girl. That's the secret to the whole thing. That's the secret to success."

And Evie did not point out the question he begged, though she was the first girl in eight generations of her family's men to walk through the gates of an Ivy, albeit Yale. Evie had smiled at him and nodded, as though they were co-conspirators. *It's getting the right girl.* She did as she had been brought up to do with older men. She agreed.

And went ahead and married Paul Schlesinger.

In their first summer, they shared a single room in a group apartment with two desks pushed against opposite walls and the mattress on the floor under the only window. They worked in utter quiet until they couldn't bear it, and one of them would turn and break the line between their desks and they'd move to the bed between. Their quiet back then had been full of desire, even when they moved to bigger places and worked in separate rooms.

And at the end of the days, they would talk. Talk with a future in it. Talk with the push behind it, talk that would lead them through dinner and into the night. They finished doctorates. Began teaching, had Seth. Bought an apartment, won tenure, were known. The years rose and sank down. They worked at home, and still in the middle of a morning, she would look up and see him standing in the doorway of her study.

She needed him, she realized as she rode the elevator back up to their apartment that evening. He'd been gone too long. The old woman crossing the street just now, Seth turning on the steps of the library, her mother returning morning after morning in the dream — life in all its pieces, going on. She needed him to help her see it all clear.

"Paul?" She stood on the threshold, listening.

"I'm in here," he called from his study.

He had his back to her, intent on tacking up a block of photographs on the corkboard above his desk. He had returned with his work done, and well done, she could see.

"Hey." She stood in his doorway, smiling.

"Hey." He turned, looking at her, and smiled back. His dark hair was silvering, but his jacket hung on his body as carelessly as it had when he was in his twenties, giving him

234

the look of an athlete, when in fact he'd done nothing but read all his life. She went to him and he pulled her into his arms and she relaxed against him. He smelled of the plane and the long ride, and then underneath that, he smelled of him. The room disappeared. She pressed herself closer.

He stiffened, as if her touch reminded him of something, and carefully pulled away.

She looked up. The storm that crossed his face was violent and swift.

"Paul?"

"Listen." He thrust his hands into his pockets, looking down.

"What?" she asked, a little frightened. "What is it?"

The buzzer rang.

"What?" Her eyes widened. "What's happened?"

"There's Daryl," Paul said.

"Daryl? Why?"

"He called me when I was in the cab. I told him to come on over."

"But you just walked in the door."

"I know." He softened. "But I wanted to show him these —" He pointed to the photos he'd been tacking up.

"The stumble stones?"

"Yeah." He nodded.

The buzzer rang again.

"Coming," he called.

Evie stared at the spot where he had just

235

stood and then fixed on the rows of pictures on the wall behind, a little dazedly. What had just happened?

"Hello, darling," Daryl Norton greeted her in the doorway, holding a bottle of wine.

One of the ruddy blond boy-men who grew like weeds all over the United Kingdom, Daryl had fled to the States in his twenties, where he could become the charming, sardonic, English bloom — an exotic in the hothouse of the graduate school where he and Evie had finished their degrees. He had been one of both Evie's and Paul's most trusted sparring partners, willing and able to shred any scrap of pretension in a new idea. The "Daryl draft" was the pass they made at an idea before anything was put on the page.

"Hello." She tipped her cheek for his kiss, still unsettled.

"Daryl brought Chinese," Paul called. "Let's eat *now*. I'm starved."

Daryl vanished from the door.

There was nothing to do but follow him down the hall to the dining room, where Paul was pulling steaming containers from the bag and putting out plates and glasses and chopsticks. He appeared to her electric with fatigue and excitement. Daryl drew the cork out of the bottle, and the three of them sat. The windows were pushed high against the June evening.

Evie sipped her wine, her eyes resting on

Paul at the other end of the table as she took the plate he'd filled for her. Daryl asked one question, then another, and after a few minutes, Evie joined in. And they were off.

Still, she watched him, catching glimpses of him as if through trees in a wood. They had fallen back into their usual patter, their banter familiar, the poking their connection. But there was something different tonight, something new. An added heat, a swiftness, as though he rappelled off her on a thread too hot to hold, looking at her and then away, a man dropping swiftly off a cliff. Just then he was listening intently to something that Daryl was saying, his head tipped as though there were music beneath the other man's words. It was a posture he took, she knew, both when he was listening hard and when he was hardly listening. The tipped head, the nod, the eyes resting on the speaker proved irresistible, working like a mesmerist to draw people out. She could see he wasn't paying any attention whatsoever to Daryl just then, that he had retreated under cover of the other man's argument to some spot to think in his head.

And it used to be that the line between them tightened just in these moments, when she would catch sight of him listening in a room with others and knew where he was in his head, when no one else did. He would nod and pause and then turn to find her with his eyes, and it was as hot and immediate as if he'd put his hand on her heart.

She watched him now, a familiar stranger. He did not look up.

"And what's on Professor Milton's clothesline these days?" Daryl turned to her equably, through with Paul. "I haven't seen you all month."

Hazel's skepticism in her office that afternoon rose to mind, and Evie flushed, pushing back against it.

"The end of my people, the last of the four hundred," she tossed. "A little monograph, tentatively entitled *The Twilight of the WASPs.*"

"Your people?" Paul looked at her.

"Kidding," she said.

"Four hundred what?" Daryl asked, undeterred.

"Families of Old New York, the ones that fit in Mrs. Astor's ballroom, and on the pages of *The Social Register.*"

"Now, *there's* a title," Daryl remarked. *"Downward from the Astor Ballroom."*

"But who owns half of an island in Maine," Paul observed. "So, not so far down."

She frowned. She hadn't been serious with all this. Why had he brought up Crockett's?

"That none of us can afford —" she deflected. "Who knows how long we'll be able to keep it. It's an old rackety-packety house on a rock in the middle of the ocean."

It was her habitual way of discussing the Island, with a practiced, wry disaffection.

"You know you don't believe that," Paul said. "You'd never say it if you really thought you were going to lose it."

"But it's a real possibility," she said, looking at him, "since only one of my cousins makes any money."

"Still," Paul observed, "somehow there is always an aunt Maud, or a great-uncle Jonathan who dies just at the right moment, releasing a tidy sum."

"It's true," she nodded, flushing. What was he doing?

"The Miltons bought it for fifteen hundred dollars eighty years ago," Paul explained. "One of these New England kingdoms where lobstermen drop off the lobster like milk in a crate every other evening. A vast hunk of rock so beautiful that no one can let go."

"Evie," Daryl drawled. "I never suspected. You've been keeping this from me."

"It's a little less exalted than a kingdom," Evie protested, looking at Paul, though she knew it was a losing battle.

"And what do you do there?" Daryl asked.

"Mess about in boats." She took a sip of wine. "Drink. Play capture the flag."

"Really?"

"Isn't that what you'd like to imagine?" She was arch. "Summer house of the patricians, tanned faces turned to a leeward breeze, hands resting on the tiller, nobility at the helm. Isn't that the fantasy?"

Daryl raised his eyebrow and looked at Paul.

"An island." Daryl whistled. "Your family owns a whole island."

He reached for the wine bottle and filled his own glass. "How exclusive, how very old-school."

She watched the fantasy take hold. The Island was always itself, and more than itself.

"Not really," she said. "There is always someone simply showing up and having to be dealt with, having to be given tea, or a drink. Always someone new landing."

Something flickered across Paul's face.

"How inconvenient," Daryl remarked dryly. "And utterly American."

"It is." Evie reached forward and pressed the melting wax down around the lip of one of the big candles, making a little barrier against the drip.

"Who owns it?"

"I do," Evie answered, "and my cousins, now that our parents are gone."

"Though Evie's going to sell her share," said Paul quietly, looking across the table at her. "That's been the plan."

Evie didn't meet his eyes.

"How much does it cost to keep?" Daryl was intent.

"I don't know exactly," she admitted. "It's

in trust."

"You don't know?" Daryl answered, incredulous. "Haven't you asked?"

Evie shook her head.

"So what's going to happen?"

"How do you mean?" Evie hadn't meant for the Island to become a point of conversation. She didn't actually want to talk about it.

"What happens when the trust runs out? How will you keep it then?"

Enough was enough. She looked at Daryl levelly. "By hook or by crook. Beggar our children, beggar ourselves."

"Sounds like a plan." He laughed amiably and raised his glass. "To the future of the past."

She smiled wanly, toasted, and drank, then stood, reaching for Paul's plate and Daryl's, and walked with full hands through the swinging door into the kitchen.

There wasn't a clear spot to put anything down on the kitchen's counters. The morning's breakfast dishes and the bags from the takeout competed for the space. It was like the last day of Pompeii in there. She set the plates down on the burners, angry and feeling exposed. What had Paul been doing out there, launching them into talk of the Island? What was going on with him tonight? She opened one of the cupboards and got a glass, then filled it at the sink and stood and drank it down.

When she pushed back through the swinging door, the dining room was empty. She followed their voices down the hall to his study, where they were staring up at the photographs of the stumble stones pinned above Paul's desk. Embedded in Berlin's streets and sidewalks, there were thousands of stones like these all over the city, set down outside the last place a Jew had lived or worked before deportation and the camps. Three of them had lain outside the door of the apartment building Paul had sublet, and when he called her on the day after he'd arrived, it was all he could talk about.

"That sounds incredibly moving," she'd said.

"It's more than moving," he'd countered. "It's everything. Everything I've been thinking —"

"How?"

"I don't know." His voice was tense with excitement. "I don't know yet."

"Before the Holocaust," Paul was explaining to Daryl now, "when someone tripped on a paving stone in the road, the folk saying went, *A Jew must be buried there.* So the stumble stones take the old folk saying and make it literal."

He folded his arms, leaning against the edge of his desk. "I had heard about the project but had forgotten it was there."

"Pavement stories," Daryl mused.

Paul nodded. "Told all over the city."

Evie came to stand beside them. Ranged in neat rows, a grid above their heads, the small brass squares reminded her of blocks of moveable type: *Here lived,* or *Here worked.* Then the name. Their birth. The date of deportation, and last, of their murder.

"Those were the ones outside the flat in Schoeneberg where I was staying." Paul pointed to the top three, what looked like a family.

Hier arbeitete
Arthur Kroner,
JG 1874,
Gedemutigt,
Flucht en den Todd, 1941

Next to his block lay his wife: *Hier wohnte* Sophie Kroner, JG 1878, *Gedemutigt, Flucht en den Todd,* 1941; and beneath her parents, Mildred Kroner, JG 1925, *Deportiert,* 1941, *Ermordert in Auschwitz,* 1942.

"Here worked and lived Arthur and Sophie Kroner." Daryl paused. *"Gedemutigt?"*

"Humiliated," Paul translated. "And flown into death, 1941."

"Meaning?"

"They probably killed themselves rather than be taken."

Evie shuddered. It looked like their daughter had been deported around the same time. That day? Earlier? It was impossible not to begin imagining.

"After I saw those first three outside my door, I started photographing the stones as I wandered around in my first days, and then I found I couldn't stop. I got the list of where they were in the city and I tried to find each one, just to stand there, in a place where they stood, before they were taken."

1930. Born. *Deportiert,* 1942. 1943. Deported. Caspar Baer. Paula Baer. *Ermordet in Auschwitz. In Dachau. In Sachsenhausen.* Born. Lived. Worked. Taken. Murdered. Julius Oppenheim. Frida Trieu. Ephraim Worrmann.

At the end of the last row were the stones of what appeared to be another family: Here lived, *Elsa, Gerhard, and Wilhelm Hoffman.* Evie read. The father was taken first, in 1936, and killed shortly after. The mother in July, 1941, and murdered in 1942. And their son — she leaned closer.

"Yeah," Paul said, noticing where she was looking. "The father died first, in Sachsenhausen, the mother in Plötzensee. Those were the prisons in Berlin. But look at that last one — the boy's."

"Ermordet Hier," Evie read. Here.

"He was killed in front of his house on Linienstrasse, in Mitte, the heart of the city. In the spot where I stood."

They stared up at the photograph.

"He was eleven," Paul said.

The ache in his voice was palpable.

"His was the one that got me. I kept coming back to their stones — they had lived not far from the Institute — and the more I walked past his stone, over his stone, around his stone, the more I wondered: Had anyone seen it happen? Who? I imagined the people in the street, who stood, as I was standing, maybe just a few feet away. The man passing by. The woman walking her dog. The ones who watched people taken away."

Daryl had his head tipped, listening hard.

"So I started to imagine another group of stones to set in place beside the stumble stones around the city." Paul pivoted from the photographs and looked at them. "A stone for each watcher. Stones for the crowd."

He folded his arms, falling silent.

"But I don't see," said Daryl, after a little, "how any of this has to do with anything you're working on."

"Where are the Jews in Henry James?" Paul challenged, looking up at him with a little smile.

"Last I checked there were no Jews in Henry James." Daryl was dry. "Except Deronda."

"And why not?" Paul answered. "There were Jews everywhere around him. In London, in Venice. Certainly in New York —"

"Go on."

"And the blacks in Nathaniel Hawthorne? Where are they?" Paul pushed.

"That wasn't his subject," Daryl retorted.

"Exactly." Paul nodded. "Precisely my point. There are no blacks in Hawthorne because he'd have to see them as real enough, human enough, for him to imagine them, put them in the story."

"Oh, for god's sake, Paul," Evie pushed back. "Of course he understood them to be human beings —"

"Really? Then where are they?"

Evie didn't answer.

"Everyone you can't see on the surface. *That's* the story. But they are buried, implicit." Paul didn't miss a beat. "That's what the stumble stones remind us. We were here."

"And?"

Paul turned to Daryl. "What if a place could remember what had happened? What if a place could speak? What if that memory tripped us up in our daily lives?"

"Okay." Daryl looked at him. "Go on."

"What if we had said what we had done here?" Paul went on. "Like the Germans. What if this country put down a paving stone for every slave — their names, the places where they arrived, the spot where they were sold — all over the South, in every market-place in the South? What if this country put what happened in the past right under our feet and said, *All right. Look. Look there. Pay attention.* Joseph, Sold. Anna, Sold. Harriet, Sold." He paused. "And resold.

"And then," he slowed. "What if there were a stone for the rest of us? What if we laid stones for all of it? A stone for the sold *and* a stone for those who watched. Who watched and turned away. What if we could mark it somehow? What if we *had*?"

"Well, there'd be no art, for starters," Daryl retorted, "as art's what tells secrets."

"But we'd have the truth."

"Yes," countered Daryl. "Then what?"

Paul broke into a grin. "Exactly. That's what I'm wondering. What's the art that comes when what happened is all out in the open? When what's been buried is laid out in stones for all to see? What would this country's stories, its paintings, its movies and poems look like if they didn't need to tell the open American secret over and over and over — this happened, is *still* happening."

"My god," Daryl whistled. "Listen to you."

Stop this, thought Evie mutinously. Stones. Memory. *Race.* These are words falling on words. *Let's stop,* she pleaded silently. But he was restless now, and on fire.

"But slavery wasn't a secret," Evie interjected. "It isn't a secret."

"No. But on a street in South Carolina, or Kentucky, or Virginia, a black man, or a

247

woman, or a child was led away with a bit between his teeth, and a white man — or woman, or child — turned away. That's what I'm getting at. That moment is somewhere in all of us — the history inside us handed down — white and black. Baldwin wrote this sixty years ago. I see it so clearly now. That moment is the one we still repeat here, over and over again, the ordinary, everyday wickedness of turning away. The American primal scene.

"And we're stuck in it, here. The black man looks at the white and says, *You you you,* and the white looks back at the black, thinking, *Not me, man, I didn't buy you.*"

"But he turned away." Evie saw where this was going.

Paul nodded.

"Though some didn't," remarked Daryl.

"Some didn't," Paul agreed. "But we repeat what we don't know, or insist we don't know — and until we recognize that, acknowledge it, we will repeat it. We are repeating it, endlessly, over and over and over —"

"We acknowledge it all the time; what are you talking about?"

"Sure." Paul nodded. "We teach it. We talk about it. But still, in this country when you meet a black person for the first time, you have to prove yourself, right?"

She frowned. "How do you mean?"

"You have to prove — both of you have to

prove — you are not *that* kind of white person."

"You have to prove you aren't racist?"

He nodded. "We have to deny the moment in the market in us. And we can't. That's the American story."

She shook her head, troubled. "You can't make an easy analogy like that."

"Which?"

"Germans and American whites. It's not so simple."

"Why not?" Paul countered.

"Because people are people." Evie fixed her eyes on him. "People have complicated *lives.* Lives that don't necessarily fall so cleanly into black-and-white choices — people are blind, but still well-intended, and see as far as they can."

Paul stared at her.

"And," Evie went on, "most people in this country don't like to be reminded."

"Most white people," said Paul.

"Yes. But why say it like that? It stops the conversation."

"Because it's true," he repeated.

Evie shook her head, impatient. "Granny K used to say that some things were better off left unsaid."

Daryl snorted. "But you don't believe that, do you? You wouldn't be where you are now if you'd sat on your hands and kept quiet."

"I know that." Evie flushed. Hazel had said

as much to her that afternoon. "But some-times I wonder about *how* we say what we say when we say it —"

"Your grandmother also referred to me as 'the Jew who married Evie,' " Paul reminded her.

"Ouch," said Daryl.

"Come on, Paul, that's not fair," Evie retorted, not hiding her annoyance. "We all know how it was in the thirties. No one of that generation would have said *Jewish.* Even Eleanor Roosevelt's letters were pocked by little dashes of irritation about 'this Jew or that one at a party.' "

"How it was?"

Holding her gaze, Paul reached into his coat pocket and handed her a photograph.

Several people sat about at a sunny picnic in a park somewhere long ago, their faces turned toward the camera, delighted to be caught. The men wore coats and ties, the women, their legs tucked under and to the side, wore skirts that dated to the thirties, Evie reckoned. One of the women had dark curly hair that seemed to have burst free of its ties, cascading around her neck. Beside her was a man whose face was turned toward her, as if trying to catch what she had said.

Evie bent her head.

"What am I looking at?" she asked, frowning at the image.

He put his finger on each of the men seated

in the grass. "Nazi. Nazi. Nazi —"

Pops, she thought, looking up at Paul. *That's Pops.*

"Yes," he said, his eyes on her. "How it was."

FIFTEEN

The day was feckless. Shafts of light plunged to dark as the sun crossed above and played with the clouds. Did one pull down or take off one's hat? The heat of the last few days remained unbroken, and the windows of the offices of Milton Higginson were shoved up as high as they could go in their narrow tracks, the wooden sashes swelling in the heat off the river, the thick heat in the air. Money moved slowly. The bondsmen called out their sales sitting down. Number 30 Broad Street, north facing, enjoyed the shade in the mornings, and Ogden Milton's secretary typed as quickly as she could. The sun would turn and begin its slow drop through the opposite window in the afternoon, finding her, finishing her. She typed. In the inner office, Mr. Milton was quiet. She stopped a minute to listen. Perhaps, she thought, returning to her typing, too quiet.

Ogden Milton was sitting behind the same polished Sheraton desk at which his father and his grandfather had worked, faced when he looked up by the same flank of mahogany bookshelves upon which ranged complete sets of MacCauley and Gibbon and the bound prospectuses of companies of interest, sunk in thought. Off his shoulder to the right, a row of windows stretched, so that from where he sat, the island of Manhattan unfurled, a granite lawn of buildings stretching to the tip where the East and the Hudson rivers met and where the great ships of Europe drew slowly upward toward the yards at Brooklyn and the piers at Chelsea. In slow majesty the old world still arrived.

At sixty, Ogden and the firm had profited from steady hard breezes moving their fortunes along after the war. Ogden sat on three boards and was the president of the American Museum of Natural History. He and Kitty had a small apartment for nights in town, but the big brick house they had built in Oyster Bay with a view of Long Island Sound meant that on most nights of his life, he was facing the water. So that most days, even when he wasn't on Crockett's, he felt near it. Pushing back from his desk, he came to stand at the window where he did most of his thinking.

Through the gaps in the buildings in front of him, a sail cut the blue distance of the Hudson on a downwind tack, some lucky guy out on the water before lunch in the middle of the workweek.

His throat tightened. *Some lucky guys,* Dunc used to say, *just a couple of dumb lucky guys.* Ogden kept his eye on the white triangle, trying to push away the thought of Dunc. It was too damn sad what seemed to be happening to his old friend. The boat glided forward, moving gloriously slow, the canvas filling and filling with wind, carrying with it the thought of Crockett's and the particular patch of dead air right at the center of the bay just off the end of the Island and how, if you caught the wind just right, you might start to fly before it past the calm, past the land's end — out into the Reach. He and Dunc used to let the sails run and turn to each other, laughing in the bright air. But that had been long ago.

It was no use. Ogden leaned his forehead against the glass. He couldn't shake it off.

The sail luffed down there on the water.

"Dad?"

He turned. "Moss."

A young man in horn-rimmed glasses, dressed in narrow trousers and a white shirt — but tieless, Ogden noted — poked his head in, pushing open the door. "Am I interrupting?"

"Some woolgathering," Ogden admitted with a sad smile. "Come in. I'm glad to see you."

"I came to see if you'd like to have lunch."

"Very much. But not today, I'm afraid,"

Ogden answered just as the buzzer rang on his desk. "That'll be the new man."

"Shall I leave?"

"No, no. Stay. It'll be good for you two to meet."

"Good for me?" Moss asked casually.

Ogden paused. "Yes, Moss. And for him, I expect, as well."

"Good of you to say."

Ogden ignored Moss's irony.

"Yes, all right." He nodded to Mrs. Meecham, who had poked her head around the door. "Send him in."

Ogden had been out of the country when Proc Smedley had telegrammed to advise that the firm should snap up Len Levy. *You won't be sorry,* Smedley had written. *Hell, you might even make him a partner.* Smedley had good instincts, always had, and proof in the pudding was that Len Levy had been at his desk only six weeks, and already he'd made an appointment with Ogden.

Ballsy? You bet, Ogden thought to himself, buttoning his jacket with one hand as he made his way around the desk.

"Sir?"

"Come in, Levy," Ogden said. "Come in."

On first glance, Levy was a big fellow, substantial, clean-cut, and with a disarming grin, a firm handshake, and a ready nod in response to Ogden's invitation to sit.

"This is my son, Moss. Moss, Mr. Levy."

"Glad to meet you." Moss held out his hand.

"Mr. Milton." Len shook his hand.

Moss grimaced. "Moss. Please."

"Moss will be coming to work for us in September," Ogden said, his eyes on his son. "You may find yourselves at neighboring desks. I've promised Moss this one last summer before the ax."

"The ax?" Len raised his eyebrows.

Moss threw himself into the other chair in front of Ogden's desk. "That's right. The chopper. The clamp."

And a job, thought Len.

Ogden moved from the window, where he glimpsed again, just before turning, the far triangle of that sail, past the channel marker and heading out to sea.

"Do you sail, Levy?" he asked.

"Sir?"

"Sailing." Ogden rounded the desk on his way back to his chair. "Do you sail?"

"I don't."

Ogden sat.

"I rowed in college, though," Len offered.

"Sit." Ogden gestured to him. "What seat? Stroke, I imagine; you've got the shoulders."

"Number two seat, actually."

Ogden raised his eyebrows. The lighter weights were usually set in the bow of the boat.

"We were a big eight," Len observed with a slight smile.

Ogden nodded. "Columbia?"

"That's right."

"I hope you weren't on the crew that beat Harvard in 'fifty-four?" asked Moss.

Len shook his head. "I was still in Korea in 'fifty-four."

"The army?"

"Yes," Len said. He didn't offer any more.

But there was more to tell, Ogden reflected. He was struck by a quite unusual calm in the young man, not seeming to need, as many men his age did, to explain himself. As if he had been born to the spot where he'd arrived, as if there was nothing whatsoever in his way. And not for the first time Ogden considered it was this single trait that guaranteed the result.

"That's all right, then," he joked. "I'm afraid there wouldn't be a spot here long for a victorious Lion."

"Understood," said Len, smiling and pushing slightly back in the chair, his hands on his knees.

What had he understood? Ogden wondered.

"Interrupting a party, am I?" Jack Higginson poked his head through the doorway.

"Hello, Jack." Ogden greeted his partner with an inward sigh.

Jack slid forward, hand extended, dressed

in bow tie and blue blazer as though he had blown in here on the way to the Yacht Club. Moss and Len rose to their feet.

"Hello, Moss." Jack gripped his arm.

"And — Levy? What brings you up here?"

"I had an idea I wanted to run by Mr. Milton," Len answered smoothly, "but as long as I've got you both here —"

He is *ballsy,* thought Ogden.

"That's my cue, I think," said Moss.

"Stay, Moss," Ogden pressed. "I'd like you to hear Levy's idea."

Moss glanced at Len and sat back down.

"Fire away," Ogden said, ignoring his partner's surprise.

"Please." Jack Higgins pointed and then settled himself in Len's emptied chair.

For the first time, Levy seemed to hesitate. Ogden wondered whether it was nerves, or whether it was the wind-up to the punch. And realized how he relished this uncertainty. He hadn't been so taken with anyone in a long while.

Len remained on his feet. "Milton Higginson is one of the great investment banks, one of the oldest —"

Jack nodded, catching Ogden's eye.

"And one of the best, extending its influence all over the country, advising all sorts of companies, from small to quite large."

He paused.

"But Milton Higginson is missing a piece

of the pie."

Here we go. Moss smothered a smile.

"In every one of these companies, there are employees," Len observed, "men who could certainly be advised toward entering the stock market."

"What's that?" Jack exclaimed. "The employees?"

Len nodded. "It seems to me, sir, that they form a vastly untapped market for our expertise. We already advise banks where to invest; why not the men — and women for that matter, why not the secretaries, too — who work here?"

"That extends quite far past our reach," Jack warned.

Len nodded. "That's the point, sir. What if you went *past* the usual parties? Opened other avenues. Created more clientele."

"Interesting idea," Ogden offered. "You are suggesting that ordinary people inside banks — clerks, accountants, even janitors — might enter the stock market."

"And *we'd* advise them."

"It's brilliant." Moss pushed himself forward. "Open up Wall Street. Invite anyone in —"

Len nodded at him, surprised.

"My son," Ogden observed with a slight smile, "appears to be a Democrat."

"That's all very well," sniffed Jack, "but that's not what this firm does."

Len fixed his eyes on Ogden. "You wouldn't be sorry."

"Of course not," Ogden said with a gleam in his eye. "Because I haven't promised you a damn thing."

"But you listened."

And in that moment Ogden realized the force of the younger man's strength, that the proposal Len Levy had just made was only the start, that Levy had leashed himself up until now, and that he had just slightly loosened his grip on the leash at that moment. He smiled.

"That I did," he said. "But then, I always make it a habit to listen." And he held out his hand.

If he heard the warning, Levy didn't heed it. He was, Ogden saw, going to keep pushing, and without thinking, without really understanding why, Ogden stood, his hand out.

"We will talk again," he promised, and caught the brief flicker of disappointment on the younger man's face.

"Yes, sir. I hope so," replied Len, shaking Ogden's hand, and then turning to Jack Higginson, shaking his hand as well.

"Listen," Ogden said.

Len paused and turned around.

"We're glad to have you on board," Ogden finished, though it hadn't been what he meant to say.

"Thank you." Len was serious. "I mean to contribute."

"Good man." Ogden nodded, an idea rising to mind.

"Put yourself on Mrs. Meecham's docket in the next week, why don't you? She can show you down to the file room. There's a record of everything we've ever done, stuffed in boxes. Why don't you get in there and dig around." He leaned forward, smiling. "See if there are any likely candidates for your idea in the businesses we hold. Make me a list."

There. He had handed Levy something. He had shown the young man he had heard him.

Len's face broke into a smile and he pulled open the door. "I will, sir. Thank you."

Moss pushed himself up out of his chair. "I'll walk out with you," he said, and followed Len out the door.

"Good work in there," he said.

Len glanced at him.

Moss nodded. "You've got the goods."

Len grinned. "Thanks."

The elevator door opened. Len put out his hand.

"I have people over every Friday night." Moss shook it. "You should come by. Twenty-nine West Twelfth," he said, stepping in. And the elevator door closed.

In Ogden's office, the two older men remained sitting in quiet.

Jack whistled. "Cool customer."

261

"I like him," Ogden said, regarding Jack.

"But the man was proposing to send Milton Higginson into the public realm —"

"So it would seem." Ogden was mild.

"That's one step above hustling in my book."

"Merrill Lynch works it."

"We are not Merrill Lynch," Jack asserted. "Thank God. Though a kike couldn't be expected to see that we don't advise employees."

Stiffening, Ogden turned all his attention to the man in the blue blazer across from him.

"What was it you wanted to see me about, Jack?"

"Addie wanted to know whether you and Kitty might make nine and ten at the table at the club this Saturday?"

"I'll see what Kitty's got planned."

"Right-o," said Jack, and heaved himself up out of the chair.

"Looks like rain," he noted, looking out the window behind Ogden. "Give us a break from this hellish heat."

The door closed behind him and Ogden remained where he sat. Jack Higginson was a fool.

It had been more than twenty years since he'd hired Solly Weinberg, and Ogden had never regretted it. He'd hired what he saw as pure genius for investment. Not a Jew.

He leaned back in his chair. He believed in

fairness. A good man could come from anywhere. Ogden had no illusions about birth. No matter how far back, no matter how much money, there had always been one man who made that move from stable to sitting room, men who were born seeing over the rim of their cradle. They were the hope of the world, and Ogden believed in a better world, built man by man.

And why should a Jew be any different? He shouldn't. These young ones coming up through the Ivies were impressive as hell. They didn't take no for an answer. They simply pushed past what was ordinary practice, asking questions like *Why not?* It was refreshing. The firm could use that.

He had spent the scant side of a half hour with this young man, and yet he wanted him around, still more, wanted Moss to work beside him. Levy could be a great influence on his son. Never mind who he was or where he was from.

If pressed, Ogden would have answered swiftly that he hadn't fought the war to save the Jews. He'd gone to war to fight Hitler, to save England and France. What had happened to the Jews had happened inside a war already so full of slaughter and brutality, it had been hard to see it clearly. No matter what Dunc insisted, no matter what Dunc had said, what happened to the Jews at the time could not have been helped. One did the best one could with the information one had. And then one gave a leg up when one could. It was the right thing; it was the decent thing. The war was over, and now one's duty was to help where help was needed. Though he was certain that the young man who had just walked through his door would despise that kind of attention. A leg up smacked of weakness. And this man, who appeared every inch Ogden Milton's match, did not seem to need anything Ogden could give, except perhaps an open door.

Which is what I can give him. Ogden returned his attention to the papers on the desk before him. *Which is why he'll do fine.*

Uptown, Joan Milton finished the letter she was typing and pulled it out of the roller. The afternoon sun had moved from the end of her desk to the middle of the office and made a hot patch in the old carpet there. Soon it would creep up the front of Whit Lord's desk and into his eyes, and he'd reach for his sunglasses and put them on, still talking, or reading, or smoking, without a pause. Just past the doorway to this room was the hall and the closet office where Mr. Rosset's desk was and where he spent the bulk of time, his feet crossed and up on his desk, leaning back in his chair. She could just see the tips of his shoes now.

The office had fallen into an eerie quiet

waiting for the decision from the judge to come down. And though the press had other titles to attend to on its list, there was the sense in here of an army at ease, hats tossed off, belts loosened, guns and swords dropped by the boots. Any moment they would hear whether they'd been shut down, or had changed the game.

"Words are nothing but clothes," Mr. Rosset had said to her early on in the job — "sewn in a specific time by a specific hand. We don't, for instance, wear codpieces anymore, or bustles, or cinch tight our waists. Lawrence takes off the clothes. Lawrence shows us to see without veils. The body in love has always been clothed by words that try to conceal. You can't suppress or conceal by concealing, he said. And if we win this, if we get the ban lifted, then we've shifted the lens, we've shown the lens for what it is: obscenity is the *clothing,* not the body."

Joan had nodded and listened and did not ask the question his little treatise begged.

But he had tipped forward in his chair and chuckled. "You don't agree, do you?"

She looked back at him and shook her head.

"Good," he said. "Tell me why."

"It seems to me we need clothing," she'd retorted. "We can't simply be *naked.*"

"Why not?" he'd returned.

She had yet to find an answer.

"I'm going," she called out now to his shoes

265

on the desk.

"Coming back?" Whit Lord drawled.

She paused and looked at him.

"Ouch." He put his sunglasses on and dipped his head at her.

"Miss Milton?" Barney Rosset called.

"Yes, sir?"

There came the sound of two feet hitting the floor in the inner office.

"Miss Milton?"

"Yes." She moved toward the closet, where Mr. Rosset appeared in the doorway. "I'm here."

He looked at her. "Where is it you are going right now?"

She raised her chin. "My sister is —"

"Oh, right, right." Her boss waved her off. "Dresses. Mothers —"

She hesitated.

"Go." He turned back to his desk impatiently. "Go on. Very important stuff."

She flushed and made for the door. He'd dismissed her like a child.

"For god's sake, Milton," Whit teased quietly as she passed his desk. "He's kidding."

She nodded tightly and didn't answer.

It was going to pour, she saw as she made her way out the door, and she had forgotten her umbrella under her desk upstairs.

Never mind, she thought, pushing out into it.

■ ■ ■ ■

And indeed, within minutes, the afternoon cascaded into a summer rain. The skies plummeted down from the tops of the gray buildings and the rain spattered on the pavement in castanets of water, snapping out a beat. And inside Mr. Bacharach's photography studio, Kitty Milton was waiting for her daughters, worried they'd be caught in it.

At fifty-four, she had the lean, upright lines she'd always had, her lovely head now crowned with silver hair upon its long neck. She had aged like a dancer, graceful, elegant, altogether on point. If this was the woman she had grown into, she thought, well, all right.

She sank deeper into one of the cushioned chairs beneath the sound of the rain, glad of a little time before the girls came, unsettled by her lunch with Priss Houghton just now.

They had gone to the Colony Club as they often did, meeting in the city for lunch. Priss was early, waiting for Kitty in one of the rose-colored club chairs perennially turned toward another, suggesting bent heads and whispers and smiles. During the day the front room filled with women, their packages and cigarettes, their hats and gloves. Coffee, lunch, tea, the club's room was the place no one had to organize or pick up, no one had to decide on whether the chairs needed recovering; it simply continued in the manner it had since they had all been children there and first allowed at tea with their grannies. The room persevered with a profound, immutable calm made possible, Kitty had long ago decided, by the gold satin underlining of the curtains. On a sunny day, the light through the tall windows shimmered through that fabric, slanting its gold along the ivory walls and calling up the summer hours between meals, the gully of the afternoon when men took to hammocks and women to sitting in the shade.

Priss had risen as Kitty came into the room, and if one didn't know her, one might take in the skirt and loafers on this sweet muffin of a woman and mistake the round edges for comfort, or ease. But Kitty could see that Priss was holding herself very carefully.

One's fifties were cruel, Kitty thought as they were seated at the little round table, pulling her napkin onto her lap. Every sorrow holds lightly on, every regret. Right there for all to see. Poor Priss. It would have been better for her if Dunc had died in the war. Something had been taken from him then, some essential thing Kitty couldn't ever put her finger on. He hadn't failed on the money front — they were perfectly well-off, she was pretty sure of that — but he hadn't held steady. He had returned without his pit, the stone at his center. And he'd never gotten it back.

"What is it?" she asked quietly.

Priss placed her hands on either side of the fork and knife, studying the cloth. "How is Ogden?" she asked.

Kitty looked at her. "Fine."

"And Moss?"

"Well," Kitty said.

"The girls?"

"Priss." Kitty was soft. "What is it?"

Priss moved the knife along the cloth absentmindedly, opening wide the place setting. Kitty watched her friend's face.

"Can one die from remembering?" Priss kept her eyes on the cloth. "Because I think Dunc is dying."

"He is not," Kitty chided softly. "He cannot. We won't let him."

Priss was silent.

Kitty put her hand out to touch Priss to stop her from turning the knife over and over on the cloth. Priss stilled.

"It's worse right now. It's always worse right now," she said. "Something triggers the memory, and then he's gone."

"How do you mean?"

"Gone in the past."

"What memory?"

"He won't say. He's never said. I just know he's lost."

Kitty didn't speak.

"This *age*." Priss looked up at Kitty, at last. "How do you mean?"

Priss shook her head. "I'm fifty-five. And I'm only just *now* beginning to understand."

"Understand what, Priss?"

Priss shook her head slowly. "I was sitting in my car the other day, waiting for Dunc's train and watching the children playing across the way in the little playground down in the village. And the mothers sitting there on the bench. So unsuspecting. They don't know how young they are. How beautiful. How *alive*."

Kitty reached across the table and covered her friend's hand.

"I wanted to roll down the car window and call to them —" Priss faltered.

"Priss," Kitty said, a little frightened.

"Take it." Priss's voice broke. "I wanted to cry out to all of them sitting there, so unsuspecting. Take this in your hands and don't let go. Grab *hold*."

"Mrs. Milton." The waitress put Kitty's plate in front of her.

Hurriedly, Priss wiped her eyes.

"Mrs. Houghton."

Priss nodded her thanks but remained quiet in front of the plate, looking down.

"There's only the one life, Kitty," she whispered sadly. "Just the one chance at it. And you can either get it right. Or wrong. And we never know, do we, as we're spinning along in it. We never know. And then one day, there you are —"

She raised her eyes to look at Kitty across the table, and all Kitty could do was nod.

"Mum!"

Kitty shook herself, turning toward Joan, who came in glowing but sopping wet. Her dress had streaks of rain running through the skirt. *Never mind,* thought Kitty. She wasn't the one to be photographed. The girl who had been assigned to their needs came into the room with a thick white towel, and Joan scrubbed her arms dry luxuriantly.

"Hello, Mum." Evelyn appeared in the doorway of the blue salon, dry and perfectly at ease, having taken a taxi, and followed by Sarah Pratt, the mother of the groom.

"I heard she took a job at Brentano's," Sarah Pratt was saying. "Even though the wedding is only two months off."

"Who did?" Kitty fixed a smile. Sarah had never learned the simple principle of beginnings, middles, and endings. Every conversation started willy-nilly and then, often, never ended.

"So you're lucky," observed Sarah Pratt, hugging Kitty.

Kitty nodded, though she wondered what it was Sarah envied now.

"Who took a job?" she asked.

"Emmy Lord."

"Ah," Kitty said, understanding. "How thoughtless."

"What is?" Joan slid her arm into her mother's elbow.

"Emmy Lord went to work just at the time her mother most needs her for the wedding preparations."

"But it's the training program," Evelyn remarked. "She has to do it."

"It's self-indulgent is what it is," Sarah commented. "Emmy Lord doesn't need to work to begin with, and certainly not six weeks before her own wedding."

"But she may want to," said Joan, dropping the towel on the back of the little chaise.

"Oh, *want* —" Kitty dismissed the idea, her eyes on Mr. Bacharach strolling toward them, his hand outstretched.

Joan arched her eyebrow at Evelyn, who smiled back.

"Evelyn," Kitty said, turning. "The dress is ready for you."

It was important for Mum to have it all perfectly in order, Joan thought, and Evelyn was perfect and in order. And best of all — Joan crossed her arms, watching her sister being shown to the dressing room, and nodding and smiling at the courtly little man who took all the bridal photographs that appeared every Sunday in the *Times* — Evelyn was in love. When one spread open the two pages at the end of the paper and studied the girls staring back from their poised black-and-white photos, the girls from the Upper East Side, from Greenwich and Oyster Bay — Miss Barr to Mrs. Lathrop, Miss Schuyler to Mrs. Southworth — one couldn't be sure of that. But the Pratts were old friends, and from Greenwich, the other side of Long Island Sound, friends who, like the Miltons, had decamped from Old New York in the thirties in search of trees and lawns an hour's train ride from the city.

One might have thought Dickie would fall in love with Joanie — she was the eldest — but Dick's eyes had slid right across the elder Milton to her twelve-year-old sister and never let go. Evelyn grew up in the shade of Dickie's eyes, unfurling slowly toward him as she too went off to Farmington, tossing her head at him when he asked her to the prom at Yale, but then writing him every single day he was in Korea — and so it seemed the only answer, when he returned from the war, really, had been yes.

This lent a satisfying inevitability to their story, as though it had been written long ago, the words *meant for each other* suggesting two souls raised in the same waters swimming blindly into each other's arms and, now having arrived there, breaking open in a joy not untinged by triumph. Watching Evelyn and Dickie together, Kitty always thought, it was as though they had won a race. Her youngest daughter was nearly always flushed these days, and full to the brim with certainty. She had done well, Kitty thought. Good for her.

"Perfect." Kitty smiled at her younger daughter, who emerged now, smooth in the white satin, her tiny waist caught up and held by the dress, the lovely curve of her shoulders allowed to slope and disappear into the long shimmering sleeves.

"Yes," Joan agreed, smiling at Evelyn, who held both arms in front of her, turning in the mirror to see the fold of her train swish behind on the pale carpet.

Outside, the rain stopped as suddenly as it had begun, and the drops upon the window glass glittered and slid down the pane. And Joan was singly, startlingly grateful.

Sixteen

The memory of the girl leaning over the balcony at Pennsylvania Station in that moment before her sister grabbed her arm had returned to Len again and again over the next few weeks, overtaking him like snatches of a song he didn't know he'd heard. He wondered if he'd ever see her again and was certain that he wouldn't. He recalled the small pulse that beat at the center of her throat while she lay on the floor of the station before coming to. He remembered the feel of her hand under his. Love, the movies would have you believe, struck like lightning. He had thought the movies lied.

Instead, he felt, sitting at his desk and then moving through the heat of Manhattan each day, the movies didn't tell it deep enough. He'd been struck dumb, cut in two — and wanted to be struck and struck again. He shook himself and looked back down at the company reports splayed before him.

Unlike his partner Jack Higginson, whose

disdain had been palpable that day in Mr. Milton's office, Ogden Milton clearly had his eye on building capital through a man's brainpower, regardless of his pedigree. And in the scant months that Len had been at the firm, Ogden Milton had made clear his regard, casting a growing and persistent light on him. He was the one to watch for, everyone knew it, and now as the summer swung fully on through the month of June, Len felt the expansive freedom of room to grow and decided he would take Mr. Milton up on the suggestion he had tossed to Len at the end of their first meeting. If he could get Milton to give him the green light, he'd show the older man what Len felt sure was a path to a broad and lucrative highway of possibility.

So one day toward the end of the month, he followed Mrs. Meecham down into the room where the files of all Milton Higginson's transactions were stored and nodded politely at her instructions — *of course nothing may be removed, Mr. Levy* — and smiled as she left him where he stood in the middle of the filing cabinets lining all four walls. *There must be dozens of companies in here that would fit the bill,* he thought. Len had a clear idea of the kind of company he would suggest to Mr. Milton: midsized, out of Manhattan, with solid returns. The kind of company that might want to reward its workers, run by men who saw themselves as forward-thinking, beneficent — canny but kind. He pulled open the cabinet nearest him, reached in, and took out an armful of folders, then tucked them under his arm, carefully turning off the light, and shutting the door behind him.

From then on, he spent the hot Friday afternoons at his desk high above Manhattan after most of the men had left to catch their trains bound for Fire Island, Rhode Island, Fishers Island, any island, he joked to Reg, but Coney Island, a solitary typewriter sounding down the hall like a sulky tap dancer on an empty stage, one of the secretaries at her job. He paged through the records of banks Milton Higginson had cultivated, of trusts the firm had advised, of companies raised from the seed of an idea (there was, in the folder connected to one of the largest utility companies in the country, a napkin from the Excelsior Hotel with Ogden's notes in blue ink) to their full impressive height. Ogden Milton had been everywhere: Germany in 1927 and in 1929, on FDR's advisory board in 1932, all the while steering the firm toward lucrative waters through the Crash, the bank crisis, and into the Depression. Len was able to read the history of the firm and see just where the man had been brilliant and just where, in Len's opinion, he'd stopped short. The history of the firm was a history of restrained success, of moderation — steady growth rather than vision. Reading the files and the notes Ogden had written in the margins, Len came face-to-face with the man he had been, the man whom Len, too, wanted to be. Though better. Smarter. Richer.

In the evenings, Len and Reg met after work and went anywhere they could to find the cool marbled bars, riding the El train out to the beach, moving in search of breezes and air. Reg had one of the new Polaroid cameras, and he'd aim it and shoot, just like the ads said. So it was often that the two men walked through the hot city, wordless as Reg held the camera up to his eye. Since he'd come home, there was a restless, waiting quiet about Reg that was new to Len, as though he hovered in the night hour just before daybreak, just before birdsong broke it and the sound of the first car's engine moved away down a street. Sometimes Len saw what Reg saw, the woman on the stoop, her child sitting between her legs, the two of them exhausted, watching the street, the man standing very straight in line for the bus. But often, it seemed to Len that Reg was shooting pictures of nothing, a child turning to see him on the street, a man staring.

They would return at the end of a night and Reg would tack up the pictures neatly, continuing the line across the living room wall.

"They don't like you," Len said, pointing to one Reg had taken of three teenage boys after baseball practice, their mitts hanging off their bats like hunter's trophies, the look in their eyes unmistakable.

"No," Reg agreed, his hands on his hips, "they don't like what they're looking at."

"You're going to get hurt," Len warned.

Reg didn't answer.

"What are you going to do with these, anyway?" Len asked.

"Use them."

"For?"

Reg looked at him and shook his head. "Don't know yet. Just collecting."

"Then what?"

Reg grinned. "Showtime."

"Be careful, Reg." Len grew quiet beside him. "These guys don't matter." He waved his hand at the wall of Polaroids. "None of them matter."

"They do, though." Reg pushed a corner straight. "That's the point."

One Friday night toward the end of June, the heat in their apartment drove them downstairs in search of a beer and some air, and into Washington Square Park, where the smart fish who swam within the netting of streets and open doorways and hot cafés and crowded jazz bars and the six-storied, slope-shouldered brick buildings that hunched

279

above Bleecker and Macdougal, Hudson, Greene, and Gansevoort streets and made up the Village gathered. And on warm nights like this one, the silent stone fountain that rarely played in the middle of the square bloomed with men and girls in clumps and stems, talking, smoking, and arguing, endlessly arguing. You could feel it, Reg thought, as they walked, feel the push, the drive on those to say it — to find the words that got what was happening. What *was* happening? A new world was coming into view. Now was the time to say it. Here we are. While the rest of the country was crowding into phone booths or jalopies in the summer days, stretching upon white beaches, sipping cream sodas on chrome stools, here on the streets of the Village and in smoky New York rooms they danced and they talked, and the talk was of sex, or the Russians, Miles Davis, or Freud, Cassius Clay's fights, *Peyton Place,* and the cheapest joint to find cold beer and hot clams.

The two walked across Broadway, then Houston, in a stream of other people out in the airless night, light and music spilling onto the sidewalks from the cafés and bars into the thick heat that slid itself over and around any moving body, through the string lights of Little Italy, then Chinatown, and the Bowery, where a trumpet was playing fast and loud above the traffic on the corner in front of the Five Spot, and Reg pulled open the door.

Inside it was hot and crowded and the smell of whiskey and sweat reached them through the haze of smoke drifting listless overhead. They stood a minute on the threshold in the darkened room where there weren't any tables, and it was too hot down there, so they turned around and kept walking.

It was then that Len remembered Moss Milton's invitation.

By the time they got there, the party had pushed out onto the stoop of 29 West Twelfth. Ornette Coleman's horn snaked plaintive and insistent in the air around them as Reg and Len picked their way up the steps and through the open front door. A throng of people stood in the hallway outside the first-floor apartment. Just to their right, a blonde with sharp-cut bangs leaned her head against a tall black man while his hands stroked her bare arms, whispering. Her eyes closed and she smiled; the two were utterly alone in the crowd.

The big front room was filled and hot with bodies, though the door to the garden was flung wide open.

There were girls from the Lower East Side and from Park Avenue, men who'd come straight from the office, a drummer Reg recognized from the Blue Note, and several uptown gesticulating wildcats mixed with the still, serious, bespectacled radicals that peppered every downtown room. There was booze and smoke, bare skin and flushed faces, and Coleman's horn sliding round and through.

Reg caught sight of a man he remembered from college, though he didn't know his name. The man had been in a singing group, Reg remembered, those men who'd stop and form a semicircle just to hear the sound of their own voices after dinner on a rainy night in October, or May, who'd look at one another and then burst into song in the middle of one of the cavernous halls of Harvard, the stone ceiling overarching as they traded notes around the air, just singing to sing. Reg would cross the marble hall, not stopping, irritated by their taking over, pushed by the voices out of the room.

Though one night they'd occupied the end of a narrow corridor outside the main reading room in the library and were blocking the passage. There were twelve of them, and in a circle, like a huddle, their backs to Reg. And this man here stood at the center, giving notes and waiting for a singer's reply. He'd shake his head and give the note again, and again the singer would try. *There,* his body seemed to nod when the singer got the note right. *There it is.*

And then he stepped back, and they fanned around him, watching. He gave another nod, and "Ol' Man River" spun up on the staff of the men's voices into the dome above. Reg stopped in the shadow of the portico, listening to eleven white men singing, their voices taking on the South, the imagined South, full of its darkies and its cotton, and they sang the sorrow, but without the terror. The past, a tragedy upon a stage, distant as an idea of terror, one thing they could imagine, but did not hold inside. And this man, the leader, was building the harmony like a mason — note by note, until they reached the final note, single and pure, all the parts of the song come together at last, in that single word, *along.*

Reg had turned and walked back through the library, past the men at the long tables in the reading room, past the librarians, out the back doors. He hated them in that moment, hated them all, these men who thought they understood, because they sang it, because they knew the notes.

Though the note, the last note, with all twelve voices holding it, had been beautiful.

Here was that man, that leader, Reg realized, as he and Len pushed forward into the sweating men and flushed girls, now roaming around the smoky room with a bottle and plastic cups, who turned and caught sight of both of them.

"Good god," Moss said, his eyes widening, "the photographer."

Reg started.

"And Levy?" Moss looked up at Len. "Len Levy?"

He deposited the bottle on a table and shook Len's hand. "How marvelous," he exclaimed, and turned back to Reg, curious, his hand outstretched.

"Moss Milton," he introduced himself. "You look familiar."

"Reg Pauling." Reg shook his hand.

"Weren't you at Harvard?"

"I was," said Reg.

"Class of 'fifty-three?" Moss grinned.

Reg nodded, smiling back.

"Me too," said Moss. "I'll be goddamned." The three stood a minute.

"Well, well, what'll you have to drink?"

"I need a beer," Len said.

"Two," agreed Reg. "At least. Each."

"Easy to fix," said Moss, and headed for the kitchen.

I'll be goddamned, he thought again as he pulled the lever on the icebox. That was why he thought he'd known him that day at the White Horse. Reg Pauling was one of the lone black men in the class at Harvard and famous for his quiet. Liked to keep to himself, everyone said. Though now, Moss saw that it must have been that no one spoke to him, that Reg had been kept to himself, because the hand that had shaken his just now and the eyes that turned on him were strong and interested and open. In the mirror over the sink, he saw that Len was shaking his head at something Reg had said, and the easy silence between the two of them was clear. Moss dropped his eyes.

When he turned around with the beers in his hand, Pres Bancroft was talking to them, his jacket sliding open on the beginnings of a paunch. He was a banker at Milton Higginson who fancied himself a writer because he'd published a novel right out of Yale. His second novel was in copy-edits at Houghton Mifflin, where apparently Reg Pauling also worked. Moss never invited him to his parties, but he always seemed to appear.

"You look like hell, Levy," Bancroft was saying. "Getting too much hump?"

"Sure I am," Len said evenly, taking the beer Moss offered him.

"Lucky dog." Bancroft drank.

"I'd have sworn you weren't raised in a barn, Bancroft," Len remarked.

"I was raised right." Bancroft smiled. "Right here."

"According to whom?"

"Whom?" Pres turned his attention to Reg. "Very nice, Pauling. You're good at that."

"I'm good at a lot of things," Reg answered smoothly, drinking.

"Get a load of this guy," Pres said to Len familiarly. Len stared back at him, wordless.

Bancroft raised his eyebrows affably, as if to say *All right, no harm done,* and ambled away.

The three of them watched as he made his way through the crowd.

"That guy," Len pronounced, "is a phony."

"He *plays* the phony," Reg said.

"Does that make him more or less of one?" Len retorted. "Cheers."

"That makes him dangerous," Reg said.

"He's not dangerous." Moss shook his head. "He's a jackass."

"No?" Reg tapped the side of his bottle. "What do you make of the fact that he introduced me the other day as a 'damn good copy editor who just happens to be a Negro'?"

What was dangerous about that? Moss eyed Reg. Wasn't that the truth?

"You can't peg him," Reg went on.

"To hell with him," said Len, turning away from them, his eyes roving the crowd. "Who else is here?"

"Can you peg anyone?" Moss asked Reg.

"I have to." Reg gave Moss a watery smile that seemed to spill over even as Reg tried to hold it back. It drew Moss to him at once.

"A black man has to know *to whom* he is speaking," Reg continued.

The word flicked again like a serpent's tongue across Moss's attention. He couldn't deny that in the beginning he had had the same response as Pres Bancroft to Reg's perfect grammar.

"More than anyone else has to know?" he

asked roughly.

Reg considered him. "Yes."

Moss looked back, folding his arms to his chest. "Why?"

Len pulled on his cigarette, looking at Reg. Something indefinable crossed between them.

Reg leaned forward and tapped Moss on the arm. "Now I know."

Moss went still. "Know what?"

"You ask the questions that get the talk on the table."

"I'm interested," Moss shot back, relieved. "I have an interest. That's all."

"Not a lot of men in your shoes ask the questions."

"Which shoes are those?" Moss frowned.

"The shoes of Ogden Moss Milton Junior," Len pronounced.

"That's only a name," Moss protested.

"Yes, it is." Len finished dryly. "And so is *Len Levy.*"

"Okay." Moss nodded, reaching for his cigarettes. "Fair enough."

"The only way for a Negro to survive this country is to flush as much toxin up onto the surface as he can," said Reg. "All the time."

"*That* sounds dangerous." Moss offered his cigarettes.

Reg shook his head. "Mistaking a white man for his manners is deadly."

"I'd guess that that would be true in the

South," Moss allowed.

The expression on Reg's face didn't change, but he went still, and Moss felt he had stumbled into the crowded room in Reg's head, into a debate going on at full tilt, and whatever Moss had said made all conversation stop, and all eyes turn on him, considering.

"Everywhere is the South, and the dream of the North, a dream."

Moss looked at him thoughtfully. "You really believe that?"

Reg considered him and took a long swallow of beer.

"It's the truth," he answered.

With a grunt, Len crossed his arms and toed an empty bottle a few inches down the wood floor. "But do you think the truth has set him free?"

Moss raised his eyes.

"Of course not," Len answered himself, "because it's a load of crap. Truth doesn't set anything free. Money sets you free in this country. And the law."

"By all accounts, then, I should feel freest of all —" Moss said.

Len looked at him. "And you don't."

Moss shook his head.

"You're a misguided soul, Moss Milton," Len teased. "But we'll drink with you anyway."

A quick shadow crossed Moss's face and

disappeared.

"To me, then," he said, and raised his glass and drank the whole thing down.

"Listen," Len said, "I'm trying to get your father on board with that idea of mine you heard the other day in his office."

"And what's stopping him? He clearly likes you."

"How do you know?"

"He asked you if you sailed."

Len nodded.

Moss folded his arms. "Do you want to sail?"

Len looked at him. "If it's the thing to do to —"

Reg snorted.

"Don't be a son of a bitch, Reg," Len tossed at him. "I'm good on the water. And I hate golf."

"It's a good sign if Dad asked you," Moss admitted.

"How's that?"

"He thinks in terms of boats. Of men and boats," Moss corrected. "And those are the principles he goes by — set sights on your goal, chart your course, and stick to it. There are lines laid out. There are oughts. I, for one, ought never to have wasted these last six years scratching musical notes onto a page."

"Why's that?"

"Nothing's come of it. I've had three or four of my pieces taken up and played down here in the Village, and there's a guy out in Chicago who wants a song of mine, but —"

"What about the music?" Reg asked.

"Yes." Moss looked at him and smiled. "Music has come of it. And the beginning of a name for myself. But none of that looks like anything to my father. And I'm running out of time."

"So, no 'to thine own self be true'?"

"Polonius," Moss observed dryly, "was a Dane."

Reg chuckled.

"Where I'm from, thine own self be damned," Moss went on. "It's family first, then country, and then, at the very last, thine own self. I was raised to do *something,* be *someone.* Not for me, you understand, for the good of the world. Any less, and I'm a failure, a grape shriveled on the vine, a white-shoe screwball." He paused, relishing the list.

"Your father's given me a fair shake," said Len.

Moss nodded. "He is a fair man. He believes in the best man winning. Believes it to the core."

"What's the catch?" Reg asked.

"To my father? No catch." Moss looked at Reg, bemused. "It's how he was raised — it's what he believes. Honor. Valor. Dignity. Truth."

"Sounds like bells," Reg reflected.

Moss looked at him, startled. Bells. Yes.

Bells.

That's it, he thought just as two hands covered his eyes from behind and someone poked him. He pulled the hands off and turned around.

"Why, hello, Jean." He grinned at a slight, crop-haired girl and her silent companion, who had just appeared at his side.

"I brought gin," said Jean, holding a bottle. "Have you got tonic?"

"That I do," he cried. "Reg, Len, meet Jean. I'll be back in a jiff." And he was immediately swallowed by the crowd.

"He'll never make it," mused Jean.

He didn't. But the silent companion, who, it turned out, was Bulgarian, went back down the stairs to get some, and then a couple of men Len hadn't seen in a while pulled him off, and Reg found himself in the middle of a conversation with Jean about Ginsberg and the Beats and all that wailing — Jean rolled her eyes — and beating their big-man chests, their poetry going right off the rails.

"You like the rails," Reg observed.

"You've got to have rails," she admonished him archly, "or you can't get anywhere."

He raised his brow. "Whatever that means."

"You've got to use the rails to ride your own trip. You can't just blow up a building, for instance," she said, growing serious. "You've got to show the building — its walls, the ceilings, the floors — and then show how you are walking straight out of it, how you're —"

"What is it you do?" he broke in, a slight smile playing over his lips.

"I'm a secretary," she answered. "By day."

"And by night?"

"By night I fuck a Bulgarian and write poems."

"About buildings?"

"About the view," she replied, and moved away.

The party opened and closed, a great mouth exclaiming into the heat of the night. The two friends were separated, drawn into conversations, drinks, different rooms. And toward the end of the night, Reg wandered out into the garden in search of Len, whom he saw standing at the very end surrounded by men he didn't recognize, and turned back around into the party. He leaned against the wall and lit a cigarette, watching Moss Milton put a record on the phonograph, turn it up, and then move around the room again with the bottle, as the Memphis Jug Band bolted into the room, the banjo and the plucked jugs and the slapping hands, singing, *Tear it down, slats and all, tear it down, hear the baby squall.* There had been countless like him at Harvard, well-born, easy, imagining they could stare down the world with a smile. Yet despite the crooked, ingratiating smile, the frank blue eyes set in a long, angular face that could shift and dance quick and easy, Reg could see that Moss was not fooling. He was all lightness in person, all play. But he wasn't playing at all. Everyone in that room belonged in the room. He was one of the few men Reg had ever met whose face did not alter or shift even slightly when he turned it toward a black man, as he was now, turned to him, a bottle raised.

Drink? He raised the bottle.

Reg shook his head.

Tear it down, the song belled high, *ow ow ow.*

"Hear that?" Moss called to him across the room.

Come on out of my folding bed, 'cause the devil want to tear it down.

Reg nodded. "Yeah."

Moss nodded back at him through the party and made his way over. "Tear it all down," he said, exhilarated. "All of it. The whole thing."

"What whole thing?" Reg glanced up at him, smiling but skeptical. "The bed, the house?"

Moss tipped his head toward the music. "That's a man ready to tear down and start again."

Reg looked at him and shook his head. "You hear the rest of that song? 'Big black nigger lying in my bed.' It's about a white man coming home and finding his wife in bed with a black man."

"It's bigger than that," said Moss. "It's

more than that."

There is no bigger than that, thought Reg, and didn't answer.

But later, after most of the partygoers had already slid out and back onto the street, when Reg and Len turned at the bottom of the stairs and waved goodbye to Moss, sitting in the window, his knees up, his back against the frame, Reg raised his hand.

"See you again," he said.

"Tear it all down." Moss smiled back at him and waved.

"What the hell does he have to tear down?" Len asked as the two of them walked away.

The hot whine of an ambulance raced up the night street. The two men kept walking through the sound into the following quiet.

Two girls passed them, their sharp heels clicking on the pavement, paying no attention to the men. The streetlight up above caught the sheen of the blond one's hair and the white of her skirt. When Reg didn't answer, Len glanced over, but he couldn't read his friend's face in the dark.

"I'd guess he doesn't want what he has," Reg answered finally.

Len nodded and flicked away his cigarette.

"These people, Reg."

"What people?"

"They have everything they need. They should be raking it in."

Reg raised his eyebrow.

"But they hang back. I've seen it again and again over there."

Reg patted his shirt pocket and brought out a pack of Kents, shaking one to Len and one for himself. "They could make a killing."

Reg lit his cigarette and held the lighter up to Len's. "Why don't they?"

"I don't know." Len exhaled with a kind of amazed laugh. "Because they won't. *One doesn't.*"

"Why not?" Reg asked again.

"It's as though they are all waiting to go through a door — there's the door, they seem to say — *You first. No you.* This decorum." Len shook his head. "It just slows them down."

"Maybe they like it slowed —"

"They don't. I don't believe it. I don't believe they even realize just how slow they are." He went on, bemused. "*Only buy from certain people. Only lunch with him. Not with him. Never with her. May I make some money? Please do.* And there's a drunk or two on every board."

"Sounds gracious as hell."

"Gracious, my ass. They are going to grace themselves right out of the race."

Reg chuckled.

But the thing niggling at Len since that day in Mr. Milton's office, the thing that had burrowed in and lodged ever since Mr. Higginson's barely veiled condescension, now pushed itself harder through his gut.

"Not me," Len vowed.

"No." Reg's smile was in his voice. "I know that."

"And to be fair, not the old man either. Ogden Milton is one in a million." He exhaled. "I'd like to show him."

"Show him what?"

"How to take the whole damn train and yank it off its tracks," Len vowed.

Reg glanced over. "Listen to the boy from Chicago."

"That's me."

They stopped on the corner of Bleecker and Seventh Avenue, waiting for the light.

"Still, I wouldn't underestimate Moss Milton," Reg said. "He is dead serious."

And that was his draw. Moss Milton clearly believed it was possible for every man to walk through any door; he believed it, and back there with him, Reg wanted to believe it as well. As if the door he held open were a real door, and he a real gatekeeper. The thought of walking through it, arm and arm with a man like Moss, was seductive.

Though it would be walking into a dream, Reg thought, stepping off the curb.

Seventeen

When Evie woke the following morning, Paul was standing in front of the open closet, his back to her. She watched as he chose a shirt. Once, she would have pushed the sheets aside, crossed the floor, and pressed her body up against the long familiar line of his. He pulled on boxers. She lay there trying to decide if she was going to pick the fight.

"Hey," she said quietly.

"Hey," he answered.

There was a plate of glass as thin as a breath between them, risen up from last night's dinner.

"Ready for coffee?" he said into the mirror.

"Yeah," she answered. "Thanks."

He closed the closet door and stood there.

"I'm sorry," he said.

She looked at him. "I hadn't seen you in a month, and that's what you did?"

"I got ahead of myself. I didn't mean to show you that last night."

He came and sat beside her on the bed and

took her hand.

"I'm sorry." He was softer than he had been before.

My life doesn't seem mine anymore, she wanted to say, her eyes on him. *My life has slipped its sprockets.*

"You remember that feeling — that feeling when we were teenagers and a song would come on in the car and you'd be driving and the song would blast and the wind blew and you could have gone anywhere, couldn't you — anywhere."

"Yeah." He smiled.

"*That* was happiness," she said. "*Open* windows, Paul."

He was quiet.

"Where is that feeling? That's what I'm missing."

"That was childhood," he said softly.

She nodded, rueful. "The phrase that keeps running through my head is from the anchoress's rule book — 'My dear sisters, love your windows as little as you can.' "

He waited.

And so she just started in. She told him about the pink room and the dark and her mother standing there, in her Keds. She told him about the sleeping house, and the door at the bottom of the stairs — and her mother, Joan, insisting and leading her out of the house and to the graveyard. She told him about the old woman crossing the street and about Seth turning on the library steps and watching her go. She told him about life in all its pieces. Going on while he'd been gone. Paul listened, his eyes on hers, and it was this quiet she'd waited for, this that she had missed.

She took his hand and put it on her cheek. After a while she made to get up.

"Stay." His arms tightened around her, gathering her in.

When she woke again, the bed was empty and she could hear him in the kitchen down the hall.

"Did you hear Seth getting up?" he said as she came down the hall.

"It's Saturday."

"Oh, right."

She leaned against the doorway, watching him moving around the kitchen with quick, efficient hands. He had pulled out peppers, onions, and eggs and was reaching for the knife.

"So," she said carefully, "when *did* you mean to show me?"

He turned. "The photograph? I don't know. Today."

She shook her head. "There's got to be an explanation for it. A reason."

"Your grandfather stood with Hiss, remember."

"And his best friend liberated the camps,

came home, and drank himself to death."

"Guilty."

"Or heartbroken."

Paul took the onion and started to peel it. "What's he doing there at that picnic with the head of German Steel, the head of Deutsche Bank, and one of the Luftwaffe heroes of the First World War, in 1935?"

"I don't know."

"How did he make his money?"

"Investments." She took a mug from the shelf and poured a cup of coffee. "You know that."

He slid the onion skins aside and looked at her. "Don't you want to know?"

No, she thought, *I don't.*

"Yes, of course," she said.

He turned back to the cutting board. "When did they buy the Island?"

"What?"

"Nineteen thirty-six, right?"

"So?"

"They bought an island in the middle of the Depression," he said. "Think about it, Evie."

He was being careful. Handling her.

"You are the second person in as many days to point this out to me."

He looked at her. "Who else?"

"Hazel," she said. "Both of you are pushing me to see something *bad.* And I just don't think it's so simple, Paul."

"Why not?" He turned back and started chopping again. "Why isn't it?"

Please let's stop, she thought. *Let's not start.*

"Paul," she said softly. "What happened over there?"

He didn't answer right away. The steady beat of the knife on the wood drummed between them.

He let out a slow breath. "I understood it all, Evie. Finally."

"Understood what?"

"There is the crime and there is the silence."

Standing at the other end of the kitchen, he seemed impossibly far away. And she saw he wasn't joking.

"And what is the crime here?"

"Deals. Handshakes. Nods. An island bought with Nazi gold."

"You don't know that."

He turned the knob of the burner, holding the *tick tick tick* of the pilot until it caught. "No. I don't."

"And that's not me. This isn't me," she said.

He reached for the olive oil. "What did you say last night? 'Beggar our children'?"

"You know what I meant."

He turned around. "Let it go, then," he said.

She went still. "No one would tell anyone in your family to *let it go.*"

"I'm not talking about your past," he returned evenly. "Or your history. I'm talking about a summer house."

"But I am," Evie said. "I *am* talking about history. Our history. Mine. It's in that place."

"It's not your history," he retorted, "it's a myth. And the danger of a family myth is that you are raised to believe it."

"And not history?"

"History can be validated. What happened when, to whom. The hero was a bastard. The mother had consumption. There are records."

"Please," she snorted. "History is a story we tell ourselves to explain how we got *here.*"

"Come on, Evie, the idea you have about that place — that there's nothing without it, that *you* might be nothing without it — it's dangerous. Worse." He paused. "It's wrong."

"But I don't believe that," Evie protested uneasily. "I don't at all."

He raised his eyebrows. "We talked about this, Evie. We can't afford it."

"But maybe we could," she said. "I don't know, maybe —"

"Evie, stop," he pleaded. "*Stop* it."

She looked down.

"Okay." She nodded. "Okay then, but I can't give it up because of some theory you have —"

He didn't answer.

"I know," she erupted. "I *know,* all right? I know how much you hate it up there — all of us wafting around being Miltons. As if that were such an awful thing."

"Evie," he said very quietly. "Wake up."

"Don't be condescending. I'm wide awake." She turned from him. "And I'm not protecting them. I'm *not.*"

Her study was flooded with the morning sun, the green windowsill bright behind the red geranium. She reached and deadheaded the crimson flower, sinking down into her desk chair and closing her eyes.

Evie, her mother's voice rose in her head. *We must go.*

EIGHTEEN

As the month went on, Len found himself
wandering through Pennsylvania Station in
search of the girl, pulling open the heavy
brass-inlaid doors with an impatience shot
through with a kind of glee. He was absurd,
and he knew it. But even as he crossed the
great vault of travelers day after day, telling
himself what a fool he was, at the same time
he checked his watch, remarking the exact
times of his crossing, as though he could
make a science of foolishness.

And then, one evening toward the beginning of July, as Len passed through Pennsylvania Station, there she was. Standing right
where she had been the last time. He stopped.
Was it her? He walked forward. Then turned
around. It wasn't, was it? But it was, he knew.
It was her. He stopped behind the information booth at the center of the floor so that
she wouldn't see him. And stared at her, leaning again into the balcony, her bare arms
crossed as she waited. Not for anyone impor-

tant, he judged, as she stared out at the crowd with a languor that suggested she was only waiting, not hoping for something to happen. He wanted to watch her, even more than he wanted to speak. He felt sure that he might never understand her, and that alone was a reason to keep watching. He had not known until this moment that what he wanted was this — mystery.

She wore a navy blue linen dress whose slim lines covered her completely and yet directed attention to her shoulders and to those long, lean arms, which uncrossed now as she reached, snapped open her purse, pulled out a handkerchief, and sneezed in one fluid, unembarrassed motion.

He stepped out from the protection of the booth and started for the stairs, looking straight ahead as if he were in a hurry and his mind were elsewhere, concentrating only on gaining the stairs, and climbing them two at a time. She stood off to his left, and as he climbed he willed himself not to turn toward her, to simply keep going up and up. If she called him, if she called out, he'd pause. He was nearly at the top of the stairs, and his heart was catapulting out of his chest. The bank of doors at the top of the stairs that gave out of the station stretched ahead of him.

"Levy!"

And even as he turned in the direction of that delighted voice, to the spot where she stood, where the voice came from, though it couldn't be her voice, he hoped.

Moss Milton stepped forward and held out his hand, pulling Len up the last two stairs, a great grin on his face. "Len Levy," he said again. "Good to see you!"

Over his shoulder, Len saw the girl see him and caught the flare of recognition on her face.

Moss turned to her. "Joanie," he said, "meet Len Levy. Levy" — he still had his hand on Len's arm — "my sister Joan."

"Hello." She smiled.

Jesus, Len thought.

"We've met." He allowed himself to look at her, and shook her hand again, standing nearly on the same spot as the first time. "In fact, we met right here."

"Did you? How incredible." Moss's smile didn't change.

"It was hardly a meeting," Joan told Moss, slipping her hand away. "I was flat out on the floor. Mr. Levy helped me up."

She shook her head quickly, a little smile caught on her teeth. "Though it's a bit of a tumble in my head."

Her lipstick was precise. Her dark hair was parted down the middle and clamped to the side, drawing attention to her neck, rising out of the soft collar of her dress. He stared at that spot with a mix of apprehension and desire.

"I see," said Moss, hesitating.

"Evelyn was with me," she explained to Moss.

"Oh." Moss looked back to Len, shaking his head helplessly. "That clears it right up."

"Are you catching a train?" she asked.

"No." He swallowed.

"Come on." Moss took his sister's arm and turned her toward the doors. "Let's go up to the Algonquin, find a cold drink and some soft chairs."

Len couldn't move. The girl in the station, the girl he'd dared to imagine his, was Moss Milton's sister. She was Ogden Milton's daughter. Joan and Moss turned around.

"Maybe another time." Len nodded at the two Miltons.

"But," she asked, "where are you going?"

"Home."

"Isn't a drink on your way?" Moss asked.

Len couldn't think of an answer. He followed the brother and sister out the heavy doors. But outside, in the bright heat, he raised his hand in a wave, picked a direction, and started walking away fast.

Joan watched him disappear into the afternoon crowd heading east on Thirty-third Street. She had forgotten his voice. How it made her want to listen. And his broad, strong hands.

"*Who* is that?"

"*That,*" Moss said, "according to Dad, is the

hope of the firm."

"What do you mean?"

"Milton. Higginson." Moss hit each name like a note on the scale.

She squeezed his arm. "He works for Dad?"

"He works for Dad." Moss nodded. "And you" — he grabbed her by the waist, steering her in the direction of the Algonquin, toward the cool clutch of good gin on the rocks — "are the boss's daughter."

"Well, that puts me in my place."

"It's the oldest song in the playbook."

"I thought he was your friend."

"Well, not exactly," Moss answered. "Though I like him. He is ambitious as all hell, I can tell you that."

"I see," she said stiffly. "So all this talk is just that."

"What?"

"Talk. Talk. Talk. You can look, but you can't touch. You can open the door, but god forbid the wrong ones go through."

"Joanie," he reproached her. "That's not fair. You're my sister."

"Never mind." She shook her head at her brother. "You needn't worry. I have a hunch he'd be the one in the story who's after the lion, and never mind the girl."

"I don't know." Moss was doubtful. "He looks the type who's got plenty of girls."

This made Joan pause.

"I kissed him, you know —"

Moss halted dead in his tracks. She nodded up at him, and then, at the sight of his astonishment, the deep chuckle that was all hers, a chortle, really, burst out. "Why not?"

"I wouldn't have thought he was your type."

"What's that supposed to mean? Because he's Jewish?"

"Yes," said Moss. "It's marvelous. You're both marvelous. Let's go drink."

Len walked several blocks without seeing where he went, his mind whirling and blank. The pavement beneath his feet shimmered with the day's heat. She was a Milton. He was a Jew from Chicago. His father was a grocer. Her father was his boss. Two men in Brooks Brothers suits veered off the sidewalk in front of him and up the stairs into the Harvard Club, its crimson flag hanging from the portico; a little farther along, there was the Yale Club. These buildings. There was no escaping. New York was full of them.

He turned around slowly and headed away from the flags, toward the Algonquin.

The Miltons were sitting in a booth in the back, and when she looked up and caught sight of him, his heart plunged.

"Oh." Joan drew in her breath. Moss followed her gaze.

"Uh-*huh*." He grinned, got to his feet, and waved Len over.

"I have some time to kill," Len explained as

309

he arrived at their table and unbuttoned his jacket. "Yes," he said, nodding at the waiter who appeared that instant. "I'll have what they're having."

"Gimlet," said Moss. "He'd like a gimlet."

Len slid into the booth next to Joan.

"Moss says you work for Dad," she said, leaning a little away from him.

"I do." Len nodded.

"What's he like?"

"Careful, Joanie." Moss looked at Len. "We don't want to break any —"

"One in a million," Len answered her simply. "He's one in a million. I'd follow him anywhere."

Joan turned to Moss. "See that?" she challenged.

"It won't matter." Moss shook his head.

There was a mole nestled in the hollow of her neck. Len forced his eyes to follow the conversation between the brother and sister, the cord between them light and strong. He didn't get it, but he did not want it to stop. He wanted to sit in this booth beside this girl for as long as it lasted. There were four inches of fabric between her skirt and his suit leg; her bare arm rested on the table.

The waiter set Len's drink on the table.

"Don't say that, Moss. It's not true."

"It is." Moss shrugged. "But Len doesn't need to hear my sob story. Let's toast." He raised his glass. "To the end of the beginning."

Len raised his eyebrows.

"It's Dad's favorite saying at the moment. Our sister is getting married in September," Joan explained.

"The girl I met?" Len asked.

Joan nodded.

"And you?" he pressed.

The face she turned toward him just then was soft and very clear. Serious.

"Joan," Moss said as he signaled the waiter and held up three fingers, "has *as-pir-a-tions.*" He hit each syllable like the chime of a bell.

"More than that." Joan shook her head. "And you know it, Moss."

It was important to her, Len saw, to be precise.

She glanced at Len. "I've got a job, right now. As a typist."

"Where?"

"With a madman," Moss teased. "And a genius."

She didn't take the bait. "I work for Mr. Rosset, at Grove Press."

Len shook his head. "Should I know him?"

Joan nodded, smiling. "Only if you believe in freedom of expression."

Moss snorted. "Or dirty books."

"Barney Rosset is suing the postmaster of the City of New York to release the books he seized and to allow the original version —

the *unexpurgated* version — of *Lady Chatter-ley's Lover* to be published. We're still waiting for a ruling from the Supreme Court."

"Get a load of *that* word," Moss tossed back dryly, swirling the ice in his glass.

"Everything should be unexpurgated," she said seriously to Len beside her. "Everything should be right up on the surface, don't you feel?"

There was that dare in her voice under the calm, and Len heard it.

"Each of us has a body, and each body is its own . . ." She searched for the word *expression.* She paused, keeping her eyes on Moss, across from her. "My brother sings, for instance. And he has that smile — that fuddled smile that looks like it hurts him." She pointed across the table at Moss, who smiled obligingly. "That's all his own."

"And I'll be damned if anyone's going to expurgate me." Moss grinned.

Joan didn't waver. Len could see she was intent on making her point. She was steady and sure, and he sure as hell didn't want her to stop.

"And your sister?"

"My sister, somehow, makes everyone want to stop and look at her. I never learned how to do that, but she can. She can walk into any room and carry it off. She and my mother, they know exactly how to hold someone's attention."

312

"And you?"

"Me?" She looked up at him beside her on the banquette. "My body has a crack running right down the middle. You've seen it. A fault line. I'm damaged goods," she said.

"Come on, Joanie," Moss protested.

"It's all right." She shrugged. "Evelyn can be in charge of all that. Something's not right about me. Never will be."

"I'd say everything's right about you," Len said quietly.

She didn't look at him. The hand nearest his reached for one of the peanuts in the bowl and then played with it, flipping it loosely through her long fingers.

"But eventually," she said, "I want to teach."

"Teach what?" He found his voice.

"Children," she answered. "How to read."

"What should they read?"

"Well, everything, ultimately," she said firmly. "Dickens. Even Lawrence. Austen. I love Jane Austen," she confided. "You think it won't work out, and then it all does. But in the beginning" — she risked looking directly at Len — "just books, lots and lots of books."

Len nodded at her, the gin and the air-conditioned cool working on him like a benediction, a space to fall into, grateful to listen as she went on. This was the difference for the girls like her, he thought. Life unfolding like a book — first chapter, second, third.

A man could be sped up or slowed down, things could be brought to bear, and a life could be plotted. He wondered what she'd make of his father's life if she were to read it — day after day in a grocery store, every single day — bread, pickles, salami, ham, bread. Rigorous in its unchanging plod. A life that went round and round in the same place, wearing down the same groove.

"I'd want them to read about other people," she was saying. "I'd want them to understand, to imagine something else."

"Other people?" Len finished his drink.

"Yes." She nodded. "Ralph Ellison, and Saul Bellow —"

"Len is from Chicago," Moss told her.

"Oh," she exclaimed. "What do you think of *The Adventures of Augie March*?"

"Don't know it." He shook his head and, seeing her disappointment, said, "I haven't had time to read much at all."

"But you must have read this, it came out years ago — it's about growing up in Chicago."

"Still," he said. "I haven't read it."

She looked down at the table in front of them, halted.

"Should I?" he asked gently.

"Yes." She turned in the booth to look at him. "I've learned something from it, about being Jewish. What it's like."

Her eyes were a deep brown. They held his

firmly in hers. And perhaps because of the feeling that the three of them were on a boat, eddied out of the heat and tides that surged outside the bar, Len pressed her.

"Oh? What *is* it like?"

She flushed, and he saw she'd heard his question as a challenge, and hesitated, not sure whether he was making fun of her. The brother and sister shared this, as though each halted an instant on an unseen threshold, waiting to be invited forward. In Moss, it was damning; he would never prevail, Len thought; in her it was — riveting.

"It seems" — she searched — "talkative."

"*Talkative?*" He couldn't help the edge that crept in.

"There's nowhere to hide, everyone's saying everything, right in front of each other. It's so — exciting. Everything's on the surface. It's honest, somehow."

"Honest?"

She looked down at the table.

"All the honesty in the world doesn't change the facts." He shook his head.

"What facts?"

"My father is a Jew who came from Germany and runs a grocery store," he said, his eyes on Moss. "We live in the Jewish section of town, because, well, the other streets just wouldn't do, the Realtor told my father. If I had enrolled in the University of Illinois, I'd have joined the Jewish fraternity, because that's what the Jews can join. There are two Jewish law firms in town, and a Jewish bank. That was growing up in Chicago. So when it was my turn, when I graduated from high school, I got the hell out of there, and came here."

He had, without meaning to, changed the mood. He felt her beside him, sitting very still, listening, looking into her drink. Moss kept his eyes on him, and Len had the sensation of having stepped off the board into the pool.

"And nothing taught me more than this: when I was ten years old, I knew there were boys my age being killed like cats. And it could have been me. Or my uncle, or my aunt, my father. You grow up knowing that, and you see it's always a struggle between who you are and what you *do.* And what I do, what I did, was move. I moved here, where I am not Levy from Skokie. I am only Levy. One man."

He had said too much. He'd said far more than he'd meant to, far more even than he'd known he thought. And for what? Why say all that to these two, whom he liked more than he could say? Why rub their noses in it, when he had wanted only to hold her hand back there?

He reached in his pocket for his billfold, not daring to look at the girl beside him. Moss stretched across the table and put his hand on Len's arm.

"On me," said Moss lightly, though his eyes held Len's. "My sister drinks like a fish."

"And this fish needs to swim off," she said, and pulled her pocketbook toward her. Len slid out of the booth without a word as she slid out beside him. She stood as tall as his collarbone, he realized. In flats. He could reach his arm around her shoulders and draw her into his chest easily if she were any other girl. Instead he stood helplessly as she leaned over and kissed Moss goodbye.

"Would you mind putting me in a cab?" She turned from her brother and looked at him. Her eyes went from dark to darker brown, and he realized in that instant that he'd underestimated her. She'd not been totting him up and tossing him off, as he had thought.

"Sure," he said, his heart in his throat.

"So long, Levy." Moss put out his hand and shook Len's.

Joan was walking away through the bar toward the door.

"So long." Len put on his hat and followed quickly, watching how the line of her body moved easily inside her linen shift. Her skin was a pale gold. And wishing he could see her face, wishing he could read the slender set of those shoulders and gauge somehow her reaction to what he had just blurted, he reached and pushed the hotel door open above her head. She turned and glanced at him quickly, then away. And they emerged back into the hot evening and stood on the curb, silent.

Len put his hand up, and a cab switched lanes, coming toward them. She would get away, he thought, she would get in the cab and he would never have touched her hand again. He would never slide his hand from the curve of that shoulder all the way down her arm as he wanted badly to do just then.

The cab came to a stop before them. Len bent and pulled the door open, and she got in, gathering her dress close around her legs, and looked up.

"Do you believe someone's life turns in a single moment?"

She was trying to tell him something, he realized. Trying to tell herself something.

"No," he said seriously. "I don't."

Joan flushed.

"Meet me tomorrow," she said swiftly. "At the Met."

"All right," Len managed to say.

She cocked her head. "All right? That's what you have to say in the face of the treasures of the ages?"

The look he gave made her catch her breath.

"All right," she said faintly. "Six o'clock."

Speechless, he shut the taxi door carefully.

The taxi pulled away from the curb. He

watched it. And it hit him then, with the force of revelation: She was his. She was his girl. She was the one in the world who'd been there, waiting. He knew it with a certainty that almost frightened him. A warm glow spread in his stomach. She would be his. There was no earthly reason for it, but he believed it with a certainty like faith.

Joan leaned her head against the leather seat and did not move for many blocks. His body standing behind her as they waited for the cab had made her feel confused and funny, and she had had to hold herself still so as not to turn around and make an idiot of herself. A little taller than her father, a head taller than she, he wore his height easily. And that marked him, this easiness, but it was mixed with a watchfulness, a waiting almost, that gave him an animal grace new to her. She had wanted him to put his hands on her shoulders and draw her to him. She wanted him with a fierce hunger she'd never felt before. Sitting beside him in that booth, she had fixed her eyes on Moss, hearing herself speak and marveling at her steadiness in the face of Len's arm on the table beside her. The drape of his sleeve. How his leg bobbed a little beside her under the table. How he did not look at her either. It didn't matter who he was; she knew him already. She had understood as she watched him flip a spoon over and over in his thumb and forefinger that the machinery up above was opening, she could imagine it slowly opening, and here for a moment without breath was the entrance, the gate, and all she needed to do was nod.

She rolled down the window and let the breeze run across her cheeks.

NINETEEN

Len went the following evening, though he half expected to be stood up. That the girl in his head was that girl, was this girl, not just any girl, she was a known girl, terrified him and called him forward as though he had been given the keys to the heavens. As though he was through some door into another world. And even as he framed that thought, he cast it off. He was an idiot. So he said nothing to Reg about meeting her, or about meeting her again.

But there she was, standing on the steps of the Met. And once she saw him at the bottom of the steps, she turned and started climbing. She could feel the warmth of his stare fastened to the spot between her shoulders, strong and sure as a hand there, guiding her up. She stepped through the enormous portals and gathered her pocketbook closer, relishing, as always, the first adjustment to the cool museum interior. When she turned, he was right there beside her.

She showed him every bit she loved — first the Italians, then the Dutch. He followed her up the vast marble staircase and into the shuttered rooms, where others stood and looked and whispered. He stood beside her and nodded when she pointed, and heard not a word. Soldiers and Madonnas stared down on him. He looked at them. He moved past them. She was the center of the earth, and if he left her side, he'd slip down into darkness. They walked backward in time, it seemed to him, until at last they arrived at the marble statues of the Greeks.

It was nearly unbearable. Their nakedness, their marble bodies, stood above the two of them. And the way she stared at their beautiful forms, at their sex hanging, small and relaxed, showed him how she wanted to hold a man, she wanted to touch a man. She didn't look at him, she'd hardly looked at him, but her hand, the one closest to his, had just grazed him as she pointed out with the other some small detail, explaining how the history of the boy was marked in stone.

"Stop talking," he said quietly.

They stood together in silence before the beautiful marble boy. The space between them, no more than a few inches, moved and coiled, drawing them together, close and closer. Her bare arms and the clean line of her dress, a deep rose, stirred him.

He took her wrist in his hand, and her

blood jumped. She followed him unseeing, back along the long hallway of the Greeks, back down the wide central stairs of the museum to the cool pavilion of the lobby, and out again, out into the waning heat of the evening, taxicabs blaring, the sky a golden eye above them. He turned and she stepped into his arms.

They stood there at the top of the steps, wordless, long enough for her to smell his skin, for him to feel for the first time how narrow she was, how small, and for the pulse between them to join and for their bodies to pull toward each other. His lips found hers and they kissed hungrily. The city vanished.

They pulled away at last and studied each other.

"Let's get on a boat." He smiled down at her.

They walked down the steps of the Met, hailed a cab, and rode the length of Manhattan. When the hot wind blew through the open windows, Len reached across her and rolled her window up halfway. It was as specific, as careful, as a declaration. He would cherish her. In quiet they got out at the Staten Island Ferry landing. He paid the taxi. Her skirt fluttered up around her knees. He took her hand and held it as though it were breakable.

A pigeon soared with a gull above the soot-black pilings by the landing. The commuters hurried to catch the boat before the iron gate clanged. Everyone around them was moving. There was a rest in time being with him, like a beat of music held. And she knew nothing about him. It didn't matter. For that moment, the hand that held hers was the only tether she wanted to this earth. She and he were joined as simply, as irrevocably, as if written in a folktale. The man and the woman walked hand in hand and lived happily ever after.

In the dark they boarded and sat on a bench toward the stern, and the island of Manhattan drew away as they rode. " 'We were very tired, we were very merry,' " she said to him, smiling. " 'We had gone back and forth all night on the ferry.' " Then she fell quiet and they rode like this, in silence together, the boat's engine thrumming beneath them, late commuters and couples just like them chattering and restless, the summer evening hanging above them in soft folds.

"Tomorrow night?" she asked him as they waited for the bus that would take her uptown.

He nodded, and as the bus shuddered to a stop and opened its door in front of them, she squeezed his hand and darted up the steps inside. After the bus pulled away, her head and shoulders pulling away up the avenue, he stood a long time, unmoving.

■ ■ ■ ■

The following day, Len got tickets to see *The Tenth Man* on Broadway and left the office at six o'clock, walking the whole way up Fifth Avenue to collect her.

She had chosen a light green silk that swirled as she moved, and she wore the pearls her father had given her on her twenty-first birthday, which always made her feel loved, and placed. And as she walked toward Len, waiting in the lobby of her building, he caught his breath at the sight of her. How badly he wanted to take off the row of pearls that ringed her soft neck like a collar.

It was a strange, talkative play with the characters speaking across and around one another, sometimes over one another as people do but actors generally don't. Len and Joan sat together quietly and did not hear a word. In the middle of the first act, he reached across and took her hand. The pulse between them beat through the cotton of her gloves. She sat very still, looking straight ahead, her lips parted. After a minute, she pulled at the fingers on her glove and slid her hand out, then gently picked his hand up and put it in hers. His thumb lay heavy in her lap, and a tremor went up from the place where his thumb rested, like a shaft of light through her body.

She turned her face toward his in the darkness and his eyes answered hers. They looked back again at the stage.

When it was over, they walked together hand and hand down into the subway, and she stood against him in the crowded car. The doors opened, and she remained in the curve of his arm and they climbed the stairs and emerged back out into the bright, hot night, the steps of the Metropolitan a white sandstone cliff, a lit dune. Her apartment was just around the corner. They hadn't spoken. He pulled the grate across on the tiny elevator, and she stepped in and he followed, pulling the grate shut again. The little chamber bounced and she fell against him.

The door unlocked easily, and she walked in ahead of him and reached for the light, but he put his hand out and stopped her. It was a studio apartment dominated by a single enormous window through which shone the great lights of the museum columns over the neighboring roof. She remained by the door, watching him as he stood at the window and looked out, and watched as he took careful account of the single room. Her bed was tucked in the corner. There was a lid on the bathtub she used as a shelf. There was a single overstuffed chair. He turned around and came toward her, and in one motion lifted her off her feet, grinning — a grin that turned into a great laugh that gathered her inside it, so she began laughing also. He was still laughing when he lifted Joan onto the board covering the bathtub, grabbing her legs and wrapping them around his waist as he stood between her and began kissing her, very slowly, his hands on either side of her chin, tipping her face to his lips. She closed her eyes and went with him, and kept her legs around him when he moved them both, at last, to the bed in the corner.

Sweetly, softly, he unbuttoned her dress, and when she lifted her arms so he could pull it over her head, he leaned in and kissed her breasts, and she shuddered. He unzipped himself and stepped out of his trousers and his boxer shorts and stood before her.

"Come here," she whispered, sitting on the side of the bed.

He reached and circled her nipple with his finger, and it rose under his touch. "Look at me," he said.

She bit her lip.

"Stay looking." He sank down beside her and pulled her onto him. She was light in his arms, and so soft.

She wrapped her arms around his neck and watched his eyes go darker. And she didn't move. They sat very still, looking at each other. Very still.

And then she moved.

Afterward, when she came back up into the city, back into the heat and the room and found him still there above her, looking down, for the first time in her life, she believed she would not die (as she had always thought) shaking, and forsaken, in a fit. He would be there, waiting, for her return. She smiled at him. He slid off and leaned on one elbow, turning her face toward him in the dark. The streetlamp reached the wall just above her face, lighting her hair and making her eyes shine.

"Hello," he said.

"Who the hell are you seeing, man?" Reg asked after a couple of weeks. Too hot to sleep, they lay sweating on their beds, the windows pushed up as high as they could go, the thick noise of the city winding up to them. It was the middle of July.

"A girl."

"Must be some girl."

Len's cigarette flared in the dark bedroom as he inhaled.

"She is."

The fan slid around slowly, hardly daring the air, and why Len didn't say who it was just then, and who he was protecting, he couldn't have answered.

They met as often as they could, evening after hot evening. They could not help it. At the end of an evening, he or she would ask about the next day, and then at the end of that one, the next. She liked the way he studied her just before he leaned to kiss her. She liked the particular shade of his dark glasses, the touch of his hand ushering her through a door. She knew nothing about him but what he had told her that first afternoon with Moss, and she didn't want to know any more. She only wanted his hands on her, roaming over her as if he knew how to find her in the dark. She only wanted him.

He'd come find her after work, always at the top of the steps of the Met, where she sat waiting. And he began to attach the picture of her outside — a pretty brunette in dark glasses sitting quietly — with the paintings she insisted on showing him inside. And forever afterward in the first few minutes of entering any museum, no matter where he was in the world, the hush and the cool and the dropping away of the noise of a city would combine with a tightening in his stomach, an urgency that brought her back to him, whole and beside him pointing out something she wanted him to see.

"Pay attention," she'd say, poking him. "You're missing it."

"I'm missing nothing." He'd pull her to him and be rewarded by the catch of her teeth on her lip as she tried not to smile.

"I don't care about this," he said one day, "about any of this."

"Well, you *ought* to care."

"Why?"

"Because," she fumbled, not wanting to say what was obvious. *So you'll fit in,* she thought.

Though he would never fit in. She smiled. Sitting waiting for him every evening, she'd catch sight of him at the end of the block, tall, dark haired, and rangy. As if at any moment he might simply start walking toward the mountains. Like Moss, he was full of motion and a restless, urgent energy which she was used to in her brother. But with Len, there was no modesty, no dimming of his light, there was just a large, healthy appetite, like a great cat, she thought, some animal stalking its prey. And she knew this was the very thing her mother would object to — no modesty, no ability to be quiet about who he was. When he turned his smile to her, his strong white teeth flashing in his wide mouth, when he smiled she saw he wanted her.

She would grab her pocketbook and run down the wide marble, nearly falling at his feet because her legs were moving faster than her feet could keep up. But his arms went around her before she reached the bottom stair and he pulled her off the stairs and into him. Cigarettes and aftershave and his freshly laundered collar surrounded her and she closed her eyes as he held her, already hard, his hands on her shoulders as he drew her to him, making her shaky, weak, making her want to sit down suddenly, lie down and take him in. With him, for the first time in her life, she was not cracked, not wrong. She was right. This life was right, and surged through her, a rich beating vein that thrummed and bloomed in his hands.

Sometimes in those first few days, Joan would stop where she was walking and hold her hand out, just to hold it, as though stopping in the middle of a stream so she could feel the current racing round her, and feel herself standing strong against it, *in it* — this hot, explosive summer that would detonate the golden, gentle gates of fall. She would stand in the heat and know that gentleness was gone for good.

TWENTY

Without Len, Reg found himself wandering more and more out into the city on his own. The summer had settled into its unremitting heat, and so even if he'd wanted to go farther afield, at the end of a day in his high, hot office, his mind had gone so slack, his head so thick and dull, that his wandering was contained to the small streets of the Village as he traveled from work to home, from home to dinner or a drink, and then again, back home.

Coming up Hudson Street on the fourth evening in a row that the city had baked in ninety-degree heat, Reg was passing the White Horse Tavern and caught sight of Moss Milton sitting by himself at a table inside.

"Hello, Milton." Reg set a pitcher and two glasses down on the table in front of Moss.

"Reg Pauling," Moss said, the smile already spreading across his face.

"What gives?"

"Not a good goddamn." Moss shook his head, rueful, pulling the pitcher toward him and pouring out the beer. "Cheers."

"Cheers." Reg touched his glass.

The night was drawing down on the bar. The secretaries and their bosses had given way to the deeper drinkers, the men and women who stopped in here for one, or two, and stayed for dinner, and for after. Over at the writers' table, there were a few men Reg recognized but didn't know by name.

"I met Jimmy Baldwin over there one night," Reg said after a while. "I was banging around down here looking for pieces to write, and he sat down at that table and asked my name and then he asked what I wanted to write about and I told him *America.*" Reg snorted. "And then he turned those big black eyes of his on me —" He exhaled, remembering. "You get caught in Jimmy's eyes, and you might as well just sink right on down."

"How's that?"

"He looks at you, and for those seconds it's as if no one had ever seen you before in your life," Reg said thoughtfully. "Not your mother, not your father, or a lover —"

Moss stared back at him.

" 'You want to write about America?' Jimmy asked. 'You've got to get out of here, then,' he said to me. *'Get out of the country.'* "

"What?"

Reg nodded.

"And?"

"I did." Reg looked up at Moss and

shrugged, smiling. "It seemed as good an idea as anything else, and I worked for the next six months or so until I had enough to buy a ticket to France."

"And?"

"I spent the next three years in cold-water flats and walk-ups, from Rome to Vienna to Berlin, sleeping on couches, and once in an apartment for a kept woman overlooking the Seine."

"Nice."

"For a time."

Moss considered him. "And did you find America?"

"I found myself homesick." Reg looked at him.

"For what?"

"Words, among other things." Reg pushed back in his chair. "English words — any words: *Cube steak. Morning glory. Five-and-dime. Heft.*"

"*Heft?*"

"*Heft,* man. *Heft.* I like that word." Reg lifted his beer. "*Kenning. Word hoard.* I would have made a good Saxon."

Moss choked on his beer. The image of an enormous blond warrior striding bare-knuckled through a bog set against the slight black man in front of him was too much for Moss. He clapped his hand to his chest, delighted.

"Glad you like it." Reg grinned, leaning his

elbows on the table. "Glad I could be of service."

"So then what?"

"Then I came back home."

"And now?"

"Now —" Reg shrugged. "I'm here."

"Here's to that," Moss said, and raised his glass. The two sat companionably.

Under the wide arch of the doorway, a few girls had kicked off their shoes and stood beside the men in blue shirts. One of them lifted and lowered on her toes as though practicing at the barre, and Moss again had the vision of a syncopated beat, but slow; a raptor's wings up and down. At the closer table here, just beyond Reg's head, a girl pulled her beret off a radiant mop of red hair. It was a bright spot in the dark tavern.

Moss's right hand rested on the rim of the table as on a piano and he tapped out the girl, the bright spot he had heard, shifting in his seat.

"What's that you're playing?"

Moss pulled his hand off the table. " 'On the Rocks.' "

"Tune you know?"

"Tune I'm writing." Moss leaned back and folded his arms across his chest. "Been trying to write all summer. Something that gets at a moment like this."

"What moment is that?" Reg sipped his beer.

Moss thought. "This time we're in, this time just before the key changes. I want to write that song." He shook his head, rueful. "*My* America."

Reg watched him.

Moss tried again. "Moments that hold inside the sense of what's coming."

"The future of the now?"

"That's good." Moss looked at him appreciatively. "Something like that."

Reg nodded. "What *is* coming?"

Moss grinned and shook his head. "New notes."

Reg raised his eyebrows.

"I can almost hear them," Moss sighed.

Reg followed Moss's gaze around the room.

"Like that." Moss pointed to a woman with the lamplight on her hair. "You see how sweet that glow is, how it warms her, makes you want to hold her, like she was a flame — a roar of D's."

The girl was talking seriously to a man at the end of the table against the wall. It wasn't flirtatious. She sank into the chair next to him, telling him something.

"And those dockworkers, sitting right beside her. They've been here drinking all afternoon," Moss went on. "They're a B, a dead B. And over there, the table of self-proclaimed cool cats, the writers, and right here, back again, us."

Reg nodded. "A white man and a black man."

Moss frowned. "Well, yes. But not only that."

Reg folded his arms.

"The *room,* man. Us *in* the room." Moss leaned toward him. "Here we are, talking. All of us in the same room, unimaginable to my parents, my grandparents. But we are here now. New notes."

Reg turned back to him, away from them.

Moss looked at him. "But where's the bass line? What holds it. I can't find the tone, the string that pulls it all together into a line. The inner logic. The notes don't add up."

"Maybe you're not seeing straight."

Moss frowned.

"It's still the country that elected Eisenhower," Reg observed. "Twice."

Moss was quiet.

"It's still the country that rebuilds Europe and lets the Negro nation —"

"The *Negro* nation?"

Reg nodded and stubbed out his cigarette. "I spent years over there seeing the fruits of American investment grow through the goddamn Marshall Plan. *Money, money, money* — and not a *dime* to sow the same seeds right here."

Moss considered him. "You should write about that."

Reg looked at Moss directly. "I should."

Moss sat back in his chair. "But what do you make of us sitting at a table, talking? We are sitting at a table *talking.*"

"So?"

"So, that's new, isn't it — that's news."

Reg shook his head. "That's Harvard, man. And random chance. Most people in the rest of the country would walk in here and see one black man sitting where he shouldn't."

Moss shook his head stubbornly. "We are sitting together, and that's the fact. Anything can happen from here on out. Anything is possible. Big ears, man. You gotta have big ears."

Reg looked at him. "You're an idealist."

"Guilty." Moss exhaled, smiling.

Reg nodded and stubbed out his cigarette. "Then *you're* the dangerous one."

His tone was unreadable. He pulled himself onto his feet and was reaching for his hat.

"But I like the sound of your new notes," he said. "I'd like to hear them, when you find them."

And the smile he turned on Moss was rich and warm and wide. "So long."

"So long," Moss answered. And as he watched Reg find his way through the clutch of people and out the door, he felt his chest catch and fill.

TWENTY-ONE

Paul had bought hamburger, three potatoes, and frozen peas — as though they still had a small child at home, Evie remarked.

"Or as if it's the seventies or something." Seth dropped his backpack in the hall.

But it was comfort food for all of them, the smell of potatoes in the oven, Paul at the dining room table reading, and the June twilight slipping through the window. In the week since he'd come home, they'd fallen into a kind of truce, picking up the regular threads between them and stepping around the tear in the surface.

She set the bottle of wine in front of Paul, who reached for it without lifting his eyes from the page. The dark mahogany table, once her grandmother's and once worth thousands but now scratched irredeemably, was set for the three of them. Around the table ranged four of the six Windsor chairs Evie's mother had shipped to California when Evie was in graduate school, a rampart against whatever wilderness Joan imagined Evie to be living in with Paul. On a strip of masking tape under the seat of each of them, Joan had written, *Aunt Minerva, 1893–1968.* Now they circled the table in varying degrees of disrepair.

"Hey, Mom. I need lacrosse socks for camp."

"You have socks."

"No. Mom. Lacrosse socks." Seth pulled out the catalog he had just brought in from the hall. "I can order them right now."

"You don't need special socks. That's absurd."

"Mom."

She looked at him. "All right, but don't close the magazine until I get the web address. I'll take a look."

"You don't need the address. Just look up 'lacrosse socks' and hit enter." He grinned. "See, that's why our generation is so much better. We just google things. We don't need to look up addresses, we can just go there."

"Yes, and when the whole system crashes, you'll be lost, and maybe" — she tapped him — "just maybe, we'll come and fetch you out of the darkness."

"Dubious," he pronounced gleefully. He took the plate she handed him and sat down.

"Question: are we middle middle class, upper middle class, or lower upper class?"

She glanced at Paul, setting down the wine

bottle, and raised her eyebrow. "Why?"

"Just wondering." Seth spooned his peas into the opened slit of the baked potato. "We just got our short answer exam questions and —"

"We're comfortable," she hedged. "You don't have to worry."

"I'm not *worried*." He set the spoon down and reached for the salt. "I just want to know whether I can write something."

"Upper middle," she said.

"But we've got the Island," he countered. "I mean, nobody else we know has an island, a whole island."

Paul was paying attention now, though he didn't lift his head.

"Yes," she said, her eyes on Paul, "we have the Island —"

"Because I'd put Larkin Reed in lower upper, wouldn't you?" Seth looked at her.

"Why's that?" she asked.

"They've got so much stuff."

"There's old money. There's new money. There is comfortable. There's rich. There is filthy stinking rich," she said blithely, and paused. "And then there are the people who know better."

"Know better about what?" Seth asked.

"About not spending money."

"So we are comfortable and know better?"

"Well," Evie admitted, "yes."

"Know better than whom?" Paul spoke for

the first time. "Who are you better than?"

"No one." She frowned at him. "We're not better than anyone; it's just an expression."

"Ask your mother what her grandmother always used to say."

"What?" Evie tried to read Paul's expression.

Seth looked from Paul to Evie, waiting.

Paul prompted. *"Always remember you are a Milton —"*

"Go on," Seth prodded.

She turned and looked at Seth. *"You are a Milton. Not a Lowell. Not a Rensselaer, a Havemeyer, or a Strong. The uprights, not the crackpots. The all-around men, the good sports."*

"Whoa. That's intense," Seth said. "What's a crackpot?"

"The Lowells," Paul answered smoothly, "are crackpots. Also geniuses, but never mind."

Evie flushed.

"So what were the Miltons?" Seth asked.

"Were? *Are.* You *are.*"

"I'm a Schlesinger," Seth said.

"Half," said Evie.

Paul looked up.

"Is that what your grandfather was?" Seth asked. "A good sport?"

"He was," Evie answered quickly, "and also the head of a major investment bank that" oversaw the end of the Great Depression, and instrumental in the Marshall Plan."

"So he was famous."

"He was, yes," Paul said, and looked at Evie without any irony. "He was, on the one hand, a great man."

"He did what he was raised to do," Evie amended.

"Which was what?" Seth looked from his father to his mother.

"Step up," Evie searched. "Work for the common good," she went on. "All of us were raised for that." She stopped. "But you know this."

Her son sat up straight. "I don't, Mom, not really."

"The boys were meant to take up the reins their fathers held — go into banking or go down to Washington and be of service. Be useful."

"Lead the country," Paul added.

"As they had for hundreds of years. They were expected to, they expected to, and they did."

"*All* of them? *All* the boys?"

Evie nodded. "Pretty much."

"There weren't any fails?"

"Fails?"

"Guys who didn't do — what they were supposed to."

Evie shook her head.

"How about your uncle Moss?" Paul said.

343

"Moss?" She stopped. "No one ever really talked about Moss. He was a little tragic, I think. He played the piano."

"What about the girls?" Seth asked, tipping back in his chair.

"The girls? We were to adorn. To adorn and to add."

"Add what?"

Evie mimicked her grandmother's tone, her eyes on Paul. "That irreducible something — color in a room, good conversation — grace."

"It used to drive your mother crazy."

Evie nodded. "And if you were going to have children, have three, but not four — that verged on Catholic, for god's sake — and two was a little pathetic."

"And one?" Seth asked.

"Mmm. Unimaginable." She smiled at her son. He tipped farther back, leaning against the wall.

(*I understand perfectly,* her grandmother had sniffed when Evie had handed her a copy of her first book, *why you would want to teach, but why on earth you need to write something that no one has any intention of reading — what is a trope, for goodness sake? — I can't fathom.*

There would be the light, appraising gaze followed by a quiet. You knew only that you had disappointed, though never exactly on what score. It was as though there were a twin beside you, the ideal twin, on whom she

bestowed her satisfaction, and even more —
her pride. There in the air beside you was
who she really sought.)

"Mom?"

She looked at Seth, returning.

"Anyway," Evie finished, "Granny K pronounced us all interesting, by which I think
she meant not a one of us stayed the course,
not a one of us carries the torch."

"Yeah," Seth continued, "and I didn't even
know what the rules were. So it's really over.
That torch is — out."

"Lord, Seth," she said, pricked. "And can
you stop tipping in Aunt Min's chair?"

He brought the legs of the chair down.
"Torches don't just go out. I'll bet there's
some dark secret hidden away."

"Oh, you do, do you?"

"There's always something." Seth paused,
thinking. *"Festering."* He grinned, wobbling
his finger.

"Oh really?"

"I'm serious. Something always happens
and then the whole world changes, *boom.*
Look at World War One, for instance."

She shook her head, smiling in spite of
herself. He sounded like all her students. "If
there is anything history teaches, it's that
nothing *happens.* No single moment. No
story. Just people going around doing the best
they can, without knowing what on earth they
are doing."

Seth raised his eyebrows, elaborately un-convinced.

"Atom bomb?" He smiled.

She snorted. Her eye fell on his plate, the knife and fork tossed down as though he were a plumber, rather than lined up side by side, correctly, at the four-twenty spot. "For the nine thousandth time, can you put those together, please?"

His smile dimmed. "It doesn't matter, Mom."

"It does."

Seth rolled his eyes. "Dad. Tell Mom. It doesn't matter where the fork and knife are. They'll get to the sink one way or another."

"There is a right way and a wrong way," Evie persisted. This wasn't what she meant to finish with, but she couldn't help it. "That's all."

"*Dad,*" he appealed to Paul. "It's not logi-cal."

For answer, very slowly, Paul moved his own fork and his knife together, so that they lay side by side. And, equally elaborately, Seth rose from his spot, cleared his own and his father's plate, took them into the kitchen to the sink, and put them down.

Then he slid out of the kitchen and back to his room. They heard his door close.

Evie stood up abruptly with her plate, feel-ing like a foreigner at her own table, and knowing she was absurd for feeling so. She walked through the door into the kitchen and turned on the tap, letting the hot water run the grease off the plate.

She heard Paul get up from the table and follow her in.

"I hate that Seth doesn't really have a sense of manners."

"He's a teenager."

"But he thinks it's funny, he thinks manners belong to someone else."

Paul didn't answer.

"He comes from generations sitting around a table knowing which knife to use, when to turn to the person on your right, when to ask a question, how to tip the soup bowl away —" She stopped. She scooped the hamburger meat and peas that had caught in the drainer, letting the water from the tap run hard in the sink. The aluminum shone. She could hear so clearly her grandmother's voice instructing all of them around the table up at Crockett's. She could conjure them all exactly. And Seth had no idea who any of them were. *I'm a Schlesinger,* he said.

How quickly the world plows us under, she thought with a pang. For two generations, maybe three, we lived on. After that, we're nothing more than a name, or — her eye fell on one of Great-Aunt Minerva's chairs standing like a sentry against the wall — a part of the furniture.

"God," she said aloud. "Listen to me."

"I am."

She turned around and saw he had been watching her, standing there very still, waiting while she thought things out.

"I'm not the enemy," he said quietly.

"But you don't see what I see." She was sad. "You always used to."

He looked at her. "You used to be in a fight with the world, with your world," he said. "What happened to Evie on the ramparts?"

She shook her head.

"You were fighting it, Evie, and now —"

"Now?"

"You're leaving, Evie — and I don't know how to stop you."

"What? No, I'm not."

"You want to disappear into the past."

"Oh." She narrowed her eyes. "I get it. This is about the Island again."

"It's not," he said. "It's bigger than that."

She watched him a moment.

"It is, though," she said.

"You want to talk about the Island? Aside from how you *got* it, we can't afford it, for starters," he said quietly. "We can't."

"Then we failed. I failed."

He groaned.

"You don't get it," she said helplessly. "That's how it seems. We have to hold on to it, otherwise —"

"What is there to get?" He looked at her. "Your mother died, and you miss her. That's what this is about."

The blood pounded in her chest. "It's more than that."

"What, then?"

"You heard Seth." She crossed her arms. "You heard him."

"Heard him say what?"

"We've got the Island," she repeated. "He said it like it was a badge or something. Like a talisman."

"He's a kid. It's paradise up there for a kid. He's oblivious." He shook his head. "But you remember how it could be? Your grandmother at one end of the table watching your father's steady pour. Your mother and your aunt Evelyn determined to keep the chatter going. Everyone under the weight, the steady weight of *being* Miltons. *We do this, we don't do that.* And your father kept right on drinking until he fell out of his chair. If you want to rewrite that place for yourself, go ahead. But I'm not paying for it. I'm not going to 'beggar' Seth to keep it. I refuse. That place has a worm in it. That place is everything you're not — it's the wrong fight, Evie."

"Fuck you," she said tiredly.

"There you go." She heard the relief in his voice.

"What if it's the right fight?" she said quietly. "Mum's fight."

Paul shook his head. "Your mother wasn't in any fight that I could see. When I think of

349

your mother, I think of someone facing into a stiff breeze with a smile on."

Evie knew exactly what he was thinking of. Her mother stepped into every room with her head tipped and her chin raised, a smile on her lips. Resolute. Forward-looking — fully armored.

"Anyway, I can't let it go right now. You know I can't."

"Why not?"

"Because of Mum," she said. "Without the Island — she's vanished. Just like that. Smoke. And I owe her something."

"What?"

"I don't know." Evie shook her head. "All I know is that Mum came alive when we were on the Island. She was her best self up there."

She paused.

"And she slipped through my hands. I spent all my life determined not to be her, not to be mistaken for her, and now that she's gone, all I want to do is sit her down and ask her."

"What?"

"What happened?"

He didn't say anything.

"What?" She pushed back at his silence. "Her life just got quieter and quieter and then just dimmed for years, almost extinguished. It's as though it never really caught."

"Well, no; she married. She had you."

"That *can't* be all," she said, tears thick in her throat.

"Evie," he groaned, "why not? Why must there be anything else? You miss her. *Her,* not the Island. How does keeping it keep her?"

Evie shook her head in frustration. The reason was just out of reach, just on the other side of a shadow, just there, ungraspable but perceived. The Island held it. The place held her, all of them. It was what she couldn't explain to Paul, because it made no *sense.*

"I can't sell the Island until I know what happened." She was firm.

"Jesus. You want the story?" He shook his head. "It's the oldest one. You lot ran out of money. You ran out of juice. The fire in the keep went out. And the people took over the castle."

" 'You lot'?" she repeated. "You are talking about my mother and my grandmother. Both of whom you knew. Both of whom knew you."

"And both of whom," Paul said, "were expressions of their time."

"So you've said." She nodded tightly. "So you've told me. But unless you truly believe that we are no more than the sum of our times — something happened. Something must have happened."

Paul shook his head.

Evie looked at him. "Do you think something is happening now?"

"How do you mean?"

"Between us," she said.

"What's your point?"

This, she wanted to say. *This moment no one sees. That tells it all.*

"Listen," he said. "There is no story until we're dead, and then our children tell it. We are just living. Your mother was living. Stop looking for what's not there. Nothing happened — life happened. Reality is not a story."

"So the only people with stories to tell are those on the stones?"

He froze.

She shook her head and turned around. "My mother wants a stone. Why does she want a stone?"

"Evie," he said. "Don't."

" 'Here'?" she reminded him. "She wants the word, *here.* Not *here,* meaning anywhere. *Here,* meaning on the Island."

"Evie —"

"Isn't that your theory?" she snapped. "Isn't that your big idea? A place holds what happened, a stone marks that fact. And facts like that, *grounded facts,* free us to leave them behind, to move on."

She was tinderous, flaming. Goddamn it.

He stared at her a minute, and then a great grin spread across his face. He leaned forward and took her by the shoulders. "Evie, that's *it.*"

"I know," she said hotly. "I'm not an idiot. I was listening."

He pulled her against him, and she let him

hold her, feeling herself slowly uncurl and open. They stood together in the kitchen.

"If Henry offers to buy you out and lets you — lets us — come up and stay?" he asked.

She pulled away. "It wouldn't be the same."

"Owning it is more important than just having it?"

"Yes."

He considered her. "Why?"

"If I let it go, then I'm not a real Milton."

"You don't want to be that — you've never wanted to be that."

She crossed her arms. "Haven't I? I feel perhaps like I've been living under a cloak."

"Listen to me," he said urgently. "You are *not* a real Milton."

"How do you know?"

"Because you married me." He reached and put both hands on her shoulders and shook them. She stared up at him, startled. "Me." He held her a minute, looking at her, and then he kissed her.

Twenty-Two

Joan and Len walked. They sat in booths. They talked. Of the trial. Of the men she watched and worked for. Of the men he did. When the ruling came down in favor of Mr. Rosset, Joan told Len how her boss had picked her up and shaken her, laughing, everyone laughing. "The genie is out of the bottle," he'd cried. "There is no turning back." Len told her about Jack Higginson and Jack Slade and the wide berth they gave him. He told her about Dickie Pratt, hired last year and engaged to Joan's sister, Evelyn, who was not too sharp, he said to her regretfully.

"I had an idea to show him how to quicken his commissions," he said. "I could show him; no one would need to know."

"Some things are better off left unsaid," she warned. "Especially with someone like Dickie Pratt."

"Someone like Dickie?"

She'd nodded her head, but that was all she'd say.

She knew most of them by name or by reputation or by the small asides she had heard her father bring home. She knew nothing about business though she was in clear possession of how things worked, of rules that didn't matter but were ironclad all the same.

And yet she broke every rule he knew for a girl of her kind. She wanted him. It took his breath away. There were no games, no hidden traps, nothing at all but her mouth beneath his, her hands on his back, pulling him to her. Pulling him down, the rich chuckle rising from deep in her, exploding.

On the other side of this time, at the beginning of August, she was going to Maine. And on the other side of that, he couldn't think. In neat compartments, like berths on a ship, he put these weeks with her. Their own ship. "We are," Joan said to him, "like members of a foreign legion."

"An occupying force?"

"No," she said, and leaned against him, "from a distant land —"

"Isn't this your city?"

It is, she thought, and nodded at him. "But not with you — with you it's somewhere else." Somewhere on the front, she thought, somewhere on the border of a recognizable life.

He looked down at her.

"Hello." She smiled up. He reached and pulled her up off the bench and into him.

"Let's walk," he said, holding her.

There was something different tonight, something urgent beneath the lips he bent to kiss her with, some trouble in his eyes.

"What is it?"

He pulled her closer at the same time as he shook his head. They walked through the trees and up the broad esplanade at the center of the park.

"I can't figure your father out."

"How do you mean?"

"Your father doesn't press advantages," he said, bemused, thinking of that morning's meeting with a client. Ogden had specifically asked for Len to watch the client's face as they went through the working of the deal. "I can't understand it."

She nodded. "He wouldn't."

"*I* would," Len vowed. "We could have nearly doubled what the guy conceded."

"We're different," she answered simply. "We don't believe in taking advantage of a situation. In grabbing for money."

We? He stilled.

"Grabbing?" He was deliberate. "I'd call it earning."

She didn't answer.

"And what about the first Miltons? Someone somewhere along the line had to grab."

She considered this. "I don't think we are a grabby people."

"You haven't had to grab; you've had it all

in your hands all along."

"My point is," she said thoughtfully, "we wouldn't grab even if we had to."

"You really believe that?" Len was careful.

"Of course," she said firmly. "We are above all that."

"All that." His voice trailed as he shook his head. "What is 'all that'? Money?"

She frowned. "It's not about the money. It's more than that — it's who you are."

"I'd say it's all about the money."

She poked him. "When one has money, one never talks about it, and one thinks about it as little as possible."

"You're joking."

"Half." She looked up at him with that dare in her eyes. "We think past money."

He snorted.

"We do," she protested.

"You *think* you think past it." He pulled her close.

But it was the kind of comment that gnawed at her, even as it made her think. What he had said about the Jews in the bar at the Algonquin with Moss had struck her and stuck deep. Listening to him, Joan had felt that his vision of the world could not be wholly trusted, it could not be the whole truth, though she felt, too, that it must be right. Jews were set apart, she knew that. Everyone knew that. But *why*? They didn't play by the rules. They didn't know how to walk into a room and be quiet, first. Yet how could they know the rules? How could they know the rules if they were always set outside?

And she wanted to give him something more than herself, wanted to come to him carrying it in her hands. Ever since she had opened her eyes in Pennsylvania Station and seen him crouched above her, she had wanted to give him something. The more she listened to him, the more she walked with him, she wanted to give him the rules. To win. Though win what exactly — her? She wasn't sure.

"You know, your father has me looking in the firm's archives," he said after a while.

"Sounds riveting."

He smiled and shifted his hand farther down her arm. "It is, actually."

"But?"

Len shook his head. "Why me? Why have me digging around? Organizing."

"He trusts you."

He shook his head. "What does he want me to see?"

She laughed. "What could there be to see?"

"How to run a firm, I suppose." He slowed. "Or how not to."

"He likes you," Joan said. "That's why. He doesn't like just anybody."

He glanced down at her, vaguely troubled.

They had reached the coffee shop downstairs from her apartment. She pulled open the door without looking up at him, and he put his hand on the small of her back and propelled them both through.

"He saved my life, you know." She glanced back at him.

He slid into the booth beside her. The air in the diner was greasy and hot around them. "What happened?"

She turned and looked at him. "Moss and I were diving for starfish, and I had just pulled one off the rock and was kicking up to the surface —"

He waited.

"It was my first attack." She shuddered. "I couldn't breathe —"

"He dove in?"

She nodded.

"Where was Moss?"

She shook her head. "In the water. He couldn't move. He was paralyzed with fright."

"Poor guy."

They were quiet.

He leaned forward across the table and took her hand. "If you have another fit, what do I do?"

She went still. No one outside of her family had ever spoken to her about her fits. He talked about it as if it was as ordinary as fixing a headache or even a tire. He must have wanted to ask that question for a long time. She looked at him, and he kept hold of her hand.

"When it happens, put a spoon in my

mouth," she said quietly.

He nodded. Their hamburgers came. They passed the ketchup to each other, salt. She sipped her Coke. He ate. The room chattered round. For an instant she saw the two of them together, past this moment, him knowing, him being there whenever she fell away from the world. She bent her head, flushing, and ate. When they were finished, he asked for the check, and she rose and wrapped her scarf around her head, making for the door, walking through it and into the night air, turning to wait. And when he leaned to put the bills on the table, she saw him pocketing one of the spoons.

Later they lay in bed, drowsing in the heat, the sheets kicked off, and a tiny breeze crossed the ridge of his body, and the hair on his chest bent and waved as it crossed in the faintest whisper like the ripple of air upon the moss at the Broads, and without thinking Joan started to describe the path on the Island, walking it in her mind's eye all the way past the old foundations, the bent spruce, the moss so deep all footfalls vanished. "When you look behind you," she said into the dark without looking at Len, "it's as though you'd never been there."

He listened to her voice describe the Big House, the small rooms, the wall above the stairs where light moved across it slow and calm. She was reverent, like one entranced.

"There's nothing to do up there but be."

"Be what?"

She wrinkled her nose. "Us," she said after a while, and turned her gaze on him. "The Miltons."

He considered this.

"It's the one place on earth where I feel right." She was soft.

"Right?"

"No, that's not true." She lifted onto her elbow and touched his face. "Here, in this bed I am right. Also."

"Then I won't leave this bed until you come back."

She bit her lip. He looked at her. They hadn't spoken about this yet. The after. After Maine. After summer. The fall.

"You'll lie here, in wait?"

He nodded, a slow smile spreading.

"I am the troll who will carry the princess off at last."

"A six-foot-two troll?" She laughed. "What if the princess doesn't want to go?"

"I'm a convincing troll."

Twenty-Three

Kitty rode the elevator up, the cut roses from the garden in Oyster Bay heavy in her arms. She stood stiffly in the car, alone with her reflection in the polished brass. She missed having an elevator man, the easy silence, the sense of weight and purpose as he spun the wheel, the grating of the cage door as he pulled it open and shut. Everything nowadays was so silent and swift.

The elevator opened onto a tiny hall wallpapered in a pale yellow silk, a Beau Brummell flanked by two slipper chairs. The bowl of pale pink hydrangeas in the table well was looking a little tired, she noted as she pushed open the door into their apartment.

Where it was quiet. She stood in the center hall, the doors to the four directions of the apartment open, and listened. Nothing came from the empty living room before her. Behind her the hall to the butler's pantry and the cool kitchen, where Jessie must be, though there wasn't a sound. To her right the door down to their bedroom. To her left, through the door to the library, she could just see the thick and rounded arm of the leather sofa. A blaze of sun lazed across the deep dark green, like the unexpected light one stumbled on in the middle of the woods on Crockett's. The lamp was on and voices started up again. Someone was in there with Ogden. She slipped out of her coat and reached for a hanger in the coat closet, trying to hear who it might be. The linen hung down, and she tucked it in beside Ogden's coat, and the voice stumbled — Dunc's. It was Dunc. She listened. It almost sounded as if they were arguing.

The two men looked up as she pushed through the door and stopped talking, as if she'd pulled a cord and a curtain fell.

"Hello, darling."

The room tensed around something she couldn't grip.

"What's the secret?" she asked lightly.

"No secret," said Ogden, the expression on his face unreadable. He held a letter in his hand.

"Hello." Dunc stood and enfolded her in a hug, the ghost of his old crooked grin snaking across his face, which both comforted and dismayed. He really was, she realized, quite terribly thin, the dear laughing man he'd once been now overtaken by this gray specter, as though he had slipped free of his own shadow, and what was left to stand for him was something airy and unsettled.

She remained in the doorway, a little less certainly now, her dress a long cool spot of blue against the dark molding.

"Can I get either of you a drink?"

"Terrific." Ogden smiled at her, but as if from a great distance.

"Usual?"

"For me." He nodded. "Dunc?"

"Bourbon," her cousin answered. "Thanks, Kitty."

In the living room the ice bucket had been brought and filled and the glass tumblers set out.

Ogden murmured something she couldn't hear, and Dunc's voice raised in answer: "I *was.* I was — we were — in charge of them. Nine hundred sixty-one of them —"

The *St. Louis,* she realized. That again. Kitty dropped three cubes in each glass and reached for the bourbon. The liquor slid golden over the ice and splashed round.

Dunc had been so lovely, the perfect expression of all of them — courteous, good-looking, strong. He was the one on whom hope rested. Frailty, Kitty thought, considering her cousin, had never occurred to her. She did not know what to do with him now. He was embarrassing, and she was ashamed of feeling embarrassed by his drinking, his provoking. Bringing up the war and what we had or hadn't done.

Kitty tipped a little more into Dunc's glass than hers or Ogden's and carried them back across the front hall on a tray, into the library.

"You shouldn't dwell on it," Ogden was saying, impatiently. "You tried to help."

"Help?" Dunc nodded at the letter in Ogden's hand. "As you helped?"

Ogden's face hardened.

"Why can't we just admit what we did?" Dunc frowned, taking his glass from Kitty. She set the tray down on the desk in front of Ogden and carried her glass to the sofa, where she sat.

"What did we do?" Ogden was being patient, she saw.

"We — the State Department — sent those people back. And you —"

"It's not so clear."

"It is. It's very clear. And we did it."

Ogden shook his head. "You did your level best. There were others —"

"Enough," Dunc cried sharply. "Enough," he repeated. He sounded exhausted.

"Ogden." Kitty remonstrated. "Dunc. What on earth is going on?"

Dunc swirled the liquid in his glass. Ogden looked at her.

"Do you remember the day we first saw the Island? There was a German woman, an old friend."

Kitty swallowed.

"Elsa Hoffman and her son," Ogden continued. "Do you remember? Who was staying at the Lowells' that weekend?"

Kitty nodded slowly. "Willy."

"Yes."

Kitty waited.

Ogden put the letter down on his desk. "She was hanged. In 1942. In Plötzensee prison. The Germans have just released the records."

The anguish on his face was clear.

"Oh, Og —"

"We were fairly certain she was dead. But we didn't know how —"

"Or where," Dunc finished.

Kitty sat forward.

"Because she was a Jew?"

Ogden shook his head. "Because she was a hero."

Kitty stared at him.

"She and her husband," he continued. "And others. She stole papers from her father's factory that proved what Hitler was planning —"

"And passed them off to the Russians." Dunc swallowed the last of his whiskey, his eyes on Ogden. "Though she had asked for our help."

"Your help?" Kitty looked at Ogden.

Ogden nodded, smoothing the letter on the desk before him. "I didn't agree with her — then."

"I had thought you didn't like her," Kitty said.

"Didn't like her?" Ogden looked at her and frowned. "Whatever gave you that idea?"

I saw your face, she wanted to say. *I saw your back stiffen. I heard your voice. You needed me to be firm that day. You needed me to help. It was so clear to me there, long ago. You did not want to be part of that woman's plan. You did not want to be pushed.*

"And what happened to the boy?" she managed. "What happened to him?"

"I don't know." Ogden was thoughtful. "I don't think we'll ever know. So many children were lost."

"We should have offered to keep him when we could," Dunc said.

Ogden shook his head. "She'd never have asked."

Elsa's urgent face on the porch that night at the Lowells' arrived whole and unopened, rising above the surface of the years and waving, like a hand shot out of the sea. The pitch, the timbre of her comprehending *oh!* reverberated deep in Kitty in that moment, like the shiver of a bell struck silent upon its rope.

Kitty set her glass carefully on the side table.

"I must change for the Wilmerdings' dinner," she said, and rose from the couch.

TWENTY-FOUR

Like a bell at the races, the first of August came, and much of Wall Street went north. Milton Higginson was reduced to its skeleton crew. Len wandered the halls of the emptied office, coming in every morning to sit at his desk and nudge along the accounts he'd been given, placing phone calls he knew would not be returned until after Labor Day, happy to be the lone man on the watch. In the motionless hours after lunch, with the windows shoved high, he continued to page through the company holdings, determined to come up with the list of good candidates for the idea he had pitched Mr. Milton by the time the partners returned.

Late one afternoon toward the middle of the month, Len pulled open one of the last of the drawers in the file room. The single file inside gave thick testimony to the fact that the firm must have had a long history with this particular company, and Len brought it back upstairs to his desk and opened it, looking for Ogden's notes. The Walser Gruppe was evidently a German steel manufacturer Ogden had courted throughout the twenties, culminating in his first investment in 1929. There was a certificate of agreement signed June 19 of that year. And then several pages detailing the inventory — mostly hairpins and kitchen faucets. Len turned the pages quickly, noting the clear evidence of a good investment — the company's numbers grew and grew over the next five years, expanding into 1935 when Len arrived at a second letter of agreement, signed in June of that year by Ogden and by Walser. Beside Walser's signature was the Nazi seal.

Len shoved the paper back as if he'd been burned and stared down.

Then, carefully, methodically, he went through every piece of paper in the file. But there was no third letter dissolving the agreement. There was nothing at all. Nothing to suggest anything other than what these letters laid out. Milton Higginson had stayed in all through the war. Could be, in fact, still invested. Len stood up from the desk and found himself, not thinking, walking toward the men's room at the back of the office, where he turned on the tap, cupped his hands, and filled them with cold water. He drank and then filled his hands and drank again, then filled them a third time, which he simply poured over his head.

Joan. Her name rose in his throat like a sob.

He looked up, dripping wet, and stared in the mirror. It was then that Len wondered if Ogden Milton had meant for him to find those pages all along.

He turned and went back to his desk, not thinking, his hands simply moving through the papers, replacing all the files back in the box. All except the Walser file. Carefully, he arranged all the pages in this one neatly back in order. Save for the two letters of agreement.

He looked at them again. And slid them into his briefcase, closed the lid, and snapped it shut. Then he walked out into the hot city, unseeing, nearly running as he headed for home.

"Reg," he called into the apartment. The rooms were still, the windows open to the heat. Len walked in, put the briefcase on the table, walked to the window, and turned around. "Reg?" he tried again.

His eyes fell on the row of Polaroids stretched in the line above the sofa. Arranged like that, it was inescapable — all the faces looking back from the frames wanted the man behind the camera gone.

Len studied them for a long while and then turned from the wall and made his way into the kitchen. The light of the icebox opened in the dark room like a fire in the woods. He pulled out a beer and went back to sit underneath Reg's photographs and wondered where he was.

The Five Spot was hot, dark, and packed that night, and Reg and Moss had found themselves a small table, two in from the edge of the bandstand. A quartet called the Ball Points was taking the stage slowly, and for now just the piano wove through the chatter in the room. The two men had fallen into the habit of sitting together in bars, comfortably silent, content to observe. Collecting, it occurred to Reg one night. There was an unspoken sense between them that this was a time in between, this summer they were treading water. Moss had shifted his chair so he sat with his back to the drum kit and faced into the room, watching it all and playing the table, tense, abstracted, and distant in a way Reg hadn't seen.

He was due to leave at the end of the week to follow his family up to Maine. *And then,* Moss thought, his eyes sliding across three men sitting at a table. All of their feet were tapping the floor. He watched. In opposite rhythm. He shook his head, smiling in spite of his sinking heart.

What did he want? The question at the back of his mind rolled forward as if tipped into the light. Rolled around and then as suddenly rolled back and away again in the dark. The maid's hands pulling down his white shirt firmly, tucking it into his waistband, yanking him slightly forward. Tucked in, tucked up, turned out, and emerging into the living room and the quick appraising glance of his mother as he appeared. *Here is Moss,* she'd say, smiling to the people sitting, having drinks in the deep-carpeted room. *Our eldest.*

He glanced at Reg, who was sitting very still, smoking, his head cocked to one side. Moss wanted to spend the month in hot cellar after smoky bar, following music, sitting and listening with Reg. Not on the Island. Not up there, the most beautiful place on earth. Where the Milton grip was so tight, he couldn't breathe.

"Do you know Lorraine Hansberry?" he asked quietly, his eyes on a couple at a distant table.

"Because I'm a Negro from Chicago?"

"Noooo. No," Moss turned to Reg, patient. "No, I mean have you seen *A Raisin in the Sun*?"

"Have *you*?"

Moss nodded.

"And?"

"It was the first time I'd ever seen my own story on the stage."

"*Your* story?"

Moss nodded, his eyes on his friend. "To see something, to want it that bad. To want and want and know that it's impossible —

it's impossible. What you want is just under the surface, just under the skin. But not yet arrived. And still you want."

Reg looked at him. "What are you talking about?" He was impatient. "You can have anything you want."

"No, Reg." Moss squared his gaze, steady. "I can't."

Reg stared back at him.

Sudden as a shot, the drums took off, and both men jumped, released, as Philly Joe Jones on the drums took them into the song, his arms working his sticks, striking the beat like matches into light, into life, lifting the room right off its bricks; and then enormous Jim Mollow with his trumpet stepped into his sound, slowly, like a girl too shy at first to come to the party, like a girl considering, while the drums banged and banged loud, so goddamned loud, Moss shouted out and turned and looked at Reg, who nodded once, and then the trumpet spun a long note, spun its gold thread above their heads, and cast Reg back to the spot in the alley where he used to meet Len to walk to school, and then further back to his father and his mother dressed in fur, his mother leaning out the window of their big black Buick, her long arms shot free of the fur, and his father, one leg up on the dashboard, both of them looking at him as he came toward them for the ride over to the lake. He saw his father's shoulders and his mother's hat, and they drove and the windows were down. It was spring, the air smelled a little rotten from the alewives washed up on shore, and they drove, and when they came to Lake Shore, his father slowed the car, pulled to the side, and then stopped, the motor running.

In the distance, to the left, Chicago glinted in the sun, and the cars along the lake darted and dipped, humming along. He heard the distant whine of the El. They sat in the car, his parents looking out the windshield. Reg reached down to pull on the handle and open the door.

"No, son," said his father.

Reg looked up.

"You stay sitting." His mother turned around.

Reg sat back against the leather. The three of them sat in the car and didn't speak. There was the city. The bright waters of Lake Michigan shivered.

After a while, his father reached down and released the brake, then turned the car around and drove back to their house. *Oh Mother,* the drums dropped down. *Oh Father,* the trumpet soared. It was life in the dark playing away up there. It was Reg's life playing down. You can wear your furs, you can go to church, you can own your house, you can pray. Lord, you can pray. And you can drive so far, and then you must turn around. This far and no farther. Life and sorrow and that beat. That beat that promised anything — anything at all might come.

Moss had sprung up on his feet with most of the room, clapping and calling out. But Reg felt he was going to cry. Like any boy, sitting in the dark, hit by memory, he was going to cry. He put his head in his hands and let the music hold him.

Mollow played the last note, played it out across the heads and the faces lifted to him, played it out the door and onto the street. He played. And when he stopped the room was quiet. Utterly still. The song hovered in their heads.

And then Philly Joe stood and mopped the top of his drum set and mopped his neck. And one by one the four musicians stepped down off the bandstand and went to the bar for a drink. Just men again.

"Christ!" Moss sat down. "That's what I want to get. Did you hear that? That moment way up there at the top of the tune. *Man* —"

Reg stared into his drink, exhausted by the music.

"That's what I want to make people feel," Moss said. "If I could do something like that, take all this fire and push, push hard on the doors, push it like Mollow did tonight —"

"What the hell are you talking about?"

Moss looked up as if seeing him for the first time and, not hearing the edge in Reg's voice, went right on.

"Mollow blows his horn — and it's his, it's all his, his story, his memories he's wound up tight in every note. But I can hear it," Moss said. "*I* hear it, too. It doesn't matter that he's black and I'm white. I hear it. And that proves it."

"Proves what?"

"It's about to happen. It's all about to happen. The bass line is exploding."

"What the hell is *it*?"

"Change, man. We are here. We're all here. But we're about to change. This is the moment. Everything's about to blow —"

"We?"

"Yes," Moss said to him.

Reg shook his head. "You are completely infuriating."

"Why?" Moss's blue eyes held his.

"Because you don't know what you're talking about," Reg said. "We don't hear each other, no matter what you think you hear. We can't."

The angry bewilderment that flared on Moss's face just then flared and as quickly was smothered. "Prove it."

Reg's heart slowed. "I don't have to prove what you can't see."

Moss shook his head. "I see something else."

"When you look at *me,*" Reg said, "what do you see?"

"Reg Pauling," Moss answered swiftly.

"First? That's the first thing you see?"

Moss flushed.

Reg nodded. "No, you don't," he said kindly. "You see a Negro. It's not a new time, no matter what it looks like to you."

But why say it like that, thought Moss. So baldly. It left no room.

"I see tribes when I look at this room," Reg said. "Men coming to sit together. Girls they allow in. Tables of tribes. No way around it. Human beings have survived because of the tribe. *That's* the fact. There's nothing we can do about that, except recognize it and listen for their drums —"

"Yeah?" Moss leaned across the table. "What are we, then, Reg? What tribe are we?"

"It's not that simple," Reg protested.

"It is."

"You're dreaming, man."

Moss nodded. "What if I'm not?"

For an instant, Reg went still. And then his dark, intent face cracked open, and the white of his smile broke through, and it got Moss, got him in his gut.

"See there." Moss grinned, reaching across the table with both hands. "See that?" He grabbed Reg by the shoulders and shook him happily.

"All right, man." Reg smiled, letting himself be shaken. "All right. Simmer down."

They looked at each other.

"Listen," Moss urged. "Come to the Island. I dare you."

The idea was on Moss's lips before he thought.

Reg looked at him. "Come where?"

Why hadn't he thought of this before? Moss shook his head, amazed.

"Come up to the Island."

"What island?"

"Crockett's," said Moss. "Where we go in Maine every summer. Where I'm going this weekend. We run boats, hike mountains, sing, eat lobster. It's terrifically, fabulously dull."

"An island?"

"On my honor," said Moss, smiling. And suddenly he wanted nothing more than for Reg to set foot on the place and walk with him and turn those considering eyes on them all up there.

"That is exactly the kind of invitation men like you toss out," Reg said, exhaling.

"Men like me? There aren't any men like me," Moss tossed back.

"And there sure as hell wouldn't be any men like me," Reg leveled at him.

"What do you think would happen?" Moss pressed him seriously.

"Nothing," Reg answered swiftly. "Not a goddamn thing. I'd be surrounded by silence and polite smiles. Like Pocahontas in London."

Moss considered this.

378

"You know I'm right," said Reg. "You were in the Yard with me."

"But I wasn't with you," Moss said urgently. "I hadn't thought it all through."

"And you still haven't."

"You think the North is a dream." Moss leaned forward. "Show me. Show me so I can see. Isn't that what you've been saying you want to do? Come to my sister's party. Come up and prove it."

He hesitated.

"Bring Len," said Moss. "Bring Len, too. I can teach him how to sail."

Reg snorted. "The Jew and the Darkie?"

With a pained expression he didn't bother to hide now, Moss stood and stretched and reached for his jacket off the back of the chair. "Come on," he said. "I dare you."

Reg tossed his cigarette down and crushed it with his shoe. "And what would we do? Hire a boat and just come over, arrive on the dock and ring the bell?"

"Something like that," Moss said quietly, and held out his hand.

Reg shook it. The expression on Moss's face was so solemn, so sweet, he couldn't look away.

"Come up and see."

"See what?"

Me, Moss didn't say. *Come and see me.*

"Us." He was light. "The Miltons. I dare you."

Reg didn't move. He watched Moss thread through the crowd, heading out of the club.

It was enough, it had been enough merely to know it, to see the lie every day and to build his wall by noticing it, by remarking it. He hadn't cared until he'd walked into Moss Milton's party and seen him turn and smile. And as much as Reg wanted to believe in the ideas that Moss believed, he wanted to prove him wrong. Once and for all, to have men like Moss see that this dream of America was impossible until everyone saw what the black man saw. He wanted to have Moss *see.* Moss stirred in him a helpless curiosity, and moving toward him was his future, or his fate. It didn't matter, Reg realized now with a kind of fear. He was helpless in the face of it.

Len was sitting in the living room, in the dark, smoking, when Reg pushed open the door. He flicked on the lights.

"What's going on?"

Len turned his head and looked at him, and then pointed to some papers on the table. Reg went over and stood looking down.

"What am I looking at?"

Len rose and came to stand beside him, pointing to the dates. "What do you make of this?"

"Jesus," muttered Reg, studying the pages. "So Milton's a Nazi."

"Well, maybe." Len was quick. "Maybe not."

Reg turned and looked at him.

"We don't know anything," said Len stubbornly.

"What do you want to do?"

"I want to ask him."

"Ask him what?"

"If we stayed in through the war."

"We? Who's 'we'?"

"The firm. Milton Higginson —"

Reg stared at him and felt older than Father Time. Old and sad, and for the first time in this room, banging the gong on his own. "Since when is that you?"

Len didn't answer.

Tear it down, slats and all, Reg thought.

"Are you going to tell Moss?"

"Moss?" Len looked at him, surprised. "Tell Moss?"

"It might break him free."

"What do you mean?"

"It might give Moss what he needs to leave."

Len looked at Reg thoughtfully. But he wasn't thinking about Moss.

TWENTY-FIVE

At eleven o'clock on the morning of the meeting, Evie pulled open the thick double doors of 30 Broad Street, where Dick Sherman's offices occupied the first floor below what had once been the offices of Milton Higginson. As long as she could remember, when presented with a knotty problem, *Ask Dick Sherman* was the reply everyone always gave. Old Dick, as her grandfather's lawyer was called, had been replaced by Young Dick, a classmate of her uncle Moss's, who was now in his eighties and had worked for the family the whole of his adult life. Seeing no one in the conference room, she pushed through the heavy door to the ladies' room, tastefully disguised as the entrance to a boardroom, where her cousin Min, short for Minerva, bent over the long row of sinks, washing her hands.

"Oh." Evie stopped. "When did you get here?"

"About five minutes ago." Min lifted her

hands out of the water and turned around, leaning into Evie's shoulder and giving it a bump by way of hello, her hands dripping.

A willowy blonde who had danced at the cotillion, cradled a lacrosse ball, and walked out the gates of Harvard Yard with the class of 1983, Min had headed as far west as she could go. Having been raised to be seen and not heard, she seemed to view quiet — of any kind — as a challenge she took up in her adulthood. Not only would she not be silenced, she would not be quiet. *She will not shut up,* Paul had grumbled nearly every summer. She believed firmly and squarely that talking things out was the only way to get to the bottom of anything, and that went for herself and for anyone else who wandered haplessly into her orbit. She was a practicing Jungian, had four dogs and a small house perched in Griffith Park, and sent out newsletters every month titled "From the Interior."

"I didn't think I'd see you," Evie said.

"Why's that?"

"It's a long way to come for a meeting."

Min looked up at Evie in the mirror, flicking water off her hands into the basin. She wore a sleeveless linen shift and blue suede Birkenstocks and still had the lithe, active body of an athlete. "Pretty important meeting, wouldn't you say?"

"Do you know something I don't?"

Min straightened. "No, Evie."

Evie nodded and handed her one of the cloth towels piled discreetly on the side of each sink. Min took it, dried her hands, and then thrust her face into the damp cloth with a sigh. Then the two cousins walked back into the office and were pointed past the receptionist's desk and into the conference room.

"Hullo, Shep." Evie smiled at her cousin, one of Min's brothers, already at the table.

Shepherd Pratt leaped up to hug the women with the fluent grace of an outdoorsman. In his late forties, he still had the bloom of a younger man and wore his suit as though he were in costume. He'd drifted in and out of nonprofit jobs, working tirelessly on behalf of orphans, flood victims, and endangered mountain gorillas until he'd tired of them all and moved on to his most recent venture, running sailing trips out of Rockland Harbor. Lovely, divorced, and untouchable, he wore his charm like armor.

"Where's Harriet?" Min asked.

"Hold your horses, I'm right here." Evie's cousin Harriet slid in. Miss Mousie, their grandfather had called her. The spitting image of Evelyn, Harriet had married young and married a Moffat, moved to Beacon Hill, given birth to four enormous boys who ran the engines high and hard on all the boats on the Island, and had already sent the last one off to college. At forty-five, she remained mouselike, her black eyes shining in a tiny, impatient face.

"Hello, everyone." Henry, the last of the cousins, appeared in the doorway, dressed as always, Evie noted, in faultless navy blue. Used to being the man in charge, the suit set off his silvering hair, and he looked crisp and ready to go. Whereas the rest of them had gone into nonprofits, academia, or the arts, Henry Houghton Pratt — the eldest of Evie's cousins — had taken the money they had all inherited and done the one thing that ran in their blood: invested it.

"Let's get started," he pronounced. "We've got a lot to decide."

And though he was competent, intelligent, and as passionate about the Island as she was, it was exactly this breezy assumption of authority that drove Evie to dig in her heels, every time. Like brother and sister, they had battled each other to be best — on tennis courts, around dinner tables, and in the winter classrooms of their college — all their lives.

"What are we deciding, Henry, do you know?" she asked.

He didn't answer, making his way instead to the end of the table farthest from the door, setting his briefcase down.

"I have some thoughts" — Shep spoke before Henry answered — "about things. Improvements that need making — some

385

small changes —"

Min groaned. Last summer, the cousins had spent a disastrous afternoon "making a list" of what ought to be done. Harriet wanted to choose new wallpaper, have a little *fun,* she pleaded, if we're going to own it, let's show it's ours, for god's sake.

"But I like the blue boats," Evie had protested. "That's what I used to count when we had to wait to be excused from the table."

"They're ugly," Harriet declared flatly. "And stained."

"Okay, why don't we look for something like them?"

"Why don't we just paint the walls. Forget about wallpaper?" Min suggested. "Try a new look — something more spare."

"I don't care what the fuck we do to the walls, let's just make a decision," Henry groaned.

They were silent.

"What's the decision?"

"To paint," Shep said, entering the fray. "I agree with Min."

"Will you guys let me at least search out wallpaper that's the same kind of color as the old blue and maybe even has the same spirit?" Evie asked.

"I had no idea you were a decorator underneath all those degrees, Evie."

"Will you?"

"What if you can't find anything? Then

we're back to square one."

"Then we paint, but keep it the same blue."

"Fine," Henry said, moving into the pantry. "What about in here?"

But Evie had not found wallpaper to match; she had not even looked. She'd gotten pulled back into her life in the city and the fall semester, and that had been that.

"Small changes," Henry said, dismissing his brother now, carrying on smoothly, "are not what we need to discuss today. We all know that the money in the Island trust can't last forever, and we're going to need to come up with some ideas for cash. We need a plan." He paused, clearly about to deliver one.

"Why don't we call Pottery Barn?" Harriet broke in swiftly. "They could do photo shoots up there."

They looked at her. "Seriously, Harriet?" But Shep was smiling. No one ever took Harriet seriously.

"Why not?" she said. "They pay fortunes for great spaces."

"Why not Ralph Lauren for that matter." Min rolled her eyes.

Harriet turned to her. "Don't be so snotty."

"What's your plan, Henry?" Evie had not taken her eyes off her cousin.

"Well, it's not really my plan. Mum thought of it before she died, so I am really just carrying on in her stead."

"Go on."

"Mum thought, and I agree, that we ought to sell a portion of Crockett's, a sizable lot that someone could build on, with a good view. Someplace set off a little from the Big House and the dock, someplace that has its own point."

"Such as where?" Evie asked uneasily.

"The picnic grounds," Henry answered her. "You have to agree, it's the perfect lot. And the rocks at the end would make a natural pier for someone to build a dock."

"We can't," Evie said immediately.

All four of her cousins turned to look at her.

"What?" Henry asked. "Why not?"

"Mum wants her ashes to go there."

"What's wrong with the graveyard?"

Evie flushed, looking down at her hands. "She didn't want to be in the graveyard; she wanted to be on the rocks there."

He shook his head. "It might scotch a sale."

"That's your response?" Evie turned in her chair to look directly at him.

He held her gaze.

"That's the spot she chose," Evie said.

"You can't."

"I promised, Henry."

"It wasn't yours to promise," he said stiffly. "The Island belongs to all five of us now."

Evie was speechless.

"And Mum wouldn't want it," he went on.

No one spoke.

"Your mother is dead," Evie said.

The sorrow upon her cousin's face caught Evie by surprise, as if his grief were fresh, his mother newly gone. He was protecting Evelyn, Evie saw. That's it. But from what? From her? He crossed his arms.

"Henry," Evie said more softly, "Aunt E is dead."

"I can't let you." He shook his head slowly. "I've got to look out for her."

Evie turned away.

"Anyway, it's not right." He exhaled. "It wouldn't be fair to Mum, or to Uncle Moss."

"Fair?"

"If Aunt Joan gets her wish on this."

"Fair?"

He nodded, but he wouldn't look at Evie.

"Henry," said his sister firmly.

Evie looked at Min. "What is he talking about?"

"You know it's not right," he said to the papers in front of him. He didn't look at Min, but he kept speaking. "You know it. Mum told us what happened. It's not right."

Harriet sat with her arms crossed tight across her chest, and Shep had started doodling on the pad in front of him. Min watched Evie, who was staring at Henry without speaking. The quiet in the room worked like a fist in the gut. It was clear they all knew what Henry meant.

"What are you all talking about?" Evie said

slowly. "What did Aunt E say happened?"

Henry didn't answer.

"Min?" Evie asked.

"Mum wanted to get rid of the whole thing, you know," Harriet tossed out quietly.

Henry looked up and frowned. "No, she didn't."

"She did." Harriet looked at him now, relishing his discomfort. "She told me so."

"Only that portion of it, Harriet." Henry sat up in his chair. "That's all. As usual, you've got it all slightly wrong. That's what I was detailing before."

"Wait a minute," Evie said. "What do you mean, Henry?"

"You think you know everything, don't you?" Harriet sat back and folded her arms, leveling her gaze at her brother and paying no attention to Evie. "But you weren't there that last morning with Mum. You weren't there."

She took in Shep and Min. "None of you were."

"Mum said get rid of the Island?" Shep was incredulous.

Harriet nodded. "She didn't want it. She didn't want us to have it."

"She didn't want *Joan* to have it." Min spoke up for the first time.

Evie froze.

(*What is Joan doing?* Evie remembered hearing her aunt's feverish voice calling from

390

the front bedroom in her last summer. *Where is Joan?*)

"Hello, everyone." Dick Sherman pushed through into the conference room, handsome, white-haired, impeccable in a tweed suit, his hand outstretched, either ignoring or not perceiving the evident tension in the room.

"Shepherd, hello. So sorry to keep you all waiting. Henry —" And he made his way around the table, handing round his greetings and his general cheer.

"Looking more like your mum every day," he said to Evie.

She gave him a tight little smile.

He nodded, moving away, ready to begin. "All right?" He remained standing. "Everyone settled?"

There was a collective pause.

"Why don't you get us down to business, Dick," Henry invited, his gaze resting lightly on Evie and then upon the lawyer.

"All right." Dick Sherman nodded and moved the folder in front of him slightly closer. "We are meeting in accordance with your grandfather's wishes that six months to the day the last of your parents had died, you would gather to assess."

"Assess?" Henry asked. "How do you mean?"

The lawyer cleared his throat. "Do you plan to hold on to the island?"

"Of course," said Evie firmly.

"Why?" Henry asked the lawyer cautiously.

"At the rate the island costs are going," Dick Sherman said, looking around at them, "the monies in trust will run out the first of next year."

No one spoke. Evie looked across at Min.

"Run out?" Shep broke in. "Entirely?"

Dick Sherman nodded.

"How much remains in the trust?" Henry asked.

"I'm not at liberty to say. Your grandfather was clear about this."

"Why not?"

"I imagine, knowing him," Dick said smoothly, "he wanted you to enjoy the place without worry."

"For Christ's sake," Henry groaned. "We're not children."

Dick Sherman made no reply.

"Now give us the bad news," Min joked. "What are the annual costs?"

The lawyer slid a sheet of paper out a folder, checked it, and answered, "About a hundred thousand a year. Give or take."

No one spoke. That was serious money.

"Can you elaborate on that number?" Henry asked dryly.

"You've got the costs on the houses, the boats — and your caretaker. Roughly twenty thousand for each of you."

"We all have that much, certainly," Henry

392

prompted, it seemed to Evie, a little gleefully.

"Not for this." Min shook her head.

"It's a stretch," Shep said.

Evie didn't answer. It wasn't realistic, but it was *almost* affordable.

Dick Sherman folded his arms and leaned on the table.

"If we decided to sell the whole place now — this year," Harriet said, "would we get whatever is in the trust, plus the proceeds of the Island?"

"Correct."

"How much?" Harriet asked.

"A conservative estimate?" Sherman considered. "I'd place it at three and a half million."

Harriet sat back in her chair.

With rising alarm, Evie sat forward. "But we're not thinking of selling."

"This is precisely why your grandparents wished you to meet." Dick Sherman looked at her. "And I have to remind you that whatever decision you do come to, the will says you must come to it unanimously. I'm afraid there can't be a sale unless all five of you agree."

"But we have until next year before the money runs dry." Shep tapped his fingers on the table.

"Why wait until the money runs dry?" Harriet pressed. "If we are going to lose it anyway, why not sell now — we'd each get at least half a million dollars. If we wait until the money runs out, we might end up *paying* for it while it's on the market; then we'd only get —"

"The Island," Evie broke in. "We'd get the Island for another year, and we'd gain time to figure out whether we can hold on to it."

The cousins were quiet, considering.

"Okay, so where are we?" Harriet asked. "What should we do?"

"Well, clearly, we shouldn't make a decision right now," Shep countered. "Isn't that the point of this meeting? Pops and Granny K wanted us to start thinking, that's all."

The mention of their grandparents calmed the waters somewhat, and there was an almost imperceptible settling in the room. Shep looked across the table and smiled at Evie, marking her, she realized with a start, as an ally in the as-yet-unnamed battle ahead.

"Can we buy some time?" he asked. "Rent the Island?"

Harriet grimaced but said nothing.

"Sounds like an awful lot of work," Henry put in. "And I'll bet the insurance on the boats would run steep."

"It's a great idea, Shep," Evie said. "It gives us some wiggle room, anyway."

"Delays the inevitable," Henry drawled.

"Nothing is inevitable," Shep retorted.

"Making a plan is inevitable." Henry shook his head at his brother and turned to Evie.

"Now might as well be the time to bring up your issue."

The band across her chest that had been tightening all through the meeting swelled now so she could hardly breathe.

"And what is that?" Dick Sherman asked.

"Mum wanted her ashes buried at the end of the picnic grounds," Evie said.

"Which might get in the way of *my* mother's plan to help us with our costs," Henry explained.

Dick shrugged, looking at Evie. "That should be fine. There is nothing in the state mandate that prevents a burial on private property."

She flashed a grateful smile at the lawyer.

"Aren't I right, Dick," Henry said, "that *all* the owners need to agree about something like that?"

Evie turned to look at Henry, sitting at the end of the table.

"Shut up, Henry," Min said swiftly.

"Bear with me here, Dick. We were talking about selling a portion of the Island, a small portion. And Joan's wishes might scotch a sale." He was stubborn. "A sale we might need. A sale that might help us to pay for the Island — to keep it." He looked at Evie. "That's all. We ought to think about that. *I* am thinking of the long term."

She looked back at him, speechless.

"Be that as it may . . ." Dick Sherman

cleared his throat carefully. "In the short term, Shepherd's idea might be realizable."

They all looked up.

"I've been approached by a man about whether he might rent the property sometime late in the month of August, perhaps the week before Labor Day —"

"It's not a property." Evie couldn't keep herself from interrupting. "It's the Island."

"Apparently he was sailing by at the beginning of the summer. Passed the place with some friends."

"What's his name?" Shep asked.

"He's a banker up in Boston, I don't think you'd know him."

"What's his name?" Shep asked again.

"Charles Levy."

"*Charlie* Levy?" Min said. "How old is he?"

"About your age, I should think."

"Did he go to Harvard?"

"I don't know," Dick admitted.

"If it's who I think it is, he was in my class." She turned to the table and grinned. "Granny K would die."

"Why?"

Min paused, clearly relishing the news. "Well, he's new money." She was ironic. "And Jewish."

"But clearly he *has* money," Harriet said.

"Oh yes," Min answered dryly. "Pots."

"Why don't we sell *him* the picnic grounds, then — kill two birds with one stone," Harriet suggested, a little smile playing on her lips. "Assuming he falls in love with the place."

She looked around, satisfied. "As everyone always does."

"I doubt he'd want it. It takes a certain kind of person — he may not even know how to sail," Henry pointed out.

"A certain kind of person?" Min asked.

"Aren't we getting ahead of ourselves?" Shep put in. "We don't have to decide all this now."

"We should, though." Henry shook his head, turning to Evie. "I'll agree to Aunt Joan's burial at the picnic grounds on the condition that you consider Mum's idea to sell that portion, next year."

"Henry, don't be an asshole," Shep said.

Henry didn't look at Shep.

"Evie, be realistic."

"To sell the part where Mum wants her ashes to be buried? To a stranger? Who has no idea what it means? To us — at all?"

"If Levy buys it, he might not care if Aunt Joan is outside the graveyard," Harriet said. "He's Jewish, isn't he?"

Paying no attention to his younger sister, Henry folded his arms and leaned them on the table, looking at Evie. "What are you going to do?"

Evie looked at him, and took in a great

breath and stood up. "Nothing at the moment."

"Damn it, Evie —"

"Are we finished?" Evie looked up at Dick Sherman.

"There's one more thing," he said.

The gravity in his voice sank Evie back down in her chair.

The five of them watched as he retrieved a familiar moss green envelope from the folder in front of him, which Evie recognized with a pang as her grandmother's Merrimade stationery.

He slid a single sheet of paper out of the envelope, and read: " 'After all, Evie may be right. What's past can be revised. I should like Moss's share of Crockett's Island to go to Mr. Reginald Pauling, of New York City, as he wished.' "

Dick Sherman pulled off his glasses. "And it is signed, Katherine Houghton Milton."

All eyes turned to Evie, who sat there stunned.

"Who the hell is Reginald Pauling?" Henry exploded into the silence.

"You told Granny K to give it away?" Shep asked.

"No," she protested. "I have no idea what she's talking about."

"Granny K wrote this?"

The lawyer nodded and reached forward and handed Min the piece of paper. Evie leaned over. It was a scribbled note, but it was clearly her grandmother's handwriting, and it was dated the year she died, 1988.

"It's in pencil." Henry was standing behind them. "It's not legal if it's in pencil. Is it legal?"

"Well," said Dick Sherman carefully, "it's a request, not legally binding, but her wishes are clear."

"This makes no sense whatsoever," Shep declared. "Pops would never have given away some of Crockett's. Why would Granny K?"

"It's Uncle Moss who wanted to give it away. It was his share."

"Wasn't Uncle Moss a little unhinged?"

"Moss?" Dick Sherman turned in his chair and looked at Shep sternly. "Not in the slightest."

"Did Mum and Aunt Evelyn know about this?" Evie asked.

"Not as far as I know."

They were quiet.

"But who the hell is Pauling?" Henry asked again. "Is he still alive?"

"We'd need to ascertain that," Dick Sherman answered.

"So the whole thing was never fully ours." Harriet spoke up. "All this time."

"Yes, it was. It is — it still is," insisted Henry. "It's up to us to *consider,* as Granny K said."

"No." Harriet laughed. "No, it never was

fully ours. It wasn't meant to be ours to begin with."

"How is that funny?" Henry snapped.

His youngest sister widened her eyes at him. "It just is, Henry."

Henry shook his head in disgust.

"Today's meeting might be an opportunity," Sherman said carefully, "for you to begin to decide if you wish to honor your grandmother's wish."

"Why *should* we honor it?" Henry shook his head. "Do we need to even tell him?"

"Granny K wanted us to do it," Min retorted.

"But are we required to do this? Look at the language, 'I should like' —"

"It's not up to us to parse like that, Henry."

"Crockett's is ours. It's ours to take on, and to run. Not someone else's. If we bring somebody in — some other person, it will —"

"Cheapen it?" Harriet said quietly.

"Don't twist my words." Henry flushed. "I refuse to be the agent that resolves some inscrutable issue of my grandparents' generation. Why should I? Why should we? What about our own children? What about the next generation?"

"When one has," Harriet said, standing up, *"one gives.* Isn't that what we were taught, Henry? Isn't that what we ought to remember?"

"Not an island," Henry protested. "Not the *Island*. I mean, who *is* this guy? We can't just give it away. It's worth millions."

"Millions we don't have," Min pointed out. "If you recall. Money."

"But it's not *about* the money," Evie burst out. "It's never been about the money. It's the place. It's our place. Our *place*" — she looked at her cousins — "and our mothers' place, and all our children's, too."

"All right." Min shook her head. "But the fact remains that we could still use the money from a renter. So what should we do? Offer two weeks to Charlie Levy? We'd need to get the house ready for him, if so."

"I'll go," said Evie swiftly. "I can do that."

"That's all right," said Min. "You're teaching, aren't you? I took the next two weeks off. I can do it."

"We'll do it together." Evie was firm. "It's the Fourth of July break next week, and both of us should be up there."

Min opened her mouth and then thought better of it and nodded.

"And what about Mr. Pauling?" Dick Sherman asked.

Evie and Henry looked at each other. Harriet rolled her eyes and looked down at her hands. Min and Shep were quiet.

"It's a moot point at the moment," Evie finally said, "isn't it? We don't even know if we can hold on to the Island ourselves."

"I think we do nothing," Henry said slowly. "For now. We wait. We *consider* what to do."

The lawyer looked round the table. Slowly, each of them nodded.

"Agreed."

"Very well." Dick Sherman rose to his feet, signaling the meeting's close.

It was raining when the meeting broke up, in the hard bursts of early summer that forced a quick think. Wait it out under an awning, or make a dash for a taxi and risk getting soaked? Evie took furious satisfaction in the fact that she lived at this end of Manhattan; she could and would walk. It made her feel somehow better than the rest of them. Walking, getting soaked, and not minding — smiling as she waved goodbye — proved something. Her grandmother had routinely pooh-poohed the rain. Turned a deaf ear to complaint of any kind. It was weak. Weak to suggest one put on a raincoat, weak to wonder whether one ought to wait it out. And weakest of all to look miserable.

The luggage shops along this block had thrown plastic down over the suitcases and the shop owners had all retreated just inside their doorways, where they stood, smoking, framed by the warm light of the deeper interiors, cozy, calling to one another over the rain in Cantonese. No one walked as she did straight down the block into the pelting rain. It may, in fact, have started to rain even harder. Her shoes were sopping wet.

The light turned green, tripping the next one, then the next, all the way up Broadway as far as Evie could see. The rain poured down and the dark stone of the buildings was punctuated by windows in which the lights of an office, a studio, the smaller lamp of someone's apartment glowed and shivered.

"Paul!" Evie shoved open the apartment door. "Paul? Are you home?" She started pulling off her clothes right where she stood, dripping onto the front mat. "Paul?"

He came around the door of his study. "Hey," he said, his eyes widening. She had stripped off her shirt.

"What's happening? What's wrong?"

"The Island," she said. And peeled her skirt off her wet legs and kicked at it to get free. "It's —" She walked past him in her bra and underwear into her study. "Hang on."

She reached for the photograph of her mother and her aunt and snatched it down.

"Evie?"

She stared at the two of them. And turned away, unable to think straight, nearly walking into Paul, who was standing in the doorway.

"Evie?"

"I can't," she muttered. "I can't —"

Shivering, she made for their bedroom and pulled on the top drawer of the bureau. It wouldn't budge. It was sticking in the humid-

403

ity. She pulled again. And then, defeated, turned and yanked open the closet door. Caged, in great distress, she batted from one place to the next.

"Stop." Paul was sharp. "Stop it, Evie. What's going on?"

"The Island," she said, and pulled a sweatshirt from the shelf.

"What? What's happened?"

She couldn't think straight. Which part was the worst?

"Henry wants to sell the land around the picnic grounds."

"Okay," Paul said again.

"It's not okay. That's where Mum wants her ashes."

"Right."

"Henry made me agree to consider the sale."

"How?"

"By making Mum's burial there contingent."

Paul was quiet.

"There's more." Evie looked away. "It's worse than that. It's not even ours anymore."

"What?"

"The Island."

"What do you mean? How? Why?"

"I don't *know*," she said again, desperate to move, to fly straight there. To erase time and distance and step off the boat onto the dock, to check it, to see that it wasn't going. It couldn't be going.

"Hold on."

"I've got to go." She looked at him, pleading. "Paul."

"Stop, Evie." He followed her back into the kitchen, where she opened the fridge and closed it without looking in. Then opened it again.

"It's not going anywhere." He put his hand on her wrist and pushed the fridge door closed.

"It is," she said fiercely. "We are going to lose it, lose what it is right now. Lose the place as we know it. As Seth knows it. It's going to change."

She paused. Her throat closed over. The tears welled up and she shook her head.

"Okay," he said, "come here." And he pulled her to him, wrapping his arms around her. She stood against him, his heart beating slow and strong on the other side of his shirt. She wanted to be calmed. She wanted to stand there and be drawn to that slow, tamed beat and be soothed.

Framed and hung on the wall behind Paul's head was the child's map she had drawn with her grandfather of the eight trails lacing Crockett's Island. He had helped her trace the outline of the Island from the map. He had encouraged her to memorize the angles of the coves, the colors of the trailhead markers, the thick inland forest and its rooted paths. He had nodded when she'd finished it and shown him. He had smiled. As if it were hers, as if it would always be hers.

"Tell me." She felt Paul's voice through her chest. "What happened at Dick Sherman's?"

"Granny K wants us to give away Uncle Moss's share of the Island."

"Give it away to whom?"

Evie shook her head. "No one I've ever heard of. Someone named Reginald Pauling. And apparently, *I* told her to do it."

"Reginald Pauling?" He looked at her, incredulous. "*Reg* Pauling? The writer?"

"What writer?"

"If it's the one I'm thinking of, he wrote for *The Village Voice* in the fifties and sixties — an African American. He was associated with Baldwin."

"That's impossible," Evie said. "Granny K would never have even crossed paths with a black man."

She could see his brain seizing hold of the idea, she could see the excitement, and it sparked the fuse. It was too ludicrous, and she didn't want to give him the satisfaction of some kind of literary detective story.

"Don't," she thrust. "This isn't some story. This is Mum. This is the Island."

"But —"

"But then, you don't care, do you? We are laughable for holding on to it, pathetic, and privileged, and *blind.*"

"Evie."

She heard the warning, but she kept going, now almost gleeful in her need to hurl it back at him.

"You said that, Paul." Her voice rose. "You said it right out there —" She pointed. *"Let it go."*

He didn't move.

"You see stick figures when you think of my family. Stick figures and cutouts. You see *Chekhov,* for fuck's sake. Or *Nazis."*

She paused, her mind spinning, the anger a dervish in her head.

"Go ahead," he said quietly. "Light the match. Burn it down."

She looked at him, the rage so high, she couldn't speak. She did want to burn it all down; she wanted to toss the match and watch it explode and have it all be done. All of this, the uncertainty, the confusion. The sorrow.

"We have always been a joke to you, haven't we?"

"That's it," he said quietly, and pushed away from the counter. "I'm done."

"You're done. Done with what?"

"For a year now, I've been listening to this — for a year? No, for longer than a year. For our lives. I've listened to you fight the Miltons, be the Miltons, love the Miltons, use the Miltons, and I was just one stick shy of the fire; I was not a Milton — and that was good, that was great — I was first-generation, a Jew with a father who listened to opera after he came home from the office. I've watched you, I've listened to you, and now you're leaving — you've somehow figured out that I was the worm in the apple all along — how? How the hell did that happen — I don't know.

"And you know what?" He shook his head in a kind of stupefied amazement. "For the first time, I don't care. I don't give a rat's ass."

They stared at each other.

"Did we lose something?" Evie asked finally. "Or did the world just catch up with us?"

"Who's 'we,' Evie?" he said quietly. "What are we talking about here?"

The gap between them opened, the silence shrouding them. Paul looked at her, waiting. She could choose to put a tear in the shroud right then. She could rip a hole in it.

"The Island. My cousins."

Disappointment flickered and faded on his face. He crossed his arms.

"Without it — we vanish," she said.

He stepped toward her, his eyes on her face. "You don't, Evie. It's an idea you have. It's the mythology. And I'm so goddamned tired of it."

He walked past her into the hall.

"Paul."

He stopped. "I'm right here."

But she had run out of air, and fire. There

was nothing to fight for, anyway.

"It doesn't matter, does it?" he said quietly. "At some point, you have to want what you have."

"I have to go. I have to see —"

"What?" He waited, his body tense, barely able to stand still, holding himself, she could see, lidding his own anger.

What indeed? The silence between them just then was windy and vast.

"What's there," she finished.

■ ■ ■ ■

THE ISLAND

■ ■ ■ ■

Twenty-Six

It was the same. The rocks and the slap of the tide, the high blue sky and the smell of wet wood in the boathouse, the same as Kitty emerged onto the bright green lawn, sloping up to the Big House. The house. The lawn. There before her was the obelisk of Crockett's gravestone, the crooked ridge of spruce behind the house, and the place, opened up to them, as on that first day. She and Ogden standing, just like this, at the bottom of the lawn, watching Dunc and Priss move forward up the hill. Years ago. Years and years, what did they matter? Time folded and refolded itself here like a shirt.

Ogden's arm stole around her shoulder.

"Yes," she said to what she knew he was thinking.

"Poor Priss," she said, looking at the empty spot in front of the house where the two of them had stood that afternoon.

He drew her closer. The sun was hot on her skin. It was midday. A dragonfly clacked in the air just past her ear. She patted Ogden's hand on her shoulder, and the two of them started up the hill.

The irises had gone leggy in the rock garden. The rosa rugosa had budded out, the pink flowers bursting from their smooth green hips and scenting the air with what Kitty always felt to be the smell of summer. Ogden went around the side of the house. Arriving at the granite stoop, she pulled the bough of the lilac toward her, burying her face in its rich purple, and then, knowing what awaited her, she turned.

The lawn stretched to the boathouse, and there stood Dunc and Priss. And there beside them stood Elsa in her skirt and cardigan. There down the hill rolled Willy, his laughter rocketing through the air. There they stood at the bottom of the lawn, as they stood every year, though Elsa had been dead all this time. Kitty's grip tightened on the bough. And Willy? Had he survived? The bright shining blade that held her up inside, the imagined core, bowed as the question found its way in, and bent and crumpled under it — a tarnish on the shine. But how could she have known? How could any of them have known what was coming? She stared at the place where the mother and the child had stood, a dark spot she'd have to walk around, a funeral in her brain she must attend now, alone. One must simply live with that. One does the best one can.

Same as Neddy. Kitty let the bough go.

The house had been swept and polished. The surfaces of the table in the kitchen and the long table in the dining room gleamed. There was a fresh coat of paint on the floorboards in the hall, and the rag rugs were tossed down at sharp right angles. Mrs. Ames had left milk and butter and eggs in the icebox. There was a fresh loaf of bread in the box, and wooden matches had been set beside the stove.

Hullo, old house, Kitty addressed the room, the chairs, the familiar hump of the granite rock out the kitchen window. She reached for a match, bent, and lit the pilot light. They were here now. Back. Again. Out the window, Ogden was already halfway up the hill to examine the new shingled patch on the lee side of the barn. Above his head an osprey soared.

Walking through to the front rooms, she took it to herself again. As she did each year. There was the chair she and Ogden had found in the little shop in Damariscotta, there were the two lamps Aunt Alice had given her after Uncle William died. Kitty had meant to switch them all these years, and then Aunt Alice died, and so they stayed. Here was the round hooked rug, a farmhouse rug, all the wrong colors, but Ogden loved it. Why? It irritated her every year, the round dull rug.

She climbed the steep stairs to the second floor and passed along the hall where the bedrooms stretched one after the other, the pink, the blue, and the yellow, the white doors pushed inward. In every room there were two twin beds, flanking a farmhouse window. Here too the organdy curtains stirred. The salt air breezed with her as she walked, the smell of the sea softened by the deeper damp wood of the old house. At the very end of the hall lay Ogden's and her room, a corner room, the bed situated so that one could lie there and see down to the boathouse and up to the barn, like the flange of a compass, Ogden had remarked.

"Flange?" She had wrinkled her nose.

The room was still. She went to the bureau in the corner, opened the drawer, and pulled out her comb and brush and the hand mirror her mother had given her on her fifteenth birthday. She set them side by side in a row. She sprang the locks on the first of her suitcases and lifted the folded underwear out, ranged neatly on top, and carried it straight to the bureau, sliding it into the top drawer. The suitcase gave its layers up — shirts, trousers, at the very bottom, her boat shoes and a pair of silver slippers. The bureau drawers filled. The sound of Ogden's hammer reached her as she opened his suitcase beside hers, again lifting the layers one by one, packed the day before on Long Island, and slid them into the other half of the bureau drawers.

In the closet, their Island clothes hung, embalmed in cedar. She swung the door slowly back and forth on its hinges like a fan to let the sea air break the winter hanging there.

Then she did what she did, had done, every night of their married life. She laid out the clothes for the evening. She pulled a full skirt off its hanger in the closet and a blouse from the bureau and laid them out on the bed. Beside them she laid a clean shirt for Ogden and his gray flannel trousers. They stretched the width of the bed, his trousers hanging just off the edge. She bent and fingered the sleeve of Ogden's shirt and then stretched it across the bedspread so that it touched the skirt, just there at the hip. Just there. She crossed her arms and stared down at the cloth couple. Kitty and Ogden Milton.

When the screen door clapped, Ogden turned from the ladder and saw Kitty striding out the kitchen door with her basket and her clippers, intent on gathering the first bayberry for the dining room table.

"Look who's turned up on the early boat," Ogden called the following morning, pushing the wheelbarrow piled with groceries and Joan's two suitcases out onto the grass.

Kitty lowered her arm. "What a nice surprise."

Ogden started up the lawn, Joan following slowly. Kitty remained where she stood, framed by the door and the tree. In her striped cotton blouse tucked into high-waisted dungarees, her silver hair pulled back in two neat combs, she appeared to her daughter to belong even more to this house and this place, though it was only for two months of the year, than to the whitewashed brick and circular driveway down in Oyster Bay. And even as she walked toward it, the daughter took this image of the mother and made swift corrections, tiny adjustments — she too would be the spirit of the place, but she'd come down the hill to meet her guests, she would fling her arms wide. She smiled.

"Hello, Mum."

"Good trip?"

Ogden kept on going around the front of the house with the wheelbarrow to the kitchen door at the back. Joan nodded and stepped up to kiss her mother on the cheek. Kitty patted her shoulder.

"Where's your brother?"

"You didn't get a message?"

"No." Kitty frowned. "What message?"

"He missed the train. Something about working late. He'll be here tomorrow."

"He'll miss our day with the Pratts, then."

Her mother's beauty, Joan realized, watching the annoyance cross over her face, relied on laughter. "It's all right, they see him in the city all the time."

"Yes, but I particularly wanted him to be here for tonight's supper — it's just our two families tonight."

"It's all right, Mum," Joan said again.

"Kitty!" Joan's father called her mother from inside the house. "Where is the — ?"

"Well, never mind." Kitty turned to go.

"I brought some samples for the chair up with me," Joan offered. "Some lovely blues, and a stripe."

Kitty shook her head. "No, a stripe won't do in that room."

"Evelyn had thought a stripe."

Something was different about Joan, Kitty thought. There was something new. "For the front room?"

"Well, I know." Joanie followed her mother into the house and into the small front room whose windows faced out to the sea. She popped the clasp on her purse and drew out the envelope of swatches cut by Mrs. Miller down at Brunschwig. It was clear the stripe was wrong as soon as she laid it on the back of the chair, but the small bluebells against a cream background were perfect. "What do you think?"

"Kitty?" Ogden Milton called again, and both women could hear the impatience this time.

"Coming." Kitty pointed at the bluebells, then looked at Joan. "I've put you and Anne in the pink bedroom."

Joan nodded. "When do they all get here?"

"Any minute. All right, Ogden!" she called. "I'm coming!"

Joan reached and pulled the stripe off the chair, leaving the bluebells lying along the top, gratified. It had been worth the race through the heat yesterday to get to Brunschwig before closing, and now with the room around her, and just outside the sea and sky, she saw how naturally the wish to adorn this place, to keep it and make it shine was part of her, would be part of her. Behind, her mother's brisk footsteps echoed through the house toward her father, followed by his exclamation, which she couldn't catch.

Joan wandered back outside, followed by the thwack of the screen door. Not a boat moved along the tide in front of her or crossed out into the open from one of the coves. She moved out of the shadow of the house into the sunny patch of lawn and lay down flat on her back, drifting into the quiet. The place buzzed and droned in the sun.

No matter how old she grew, up here the general order of things never shifted. On and on. Nothing ever changed. Sunlight. Twilight. Drinks on the dock. A cardigan sweater thrown over a chair. And though the tumult of the city, the confusion and the excitement that reached her at her desk, came through her very fingertips and out through her smile into the world she was running to join, she belonged to this spot. Here, the girl with the shakes, Miss Milton at the typewriter, Joan Milton holding Len Levy's hand on the street, fell away. Up here the whole question of marriage, whether she could, what she wasn't, needn't come up. Here she was single, clear, her father's daughter. Joan Milton, the keeper of this place.

"Joanie!"

She rolled over and pushed up on her elbow and saw her sister standing in the frame of the boathouse door, waving once before she turned, vanishing back into the dark interior. Evelyn had insisted on traveling up with Dickie and his mother and father and sister, Anne — as though she were already a Pratt.

Slowly Joan got onto her feet.

A peal of surprised laughter burst from down the hill, and Joan halted as she saw Dickie grinning ear to ear, carrying Evelyn in his arms and pretending to take a giant step over the threshold of the boathouse onto the sunny lawn.

"Put me down, you great dope," Evelyn cried, squirming and laughing. "You have to wait."

Dickie hugged her closer to his chest, the big Yale lineman carrying Evelyn as if she were firewood. Behind them, the shadows of his family gathered and emerged past the couple.

"Hullo, Joanie!" Anne Pratt waved at Joan.

Dickie dropped Evelyn on the grass, having carried her over the threshold of what was not *their* house, thought Joan fleetingly, but never mind, and she walked down to the merry group with a smile on her face.

"Hello, Joan." Mr. Pratt reached a hand toward her.

"Hello!" She was pulled into his bear hug.

"Hello, dear." Mrs. Pratt smiled. "Take this, will you, Annie?"

Anne Pratt, Joan's roommate from Farmington, rolled her eyes over Joan's shoulder and winked.

"Joanie, take a look at what Dickie brought!" Evelyn cried.

"What?"

"Show her!"

"Hang on," Dickie said as he kissed Joan on the cheek. "Hello."

"It's the most terrific pillow, Joanie — you'll see." Evelyn was already moving up the lawn toward the house. "So precious and funny."

Joan and Anne grabbed the Pratts' duffel bag, a handle in each hand, while Mr. Pratt carried two satchels full of liquor bottles on his shoulders. Dickie swung two suitcases up in his arms, and the pack of them followed Evelyn.

"Hello, Pratts!" Ogden came round from

the back of the house, beaming, his hand outstretched. Kitty followed.

Evelyn ran the rest of the way up the hill and threw her arms around her father, and then, laughing, murmured to her mother and turned and called back to Joan, "Come on, slowpoke, I have to show you —" and disappeared through the front door.

"Lord have mercy," Joan called after her. The delight of her sister was all the flash and patter, the sheer abundant life burst free from the bobbed head and the smile, the great Milton smile, which promised everything but gave away nothing.

"What is it?" she said, letting the door slam behind her.

"This is perfect!" Evelyn said, turning to her with the sample of striped blue fabric in her hand. "It's just right."

Joan frowned, looking for the bluebells.

"Mum and I thought the other."

Evelyn sniffed. "God no, that's as bad as the Lowells."

"I thought it was pretty."

"Yes, but it's so old-fashioned. Let's bring some spirit into the old girl."

"The old girl?"

"Here." Evelyn picked up the pillow that Dickie evidently had bought. "Look — isn't it darling?"

Across a field of bold red stripes had been embroidered the phrase *Reader, I married him.*

Joan only smiled.

"You see why we have to go with the blue stripes now, don't you?"

Joan looked at her sister. "To match Dickie's pillow?"

For the first time Evelyn heard the trouble in Joan's voice. "Yes, Joanie. To make him feel welcome. To make him feel like the place is his."

"His?"

"Don't be an old stick-in-the-mud; you know what I mean."

"I'm not an old stick-in-the-mud."

"Joanie."

For an answer, Joan reached across her sister and very carefully retrieved the bluebell swatch and placed it along the back of the chair, then turned around and walked out of the room.

"Oh, for god's sake, Joan," Evelyn sighed behind her.

There was lunch on the lawn in the front of the house and a sail on the *Sheila* in the long afternoon. Roger Pratt napped in the shade. There was the *pock* of tennis balls hit across the cove on the court, and old Mrs. Hunnicutt arrived with her boatman for tea. Croquet was set up on the flat spot by the dock and the *whack* of a wooden ball hit too hard floated up to the house spun with protests and laughter. They were a comfortable group,

424

the Pratts and the Miltons, joined as they had been by Anne and Joan's friendship at boarding school, and now even more resolutely by the young couple and by the bringing in of Dickie to Milton Higginson. The day unfurled slowly, as lightly as one of Kitty's irises, the hot drive up, the city forgotten, all of it peeled off them, so that by the end of the afternoon, they had fully arrived. The Island held them all in its hand, Kitty thought, sitting on the green bench in front of the house and shelling peas for dinner.

The prow of a lobster boat coming from the mainland crossed out of the sun in the middle of the Narrows and into the cooler dark of the shadowed cove.

"There," Kitty said from where she sat on the bench, as Ogden came round the side of the house with a pair of clippers and a saw, "that must be Priss."

He nodded. "That's all of us now."

Or almost all, she thought, and stood up.

"Hullo!" She waved as Priss appeared in the boathouse doorway in an enormous purple sunhat, carrying two small bags in either hand and making her way slowly up the hill.

"Leave your luggage," Ogden called to her. "I'll come down and get it later — Joan." He held up the clippers. "Let's get to the trail down to the picnic grounds before tonight."

"All right." She pushed herself up off the

lawn, coming to stand beside her father and mother as Priss arrived at the top of the hill, dewy with the exertion, smelling faintly of bourbon.

"All in one piece?" Ogden smiled down.

"Hullo, Priss." Kitty kissed her.

"Hello, Miltons." Priss kissed them both.

"Hello, Pratts," she said brightly to Sarah and Roger coming round the corner of the house.

"Hello, Evelyn. And Dickie, hello! Hello, Joan dear."

"Come in." Kitty patted Priss on the shoulder. "I've put you downstairs."

"Come on." Ogden looked at Joan. And she took the clippers from her father and followed him into the woods.

They went at the trail in silence, clipping branches and sawing boughs and dragging the brush farther into the woods, clearing the path of what the winter had wracked, the winds and furies of January raging through these same trees. Snow in here where they only knew rain, or fog, or the single shafts of sun stretched across the deep green. They worked together as the two of them always had, with a patience and a memory restoring the path of the previous summer, clear from the dock to the rocks at the edge of the picnic grounds, where dinner would be tomorrow night. Distantly the foghorn in the Thoroughfare moaned. A woodpecker worked away high above their heads, his sound like corks popped from bottles, *pock pock pock.*

Ogden reached up, testing the limbs of the tree that had been hit by lightning and now leaned across the path in front of them.

The clippers snapped the wood, and the bough fell with a soft thud into the moss at his feet.

She dragged it off. Her father lifted the clippers to the next. The branch fell. Ogden threw it to the side of the path and straightened, looking through the cleared brush to the water. He seemed far away.

"Dad?"

He turned. "One is never enough, Joanie. It's never enough."

"What isn't?"

He looked at her. "When you are young you think you can change the world — make it over, straighten it out. I did — your godfather, Dunc, did too."

She waited. She couldn't make out what he was telling her.

He looked back out at the water. "But the world doesn't change; only you do. And then you are left with the places that remind you —"

He toed at a mushroom on the side of the path, looking down at the moss.

"Damn it, Joanie." He was soft. "Dunc should be here."

Joan glanced at him in surprise.

"I thought he was coming?"

"He's not feeling himself." Ogden put down the clippers and slid the curved saw out of its leather casing, setting the teeth on the biggest bottom branch. "Priss phoned last night."

Wordless, Joan went to hold the branch steady as Ogden drew the blade back and forth. The branch cracked, and she leaned on it as her father sawed. It cracked further and then snapped off in her hand. She turned and tossed it into the brush behind her. Her father put his saw on the next big limb and looked up, and she moved to stand across from him, her hand on the wood to put the pressure where it was needed. He drew the saw once across to mark the line and then went at it, his arms working in a steady even rhythm, his chin and cheek all she could see under the visored hat.

How she loved him, she felt, standing there waiting for the tree to split. He stood for the good; he was everything good. She moved her hand farther down the limb.

After a few minutes, the limb fell. Joan bent and dragged it off the path and into the brush.

"You know, Dad," she said, coming back to stand beside him. "Up here, on the Island, is the only place I ever want to be."

"Isn't that funny." Ogden smiled. "It's just what I'd say myself."

She nodded at him. "And you can count on me. I'll take care of it. I won't let the place down."

Ogden turned around and looked at her, clearly moved.

"You are a good soul, Joan Milton," he said gruffly. "But don't make promises you can't keep."

She lifted her chin. "But that's one I can keep."

Ogden shook his head, though he smiled. "You'll have your husband to consider."

"My *husband*?"

"He may not want to have anything to do with the place," Ogden pointed out.

Joan flushed. "But I may not marry."

"Don't say that, Joan. I'm sure you will." Ogden looked at her seriously. "I hope you do."

"What about my —"

"It shouldn't matter." Her father shook his head. "You haven't had a seizure in years. What the doctors said at the time has been borne out, hasn't it? The medicine is working."

She didn't answer.

"*If* I ever marry," she finally said, "it will have to be someone who will love this" — she nodded at the trees — "*all* of this, as much as I do."

Ogden considered her a minute, then broke into a smile.

"That's the stuff," he said as the kitchen bell rang from the house, a distant clang through the trees.

TWENTY-SEVEN

"Grab that, will you, dear?"

Jimmy Ames pointed to the bumper on the stern, and Evie tossed it over the side as he brought the *Katherine* smoothly into the dock, the bumpers nudging them back from the wooden edge. He cut the engine, and the sudden quiet tightened the evening into parts: the stark angle of the boathouse roof, light on the water splashing the granite rocks as the boat's wake shuttled in, shuttled out. Evie stood in the stern, staring up past the boathouse, where the great green lawn stretched to the Big House perched on its granite foundations on the hill overlooking the cove of Crockett's Island. Granny K's green bench sat beneath the front windows, and on either side the white wooden slat-back chairs with the arms wide enough for a book laid out flat. The high corner of the oldest Crockett's gravestone poked up to the left of the house over the shoulder of the hilly field of timothy grass. The flag blew a straight

431

rectangle at right angles to its pole.

No matter that she arrived just like this, every summer, year after year, there was always this moment when she felt that she had cheated time, that this was the place on earth that unfolded and opened, bending toward her and saying, *Child.* Standing there in the boat, looking up at the house, she felt the hand of the place; the sky and the water retook her. She forgot this moment as soon as she left the place, and then always, on the return, there it was, there she was. Here, like nowhere else, she belonged.

The first time Evie had brought Paul to the Island, twenty-five years ago, their books, bathing suits, and some sweaters crammed into duffel bags, they had rounded the point, and when it sprang free and separate on the water, the line of spruce trees arching into the sky, Evie couldn't deny the flush of pride. *See that,* she would never have said aloud, but felt — *see that, that is mine. I am that.* And the picture of the two of them, in the stern of her family's boat ferried by Jimmy Ames, their caretaker, unimaginable to Paul's family, like something out of a postcard, also made her proud. Look what she could bring him. An island in Maine. Look what she could offer, her hands full.

"So," he had teased. "This is your 'little old place'?"

"Come on." She smiled. "Admit it. It's

beautiful."

He slid his hand around her waist. "Of course it's beautiful."

But now, twenty-five years later, it was Paul's words in her head as Jimmy and she stood in the stern of the *Katherine* looking up at the "little old place."

"Same as always," Jimmy commented in the silence. A heron lifted from the rocks beside the boathouse.

Evie nodded at him. But it wasn't the same. It wasn't at all the same.

"When is your cousin due in?" Jimmy pulled her bags out of the hold and slid them down the boat deck toward Evie.

"End of the week."

"So you've got a little time on your own, then."

"That's right." She smiled at him. "I thought I'd clear out some of the closets, get ready for this guy."

"He sounds nice enough."

"A stranger renting Crockett's? Granny K would turn over in her grave."

Jimmy hoisted himself up and over onto the dock. "She might have surprised you."

Well, yes, thought Evie, *she certainly has.* She looked away.

"Will Min come in the same time as you?"

"I don't know what she's doing." Evie tried to keep her voice neutral. "She ought to call you."

"Just like her mother," he chuckled. "Keeps us all on our toes."

"It would be nice if she let people know what she's planning."

"Sure." He whistled appreciatively. "Sure it would."

The first wave of annoyance washed over Evie. Just like Aunt E, Min was going to be given a free pass by Jimmy, showing up and simply expecting to be taken care of, to be driven. As if Jimmy worked for her alone.

They piled her two duffels, the boxes of groceries, and her laptop into the back of the tractor, and Jimmy pulled away. Evie followed slowly, her eye on the house looming above him.

When she was alive, her grandmother would climb to her feet, holding on to the branch of the lilac by the front door for balance, and stand there, watching as her children and grandchildren walked up the lawn to her. Every summer, no matter how many times they'd seen her throughout the winter, or even just weeks ago in the spring — it was this veil of scrutiny, this gaze that they all passed through that seemed to mark the beginning of the year. How you appeared to her on that day, the first day, was who you would remain.

"You've put on weight," she'd say, eyeing Evie. "What's happened to your hair?"

"Aren't you sleeping, then?" she'd ask Joan,

though her voice was softer, always softer, with her.

And Evie's mother would tilt her head to the side and say nothing, leaning forward to kiss her mother's cheek. Silence had been Joan's weapon and her shield, though Evie hadn't understood the difference until well into her forties.

Her mother was all around her now as the tractor climbed in low gear up the hill toward the Big House door her grandmother had vanished from twenty years ago.

Jimmy rolled in a wide semicircle and parked the tractor to the left of the steps. He kept the engine running and slid off the seat, reaching for the luggage and walking it up to the top of the stairs, where he left it for Evie to carry the rest of the way in. She was one of the grandchildren, after all. Not her grandmother, her mother, or her aunt, whose bags he would have carried all the way up the stairs to their rooms.

"Need anything?"

She looked up at the house from the bottom of the steps, the box of groceries in her arms, then turned around to him and shook her head. The paint around the front door was peeling, and the green bench where Granny K had poured tea, watched capture the flag, and waited for picnickers to come up the lawn tilted dangerously backward on a rotten leg. The lilac's dead wood had grown so dense it blocked the outside light. Evie reached for the handle of the screen door and noticed Jimmy had filled the pot on the granite step below the door with geraniums, like lipstick on a dowager. Someone else knew how it had looked once, how it was meant to look now.

"It all looks great, Jimmy," she said.

He nodded. "It made it through. Hard winter."

He had stopped at the bottom of the steps, facing the water, and she turned around beside him, trying to think what else to say. Though the sweep of the lawn, the late afternoon draped golden on the great rocks either side of the boathouse was what there was to say.

"Will you need the boat tomorrow?" Jimmy asked.

"No," she said. "I'm all set."

"I'll be going into town, then, to pick up the inspector."

"Inspector?"

"You can't make any changes without calling in the state these days — even minor ones."

Evie looked at him. "What changes?"

"To the boathouse."

"What?"

Jimmy frowned.

"Sorry," Evie said. "Catch me up."

"Your cousin thought a dressing room

down by the dock would be handy."

"Which cousin?"

"Shepherd."

"Shep did? Handy for whom?"

"His passengers, I guess." Jimmy reached for his cigarettes. "Not a bad idea. It's a long way to come all the way up to the house to change or freshen up."

"But . . ." Evie tried to think whether Shep had said anything about this in Dick Sherman's office. "We haven't paid anybody."

"It's all done. He wrote a check."

Did Shep just think because he had paid for it, he could go ahead and make a change like that? Did he expect to get reimbursed?

"It's a good idea." Jimmy bent over his cigarette, cupping his hand around the flame. "You could do with a place to store things while you're out on picnics."

He climbed back up on the tractor and shifted into gear, the growl of the engine his goodbye.

"See you in the morning," she called, and he waved. Sound followed him down the hill, trailing like gulls behind a lobster boat, leaving her standing with the box in her arms, staring after him, the thick, familiar territorial rage rising as she watched Jimmy pull the tractor into the boathouse. Shep's "improvement" was the kind of thing Aunt E would have done, making little changes here and there "because they made sense," catching

437

her mother off guard at the start of every summer, changing the house in her own image, not consulting anyone else, so the hurts and slights of years up here walked hand in hand with the beauty of the place itself. *Don't be ridiculous, Joanie,* Aunt E would say summer after summer. *Don't be a stick-in-the-mud. It's only wallpaper.* Or curtains. A spot of paint. What did it matter? Though of course it mattered terribly to Aunt E, too.

Evie turned around and yanked open the screen door. She needed Paul, she realized standing in the doorway, alone in this house for the first time in her life. He would have been right behind her now, would have heard Jimmy's comments about Shep, about Min, would have walked up the hill with her, carrying his books, and known exactly what those comments meant to her and how they pricked. How Evie's good manners would have triumphed over her outrage, and what not saying anything more to Jimmy had cost. He was the one who'd been beside her all these years, watching, all this time. But their fight had opened a gap between them that was raw and frightening. And she didn't know how to stitch it closed.

"Listen," he'd said as she got in the car that morning, "I've got to nail a draft of this essay down, and then Seth and I will be up Sunday or Monday."

Evie had turned the key in the ignition.

"You don't have to," she said stiffly.

"I want to be there to bury your mother with you," he said quietly. "Of course I do."

She couldn't answer. She stared straight ahead out the window.

"Okay." She nodded and then looked up at him.

"Okay," he said. And patted the open window of the car.

Inside, the hall floor had been freshly painted and the gray boards shone straight back to the dining room, the battleship-gray floors familiar and necessary to the rightness of the place. It was as spare and as pure as a church — about as far from Nazi gold, she decided, as you could get. Here was the front room with Granny K's chair, the china shepherdess on the white mantel, there at the end of the hall was her grandfather's soft-visored sailing hat on its hook. In the kitchen, in the cookbooks, Granny K's script wove in and out of Aunt Fanny Thompson's recipe for oysters in cream, beside William Alfred's Roman punch. It was simply the place they all were. The place they all belonged.

She pulled the Polaroid of her mother and Aunt Evelyn and Uncle Moss standing in front of the house out of her satchel, and leaned it up on the tiny white mantelpiece.

Then Evie walked through the dining room into the kitchen, setting the box of groceries down on the table. The evening sun planed the kitchen linoleum, mopped and clean. She reached to push up the old wooden frame of the kitchen window, having to give it two sharp knocks to loosen it from the winter warp. Slowly it gave, and she smelled the salt air on the breeze.

And why *should* she be ashamed, the protest in her head aimed at Paul continued. Why make a rueful joke out of the place as she always had done? Why not simply say yes. Why not take it on? Even the lies, the handshakes, and the deals he was so certain of. Why not?

Evie turned around and tried to see with the eyes of someone renting, and saw the mismatched kitchen chairs, the spindles broken on some of the backs and taped with silver duct tape, chipped china — Wedgwood or no — and fifteen wineglasses that Evie had never seen before but had clearly been pulled from the attic by Polly. Crystal bowls on squat pedestals, they were shapes from another era, designed to be cupped in the palm of one's hand, taken out onto the green close-cropped lawns of the twenties, where laughter beckoned on a string of pearls. Something her grandmother must have brought up from Long Island.

She touched the rim of one of these. The house, as Paul had said, was still here. Evie turned round and looked through the pantry to the dining room, a woman at the end of a long line of women in a house full of ghosts. Polly Ames had polished the dining room table, and the high backs of the twelve Hitchcock chairs were pushed in and ready, looped one after the other around its polished oval. Through the organdy curtains, the new green grasses waved high in the back field.

The copper vase stood at its usual spot in the center. Granny K used to get off the boat and walk directly up from the dock to the patch of bayberry behind the kitchen and start cutting, her city coat still on. Filling the vase was the first thing she'd do on the Island. The cut bay on the dining room table was the announcement: summer had started. The Miltons had come. Evie walked forward onto the threshold, noticing the organdy curtains were tattered, and two of them were missing their ties. A new yellow stain rippled down the far corner of the dining room wall, the paper buckled and hanging.

Never mind. Evie lifted the empty copper vase from the middle of the table, opening the screen door to the back garden. Never mind.

She grabbed for the rusted scissors hung on the nail by the door and climbed to the top of the hillock behind the house where they all lay. The sky ricocheted blue above her head, filled with the motion of gulls. The humps of granite were so much smaller than

441

in the dream.

Ogden Moss Milton
Nov. 11, 1899–Oct. 4, 1980

Katherine Milton
May 4, 1905–Sept. 10, 1988

Ogden Moss Milton Jr.
March 17, 1930–Aug. 22, 1959

Evelyn Milton Pratt
April 18, 1937–March 24, 2017

She stared down at the names and the dates. The picnic grounds were far from here. *Why, Mum?* She turned.

Bayberry branches scratched her legs as she waded right into the center of the big patch and started cutting the silver-green stalks. An airplane crossed, and she followed its vanishing, soundless above her, into the blue heaven. If her grandmother were looking down, she'd see Evie filling the vase as it had always been filled and approve.

Evie cut an enormous bouquet of bay, jammed it into the mouth of the vase as she backed out of the bushes, and went into the house, the screen door clapping behind her. She set the copper vase in the center of the dining room table, The smell of the cut bay mixed with the salt breeze through the open windows. There. The evening shone and slanted along the wooden surface. The flap of the flag on the breeze beat time.

She was back on the Island, one of the Miltons. Acolyte. Priestess. She would do what had always been done.

And the peace of this place descended, a sense of order that Evie hadn't felt for a long while. There was nothing more to do this evening. No one else to distract her. It was the kind of peace she associated with days in the library stacks, surrounded by scraps of paper, piles of books. Through the old window glass, warmed by sun and waved by age, the lawn down to the boathouse shivered from this angle. The past walked, and had always walked, up and down this green fairway, and she had grown up watching without knowing that she watched. If a historian is trained by hours in a library, the longing to be trained like that, to keep your eyes seeing backward surely comes from the child's watchfulness, the need to chart the family seas, put signs upon the water, divide it up between navies and quadrants and coastal routes and understand the quiet.

In the front room, she shifted the chairs so they tipped slightly toward one another, filling them: Granny K in her Morris chair, her mother sitting opposite in the faded wing-back with the bluebells.

The room waited. Dinner could be in an

hour. Someone could be in the kitchen. The bell outside the back door would ring and pull them, the children — Evie, Min, Shep, Harriet, and Henry — up into the evening hour, pull them from their games, out of books, or from low tide down at the cove. The first bell warned them. The second bell summoned them down to the dock. On the third bell, they knew Granny K had set her Dubonnet on the cocktail tray, walked back up the lawn, and come through to the dining room, taking the head of the table, where she waited for her daughters, their mothers, to come take their places.

TWENTY-EIGHT

By six o'clock, Evelyn had organized them all, and the families wandered through the woods to the natural clearing where Ogden had dug firepits and built benches along an old stone table. At high tide, the grassy spot ran down to the granite boulders and from there to the water in one long, even line. At low tide, the water pulled way out leaving bare the massive granite ledge that lay just below the surface.

Kitty deposited the bowl of nuts and the block of cheddar cheese on its plate and turned around. Ogden was already pouring drinks, and the little party ranged upon the grass. Evelyn had taken Dickie by the hand to walk all the way out to the last boulder, and there they stood, hands clasped, alone for an instant. Kitty remembered that feeling, when the whole world beat in the clasp of your two hands.

She smiled and sought out Ogden, who was laughing with Roger Pratt. Though they were roughly the same age, Ogden seemed much younger, having taken the turn for the better that happened for some men as they aged. The sleeves of his broadcloth shirt were rolled, navy style, revealing arms tanned by work out of doors on the Island — an older man at the height of his power, she thought. A man one approached with a full deck of cards in one's hands, or not at all.

Priss was standing beside the two men, gazing at Ogden with an unprotected wistfulness that cut Kitty to the quick.

Anne and Joan sat against the rock ledge with their knees up, drinking their bourbon in the paper cups Joan had brought from the city. Paper cups made life so much easier, Joan had pointed out to her mother, and when you were done with your drink, you can just toss your cup into the ocean. *Like a Russian,* Joan thought now, tossing hers forward off the rock. It floated away on the outgoing tide, heading for the middle of the Narrows, the channel of water between Crockett's and Vinalhaven, the neighboring island, where, over the years, several friends of the Miltons had bought summer places, among them the Welds, whose dock Joan could just see at the lip of the opposite cove. She stirred uneasily. She hadn't seen Fenno Weld in weeks. Since Len.

Dick and Evelyn were still standing at the edge of the long rock sloping down into the tide, now listening to Roger Pratt, who had ambled over to join them, the navy blue of Dick's Shetland sweater beside Evelyn's lemony-yellow blouse making them a primary pair, thought Joan.

"I wonder who *I'll* marry," Anne mused, her eyes also on the couple. "It's so strange, really, to think about."

"What is?"

"That unknown someone, that something else, ticking away. Somewhere out there in the world is the man I'll marry. Somewhere *right now,* he is turning his head to listen to something someone is saying and laughing."

Joan smiled. Prattle, they had nicknamed her early on at Farmington. And the funny thing was she always managed to get something substantial in between a torrent of words.

"I could meet him any minute, or in a few years — that's what is so odd about things: you never know."

"Maybe you've met him already."

"God, I hope not," Anne declared.

Joan considered telling her just then about Len, but if she said it aloud, he wouldn't be just hers anymore. Right now, he was a secret she wanted to keep a little while longer. He could be, like her apartment, something only for her, with a lock only she could open.

"I'm not going to marry." She took a drink. "It would be unfair."

"Don't be ridiculous."

Joan looked over at Anne. "I'm not. I don't think one should marry a man if you can't have his children. It wouldn't be right. It's not fair to him."

Anne frowned. "That's a bit puritanical. What if you love him?"

Joan sat up on her heels. "If you love him, you would give him what he wants — what all men want."

"Really? What is that?"

"A home and a hearth and a child." Joan chuckled and stood.

"Oh please," said Anne, rolling her eyes.

The evening pinked, stretching long clouds across what had been a clean blue, leaving traces and trails, extending with the gin and the bourbon through the little band.

"Tap, tap," Dickie called out.

"Look," Anne drawled. "Dickie is going to make a toast. Go on!" she called.

Slowly and wordlessly, her brother raised a pole he had in his hand and carefully, happily unfurled the fabric around it, then held it high and waved it.

EVELYN, the flag proclaimed.

"Oh!" Evelyn cried, delighted, and laughed. "Oh, Dickie!"

"Today —" He stopped, his throat closing suddenly. "On this day," he tried again.

How extraordinary, Joan thought. She'd

never thought Dickie had it in him to be undone.

"I am —" He cleared his throat and then looked directly at Evelyn, who slipped her hand again into his. He looked down at her, and the face she raised to his gave him everything, all of it, all of her.

"Evelyn's!" he cried, his right hand lifting the flag in the air, his left lifting Evelyn's. "I am Evelyn's! And I claim this land for her!"

She laughed again. He turned and thrust the pole between the slit in the two rocks at the end of the picnic grounds.

Joan raised her eyebrow and glanced at Anne, who nodded, aware of Joan's gaze. Anne had grown up in the shadow of her brother's princely self-regard and long ago determined not to play the scullery maid.

And now, where the water stretched its widest, a deep purple where the sky and sea collided, a single rowboat was setting out from across the way on the opposite shore.

"Milton!" a voice cried out from the boat coming toward them. "Any Scotch?"

Ogden Milton chuckled and went to stand at the water's edge. "Not for you, Weld. But if you've got your bride on board, there's plenty for her!"

The oars crossed silently back and forth, and they all heard the silvery ripple of a woman's laughter. And as they drew closer, it was clear there were four people in the boat, and a dog.

"I have mussels to cook," Fanny Weld called across the water.

"I have butter!" Kitty answered. "Who have you got there?"

The rowboat had crossed the halfway point of the channel, and the last sun slid across the backs of the two young men in the bow.

"It's Fen, Mrs. Milton," Fenno Weld's deep bass sounded across the water.

"And me, Mum!" Moss Milton turned, and they all saw him. "I'm afraid they've got me."

"Moss!" Kitty cried. "Moss Milton, you're here!"

The Welds had brought two buckets of mussels, "having been left at the altar," crowed Fanny Weld. "Yes! That is what I mean," she said, climbing out of the stern of the rowboat gracefully and nodding hello to everyone, being handed up to dry ground. "It *is* what I mean, Ogden, don't tease. We had guests due for dinner and they missed the last ferry."

"And then I showed up and needed a row across," called Moss, kneeling in the bow to fend off from the rocks. "And here we are. Hello, Pater," he called to Ogden.

"Here we are," Kitty repeated, smiling.

Yes, thought Joan, her eyes on Fenno as he leaped from the bow with the rope in his hands and clambered up the rocks easily, handing it to her.

"Joan," he said.

And she took the end of the rope and climbed to the tie-up tree, looped the rope in a half hitch, and turned around. Fenno was helping haul the mussels out of the boat, saying something to his mother Joan couldn't catch.

Of course, now there could be no talk at all of the Welds leaving; they had to stay for dinner. Joan and Anne were dispatched to get the big steamer pot and a stick of butter from the kitchen and tell Jessie there would be four more. The grate was put on the fire and water set to boil. What had been a loose clumping of two families soon to be joined became something closer to a party, and the spirit of an evening suddenly pulled together colored the fun. Fenno had brought his ukulele, and along with the mussels, there were green glass jugs of the new California wine, chilling now in the water just off the rocks.

Ogden was gay tonight, fueling the fire with the driftwood boughs, stirring the flames higher so the broth boiled around the mussels, directing Kitty to line the paper cups up to receive the butter. Joan felt the heat of the fire on her sunburned skin. The sky lowered from its pink to the deeper curtain of dense blue, and the fire made a room around them all, gathering.

Aldo chaired the philosophy department at Harvard, and Fanny was a lecturer in classics. The minute the spring term ended — the *second* it ended, said Fanny — they decamped up here. Not long after Kitty and Ogden, the Welds had bought a boathouse across the Narrows from Crockett's Island and refurbished it with two studies, a kitchen, and a long dining room that faced the water. Fanny was English, had won a first at Oxford, but when she had first met Kitty Milton, she told Joan one summer, "I was *terrified.* American girls seemed capable of doing *everything* — they were smart, had gone to college, and could speak French, play tennis, ski, sing. Unlike me" — she paused — "dull as pond water, able to do nothing at all but turn a phrase."

"But Mum didn't go to college," Joan had pointed out.

"It doesn't matter," Fanny Weld pronounced. "Look at this place. Your mother creates worlds out of *air.*"

"Good trip up?" Fenno arrived beside Joan on the rocks.

"It was all right."

"Hot?"

She tossed her paper cup off the rock. "Come on," she said, turning and squinting up at him, "you can do better than that."

Her teasing broke the wary hold he was clearly keeping on himself. His shoulders loosened, and he looked down at her and smiled.

And then she found it easy to smile at him, after all. Easy because he was familiar, and having him there beside her made it clear that that was how it would always be. She needn't say anything at all. He was as much a part of this place as she was. Nothing more.

"Look," cried Evelyn. "Oh, look, everyone. It's going —"

The pink-and-orange orb hung above the evening sea, and the color stretched across the sky and touched the granite at their feet into a white glow.

Kitty glanced over at Ogden. *There,* he seemed to say, holding her gaze. Her eyes softened, and she nodded.

No one spoke. The sun lowered slowly into the black below. And then in an instant it was gone.

"There," said Kitty, pushing her long body up to standing. "We can't keep Jessie waiting."

"Come on, then." Ogden crossed to her and offered her his arm; she cocked her head and slipped hers under his. The two of them led the way up the path through the woods, leaving Fenno and Moss to gather the beers and the wine, and as Joan trailed her mother and father, the laughter of the two men on the rocks curled after her. Fenno's low, deep chuckle clapped against the higher notes of Moss's delight.

■ ■ ■ ■

There were candles stuck in driftwood candelabras. There was bread, butter, the jugged wine. And lots of it. There was the genial quiet brought on by food. And when Jessie poked her head round the swinging door with the Irish stew, a cheer went up. Though the Miltons were possessed of one of the most uninspired cooks on the Thoroughfare, Jessie made up for it with a sense of ample portions. Unlike the Lowells, or the Hunnicutts, the Stinsons, or even the Welds, at Crockett's there was always enough to go round for dinner.

Jessie nodded her thanks without so much as the trace of a smile, put the pot down in front of Ogden, handing him the ladle, and vanished back into the kitchen. Kitty followed the swing of the door behind her cook. Jessie had come up with them every summer since the first, complaining bitterly about the difficulties of preparation on an island, she'd sniff, *an island, for the dear lord's sake,* but was the very first to have her bag packed and ready to be shipped up waiting in the back hallway each June.

Kitty sat at one end, with Aldo and Roger Pratt. Her eye rested on Priss, seated at Ogden's right at the other end of the table, with Moss next to her. She caught Ogden's quick glance at his son and felt how keenly happy Moss made him. It was all in line tonight. Complete.

"Dad," Evelyn appealed. "Help me out. I'm telling the Pratts about the Worthington Bartletts."

Ogden tried to recall them. "Your friend Abby? Who just married?"

"That's right." She nodded. "And they are happy as clams except for one thing."

"Her cooking?" Mr. Pratt hazarded.

"Not at all." Evelyn shook her finger at him playfully. "Abby took classes at the Alliance Française. No," she said, and paused. "Worthy finds his father-in-law hard to take."

Og set down his glass. "Griswold Adams is a good man."

"Of course, Dad. It's his politics."

"How on earth do you know that?" Og frowned.

"Abby told us."

"*Abby* did?" Kitty asked, astonished, from her end of the table. "How extraordinary."

"Don't you ever let me hear you talking aloud about Dickie or what Dickie thinks, young lady." Og was firm.

"Damn right." Dickie Pratt raised his glass. "Thank you, sir. We men have to stick together."

Evelyn swatted him.

"You see that?" he protested, smiling.

"It was all among friends, Dad." Evelyn

455

turned to her father. "Good friends."

"I don't care how good a friend you are," he answered. "The beauty of marriage is that it's private. A jewel. A wife ought never talk about her husband. And certainly not about his family. Talk tarnishes."

His eye rested on Kitty, who gave him back her smile.

He raised his glass. He had been serious, but it needn't be punishing. "To untarnished love," he said.

"Untarnished love!" Mr. Pratt echoed.

"And the code of silence!" Aldo Weld teased. "Upon which it rests!"

"All right, all right," Ogden grumbled cheerfully. "But you know I'm right."

"Did anyone else catch Mike Wallace this week?" Aldo Weld asked into the quiet that followed as the table started eating.

"Horrible." Kitty grimaced, looking up. "I turned it off."

"She tried to turn it off," Ogden said. "I wouldn't let her."

"What's this?" Roger Pratt asked.

"Wallace did a show on some Negroes up in Harlem preaching race hatred."

"Race hatred?"

"Whites are the blue-eyed devil —"

Moss put down his fork. "It was called *The Hate That Hate Produced* —"

Ogden looked up and nodded. "Yes, that's right."

"For a reason," Moss continued. "Negroes have a right to be —"

"But why say it? Why have it all out there on the surface?" Kitty asked. "What good does it do? Everyone has the blacks' interest at heart."

"Not the citizens of Montgomery, perhaps," Fanny decided.

"I meant," Kitty said, "everyone at *this* table."

"It's not enough," Moss said quietly. "It's not nearly enough. Something's got to break —"

"Not by calling each other names. Everyone needs to keep a cool head," Roger Pratt said. Ogden nodded.

"Eisenhower was for integration, but gradually," Aldo Weld said, leaning back in his chair, "Adlai Stevenson was for integration — but moderately. Isn't that how the joke goes?"

"But it's true." Ogden frowned.

"Don't you see the joke, Dad?" Moss asked.

"I see the joke, of course I do. One white man is like any other —"

Moss frowned. "Well, no."

"They are good men, both of them, who meant well," Ogden said, "and the country has profited by that sort of man."

"The country?"

"Yes."

"What about —"

"We do our best and move forward, Moss. That's the only way, move forward."

"I disagree." Moss shook his head. "I'd say backward. You have to go backward. You have to turn around and look at what happened and see why —"

"What exactly are you talking about?" Aldo Weld leaned and reached for the wine, topping up Sarah Pratt's glass beside him.

"I'm talking about hidden laws," Moss answered.

Ogden considered this. "Laws are not hidden."

"Unwritten laws are hidden. Unwritten rules."

"Hidden and inexorable," Fenno agreed.

Ogden looked from his son to Fenno, and said to Aldo, "The younger generation seems to be ganging up."

Hidden laws, Kitty thought impatiently. *Why can't we just sit at the table together? Why the need to talk, to raise things up and examine them — to set up separate tables and say,* I'm here, you're there.

"Listen." Ogden leaned back in his chair. "I have no illusions whatsoever about the blacks. They have been poorly treated, ill-used from the start. All right, then. How do we bring them in?" He looked at his son and smiled. "Slowly," he answered himself. "That's how civilizations hold. A leaking, fractured bucket

458

cannot hold new water."

"No," said Moss, "we need new buckets. Or something. Bad analogy."

He pushed back from the table and stood up. "Beer?" he asked without looking at anyone.

"I'll take one since you're up," Dickie called out cheerfully. "In a bucket, or not."

Moss nodded absently, moving toward the pantry and out into the night, where the stars hung a distant canopy over the sky. There were acts to every meal, he thought, creeping forward in the dark toward the rock shelf where he had wedged the beers brought up from the picnic grounds. Like a play — or better, an opera — a dinner like this one could set new patterns, the dips in voice below the surge of opinion, the scraping in and out of chairs, the chatter that didn't add to much, the quick, considering glances and the replies. Act One was nearly done in there, and now came the complicating Act Two, where people settled into their food and the conversation, and one could begin to hear the pure blue strain, the single strand that would bind or divide them. The melody.

Break it down, Moss hummed to himself. *Break it down, break it down, let it go.* He didn't worry about what he meant. What it was that needed breaking down. Somehow he knew enough to know that that didn't matter. If he could capture that dinner table in a chord — his father's blind assurance, his mother's watchfulness, the ease and arrogance of the old men's talk, his sister's laugh — and then step away so the chord disappeared, leaving its echo, the moment's trace, then he'd have done something. *Find me some new notes, George,* Miles Davis had said to his drummer ten years ago, and Moss had set his course by that phrase ever since.

Find me some new notes, indeed. Moss pulled a beer off the rock ledge and dug for his pocketknife. The talk in there at the dinner table did not break its borders, though he knew his father thought himself an open-minded man, able even to talk of Malcolm X at the dinner table. Like an old song sung a cappella, the old men relied on chords, moved their voices in fours up and down in tight harmony, the single chute of sounds — alto, bass, tenor — combined, but never lost. Separate but equal. He set the can on the rock and opened it by feel, finding the lip of the can under his fingers and setting the opener there. Segregated sound, each note kept firmly in its place.

A star fell above him in the new night sky. The single light simply dropped into motion, as though pushed from behind off its black shelf. He followed it all the way down out of sight, his eyes resting at the end, then returning to the squares of light blazing from the dining room out into the night where he stood. He took a long drink. He had a sudden wish that Reg had come, that Reg could see all this. He'd see who Moss was. Or rather, who he came from, and what Moss was talking about when he was talking about wanting to find new notes. Reg would see what Moss saw, and see the need to *tear it down.* He smiled to himself. Reg would see it and take it in — this impossible beauty — held tightly in the Miltons' well-behaved, *civilized* hands.

Moss tipped the rest of the beer down his throat. He found himself transfixed at the window, unable to go back inside. Around the table a lively, inaudible conversation was going on. His father was leaning in his chair, listening. Moss opened the second beer in his hand and drank, watching as Mr. Pratt told a story only half the table paid attention to. Fenno spoke to Anne and his mother tapped the top of her chair. What's in between? What's in between? The rhythm of her fingers caught him.

Phrases swallowing other phrases and rooms, one room joining another and moving past it and then stop. Then stop. And start. Start again. He could hear it, just on the outside of the conversation, just past where the talk stopped, there was music. And for a minute, for a small instant, he had a glimpse of what he was trying for, a glimpse of how to get all of it — the room, these people, the candles and the stars — out. Out into words. But past words. Where it mattered.

An easy golden haze spread through him. Evelyn sat just out of the window frame, across from Joanie, whose brown head was very still, listening also. Tonight, as he'd crossed with the Welds in the dinghy, it had been Joanie's figure, sitting on the rocks, he'd caught sight of first.

It was always Joanie he looked for in a crowd to reassure himself that she was still there. He sipped the beer. He couldn't help it. Anything might happen. He'd grown up in the shadow of that morning she had almost drowned. They had been together, and then he'd turned around and she'd simply vanished. She'd been too close to the water tonight, he'd felt, watching Fenno Weld shift in his chair; and Moss saw he was listening to Anne, but he was watching Joan, who had leaned forward to press the wax at the top of the candle. Fenno gazed on Joan with an unguarded confusion. And Joan was somewhere else, Moss could tell. He wondered where. She stood and reached for Mr. Pratt's plate and then her own. Whoever got her would be lucky.

"Moss?" Joan stood in the kitchen door silhouetted against the pantry light.

"Out here."

The screen door clapped shut, and he heard her cross through the grass toward him. The two of them stood silent together outside the house.

Moss raised his beer to the scene inside. "The immortals at dinner."

Joan smiled. He was right. Everyone inside looked like they were suspended in time.

"It makes me want to break something."

She glanced at him, startled. Half-lit by the window, he looked like he was listening to something they couldn't hear, and he looked thrilled. He poured the last of the beer down his throat.

"Why?" she asked.

He looked at her. "You can't see anything until it's broken."

Was that right? She folded her arms. He reminded her of her boss just then, this same excitement, taking on the world.

"Then you just have pieces," she said.

Beside her, he shook his head. "Pieces to make other pieces."

Joan considered this.

"You know that feeling you have standing in front of a painting, or hearing the last few notes of a perfect song? Like a bolt shot straight into you. A recognition. You are not alone."

"But you aren't alone," she said. "Look at all of us, look at all of this here."

"But if I could make something bigger" —

he was urgent — "something bigger than all of this —"

"What is bigger than this, Moss?" she asked simply. "This place is everything. It's clear, complete. Everything's right here, in this place."

He didn't answer right away.

"It's all wrong, Joanie." He shook his head. "Or I'm all wrong."

"You are not."

"I don't have the goods for this place."

"You do," she protested.

In the dining room, Kitty rose from her chair and began setting out the dessert plates at everyone's place.

"I don't want them, then."

"What do you want?"

"I want," he said softly, his eyes on his mother, "for someone to look at me, and only me, and not the air beside my head, as if they are always looking for someone else."

Joan watched their mother sit back down. She put her hand on her brother's arm.

"Come on," she said, and squeezed. "Let's go in."

"There you are!" Kitty called, catching sight of the two of them. "Come in. Poor Dickie has been very patient and parched here at my side."

"Hardly, Mrs. Milton."

"Hardly patient?" Evelyn teased.

"Hardly parched." Dickie smiled.

Moss handed a cold can of beer to Dickie, followed by the can opener, still in the grip of what he had understood out there in the dark behind him, and without thinking, without pausing, cleared his throat and raised his beer.

"Toast!"

One by one, their faces slowly turned toward him. He pushed his glasses up along his nose.

"There is a genius out there in the world right now," Moss began slowly. "A man who has figured how to make us hear great rooms of sound, in which anything is possible. Mr. Miles Davis —"

He was quite alert suddenly. He stood at the edge of a dive. His mother's eyes rested like hands on his shoulders, willing him to sit down. He could simply step and jump. He glanced at his father, who watched him, waiting. *Get on with it* — he could feel his father's mood. *Get on. Get on.*

And against that push, Moss straightened. He slowed. He took a good long look at his mother sitting at the end of the table, and he smiled.

"And though the order of business here this weekend is you two, Evelyn and Dick, I'd propose a toast first to infinite varieties —" Moss stopped. "To sounds that leap their barriers, notes that don't stay put. To love in the key of blue." Moss held his beer up.

In the puzzled silence Moss put the beer to his mouth and drank.

"Whatever the hell that is," Dickie said, raising his beer good-humoredly, "I'm for it. I'm for you, Moss."

Moss was drunk, Ogden realized. He would have to shape up; he must know it was time to give all this up. Kitty caught his eye and held it. *All right.* Ogden almost nodded. *All right, I won't say anything at all.*

He rose with his glass in his hand.

"I leave music to Moss, but love brings me to *my* feet." Ogden began. "In my experience, men make lonely music until they find a woman. We are just sounding brass" — he paused — "or a clanging cymbal.

"Behind every successful man is a good woman." He smiled. "Or so the saying goes. But I suggest a good woman is the reason men put up walls and gardens, churches. The reason men build at all. At the *center* of every successful man is a good woman."

He raised his glass and bowed slightly, first to Sarah Pratt, to Fanny Weld, and then to Kitty. "Tomorrow we'll be overrun. A toast tonight, to the good women at the center — to Sarah, to Kitty, to Fanny, to Priss, and — to Evelyn, soon to be there."

Moss raised his beer in answer. How cleanly his father worked, how cleverly. He had deflected the conversation, and yet it seemed he had taken it seriously, nonetheless. He drank, his eyes on his father.

Evelyn flushed with pleasure. She had gotten her ticket. She would be all set now. And seeing the look on her face, Dickie's own dissolved into a boyish happiness, nearly alarmed by his good fortune. They were exactly right together, neat as pins, Joan thought without jealousy. And Evelyn had always been that way, light, quick, neat. Did sisters always fall into these patterns, the light and the dark? The beauty and the brains? Although, she thought as she moved the saltshaker to stand alongside the pepper, she was hardly the brains. Her stuffing leaked. But — she tapped the glass shaker with her butter knife idly, a little smile on her lips — it leaked gloriously and in hidden ways.

"Come on," Joan said to Anne across the candles. "We good women ought to lead a party down to the dock."

Laughing, Joan and Anne rose, their plates in their hand, and Evelyn and Dickie rose as well. Through the door and out into the dark they went, their voices drifting past the open window at Kitty's side and into the emptied room, where Moss remained, turned in on himself. Kitty looked at her son, puzzled.

"Go on," she said to him.

He roused at her voice and looked at her, and as she held his gaze she realized with a start what she had pushed away all evening.

He reminded her of Dunc.

He stood and stretched and gave her a little bow, clearing his plate and his beer. The swinging door into the pantry closed behind him. And then the screen door slammed.

The older generation sat a moment in the quiet behind them. It was as though they had all shrugged off a coat. No one would say it, but now they could breathe.

"I want to take the Herreshoff out tomorrow, if it's clear," Ogden said to Kitty, "early."

She nodded, enjoying the faces round the table, all of whom she could count on, all of whom understood their roles, their places, she thought, rising from her end of the table.

Sarah Pratt and Fanny Weld rose also, gratefully. Priss did the same. Released. Happy to follow Kitty out of the dining room and outside to stand in the cooler air, into the night and the quiet. Kitty reached for the limb of the lilac arching over the door, the familiar branch like an arm. In front of her, the long lawn vanished in the dark. It was a clear night. Ogden would get his sail. Down on the dock, the tiny lights of the children's cigarettes moved slowly, back and forth.

TWENTY-NINE

Kitty woke in the earliest part of the morning, her heart pounding. Neddy needed her somewhere, and quickly. Where or why, she never knew, though the dream was always the same. The dream never left traces like other dreams, there was never a moment in the waking day when something left over would glide through the air, when she'd catch it and remember, *Oh, that's what it was, that was the dream.* This one came and sought her, and she'd start running in her sleep, running in the grip of a nameless fear toward him, to get him.

Lying there on her back, she put a hand up to her forehead and felt the sweat. Her eyes adjusted to the dark in the room, and the shape of Ogden's body beside her rose like a soft wall between her and the drop of the bed, the window beyond. A comforting dark. A quietening one. She lay there. But this dream had been different, somehow. She tried to pull it back as her heart slowed. It hadn't been Neddy. It had been someone else. Some other child she must get to. Some other child who needed help. She lay there, a breeze coming up from the water pulling through the window at the foot of their bed, blowing the shade forward toward her. Who? She couldn't recall.

She knew if she slid off the bed to lift the shade and look, there would be no light in the sky. During the moonless nights of the month here on the Island, night was pitch-black and fathomless as if colored by a child.

But full of sound. Trees shifted in the wind, and their boughs sighed. On windless nights, when the trees were still, one could hear the tide pulling back and forth, combing over the black rocks in the cove. The only animals on the move, full of the same silent sound as the rocks and trees, were bats winging in tight circles above the barn.

The sweat cooled and she pulled the comforter up closer around her neck and chest. Ogden rolled over and put his warm hand on her collarbone. "All right?" he murmured, half-awake.

"Yes," she whispered, "go back to sleep."

He grunted, already gone.

Moss. That was it. *Had* it been Moss? It must have been. Something she had seen last night must have set off this panic. Something so small, she wasn't sure she could find the word that would haul it up to the surface so she could think about what she had seen, understand it somehow. Name it. It was his toast, wasn't it? Or it had happened before the toast, something he had said in the middle of a conversation?

It was the way he had stood from the table, wasn't it, the way he had stood as if — she searched, thinking of Moss moving off toward the swinging door, nodding *Sure, Dickie* politely before disappearing outside. What was outside that couldn't be found in here? Kitty turned on her side, away from Ogden, so she could think in the dark.

As if he wanted to flee. Flee the table. Why? A dinner like that, with so many old friends who'd shared so many meals up there, and then again down in the city, carried the world in it, carried the ease of the world and all the givens. Ogden at one end of the table, herself at the other, the guests ranged around the sides, the plinths. She liked to ask a question from her end and watch the men take off. She liked that she knew enough to follow where they led, to make sure the conversation stayed its course, to divert it when the course was fraught. She'd never take up the argument, but she rode it, she made certain it kept up its paces. When a man refused to take up the bit, it shook her. When a man neglected his duties, failing to fill someone's glass when it was empty, failing to be the host, it was the sign that something had gone off. Something had slipped.

And Moss had stepped out of the circle round the table. Moss had ducked the halter. She sat up. The faintest glimmer of light rimmed the shades. The flashlight on the nightstand was heavy and cool in her grip, and she pointed it to the floor and stood up in its beam. There would be no more sleep tonight.

In the mudroom downstairs, she fished a wool coat off its hook and a hat and pulled on the tall rubber boots she used to pick mussels. It was still night outside, though a paler shade of dark. Softly, she made her way through the dining room and the pantry and toward the dim glimmer of the pilot light under the burners of the stove. She turned the knob, and the flame thrust its blue claw above the iron burner. In the big dormitory room over the kitchen, Moss turned in his sleep.

She reached for the kettle, set it on the flame and picked a teabag out of the canister, setting it into a teacup. Kitty pulled the coat closer around her nightgown, waiting for the kettle to boil.

The urgency on Moss's face had frightened her last night. He had seemed almost — desperate. And that smile, that crooked grin that stole over him, had been all Dunc, she realized, standing there. Moss had never quite taken, never gelled. He had a gift for people, a gift for gathering strangers together; he always had. But there was something missing, a rope that had never found its ring.

She folded her arms over her chest. Moss was *not* Dunc.

The kettle started the roll before it squealed, and she snapped the flame off, reached for the cup, and set it on the counter, pouring the hot water. Now the pale glow of the big rock began to show through. It would be dawn soon. There was something coming, something she couldn't fully see yet, an argument whose words she couldn't quite make out behind closed doors and felt, therefore, powerless to affect.

Overhead there was a quiet thud, then another as two feet climbed over the side of the bed and onto the floor. Kitty waited. Moss would be coming down the narrow stairs, most probably to find the bathroom at the end of the hall. She picked up the teacup and headed for the kitchen door as the footsteps crossed. The door opened, and she pushed through the screen and out into the morning.

A low, dense fog hung above the lawn, heavy with dew. Ogden's clear day, the promise of the day offered by last night's star-struck clarity, had shrouded. She walked forward into the paler gray that was the air, distinguished from the dark shapes of the spruce at the water's edge. The first of the engines hummed just past the point, as someone hauled his pots in the thick damp.

When fog wrapped the trees and stalled in the air like this, it used to frighten Moss so. He used to see people flashing in and out of the dark trunks. *No, you don't,* Kitty had tried to soothe him. *Of course you don't.* But he would stand there, patiently stand in the upstairs hall looking out the single frame window, her boy in his short pants, his hair combed, his teeth brushed, his back straight as he waited for the ghosts from the woods, as though by watching he could protect them all.

Kitty shivered. There were the shadows underneath the spots of time.

Or rather, there was a spot in time up here that did not hold sunlight or square dances or weddings or the other children running down the hill to catch the boat. It drifted up to the surface of memory only when a certain present stumbled across the past and called it up.

That morning, Moss had wandered down the hill in the fog toward the boathouse holding Joanie's hand, following Ogden, and it had seemed to be one minute Kitty had said, *Okay, dearie,* from where she was bent among the roses, and the next minute, she looked up and there was Ogden carrying the little body in his arms up the hill and Moss was running toward her, dripping wet and sobbing. It was

Joanie. Ogden was carrying Joanie in his arms. Water was pouring off his shirt.

"We need a doctor" was all Ogden said.

Kitty dropped her trowel.

"Mum," Moss cried.

She turned around and held open her arms.

"Come on, love," she whispered, "we need a blanket."

"Joanie was shaking." Moss turned his blue lips to his mother. "She fell."

"In the water?" Kitty could barely breathe.

"I couldn't stop it, Mum. I couldn't stop — she was going under, and I saw her face —"

"It's all right, Moss." Kitty pulled open the front door, still holding his hand. And they climbed the stairs together to the linen closet, where she grabbed several towels.

"I couldn't do *anything*." Moss trembled.

She sank to her knees and folded him in a towel. Her proud little boy, her stalwart.

Oh. Kitty paused now, her mind run up against that morning again. It had been so long ago, all that.

She walked through the boathouse and out onto the dock, where the fog hung loose upon the water, upon the dark angle of the roof, running down into the wide granite rock that formed the tip of the cove. Water dripped from the floorboards of the boathouse onto the rocks.

She worried about Joan. Everyone did. The

doctors had warned that a fit could take her anytime. She might drown or crash a car, she might fall down in the middle of a street. She ought never marry — it wouldn't be fair to ask of a man. Unless it was someone who knew her, unless it was Fenno. Kitty searched for the Welds' dock across the way, but the fog was in too thick. She had always liked him. Fenno knew all about the fits. Fenno would be kind.

There were footsteps coming through the boathouse, and then on out onto the pier behind her. Someone paused at the top of the gangway, and she turned around.

"You're up early," she said.

"Something woke me." Moss yawned, pulling open the gate and padding down the gangway in his bare feet. "Thickafog," he pronounced.

She nodded. "Evelyn will be worried about people coming tonight."

"It'll burn off."

"Perhaps."

They stood together in the quiet.

"I was just thinking how it used to frighten you."

He thrust his hands deep into his pockets and nodded. "Fog always seems like it's waiting to get you."

"Tell me something," she said after a while.

He looked at her.

"What on earth were you talking about last night?"

"Which part?"

"Looking backward."

He shrugged. "Why are we here? How did we get here?"

She frowned. "Here? On the Island?"

"No, Mum. Here. To this point in time. The situation with the Negroes. Dad was talking as if it didn't matter what the television show was called, just that the blacks were sounding off." He shook his head. "But *why* are they sounding off? It's the why that has us here."

But where was here? she wondered, bewildered. What was he talking about? His row would be harder to till, she thought apprehensively. He was making it more difficult for himself with these interests, these passions. He'd have a harder time slipping into work for Og.

"Enter every room with a smile," she said. "Speak to everyone, regardless of their place, as another human being, a reasonable person — so as to create an atmosphere of goodwill. That is the best defense against people who haven't been brought up to know better. You just leave them alone. No one can touch you, then. And you show others the way to be. You lead by that example."

He nodded, unconvinced.

She paused. "Of course they don't like being treated badly. No one does. But these things take time. They take patience."

"Whose patience?"

She wanted to shake him, just then. Hard. He had the same overabundance of conscience as Dunc had. Responsibility was not an absolute. We were kind, we were generous, but we did not owe more than we could give.

"Moss," she said sharply, "why *identify* yourself so?"

He shook his head. "What else is there?"

And something in his face, the careless confusion, called back that moment so long ago, the boy who did not see the danger, turning to her in front of that window. She shuddered.

"Moss." She rested her hand on his arm, frightened. "I mean it."

"I know you do," he said, and gave her one of his sweetest smiles and turned away.

The fog had come in and sunk down, Joan saw with satisfaction, lying back on the pillow. She loved the fog. She looked up at the ceiling, picturing the men in North Haven right now who'd pulled out their charts and their straightedge and were plotting the course over here. Those who were coming would stay the night, which meant — she rolled over — there'd be mattresses to pull and sheets and blankets to haul up to the barn. It was delicious. A party that would begin with dinner and drinks, move to dancing, and then last and last right through the dark.

Anne lay profoundly asleep in the four-poster next to hers.

Joan pushed the pink covers off and sat up. Her eyes rested on her shorts, folded over the arm of the wicker chair at the foot of the bed, her sneakers pushed in underneath, dutiful as a child. She brushed the floor with the soles of her feet and stood, pulling her nightgown over her head in one long motion. Her nipples rose and she cupped them, imagining Len's hands on her waist, pulling her into him. Len. She caught sight of herself in the little mirror above the bureau and shivered at the clear longing in her eyes. Len Levy.

"Of course people will come," she said to Evelyn, who was standing at the bottom of the stairs, staring out the screen door into the fog. Moss and Mum were walking slowly through the gloom, Moss's white shirt glowing against the gray.

Evelyn turned around and looked at Joan gratefully. "Do you think so, really?"

"I do," said Joan. "They're mad for stuff like that over there. A test of valor and all that." She rolled her eyes, and Evelyn smiled.

"Hello, Mum," she said.

"Good morning," Kitty answered. "Is there coffee for the Pratts made?"

"They aren't up yet," Joan said, but she

picked up the kettle and filled it with water.

Dickie was up and toasting bread over the open burner, watched with suspicion by Jessie.

"Don't worry," he said to her cheerfully. "I'm a professional."

There was much to be done before the party. The rowboats would need to be pumped out and then pulled off into the cove to make room for the boats from North Haven and Vinalhaven. But first, Kitty warned, "We'll need to figure out about the piano, how to get it up that hill."

"Oh god," Moss groaned.

The piano was an upright, a Steinway that one of Kitty's aunts had left her after the war. They had brought it across on the gasboat and then wheeled it up the lawn on a wooden dolly, getting it inside the house with considerable effort. Kitty had long planned to take it the next distance up to the barn, and the promise of so many young men handy for the job made it impossible not to do, even as it seemed well nigh impossible to push a quarter ton of mahogany, steel, buckskin, and glue up a hill pocked by voles.

The improbability of it made it just the kind of plan Ogden relished, and on a foggy day provided them all a physical challenge equal to, and more useful than, a walk in the woods, which Ogden had also suggested for the morning.

"How were you thinking of doing it?" Moss asked.

"With the dolly, just as before," she answered.

"The dolly? What dolly? That went over the side of the dock years ago."

Ogden frowned. "He's right — do you remember?"

Kitty shook her head.

"It should be easy enough to rig something else up," Dickie said as he appeared in the dining room, "if you've got a wheelbarrow and some boards."

Ogden turned. "Have you got a plan?"

Dickie grinned. "Always."

Moss rolled his eyes at Joan.

"Good man," Ogden said. "Go on, then."

"We'll still have to manhandle it onto the wheelbarrow and then down the steps."

"Manhandle," Evelyn chirped from the kitchen. "I like it."

"This is all for you, Ev, you realize," Moss called.

"Me? This is Mum's idea."

"It's your party. Yours and Dickie's."

"Don't give me that." Evelyn paused. "You'll have the whole barn now to play in without anyone listening."

"I like people listening."

"Do people?"

"Go on," Ogden said. "You better get

481

cracking if we're going to get it up the hill by sunset."

"We'll get it up there, don't worry, Mr. Milton." Dickie appeared behind Evelyn, towering over her. "I'll get these guys moving like a team."

"A manhandling team," Evelyn tossed at him over her shoulder as he gave her a squeeze and went out. The screen door slammed.

Joan came through the kitchen door with bayberry she had cut from the big patch out back, and Kitty held out her hands to take it.

"I hate bayberry," Evelyn remarked idly. "Why do you always choose bayberry when there's so much else out there?"

Kitty set the greens down on the dining room table and looked at her youngest daughter. "If you can't say anything nice —"

Joan took the copper pitcher at the center of the table with her into the pantry, where she filled it with water from the sink.

"Don't say it," Evelyn groaned. "I know."

Joan turned off the tap and dried her hands on her shorts.

Kitty held the cutting shears and motioned Joan to set the pitcher on the table in front of her. Mutinous, Evelyn folded her arms against the silent agreement between her mother and her sister. There was wild yarrow, Scotch heather — anything but the bayberry. But Joan's ideas were always seconded by their mother. She was the favorite, the pearl.

"But Mum —"

Kitty raised her eyes and looked at Evelyn, who chose to keep whatever else she was going to say to herself.

"Beds?" Joan suggested. "Shall we pull out the blankets and pillows and bring them up to the barn?"

"Good idea." Kitty nodded, beginning to stuff the bayberry branch by branch into the vase's narrow mouth. Beneath her hands a green bouquet grew, cantilevered over the lip of the copper, filling the room with the sharp smell. Kitty set the pitcher at the center of the table and then swept the cuttings into the wastebasket she had brought in from the front room.

"There." She smiled at the arrangement.

Anne Pratt woke at last, and she helped the sisters drag all the bedding they could find out of the linen closet, folding it neatly on the spare beds in the upstairs front room. Hudson Bay wool blankets from Granny Houghton's camp in the Adirondacks, down pillows, pillowcases, and cast-off sheets from the Ausable Club.

After a little while, the men's voices snaked through the fog and the open window as they returned from the boathouse and lay boards across the granite steps in the front. Moss was in high spirits, and the girls heard them tramp though the front door and down the hall to the living room.

"Fog is thicker than ever!" he called to the house.

The opening chords of a song reached through the house to where the three young women stood, and the slow, bewildered strains of "So in Love" climbed as Moss sang above the notes he played. *"Strange dear, but true dear."* Joan smiled at Anne, who had sunk down onto the folded sheets to listen. It was something about how slow the song was, the mood of it perplexed and thoughtful, not gay, not the usual Cole Porter. *"When I'm close to you, dear."* The low thread of longing that ran through it suited the thick air, the sense of a party coming, of something about to happen. Joan folded the blanket in her arms and then hugged it.

Her father's voice cut in, and Moss's hands came abruptly off the keys.

"Joan?" her mother called from another part of the house. "Joan?"

"Coming!" she called back.

The bell on the dock clanged down in the cove.

"Girls," Kitty Milton called to them as they rounded the top of the stairs. "Go and see who that is, will you, and then bring them up here."

Joan nodded, and she and Anne came down

the stairs and out the front door and into the fogbound morning. Somewhere out in the Narrows, the low thrum of a boat's engine flared and caught and pulled away into the invisible ocean. The scattered gray humps of the granite in the lawn vanished into the air, even the bright green of the grass seemed to have turned its color down.

"Who on earth got through this pea soup?" Anne wondered aloud.

"I'm telling you, these sailors up here are mad." Joan smiled and walked forward into the gray.

"Anyhoo," said Anne, "I meant to ask. Do you have your own checking account?"

"Yes." Joan glanced at her. "Of course."

"Well, of course nothing. Mum thinks it's dangerous to give me one, that I'll have one soon enough when I'm married, and I'm not sure, but I don't agree. Maybe it's best to leave it with the men," she mused. "We don't ask them to make hollandaise."

Joan snorted. "For god's sake, Prattle. It's 1959. We've got washing machines and dryers. We've got no-wax vinyl floors. You ought to have your own checking account. Don't you want to be practical?"

"Of course I want to be practical," Anne returned cheerfully. "I want to be more than that. I think marriage ought to run on two rails. His and Hers. Without dipping your finger into each other's pots. That way you can concentrate on loving each other."

"Love involves pot-dipping," Joan tossed back, smiling. "At least the love I want."

Other than Anne's feet right beside hers in the moss, there wasn't a sound. It seemed they were walking straight through a cloud. It was impossible to see farther than five feet in front of them, and when the gray shadow of the boathouse loomed ahead of them, Joan almost started.

"En amour, moins on se parle, mieux on se comprend," Anne pronounced grandly.

"That makes no sense to me whatsoever," Joan retorted, smiling. "I would think you'd want to be talking all the damn time — otherwise you'd bore each other to tears."

They had passed through the gray wooden room and out again into the vapor on the other side, making their way to the end of the pier and looking down.

And there, standing at the end of the dock with his back to them, was Len. Beside him stood a black man with a camera.

"Oh." Joan stopped, weak at the sight of him. *No,* she thought, *not here. Not* here. *I'm not ready.*

"A Negro?" whispered Anne.

"Come on." Joan walked forward as naturally as she could. "And put a smile on."

THIRTY

The wind had come up suddenly, and the waves crashed over the dinghy with its one little sail, skimming across the water at a terrifying clip. She wasn't sure how long she could hold on to the main sheet if the wind kept blowing across the bow this strong, and at the same time she couldn't let go. She had fallen behind the rest of the sailing class at the turn of the race, tacking badly, the lines getting caught through the pulleys. The water was pooling in the bottom of the dinghy and the seat was slippery and wet and the pitch of the boat was so steep, she knew she couldn't stay on the bench for much longer. "I thought you could *sail*," the sailing instructor cupped his hands and taunted her from a dinghy beside hers, his hair wet from the spray, his slicker open.

"I *can* sail," she cried, "I'm just tangling all the lines."

Evie woke, furious. *I'm a good sailor,* she

protested to the bedroom around her. *I won my class.*

The shade pull tapped on the glass of the window in the dense silence of dawn. The grumble of diesel engines circled far out in the bay; the first lobstermen had gone to work. The morning had started. Someone else was out there, threading the day into cloth. She lay back on the pillows, listening to the engines. Lay there like the child she wasn't, her knees poking the top of the blanket up like a tent pole.

God, she thought. *Sailing dreams?*

Though at least it had been a new dream, something other than her mother coming and standing at the foot of this bed, waiting for her in this room that was the room in the dream, and where she had always slept, the twin four-posters with the pink quilts, lined firmly one against each wall, a window above a nightstand, with the shade pulled down. In the space between the beds lay a metal grate, cut into the floor to let the heat into the upstairs rooms from the fireplaces down below. The dining room lay directly below this bedroom, and all through her childhood, night after night, Evie would wake up in the dark, having fallen asleep chin in hand, and catch the low, incomprehensible adult world in murmurs and bursts of laughter, spooling outward down below.

She turned on her side and rose on her

elbow, lifting the shade to see the weather. The wide lawn down to the boathouse shimmered in dew, a shining path to the dark perimeter of spruce at the water's edge. It was a clear morning, no fog, not a cloud. She dropped the shade again.

Downstairs, the morning filled the house with light. She tugged the Chemex coffeepot out of the cupboard and gave it a rinse, filled the kettle, and set it on to boil. Around her, it was as quiet as prayer. Framed by the doorway, the dining room table stretched, crowned by the vase of bayberry. Dogs piss, men argue — and women put flowers in their grandmother's vases. She smiled. She had carried the torch. She had taken Granny K and carried her forward. For the next couple of days, until Min got here, the Island was hers alone to get ready. Hers alone.

Someone had moved the china cow from the windowsill in the kitchen. Evie looked on the pantry shelves. It must have been put in with the daily china. The cupboards had just been lined by Mrs. Ames's granddaughter, who did the cleaning now, and the smell of Lysol undercut the old wood.

The kettle gathered its steam and blew. She flicked it off and poured the water through the coffee in the filter, and the smell of the grounds rose sharp and rich in the air. The wooden corset around the Chemex was cracked and missing its leather tie. It had been that way for as long as Evie had been drinking coffee, and the idea of buying a new one had never occurred to her. In this, she was her mother's daughter.

Always the first to arrive on the Island in June and the last to leave in September, Joan sat in Granny K's Morris chair, her face turned toward the lawn, staring down to the dock. On sunny days, Joan would set up outside on the green bench with a pair of binoculars, a box of Triscuits, and a thermos of tea. *You go on,* she'd say if anyone asked if she'd like to walk. *I'll man the fort.*

For some reason, this drove her aunt Evelyn wild.

Evie would come in June with her mother and follow her around the rooms as Joan removed a snapshot of Evelyn and Uncle Dick left upon the mantel the previous summer, one of the Pratt grandchildren's drawings on the shelf in the front hall, a collection of periwinkles along the rim of a bench, and put them in the kitchen, or along the windowsills in the pantry. Then she would move the things that "ought to be there" back into place. The china shepherdess on the white mantel. The brick doorstop covered in mattress ticking out from where it had been shoved under the sink, to the pantry door. The organdy curtains up again in the kitchen windows.

"Evelyn always wants to change everything," her mother muttered. "Always adjusting, always moving things around."

"What's wrong with that?" Evie had ventured one summer. She was perhaps eleven.

"Then you forget," Joan said.

"Forget what goes where, you mean?"

Her mother's eyes rested on her.

"Yes," Joan said, and Evie understood that was not what her mother had meant at all.

"Well." Evie had flushed, hot and confused. "That thing" — she pointed to the doorstop that held the pantry door open, its cloth cover stained and tattered — "could be forgotten. It's so ugly."

Joan turned and looked. "Yes," she agreed. "It is."

But it remained right where it belonged, keeping the pantry door from swinging shut by Joan, and pushed under the sink when Evelyn walked by.

Enough. Evie pulled a mug off the kitchen shelf and poured her coffee. *Enough,* she thought as she crossed through the pantry and into the dining room, kicking at the doorstop brick on her way. That's enough. The door, unmoored by the brick, banged against the jamb.

She would start in the bedrooms, she thought, clearing out closets and drawers, and climbed the stairs to the pink room, where she was sleeping. The closet there opened on to shelves to the left piled high with games and the tea set her mother had found at the Rockland Ladies Auxiliary one afternoon while they waited for the ferry some weekend in the sixties. The stack was exactly as it had been left and made its own pattern of color and memory, seen and disregarded every intervening summer as Evie hung up shirts on the hangers to the right, slid her shoes below, and threw the duffel bag in the corner.

She began on the top shelf, pulling the games off one by one and stacking them on the bed. Behind where the games had sat on the shelf was a single child's sneaker, some cutoffs Evie vaguely remembered — had they been hers? Min's? — and a pair of binoculars whose rotting leather strap came away in her hands. Each of these she placed next to the games on the bed, and then on tiptoe reached with her hand for the spot she couldn't see, for the farthest back corners, to sweep them clean. Something rolled from her fingertips and she reached again and closed over a bottle, like a film canister. A pill bottle, she realized, looking down at it. DILANTIN, the label read on the outside. MISS JOAN MILTON. 460 EAST 81ST ST., NEW YORK, NY. MURRAY HILL 3467.

She moved out of the closet, carrying the tiny vial into the light cast by the dormer window, and pulled off the top, shaking it, releasing a faint odor like chalk, followed by the rim of a tiny scrap of paper.

Ask Fenno —

What? She stared at the piece of paper, her mother's handwriting — its tiny, careful lettering, clear and sharp.

Evie sat down on the bed, the memory of her father so strong, she had to close her eyes. It wasn't even a note, it was a dash in Morse code — *Ask Fenno* — a stitch made in the fabric of their marriage, a girl risen from her seat to say something, halfway out the door and then stopped. Ask Fenno *what?*

The picture of her father, spindly, standing to the side, always extra, came to mind. It was clear that her father adored her mother, though why her mother had married him, Evie couldn't fathom. She had grown used to the silence in their house, her mother in the kitchen, her father seated in a chair in the living room, joined by the music he had put on the record player. The biggest extravagance he had ever allowed himself were the shiny square speakers he had bought and installed for the kitchen in 1975.

Her father had been one of the editors of the *World Book Encyclopedia.* "Good for nothing," he'd say lightly, and smile — "except the B's the D's and a smattering of the R's." He knew a hell of a little about a lot. A *generalist* — he'd stress the word, bemused. A man marooned by time.

"Meaning what?" Evie had asked once.

"Meaning" — her father looked at her — "better for me the nineteenth century; even better perhaps, the eighteenth. Encyclopedias. Lists. Maps. Codes. But *this* —" He'd gestured out the window of their apartment in New York.

Evie had turned her head as if he were pointing to something she could see. She looked back at him.

"Take me out, Coach," he finished helplessly, sitting as he always did, with a drink in one hand and a Kent cigarette in the other, smoking the evenings away. *Taking it easy,* he'd answer if anyone asked. *Man of leisure,* he'd chuckle as though it hurt. Gentleman. Whiffenpoof. Drunk.

Hapless drunk, she thought, adding the word he had given her one afternoon when she'd stolen into his study looking for the dictionary, thinking he was out. "Aimless?" she'd wondered aloud. "Hapless," he'd said, looking up from the chair in the far corner. It was the only time she could remember her father looking straight at her. The following morning she had gone back to graduate school.

Two months later, he was dead.

She shook herself. She had been twenty-eight.

The bell rang down on the dock, and Evie sprang up, as though she'd been caught doing something. She crossed the long room to the front window that gave onto the lawn. The bow of a boat stuck out off the end of the dock, but the boathouse sat between her and whoever it was. When her grandmother was alive, people were always just showing up at the dock, ringing the bell and marching gaily up the lawn to the Big House, in search of a cup of tea, or a good Scotch, depending on the hour.

She climbed down the narrow stairs and passed through the kitchen. Ahead of her, the open door at the front of the house showed the flag listless on its pole. She pushed through the screen and stood in the doorway on the top stair, looking down the lawn.

Anne Fenwick (née Pratt, as Granny K would say), her mother's oldest friend, and her husband, Eddie, emerged through the boathouse into the sun at the bottom of the lawn. Evie caught her breath. They had outlasted them all. Aunt Anne had gotten smaller, Evie thought, though at eighty-four she was as tidy and crisp as ever, her straight fine hair parted sharply on the side and pulled back in a barrette, as she had done ever since Vassar. She walked beside her husband in Keds and a wraparound skirt, festooned with purple seahorses set upon a sea of navy blue linen. Uncle Eddie carried the canvas bag, trim, tall, and impeccable in his khakis and a sky-blue Shetland sweater.

She could hear Eddie Fenwick as the two

climbed slowly up the hill.

"What's that you say, dear? What, love? What, sweetie?"

"Hello, dear," her godmother called up the hill.

"Hello." Evie smiled, waiting, her hand on the lilac by the door.

"We saw you come in yesterday," Anne explained, still walking.

Evie stepped down the stairs.

"How like your mother you look." Anne folded Evie in a big hug, bringing tears to Evie's eyes. Eddie patted her quietly on the back.

Anne pulled away, her gaze resting lightly on Evie, like a hand testing for fever. "How are you?"

"Fine," Evie answered, a little dazed by the two of them. "Other than being haunted by ghosts, racketing around in the Big House by myself."

Anne wrinkled her nose. "Well, of course you are. Ghost stories belong to the middle-aged, though it's always the young who play the dramas. All our memories crowding one on top of the other — thronging. Especially up here."

Evie didn't say anything.

"Now, how old was Odysseus, do you suppose, my love?" Eddie mused beside her.

"How's that?"

"Odysseus — you remember," Eddie answered. "Down in Hades, and all the shades *thronging,* coming toward him, so many he couldn't speak." He raised his eyebrows jovially. "That was middle age, I'll bet."

Evie wanted to hug him, hauling the ancients around and pulling them out of his pocket. It was just this playful wearing of the classics on one's sleeve that Evie had grown up with. Useless, erudite, familiar.

"In Greece, in the sixth century *bce*?" she answered. "Middle age would be around thirty."

"Ha!" He was delighted, and pointed to the green bench at the front of the house. "Let's sit where your grandmother liked to."

They had brought their own orange juice in a thermos, and Eddie, always elegant, poured his juice into a paper Dixie cup — a thimble really, Evie thought to herself as she took his offering.

"What's that you've got in your hand?" Anne asked.

Evie looked down and saw she still clutched the pill bottle. She showed it to Aunt Anne, who looked at it and nodded.

"Your poor mother."

"I never knew anything about Mum's epilepsy until the week she died."

"She never told you?"

Evie shook her head. "She never told me much of anything."

"She was ashamed of it. One was, you

know, in those days. We never spoke about things like that, about sickness and the like."

Evie smiled at the older woman. "I can't imagine you were ever quiet."

"Heavens, no," Anne agreed, "we talked all the time. But we didn't blow on about ourselves if that's what you mean. We didn't *protest* so much about this and that." She landed lightly on the word and pushed off. "And we were all so *hopeful* then — though perhaps it was just that we were so young."

"I'll bet Mum never said much, though."

"Not true at all," Anne said swiftly. "Your mother had plenty to say."

Evie stretched her legs out before her. "Not to me. To me she was lovely and vague — and silent."

Children believed they knew so much, thought Anne, considering her old friend's daughter, and looked away down the hill.

But what did they know, the proud men and women who were still strong in their middle-aged youth, though they complained of needing glasses, of fatigue and irrelevance, complained because such things were still so new, so remarkable. They had no idea. There they were at the middle of their lives, at the tipping point, when their strength could be in the seeing. And they thought they saw. And they saw not at all.

"Everyone these days is so proud of them-selves for knowing what they want," she erupted, "as though that's a mark of distinction, as though knowing yourself is as easy as knowing what you want."

She stopped, caught off guard by her own vehemence.

"But knowing what you can't have seems to me equally useful. And exemplary simply to accept it."

"Okay," Evie answered carefully, her eyes fixed on the older woman, waiting.

Anne turned her head. "Your mother was honorable," she said firmly. "She was the most honorable soul I ever knew."

"Honorable?"

"A good sport," agreed Eddie.

"Your mother felt she oughtn't marry, you know. That it wouldn't be fair to burden a man with her condition. She'd made a sort of vow."

"A vow?"

Anne nodded.

"What happened?"

"Well," said Anne, looking at her. "You came along, didn't you?"

And Evie couldn't be certain whether there was an accusation under the smile.

"Let's have a look at the barn, shall we?" Eddie suggested into the little quiet that followed.

"The barn?" Anne sighed. "All the way up there?"

He nodded. "Come on, love. It'll do you good."

Anne brushed the front of her skirt and stood as well, holding on to Eddie's arm as she rose. The three of them moved slowly round the corner of the house and toward the bottom of the path that wound through the field to the barn set at the top of the hill, the sharp angle of the enormous roof cut sharply against the blue day.

"So wonderful this place will carry on — extraordinary really, isn't it?" Eddie mused, his elbow tucking Anne's hand tight against his side.

Evie said nothing. The ground was uneven, though it wasn't a steep climb.

"Your grandparents had such wonderful foresight," Anne remarked, her eyes on the path, her arm under Uncle Eddie's. "But exhausting. They expected the moon, and they got it. And they got it all, all the while impeccably dressed."

"You and Eddie are pretty natty, I'd say."

Anne stopped walking, turned, and looked at Evie. "Eddie and I are shades by comparison, dear."

"I don't know."

"There are those who follow the rules, those who break the rules, and those who make the rules. Your grandfather made the rules."

"And what about Mum and Aunt Evelyn?

What about Uncle Moss?"

"Moss," Anne answered, her attention snagged. "Yes, well. Moss did his best."

"To do what?"

"To be his father's son."

"Now, how will you all run the place?" Eddie mused aloud. "There are just the five of you, isn't that right? Just you and the Pratts."

"Yes," Evie answered, "and I'm not sure."

"Eddie, darling, what's that bird?" Anne pointed to a kestrel slicing downward, diverting her husband's attention.

"A hawk, my love," he said.

"So it is," Anne answered. They had arrived at the barn.

Evie took hold of the sliding door and gave it a huge shove. The door groaned and slid a few feet, and then slid a few more with another push. They stepped through. The oak floors with their wide beams, planed smooth by years, smelled of salt and winter's shut-up air. Mouse droppings littered the wide window seats covered in duck cloth fabric along the windows. Inside, the space rose three stories in the empty air. Cut high in the eaves, on either side, a single large window let the sky come shooting down onto the floor. As children, they'd beg to have sleepovers up here, though the bats flickering overhead in the wide night space, their wings whispering, terrified them all. The barn had begun to list slightly, like an old man leaning at the waist.

"There were such parties in here, do you remember, love?"

"Oh yes!" Eddie grinned.

"We had square dances," Anne said, and stopped in the middle of the room, as if calling memories toward her, standing there at the center. "Oh my, that piano."

They stared at the battered upright piano that had stood in one corner of the barn always. And always, Evie reflected, with the sheet music for "Night and Day" or "So in Love" spread open, as if anyone might just sit down and tickle the keys. Though all she'd ever heard played on it was "Chopsticks."

"It took four men and an entire morning's work to get it up here, and here it remains," Anne said. "Rotting, probably. That was for the party, Eddie dear." Anne turned to him. "The night I met you."

"Ah." Eddie smiled at his wife, the love in his eyes so soft, so clear, Evie had to look away.

"When was that?" Evie asked.

"Nineteen fifty-nine," Anne replied "The last good year, my father always said. Before everything in this country got so —"

"What?"

"Complicated, was what he'd say." Anne was thoughtful. "But really, I think he meant unfamiliar."

"Everything happens at a party." Eddie wandered toward the piano. "Who said that?"

"Austen, most likely," Anne said. "She said pretty much everything needing saying."

Evie snorted. "I hate Austen. I'm with the Brontë sisters, banging around in beautiful fury on the moors."

"My word. And you can't have both?" Her godmother was mild.

Evie smiled, the question catching her off guard.

Anne nodded at her. "I'd have thought you'd appreciate Austen. You always seemed to me made of cooler stuff. Like your grand-mother."

But I'm not at all like my grandmother, thought Evie a little mutinously, drawn toward the big barn doorway where the grasses waved outside.

"Was that the time the Negro man was here?" Eddie wondered.

Evie turned around, startled. "Pops had a black man working here?"

"No, I don't think he was working here, was he, dear?"

"No," Anne said firmly. "He was a guest."

"Yes." Eddie sailed proudly back to his wife. "They were quite a pair, your grandparents. Everyone welcome on board."

Evie saw the flicker of something she couldn't read, something strong, cross Anne's face.

"Aunt Anne?" Evie probed.

Anne looked at her, her mind clearly somewhere else.

"Come on, love." Eddie offered his elbow to take the step down outside. Anne reached for his arm and he snugged her tight. Gently, together, they eased over the wide threshold onto the granite slab that formed the stoop. Evie was left standing, her mind racing. The wide door framed the older couple.

"When was this? Do you remember?"

"Haven't a clue," said Eddie cheerfully.

"It was the party, Eddie."

Evie concentrated on pulling the door shut, not wanting to look at her godmother, not wanting to nudge her out of the place in the past where she had clearly fallen. They stood outside a minute, looking down the hill to the Big House and beyond that to the water.

"Coming, love?" said Eddie.

She nodded, and the three of them wandered slowly down the hill, but when they got to the Big House, Anne sank down gratefully on the bench in front. Evie sat beside her, and Eddie took the picnic basket and their sweaters, continuing on down to talk to Jimmy on the dock. They watched in quiet as he reached the end of the lawn, disappearing through the square of the boathouse door.

"Do you know," Anne said after a while, "I've been going through our family papers, trying to put everyone in order. Not, thank goodness, Eddie's side, just my own. And it's been so *instructive.* There are quite a lot of them, you see, going all the way back three hundred years. And what strikes me, Evie, is just how little *difference* there is between us all —"

Evie glanced over at her. "But there are huge differences in the way we all live."

"Yes, of course," Anne conceded, "of course, cars and the like. But I mean except for that, really — they were born, grew old, and died just as we are. Over and over and over. And Evie" — she put her hand on Evie's knee — "dearie, what does it *matter*?"

"What does what matter?" Evie swallowed.

"Well." Anne considered for a minute. "This."

"What is this?"

The older woman turned her head to face down the lawn. Eddie would be waiting, sitting in the shade of the boathouse with Jimmy. Eddie, who used to come to her in the middle of the day, straight from the office, in between appointments, and love her. Sometimes even with the babies awake in the playpen. It would be so quick and urgent and you never know, do you, that that part will be over because it stretches for such a long time, the hot, tumescent quiet of one's twenties and thirties, even one's forties. Mornings in the city, scorching mornings when the windows open far above the street can't keep the street away, or the heat. And the babies are listless, and the children whine, and Mrs.

Marstead is cutting carrots in the kitchen for the children's supper. And suddenly, here you were on a bench beside one of those babies, Joanie's little girl. Anne's eyes rested on the dark rectangle of shadow stretching across the wide boathouse door. Poor Joan.

She shook her head.

"Us," she said quietly. "Not this. Us. All of *us.*"

Evie searched Aunt Anne's face. Long ago, stuck in the top carrel in the library stacks, Evie remembered feeling she could hear the voices speaking from the pages she was reading, times when she could almost understand the world below the words, see the eleventh century whole. But she had to skirt around it so as not to scare away what she thought she understood. She had the same feeling just now. There was something she might miss if she thought about it too hard. Something that might pertain.

"Hang on a sec." She stood and went into the house, letting the screen door bang behind her as she moved into the front room and pulled the Polaroid off the little mantel.

Evie came back out. "Have you ever seen this?"

Her godmother looked down at the Polaroid Evie handed her, in silence.

Joan, Anne thought. *Oh, Joanie, there you are.*

"Well, they were something, weren't they,"

she said, turning over the Polaroid and seeing what Joan had written.

"What does that mean, do you think?" Evie asked. " 'The morning of —' What morning, do you know?"

Anne looked up at Joan's daughter, who believed she knew so much but who had never known her own mother — had never really tried, it seemed — and was exhausted by it all. She knew precisely what Joan must have meant by "the morning of." But she wouldn't say. It wasn't hers to tell.

"I haven't the faintest idea," she replied, turning away.

Damn it, Evie thought, looking down at her mother's oldest friend. Here it was again. This quiet. The familiar quiet around her, the quiet she'd grown up in. A quiet that robbed her, that continued to rob her some-how, though she couldn't see how, or why — or who was the thief.

"How like your grandmother she looks."

Evie turned and followed Anne's gaze.

A tall blond woman was coming through the boathouse, pushing Grandfather's wheel-barrow with her luggage on it and talking to Eddie and Jimmy.

"The spitting image," Anne said approvingly.

"Min." Evie's heart sank. "She's come early."

THIRTY-ONE

"It's all right, Reg," Len said quietly. "We were invited."

"In New York." Reg lifted the strap on his camera and settled it off his shoulders. Moss's invitation had been tossed out so easily the week before last, so blithely, that the plan had seemed indeed nothing out of the ordinary. They had booked two tickets on the overnight train from Manhattan to Maine, walked the two miles to the ferry landing and into a watchfulness that had felt like another kind of waiting. It was, in part, what he had expected, but he was already weary of bracing for something he couldn't see coming. Up here, he seemed outlined by the stark light, by the severe angles of the fishermen's white cottages, the single street rising straight up from the ferry landing to the market at the end. New England. Up here, there was nowhere to hide.

They heard voices coming toward them through the fog. Len took his hands out of his pockets. Beside him, Reg folded his arms over his chest and then in the next motion unfolded them. They couldn't see past the lip of the dock. To their left a black tar-papered ramp stretched into the mist, ending above them in a pier.

Footsteps sounded on the wood coming through the boathouse and then paused behind the gate above Len and Reg at the top of the gangway down to the dock. Two women stood above them looking down. The one in front was tall and lovely standing there, her long bare legs emerging from a pair of dusty rose-colored shorts, dark hair resting at the neck of a fisherman's sweater.

"Len." She hesitated, her hand on the gate. "Len Levy."

Len was frozen beside him.

"Jesus," Reg muttered. "You know her?"

"Hello, Joan," Len answered.

"Len?" Reg asked again.

"This is Moss's sister," Len said, raising his voice. "Joan Milton."

She pushed open the gate and came down the gangway, her eyes on Reg. "You must be Reg Pauling."

"Yes."

"Moss has talked about you." She held out her hand.

Reg took it. Len was stiff beside him. This girl knew him, and except for the slight toss of the chin, she was not going to let on how well. Len fixed his eyes, as steadfast as a drowning man, on the other girl.

Goddamn him, Reg thought.

"Have we met?" The second girl scrutinized Len.

"No." He shook his head. "Never."

"I didn't think so." She nodded. "I'm Anne Pratt."

"But how on earth did you get here?" Joan asked Reg.

"By boat."

Joan looked. The dock was empty.

"A lobsterman dropped us off," Reg explained.

"A *lobsterman?*"

"We got a ride."

"So you are marooned," said Anne cheerfully. "Castaways. Now you'll have to stay for the party."

There was a single instant of intense silence and then a hot blush bolted across Joan Milton's face. She would be damned, Reg saw, to be seen as rude.

"Yes, yes, of course," she echoed Anne. "Come and say hello. Moss will be so happy to see you. *We* are so glad you made it."

She turned and started up the gangway into the boathouse.

"This is the girl?" Reg said to Len under his breath. Len nodded.

"Let's go," Reg said. "Let's get out of here. Let's just not go up there. This is a mistake."

The broad blank face Len turned to him was as clear as a hand put out palm first: *wait.*

"Reg," Len said.

"Coming?" Joan stood at the top of the gangway.

"Right behind you." He reached down and grabbed his bag without looking at Reg.

There was nothing to do but follow the other three through the old wooden building and into the fog on the other side, which was moving, Reg noticed, as though the air breathed. Len was walking in front of him without a word. Since he had discovered the Nazi papers he had been as restless as a cat, anxious, going into work every hot morning hoping, Reg knew, to find something to contradict what he had already found in the files. But there was nothing more. Nothing was there. There was nothing to exonerate Milton, nothing to set Len free of his suspicion. "I have to ask him," Len insisted.

"Why can't it wait until the fall?"

"I can't wait," Len said.

"Why not?"

"I *can't.*"

Because of the daughter, Reg understood. This girl. This Joan Milton, leading the three of them up the hill.

Through a sudden gap in the fog, an enormous white house at the top of the lawn appeared, a solid through the mist. In an open window, a curtain blew out into the air slowly, like a kerchief waved by a prisoner.

"The most beautiful place on earth," Reg said quietly. Joan glanced at him, surprised.

"That's what your brother called it."

"And he's right," she said, liking Reg immediately.

"What kind of camera is that?" Anne asked Reg, barreling forward up the hill.

"A Polaroid," he answered. "A Land."

"Will you take our pictures?"

"Of course," Reg replied.

Ahead at the top of the hill, a loose group of people stood clustered around what looked like a piano, their backs to the lawn. The door to the house was wide open and the screen door tied back against one of the shutters. And, Reg saw, it was in fact an upright piano balanced in a kind of wheelbarrow and towering above the men and women standing there.

Moss was nowhere to be seen.

"Mum!" Joan called. "Dad! We have guests."

An older man turned around.

"Sonofagun! Levy?" Ogden exclaimed, the surprise on his face mixed immediately with delight.

(And watching the two men walking toward them through the fog behind Joan, Kitty was overtaken by the brief impossible thought that here was that little boy coming toward her. Alive and returned. She shuddered, fixing her smile. Of course it wasn't him — but here was the mess, here it was, coming.)

"Hello, sir." Len closed the distance between them and stuck out his hand.

"Kitty," Ogden said. "This is Len Levy."

"Levy?"

Reg thought he caught the barest shiver and then the swift correction as Mrs. Milton came toward them with a firm smile on her face, drawing the place with her, her silver hair tucked behind her ears, tiny clippers in one hand.

"Mrs. Milton," Len said.

"Len hails from Chicago," Ogden told her, apropos of nothing. But she nodded. Then she turned to Reg.

"This is Mr. Pauling," Joan pressed quietly.

"Hello." Kitty extended the other hand. "I'm afraid you've come just in time to help with the piano." She smiled.

"Levy?" A man Len's size stood in the open doorway. "Is that you?"

"Hello, Pratt." Len nodded at him easily and crossed the rest of the lawn to shake his hand as Dickie came down the front steps.

"My sister, Evelyn." Joan pointed to the girl at the bottom of those steps who Len was greeting now.

Reg saw the same expression on the sister's face as had rested upon her mother's. A vague worry, smoothed away.

"But where on earth have you come from in this fog?" Kitty asked him.

"Reg!" Moss shouted from the doorway, grabbing Evelyn from behind and moving her gaily down the steps and out of the way. "You *came.* I don't believe it! You've come!"

He put his hands on Reg's shoulders and grinned, elated.

"You asked." Reg grinned back at him, shaking his hand, the door in his heart kicked open.

"That I did."

"We heard you needed a hand with a piano?"

"That we do," Moss answered him happily, "and a whole *hell* of a lot more, besides. You brought your camera! Good.

"Hello, Len," he added, giving Len's shoulder a squeeze.

"All right," Ogden announced. "I hate to say it, but if we are going to move that piano, we've got to start now."

"Where's it going?" asked Len.

And when Ogden pointed at the barn at the top of the hill, Len didn't hesitate. He nodded and walked over to the cart, picking up one of the long wooden handles.

Not to be outdone, Dickie stepped forward, and then Moss and Reg, the four of them grabbing hold of the wagon and advancing, slowly, foot by foot across the lawn and around the corner of the Big House. The mahogany form — still and somber against the gray moving air — gave the procession a reverence out of all proportion to the thing itself, like the elephant in *Aida,* Joan thought, crossing the vast stage of the Metropolitan Opera and turning its slow head toward the audience beyond the lights. It was fantastic. Impossible. Absurd. She smiled as she and Anne and Evelyn followed the piano bumping slowly up the hill, until they were at the top and the angle softened, and Len lowered the handle and they could wheel the wagon right up to the barn doors and set the handles on the haying ramp to the side of the door — and suddenly it was done.

"Thank god," Dickie gasped, and grinned at Evelyn.

"Good job, darling."

Moss threw himself down and spread-eagled his arms and legs in the grass. "Christ," he sighed.

Len and Reg leaned against the wagon, catching their breath.

"All right?" Moss asked.

"Looked like you might lose the whole thing back there." Ogden came into view.

Len straightened up. "Almost did."

"But we figured it out," Dickie corrected him smoothly, "didn't we?"

"They did," Evelyn exclaimed to her father, "they were terrific, oh, isn't it the nuts, Dad — we'll have music tonight, after all."

Tonight? thought Joan, her eyes sliding off Len's back and darting away. How could she think about a tonight, or even an afternoon, with him here? What was he doing?

Ogden grabbed the handle of one of the barn doors, pulling it open on its runners. Moss got on his feet and grabbed the other door, pulling it in the opposite direction, so they all stepped up and into a vast open space, the roof pitched three stories above the floorboards where they stood, the great crossbeams stretching overhead like the spars of frigates, fifty feet up. Inside it was empty, wooden, and yet somehow sepulchral, Moss felt — had always felt. The sudden opening, the stumbling into air and light. Along one side of the barn, where stalls once held cattle, benches had been built to hug the three walls of each stall, and cushioned in a gay yellow stripe, around a table set in the middle of each. Extending down on a long rope from the crossbeam, a lantern hung above each of the three tables. The effect was that of a makeshift lounge, comfortable and rakish all at once. It was the kind of charming arrangement Kitty excelled at. The piano was to go in the corner at the edge of one of these booths.

The men pushed the piano safely over the doorjamb onto the smooth wooden boards and across the floor, the heavy piece moving easily on its caster wheels, and set against the wall at last.

Clap. Joan pushed the wooden shutters off

the far windows at the end of the barn. *Clap, clap.* She folded them back and now the gentle gray light of the fog pushed through from the other side of the barn, the room filling with the low glow. She felt the heat of Len's attention on her back and turned around. And for a moment, the longing on his face was so clear, so naked, Joan wanted to put her hands on either side of his chin and kiss him. The moment ticked. Something was happening right that second. Here she was. There was Len. She felt him in her knees.

Oh god, what will happen? she thought. *What will happen now?*

Moss raised the lid and lowered his fingers down, and the full chord of a middle C rose up. There, he set them again, and the chord repeated. Anne pulled over a chair and Moss sat, without letting his hands lift, running up and down the keys, in shivering sound, one note tripping over the other, up and down, looking to settle, a little variation, a little repetition, this note, that one, he roamed, and the notes laughed into the exorbitant empty possibility around them, up and down the keyboard, finally settling once again on that C.

Through the kitchen window, Kitty watched them all coming back down the hill. Trailing the men, Joan and Evelyn were walking arm in arm, a habit they had never left behind in childhood, and even now the fact that the younger sought the older's arm made Kitty glad. She pushed open the screen door and went out to the sunny patch of granite just behind the back door and stood there waiting for the triumphant group to arrive.

Moss walked slowly, his hands in his pockets, saying something to the Negro man, who leaned toward him, listening intently. He laughed. The other appeared not to hear, perfectly at ease here with his big bones and his broad shoulders; she saw that Ogden set great store in him. He stood a little too tall in his shoes for her. She watched him carefully now.

And so she saw it then, saw Mr. Levy glance backward up the hill at the girls. As though he had left something behind. Something irretrievable. And the quick, sharp turn of his head, the easy assurance of a great man's body in the world, checking something behind him while still in mid-stride coming toward her reminded her, improbably, of Ogden. As though he were his match, his equal, his inheritor.

No, she thought. *I don't like it —*

"What's that?" Og came up behind her.

She flushed. She hadn't thought she'd spoken aloud.

"I don't like lunch to be kept waiting." She managed to smile at him. "As you know."

THIRTY-TWO

"So what's our plan?" Min asked as they stood on the dock watching the Fenwicks putt slowly off into the Narrows.

Evie didn't answer right away. In fact she didn't have an answer. She watched Anne and Eddie's boat disappear around the point on Vinalhaven where the Narrows met the larger waters of the bay and wished Paul had seen them standing there in the middle of the big empty room in the barn. He might have understood something that she couldn't put her finger on. Something other than that the Fenwicks were a lovely old pair. She turned around.

"*Our* plan? I don't know. I thought you weren't coming until the day after tomorrow."

"Yes, well, I've come today. Hand me that, will you?" Min had lowered herself into the dinghy tied up to the end of the dock. She pointed to the hand pump that Jimmy Ames kept down on the dock.

("Min," their grandmother had observed to

her mother, sitting in the blue chairs above the dock, "likes to get things done around here."

"As does Evie," Joan had protested.

"Evie likes to *think,*" Kitty demurred.

Evie, who had listened quietly to this kind of conversation shuttled back and forth between her grandmother and her mother and her aunt all her childhood, the three women totting up the children — who was this, who was that, what this one had, what the other did not and never would — and who had never once let on that she heard, turned around on the dock and stared at her grandmother. She was seventeen. In two weeks she would leave for college. Enough, she thought to herself hotly, was enough.

"Hello there." Her grandmother had answered Evie's stare mildly.

And Evie, who had not yet learned that venom is best defanged by calm, had thought somehow she had won. It was only much later she understood that she had been handled.)

The water sluiced from the pump out of the bottom of the rowboat in a dirty stream. For a long while the two cousins stood in silence, the regular, even slap of water hitting water between them as Min emptied the boat of its winter bilge.

"How did we get here, Min?" Evie asked quietly.

Min didn't look up. "How do you mean?"

"Here. To the end of the Island."

"We ran out of money. Full stop."

Min stood with the pump between her legs, the long hose trailing off the gunwale into the water, and started pumping again. The water burbled out once and then gushed in a thick, steady stream over the side of the rowboat into the sea.

"That's it?" Evie sat down on the end of the gangway and watched. "I can't help thinking there must have been a starting point where it all began to go wrong, when we started to lose this place from under our feet."

Min looked up at her, curious. "Why do you want this place so badly?"

"Why don't you?" Evie stared.

Min held her gaze a moment and then looked back down at the pump.

"We didn't lose it, Evie. We made other choices. Choices that don't involve making money, for instance," she added wryly.

"Except Henry. He can afford to buy us all out."

"Henry?" Min kept pumping. "Henry is a fabulist."

"Is he?" Evie asked. "Was he making up what he said about something your mother said my mother did? Something that happened?"

Min looked at her. "Would it make it easier

if something bad had happened?"

"Yes."

"Something we were all being punished for?"

"In a way, it would." Evie nodded.

"It would mean that things don't just come to an end. It would be part of a drama, in some way or another. With a meaning."

Evie looked at her. "You sound like Paul."

Min raised her eyebrow, diverted. "How is Paul?"

Evie folded her arms. "Paul is fine."

Though we may not be, she thought.

Min looked back down and started pumping again. "Let me tell you something: there are no hidden secrets that will burnish our story, nothing romantic or gothic or whatever the hell flavor you want. Life is simply this. Just this. Two people."

"Arguing?"

"Arguing, sitting together. Making love. Not making love. It's always this, ordinary and simple."

Evie studied her. "You realize, don't you, that you may be the only shrink on the planet who has come to the conclusion that life doesn't revolve around untold secrets. That life is caught best by its — surfaces."

Min shook her head impatiently.

"That's what I'm trying to say, Evie. *This* is not a surface. This is it. But no one wants to admit it. If I've learned anything at all in all these years of listening to people, it's that the urge to see causality, the need for A to lead to B, and then, blindly and without fail, to C, is stronger even than the urge for sex." She looked up at Evie with a broad grin.

Evie smiled back.

Min shoved the lever down on the pump to clear it, shaking it dry. "It's just the end, that's all. Our time is up. We're history. Toast."

"You sound glad."

Min turned around and looked at her. "I suppose I am. I mean, look at it. We could limp along like this — killing the place teaspoon by teaspoon, this belongs here, that belongs there. We don't replace the teapot, we don't use the floats; if the roof leaks, put a bucket under it and move your chair. We could do all this wryly, gaily as we were taught. *Oh, never mind. Oh, don't bother yourself about me. Oh, I'll be fine. Just fine . . .*" Min's voice trailed off. "Or we could sell it. We could let it go. We could let it *go.* And we could move on."

"Then who would we be?"

"Ourselves." Min shrugged. "With a little more money."

Evie followed her cousin up the gangway and into the boathouse, where Min tucked away the pump. The wide rectangle of the boathouse doorway framed the Big House. The lilacs were in bloom beside the door. A fish hawk lifted off the top of one of the spruce by the barn. How could they let this go?

When her cell phone rang in her pocket it took several seconds before she registered the sound.

"Hello?"

"Hi, Mom." Seth's voice curled through the phone.

"Hey." She smiled, and nodded at Min, who kept going up the hill.

"How's the Island?"

"It's good." She watched Min touch one of the limbs of the lilac before opening the screen door. "Great."

"Foggy?"

"Not a cloud."

"Okay."

She waited.

"Okay." He yawned. "I just wanted to say good morning."

"It's almost lunch."

"Mom." He was patient. "Are you familiar with the concept of summer?"

"I am familiar with the concept of sloth," she teased. "Anyway, sweetie, hearing your voice is the best thing ever."

"God, Mom, I hope not."

She smiled. "Is Dad there?"

"Yup. Do you want to speak to him?"

She rolled her eyes.

"Bye, Mom. I love you."

"Love you too."

Two lobster boats raced through the Narrows at full throttle, heading for the wide waters at the end of Crockett's, the turrets of their radars flashing through the gaps in the trees. Min was clipping blooms from the lilac out front. She did look like their grandmother, Evie thought.

"Hey." Paul came on. "How is it? How are you?"

Her throat closed at the sound of his voice.

"Haunted," she answered.

He was quiet.

She cleared her throat. "It's okay."

"Okay?" he asked.

"Min's here," she said, lowering her voice.

"That's good," he answered. "She can help."

"I don't really *want* her help."

"It's a big job."

"Yeah." She didn't want to talk to Paul about this. She didn't want to hear it was a big job and Min was a big help. She wanted him to understand something else — that she was standing in the boathouse door looking out at the yellow grasses waving under a midsummer sky, the Island around her. And that when she was here, here was all there was. That was what she wanted to say, though it said nothing. Words said nothing at all, at times. Words were just empty boxes stacked on a shelf.

"Did you tell her about the photograph?"

"Which photograph?"

"*Which* photograph." Paul was incredulous. "The one I showed you."

Evie straightened. "No."

"Why not?" Paul pressed.

Because, Evie thought. *Because I don't believe it.*

"What would it explain?" she asked.

"It doesn't have to explain anything." Paul was impatient. "It's a fact. Min might have something to say. She might have heard something growing up."

Evie didn't answer.

"Evie, this is a big deal —"

"All right," she said. "It's a big deal, all *right.* I can *see* that."

He didn't answer.

The phone was pressed so tight against her cheek, it hurt. "Paul?"

He let out his breath. "I don't know what you see sometimes, when it comes to that place, or your family up there —"

"He was *not* a Nazi sympathizer, Paul."

"I'd want to know for sure. I'd want —" He stopped himself.

"Tell me this, Paul. Explain this," she pushed back at him, her voice catching. "Why do I feel I have to hold on to it — this place, all of it — at all costs?"

He was quiet.

"Evie," he said so gently, she closed her eyes.

He stayed with her, on the other end.

"Listen," he said, after a little, relenting. "I've been digging around on your Mr. Pauling."

"He's not *my* Mr. Pauling —" Evie drew in her breath. "Wait."

"What?" Paul asked.

"This morning, Aunt Anne was here, and Uncle Eddie mentioned him."

"By name? What did Anne say?" Paul pushed.

"No, no. It had to do with the piano in the barn."

"And?"

Evie frowned. "We were looking at the piano, and Eddie remembered 'the Negro,' as he put it."

"That's it?"

"No," Evie realized. "The way he said it, I thought he meant that Pops had a black man working here, but Eddie corrected me. Apparently, he was a guest."

"It *could* have been Pauling, then."

Evie nodded. The thrill in his voice was taut. She could see him holding the phone, his elbow sticking straight out in his excitement.

The sun splintered on the water, bouncing in light pockets in the waves.

"You would have thought you'd know about

a black man coming onto the Island," he said.

"Yeah, well." Evie was wry. "Same old story — isn't that what you were telling me and Daryl that night you got back from Berlin?"

"How's that?'

Hazel's word rose up in her head. "The invisibles."

"The invisibles." She heard his smile. "Market that one — the unsung action heroes."

"Unsung," she said, and smiled back, "doesn't even begin to describe it, and I can't claim it. It's Hazel's."

"Riffing off Ellison," Paul remarked.

She nodded into the phone.

"Anyway," Paul went on, "this Reg Pauling, the one I'm thinking of, is still alive, you know."

She tensed. "I would have thought Dick Sherman would have found that out."

"Probably so," Paul allowed.

She nodded against the phone.

"Why don't you check the guest book?" he asked.

She had forgotten all about Granny K's guest book. She felt a tug of excitement, the pull toward research, of digging into a question. The pull toward Paul, she realized.

"Evie," he said. "Are you there?"

"I'm here." She nodded.

There was a pause.

"Evie," he said again, more softly. And she

heard what he didn't say. All the distance and all the time they had traveled together, their past. The nights and the mornings, the long afternoons. She heard Seth's wail and his small boy's voice in the night. In Paul's voice just then, she heard all the years that were gone, and were still there, between them. His love.

"You're okay?"

"I'm okay." She smiled.

"Dad?" Seth called.

"Go on."

She turned around, still smiling, and started back up the lawn. Ahead of her, Min emerged from the side of the house with the copper vase from the dining room and gave it a great heave. The bayberry sailed out of its pot and into the grass by the side of the kitchen door.

"Min!" Evie shouted.

Min looked up.

"What are you doing?" Evie was charging up the hill.

"Mum hated that stuff," Min said.

"But Granny K loved it, and Mum did too."

"The lilacs are in bloom," Min answered. "We're never here when they are in bloom."

"But Granny K always filled that vase with bayberry."

"So? That doesn't mean we have to."

"Yes. It does."

"For Christ's sake, Evie." Min laughed in disbelief.

They stared at each other.

"Why did you come anyway?" Evie blurted.

"I told you. I thought you might need some help."

"No, you didn't," Evie saw suddenly. "No, you didn't. You just didn't want to let me be here on my own. You're exactly like Aunt E. You just take over."

"Evie." Min turned away, disgusted, and yanked open the kitchen door. "You're no better than Henry."

The door slammed. Evie stood a minute and then pulled the kitchen door open, furious.

Min was pulling fixings out of the fridge to make sandwiches. Evie's breakfast dishes lay stacked to the side of the sink. The coffeepot squatted on the stove. She should have put everything away first; she should have tidied. Mum and Granny K would have cleaned the kitchen before going outside. The breakfast things on the counter were a reproach. Automatically, Evie took the jam jar, tightened the top, and put it in the fridge. Min wouldn't look at her.

She was laying out soft brown bread, Hellmann's, and a thick cucumber she must have bought at the farm stand along Route 1. Evie had forgotten about cucumber sandwiches, but now, standing there in the kitchen, Min busy peeling the green skin off in long strips, all the lunches at this table with her cousins and the impatient efficiency of Granny's cook, Jessie O'Mara, returned.

A dragonfly bounced off the screen door and then nattered by in the heat, its castanets vanishing.

"Can I have one?" Evie asked, her anger cooling.

"Sure," Min answered tightly, and set out two more slices of bread.

Evie leaned on the counter and folded her arms. "Why are we stuck in this fight?"

Min spread a thick swath of mayonnaise on two of the pieces of bread and began to lay down the slices of cucumber like tiles.

"Because they were stuck in it."

Evie went to the kitchen table and pulled out a chair.

"Do you know your mother never thanked my mother once?" Min said, her back still to Evie.

"For what?'

"For protecting her."

"Protecting her? She obliterated her."

Min turned around.

"You never see what is right in front of you, Evie. You never have. Mum protected Aunt Joan all the way through. Without my mother yours would have died from her seizures."

Evie frowned. "I never heard anything like that."

"Exactly." Min put the knife down. "That's exactly my point."

"Listen, Min, I didn't even know she *had* seizures until just before she died."

Min stared. "How can that be?"

Evie nodded.

Min cut both sandwiches in half, put one in front of Evie, and sat down herself.

"I hated how our mothers fought up here," Min said. "I hated who they all became. There's no such thing as the past here — I mean, look at us; the minute we're here, we're our mothers fighting over flowers in pots, over what goes where, over who gets what. Nothing is ever finished, it's just carried along, carried onward. No offense," she said, glancing across the table, "but that's why history always seemed to me so —"

Evie narrowed her eyes. "Useless?"

"Silly," Min said quietly. "As if things that happen could really be put in a box or a book and let rest. What's over is always under. And that goes double up here."

"How do you move forward, then, without seeing the past for what it was?"

Min shrugged.

"So who cares what happened?" Evie poked.

Min folded her arms and looked at her cousin. "You know, Evie, lots of people finish my sentences for me. I'm used to it. But you are the only person on the planet who finishes them wrong — every time."

Evie tucked her chin, watching her cousin warily.

"It's not who cares what happened," Min went on, "but who knows what happened. After a while, I don't think even they did."

Evie shook her head. "But that's not what Henry thinks, or Harriet — they think Mum did something to your mum, and that's why they won't let Mum have her rock."

"Mum was saying all sorts of things at the end. But the fact that Aunt Joan wanted to put a rock down — some marker — drove her wild."

"But it was where she wanted to be buried, that's all. It was something about *her* life," Evie protested.

"It was more than that, I don't know what. But for Mum it would be as if Joan had had the last word."

Evie stared. "On what?"

"I don't know." Min shook her head. "But we're stuck like this, Evie — I know you know it. And I can't stand it. I don't want this place. I want out. I want to be free of it."

The two stared at each other.

"But —" Evie said. "This *place.* Look at it, look at that." She pointed to the sunlight divided into the nine squares of the old kitchen window, stretched and held against the faded wall. Time stopped. Light. Sky. Nothing changed here but the light of day. The tap in the pantry dripped single notes into the sink. A cloud crossed the sun in the sky and the light dropped in the room.

"Yeah." Min shook her head. "I've had enough. It's sad. It's broken. It's a shell — why hold on to a shell?"

"It's where everyone is."

Min exhaled. "Really? What about Paul? Seth? Aren't they everyone too?"

"Of course," Evie replied uneasily. "You know what I mean."

Min nodded, picked up her sandwich, and took a bite.

They had reached a kind of truce. They ate in quiet, and it seemed to Evie that she had sat in this chair, her bare feet flat on the blue linoleum, eating with Min for years and years and years.

"Poor Mum," Evie said at last. "This was the only place where she was happy."

"What made you think she was unhappy?"

"She never got out of the gate, somehow." Evie was thoughtful. "She and Dad always seemed to be living just to the side of their own lives." She shook her head, rueful, and looked at Min. "Whereas in your house, everything added up. I used to study your Christmas card, you know —"

"Oh god."

"I'm serious." Evie smiled.

There was a certainty there, a rightness that Evie never felt anywhere else. And it created great calm. One went to Aunt Evelyn and

Uncle Dickie's enormous house in Greenwich, Connecticut, overlooking the sound, where the silver was polished, drinks were at six and dinner at seven and everything had its place. There was a right way and a wrong way to do things, and at Aunt Evelyn's it was right. In this spirit, she had borne four children, all of whom knew how to ski, play tennis, speak French, decode Latin, throw a good party, drive a boat, a car, and, if need be, a tractor.

"Everyone else had mothers who talked to them, fought with them, took on the world. Not mine."

Min listened.

"Why does someone retreat like that?" Evie asked her. "Say no to the world? Pull back, raise the drawbridge, turn away?"

She looked at Min. "It was as if Mum had ceded the field to Aunt E and Granny K —"

"Granny K was a big bully," Min said crisply. "If you didn't do as she liked, if you didn't sit up, speak when you were spoken to, adore lobster, blueberries, and wildflowers, speak French easily, go to Yale or Harvard, or *marry* a man from Yale or Harvard — you simply didn't exist."

"That's a little exaggerated," Evie protested, but it made her smile.

Min raised her eyebrow and said nothing.

"Anyway," Min said after a little, "Aunt Joan never seemed unhappy to me. She seemed —"

Evie looked over.

"Devoted," Min decided. "She was a devotee."

Min reached for Evie's plate, stood up, and carried both to the sink.

"Of what?"

"The Island," Min answered. "Everything always had to be right where it belonged. The geraniums in the barrels at the front of the house. The marguerites, the cosmos, and the phlox. She was a stickler for details. Don't you remember, in the eighties, when Granny K got too frail to go down to the picnic grounds for drinks, Aunt Joan rented a golf cart from the mainland to carry her up and down the lawn. 'We always have drinks down there,' she insisted. 'Why stop?' "

Why stop? Evie's throat caught.

"It drove Mum crazy. She hated it up here, you know," Min said.

"No, she didn't."

"She did. The older she got, the more she hated it. At the end of every summer, she'd say to me, 'There, that's done.' Like a test she had passed yet again."

"But I thought Henry was carrying on the way she wanted. She always wanted to be in charge."

"They were sisters." Min wrinkled her nose. "She just didn't want Joan to be in charge."

"But" — Evie was incredulous — "Mum

was never in charge; your mother always made all kinds of decisions without telling Mum."

"She had to," Min answered. "I loved her, but Aunt Joan was the most stubborn person on the planet."

Evie snorted. "Mum?"

" 'Unforgiving,' according to Mum." Min nodded. "Both of them. Joan and Moss. And Mum always seemed to feel it more up here."

Moss? Evie thought.

"What had your mother done that needed forgiving?" Evie started stacking the breakfast dishes in the drainer back up on the kitchen shelf.

Min paused so long, Evie turned around.

"I'm not sure whether I believe this, but apparently there was a man," she said cautiously.

"A man?"

"Between them. Somebody —"

"How do you mean, between them?"

"I'm not sure. I think in the obvious way."

"Someone who came here?"

Min shook her head, mystified.

"Wait a sec." Evie remembered what Paul had asked. "Hold on."

And she walked to the front room where the row of leather-bound guest books sat on the little bookshelf beside Granny K's chair. The embossed gold of CROCKETT'S ISLAND still held a faint glow on the oldest one in front.

"Evie?"

"Hang on." She pulled the guest book marked 1959 and walked it back into the kitchen, laying it down on the table between them.

"What are we looking for?"

"Reginald Pauling."

Min was startled. "The man Granny wants Moss's share given to?"

Evie nodded.

"But who is he?"

"Well, the one that Paul knows of is an African-American writer."

"A black man? Here? That would never have happened."

"We'll see."

Evie slid her hand across the smooth green leather cover before opening it. The musty smell of old paper rose up, mixed with something else. She leaned down. Camphor? The thick paper of the pages cascaded in her hand, stray words and phrases in various inks and handwritings cast up like jetsam. *Marnie . . . true friendship and . . . without ovens or time . . . picnic . . . more time in your company.* She riffled them all the way to the end of the book and then, more slowly, started at the beginning again, paging through the names in the early part of the summer, slowing down as she neared the end. There was nothing, no one named Reg, not even an R. Pauling appeared on any of the pages.

"He's not there," she said, disappointed.

The last name in the book was Leonard Levy. She flipped through the rest of the pages to be sure.

"That's weird — it ends on August twenty-fifth —" She looked up. "Shit."

"What?"

Shit. Shit. Shit. Evie walked back into the front room, pulled the Polaroid off the mantel, and then brought it back to Min, tossing it across the table at her.

"Where did this come from?"

"Mum had it."

"God." Min studied it. "Look at them."

Evie nodded.

"Who took it, do you think?" Min looked up.

"No clue." Evie reached and turned it over and pointed to her mother's note. "But look at that."

Min looked down again.

"I asked Aunt Anne about it," Evie said. "But she didn't have any idea what it might mean."

Min shivered and looked up at Evie.

"I don't know what 'the morning of' means either, but look at the date."

"So?"

"I'm pretty sure that's the day Uncle Moss died."

THIRTY-THREE

"Where's your camera, Reg?" Moss asked, coming around the corner of the house. Reg pointed to the Polaroid, sitting where he had left it on the green bench at the front of the house. Moss turned and shouted back to Evelyn and Dickie, "Come on, you two, come get documented — it's the morning of your big party!"

Evelyn and Dickie walked toward them all and stood a little awkwardly together. "Where?"

Moss pointed. "Up there, on the steps of the house."

So the two lovers stood very straight together in front of the Big House and looked politely into Reg's camera as he lowered his face into the visor and shot. The flash went off, and the film whirred its way through the machinery to the light. Reg rolled the image out of the back of the camera and laid it on the green bench to dry.

"My turn." Joan pulled Dickie away, smiling, and slid in beside Evelyn. The two sisters stood arm in arm together, and when Moss said, "Come on, Evelyn, smile for Reg," the wary expression on her face softened just a little. Joan allowed herself a glance at Len standing off to himself behind Reg. At the last minute, Moss jumped into the frame, cupping his cigarette and giving Reg a look that was part sweetness and all dare.

"Take me," he said. "Right here."

Everyone laughed.

Slowly, Reg pulled the camera up to his eyes and held it steady. Through the viewfinder, Moss looked back at him, and there was no mistaking the look. Reg closed his eyes and snapped.

"Christ," he heard Moss chuckle. "That's bright."

Reg lowered the camera and looked at Moss.

And Moss nodded slowly back.

In a little while, it would be lunch. The sisters went inside to help their mother. Dickie brought out a football and tossed it to Reg, who threw it to Len. Moss lay back down in the shade of the house, listening to the slap and tuck, the sound of skin on leather. The flag hung listless on the pole. The ball tossed back and forth. Slap and tuck. Behind the men, through the windows at the front of the house, there was the murmur of women's voices.

Joan had stalled at the window in the front room, watching Len twenty feet from her on the other side of the glass. And though she was staring, though she was a figure at the window anyone could have seen, she didn't care. She wanted him to see her. If he looked up and saw her, he'd know.

But he hadn't looked up. He hadn't stopped from his game. Aside from that one look he had shot at her on the dock, he hadn't looked at her again. He seemed determined about something, as though he had a job to do before he could catch her eye again. He had thrown the ball, round and around, and then, uncomplicated as a dog, had thrown himself to the ground, laughing. Then gotten up to throw again. Men could do this — lie around, bat words up and down, or say nothing. Even through the glass she could feel the slack good humor, the fellow feeling that bound them. Four men on the grass.

But why had he come?

"I've just realized who he is." Evelyn was watching them, beside Joan, her hands on her narrow hips.

"Who?" Though Joan knew full well. "Reg or Len?"

"Not Mr. Pauling." A hard expression settled on Evelyn's face. "I have no idea who he is. And anyway, I don't like him."

"Evelyn!"

"I don't. And Dickie doesn't either." She

frowned. "He is watching us all the time, making judgments about us, I'm sure. What does he think? That we'll behave badly? Of course we won't. None of us would say a word to offend him. He's welcome here."

"No, he's not," Joan protested. "I don't think that's right at all."

"Pay attention. You'll see." Evelyn leaned her arms on the sill. "No," she said quietly, "I meant Len Levy. He's the man who helped us that day in Penn Station at the beginning of this summer. I'm sure of it."

Joan turned away so Evelyn couldn't see the flush on her cheeks and started stacking the week's newspapers. "It's all right."

"All right? It's not all right, it doesn't feel a bit right."

"He works for Dad." Joan set the guest book on top of the papers, lining up the corners.

Evelyn nodded. "Dickie says he's full of himself."

Joan bit back a retort.

"How did he get here?" Evelyn asked. "Add it up, Joan."

"Add what up?"

"One doesn't just show up on the dock and expect to stay for lunch."

"He didn't expect anything, I don't think."

"Don't be so dim." Evelyn rolled her eyes. "Of course he did."

"Moss *invited* them, remember?"

"Was it a real invitation, do you think?" Evelyn was dubious.

"Of course," Joan said stoutly. "I'm sure it was."

"Pretty nervy to just come. Moss seemed as surprised as any of us."

"Moss said you should come, and Len did," Joan said quietly. Though she knew exactly what Evelyn was driving at. One didn't generally just take an invitation at face value. And either Len didn't see that, or — her heart tossed — he didn't care.

"What about the party, Joan? Now they'll have to stay. He's going to ruin my party."

"No, he's not."

"He is."

"He is a friend of Moss's," Joan said again patiently, "and he works for Dad."

Evelyn looked right at her. "But he's staying because of you."

Joan flushed.

"He is," Evelyn vowed. "He's watching you. All the time. You kissed him, remember?"

Joan turned from the window, straightening the shells on the hanging shelf without seeing what she touched.

"He thinks there's something there," Evelyn concluded.

Joan lifted her head and stared out the window. Dickie had the ball in his hand and was pointing down the lawn at a spot, and Len nodded, running just as the ball arced in the air toward him, leaped, and caught it, tucking the ball into his chest and folding his arms around it. She wanted those arms around her. She shivered and looked down.

"The whole mess is typical of Moss," Evelyn fumed. "He hasn't thought about this at all."

"What is typical?" Kitty paused in the doorway with her flower basket.

"These friends." Evelyn was dismissive. "Where will they sleep?"

Kitty stiffened. For a long moment, she studied her youngest daughter.

"We are not," she said quietly, "we are *never* the people about whom it shall be said we have made anyone feel uncomfortable. Or unwelcome."

Kitty drew the basket onto her hip and turned. "And I don't think Moss knew they'd come today," Kitty said on her way out the front door. "Though what possessed them to come all the way out here in the fog, I can't think."

"I know exactly what possessed them." Evelyn looked at Joan.

Lunch was set out on the pier so as to catch any breeze from off the water. And though the fog had lifted slightly, the damp air still hung a thick curtain, blocking the view down the Narrows to the mainland. They had eaten the sandwiches and drunk the lemonade, and the group had loosened and scattered slightly, like petals fallen from the stem. Fenno Weld had appeared out of the fog, his white shirt lifting and lowering as he rowed forward, a ghostly apparition. Priss and Sarah Pratt had gone up for a nap. Roger and Ogden were in the boathouse filling the kerosene lamps for the party. There was much to do, but Kitty rested in this little gully of time after lunch. The others were arranged before her in clumps, Evelyn and Dickie down on the dock, Joan standing with Len Levy and Reg Pauling beside them, his back to the water, leaning on the railing, talking. Moss sat near her with his knees up against the slats of the pier, his eyes closed.

The tide was going out, and the dock rocked slowly, keeping time to the swells carrying the waters of the bay back out to the sea.

Len Levy shifted beside Joan. The man wanted, Kitty could see, to put his hands somewhere; he had thrust them down in the pockets of his jacket, but they crept back up and out. He was quite attractive, though Joan seemed not to notice, she seemed miles away. Good for her, Kitty thought. She was not taken in by all that *brio.*

A fish hawk wheeled from the top of one of the trees in the cove, its broad wings as taut as sails. And Reg Pauling's eyes followed the point of the bird, his eyes sweeping over the group, resting briefly on Dickie at the end of the dock, pointing something out to Evelyn. Kitty felt the perception in him, the fine adumbrating mind that sorted and classed even as it took in the navy blue sleeve of Dickie's Shetland sweater. She wondered what he thought of it all and wondered if she'd ever know.

And the fact of him, the physical fact of him, a black man standing there listening to the talk, talking himself, startled her at the same time as it soothed. This is what it looked like. Nothing more.

"Mr. Pauling," Kitty called, "come over and talk to us."

Reg turned. She patted the spot beside her on the bench. "Moss tells me you know the Lowells," she said to Reg. "How is that?"

Perhaps his mother had worked for the Lowells, she thought.

Without opening his eyes, Moss drawled, "Reg was in Lowell House, Mum."

"Well then, that explains it," Kitty said, without missing a beat. He must be one of Jolly Lowell's "projects." "And what did you study there?"

"English," said Reg.

And she smiled at him. She liked how still he sat beside her, how he tipped his body toward her when she spoke. Kitty liked this neat man beside her.

"It's going to clear," Ogden declared, coming out of the boathouse with two lanterns, followed by Roger Pratt. Kitty turned toward where he pointed. Far down the Narrows a rip in the fog had opened a bright impossible blue and a spot of sun just at the end of Vinalhaven.

"So it is." She smiled.

"Dickens or Trollope?" Roger Pratt asked Reg.

"Excuse me?"

"You studied English. Are you a Dickens man," Roger asked, more slowly, "or Trollope?"

Reg turned around and regarded him.

"Anthony Trollope," Roger offered.

Reg smiled. "Yes, I know Trollope."

"I ask the question to everyone now —" Roger set the hurricane lamp on the table beside Kitty.

"What is the difference?" asked Reg.

"I'm sorry?"

"What is the difference between the two?"

A swift look crossed the older man's face, close to something like worry.

"The difference?" he said. "Why, it's enormous. One of them cares about systems, the other about people. Writers always break down into those two groups in the end."

"Do they?" Reg asked.

Moss grinned. "Reg is a writer," he offered, opening his eyes.

"A copy editor now," Reg corrected. "But I

was a stringer in Europe the past three years."

"What's your impression of it over there, now that the Marshall money has run its course?" Ogden carried three more lamps out onto the pier, setting them at intervals along the railing.

"In Germany? Or Italy?"

"Germany."

And as Reg answered, describing the wealth he had observed over the past few years, Ogden listened, clearly satisfied.

"This is what I've been saying — this is what Marshall saw in 'forty-six. Money, men, and know-how saved Europe. You sow good men, and good men mean good business, no matter where they come from. It worked in Europe, and it's working here. Good men. Good ideas. Money to seed them."

"Agreed." Roger Pratt nodded.

"So why is it, then, do you think, there was no Marshall Plan for the Negro?" Reg asked quietly.

Moss sat up and looked at Reg.

"For the Negro?" Ogden folded his arms, perplexed. "The Negro is an American, not a war-torn nation. There is no need for something special; it would be demeaning. America is surging forward, and the Negro — with everyone — rides the tide."

"And wasn't the Negro devastated by war? Aren't we a war-torn nation?"

Roger Pratt was mystified. "I'd say we all

profited by the war. I mean," he corrected himself, "not those poor souls who lost someone, but in general the late forties saw nothing but growth."

"I think Reg means the Civil War," Moss put in swiftly. "You are working on a theory, isn't that right, Reg? Something for *The Village Voice*?"

The name meant nothing to the older men, but the question had safely been deflected. Moss had caught it, held it, and diverted it from its mark, and the window was open between him and Reg there on the dock.

"That's right," Reg said evenly, giving Moss a slight smile, as if to say, *See that? There you go.*

But Ogden was shaking his head, still struck by what Reg had described in Europe. "It's the way to ensure peace."

"Money?" Roger shook his head. "Money alone won't do it."

"There is a right way and a wrong way," countered Ogden. "French Indochina will prove that to be true in the end. You'll see, Pratt."

"Nothing is black and white about the truth there." Roger shook his head. "You've got to have an endgame. You've got to give a people the tools to get them there."

"Speaking of which, Levy, tell these characters what you told me."

"What's that, sir?"

"How we are missing" — Ogden glanced at Roger — "a market."

Len pulled his hands out of his pockets and straightened.

"Honestly, Ogden," Kitty protested. "It's Saturday."

"Tell Dickie," Ogden said, waving Dickie forward, "what you were telling me in my office about expanding."

"Expanding?" Dickie pushed through the gate, joining them on the pier.

"Len thinks maybe we might expand a little. Instead of just advising companies where to invest, we advise the people who work there, as well."

Len nodded at Dickie. "If you take Milton Higginson out into the rest of the country, you would open Wall Street wide — you would show that the financial center need not remain in one place — and everyone profits."

Roger Pratt shook his head doubtfully. "Wall Street is Wall Street because it is run by men who understand the business, just as Washington is run by men who understand statesmanship. I was sent to Vietnam, for instance, because I know what I'm looking at. Doctors are trained, lawyers likewise."

"Granted, sir" — Levy didn't skip a beat — "but a carpenter might *invest* in a corporation. A carpenter might take financial power into his own hands. And if it were poised in various offices around the country, Milton Higginson would have put it there."

(*How the man talks,* Kitty thought, looking past him down the Narrows. *How he just steps in and takes over.* She watched him bend toward Ogden like a conspirator, and she frowned. As if he were in on something. As if he believed he could be in on something with Ogden.)

"See that, Pratt?" Ogden approved.

Dickie looked from Len to Ogden. "Are you proposing to send Milton Higginson into the public realm?"

"No," Len answered mildly. "Just looking to expand where we already are."

A mulish expression settled on Dickie's face at Len's use of the word *we.*

"I'd say where we are, at the heart of New York, is pretty much dead-on."

"There are many people who don't put New York as the only center of the country's power," Len said.

"And they would be wrong," Roger Pratt answered comfortably, rising to his feet. "The centers of power have always been right here."

"Yes," Len pointed out smoothly, "but centers move. They always have. And they move before people know they are gone. For instance . . ." He turned to Reg. "Tell them what you told me — about Gary Cooper in Paris."

"Paris?" Dickie whistled.

"The scene in the saloon?"

Len nodded. Reg folded his arms, looking at the group.

"The French are nuts about the movies," he said. "American movies, and Westerns, most of all — I'd say there's a theater tucked in just about every corner of the city. Last fall I saw there was a showing of *High Noon,* in a tiny theater just off the Rue de Rivoli, so I went in. The place was full of Frenchmen. I may have been the only American — I was certainly the only Negro."

That was the second time he had done that up here, Moss realized. Called attention to himself like that. It worked like a bell they all heard, a finger tap on the skull. It seemed to Moss that Reg was enjoying himself. As if he'd loosened his tie and dove in.

"In *High Noon,*" Reg was saying, "Gary Cooper pushes into a saloon, throws his hat down, slams his fist on the bar, and shouts: *Give me three fingers of red-eye!*"

Ogden grinned. "Go on."

Reg smiled, pulling back the arrow before he let it fly.

"But in Paris, Gary Cooper walks into the bar, slams his fist down, and demands: *Une verre de Dubonnet, s'il vous plait.*"

There was a little pause, and then everyone on the dock burst out laughing.

"See that?" Len was buoyed by their reaction. "The cowboy is what's coming, and the French don't know how to translate him."

"Why, that's not the point at all!" Dickie remarked, dismissing Len, appraising Reg newly. The man spoke French.

Moss laughed with the others, his eyes never leaving Reg's face.

There comes a turning, a turning point, not a climax, not the top of a song, but a turn when you realize the bass had been there all along, all along and under. Suddenly, you understand the steady, rich, insistent note was the tie, the bass was the tide. And Moss saw Reg was that. Reg was the anchor. Reg was the steady beat. With Reg at the center, with Reg telling stories here on the dock, Moss understood, they could all listen, they could imagine themselves to be the good men they were. They could believe a dream about themselves, and about the country. Why not? They were all standing right here. In fellowship. Laughing together.

But Moss heard another tune. His eyes upon them, Reg answered and asked and beat the bass to the bass, the note that troubled, disturbing, even as it preserved the tune. The men on the dock were on their best behavior, behaving around him, *for* him; and the notes Reg played, played them — and showed the sham of fellowship, showed up the stage. Watching him, Moss had seen for the first time what they all must look like to Reg.

Moss saw white. He saw black. The dream of themselves was a dream.

Reg was the bell *and* the crack in the bell, the steady note that tapped at the back of the skull and wouldn't stop.

That's what it was, Moss realized now. The slow beat of race — heard, unheard, and heard again. Always there, always sounding. Here was Moss's song for America, this moment right now. Moss's pulse quickened; he knew he was right. Reg was the ground. Moss stood up, hearing the notes in his head, hearing how to get this, how to show what he had seen here on the dock, in music. That was the center of the song. And it had always been here. There was no American song without it. Reg was the bass. Reg was the bell.

"Moss?"

"I just need to write this down, Mum," he said to her, but looking at Reg, his face opened into his crooked, contagious grin.

"You're the bell, man. You're it."

"No need to get carried away." Reg looked back at him, smiling. Moss chuckled and turned away.

"Don't vanish, Moss," Kitty called after him. "Dad will need you soon to dig the firepits."

"Sure thing." Moss nodded without really hearing, hurrying toward the boathouse. "I'll be quick."

His footsteps pounded away and then were

muffled by the lawn.

He would never give up this music, Kitty realized, as he disappeared into the fog. He would go and work for Ogden, but his heart would not be in it. It would not hold. A sudden spasm of fear gripped her.

"Joan," she said sharply. "Joan, these dishes need clearing. Where is Evelyn?"

Joan stood up abruptly from her spot beside her mother and started gathering plates.

"Can you give me a hand?" she said over her shoulder to Len.

Swiftly, Len pushed away from the railing, held the big wicker basket for Joan as she lowered the stack down in. They didn't exchange so much as a glance.

Kitty watched them. *So that's it.* It was the oldest trick in the book. The man worked for Ogden but wanted Joan.

Well, she thought. *Well, well.*

Beside her, Reg bent and lit a cigarette, and then, exhaling, kept his eye on Len following Joan through the boathouse until the two disappeared.

Joan walked straight through the boathouse and up the hill without pausing, stopping at last at the top of the lawn, where Len caught up with her and put down the basket. Though they had left the group behind, they were not hidden. Anyone could see the two of them standing together on the lawn, side by side.

She held herself very still beside him, refusing to look at him, which only underscored to him their bond. He'd not been able to look directly at her himself. So this was how it would be.

And yet, what had he thought? That he could stride up here and ask her father, his *boss,* what he had done in the past — or what it *looked* like he had done? That he could whisk the girl from the castle? Here she was beside him, and it was clear she belonged to the castle.

The fog had lifted enough to show the low line of the opposite docks across the Narrows. A sail angled across the Narrows, heading toward the point, three heads turned into the wind.

He crossed his arms. A single gull swept across the sky before them and disappeared behind the darkening fringe of spruce trees in the cove across the lawn.

The air was very still. Music came from the piano up at the barn.

"You are driving me crazy," he said, very low.

And then she turned, at last, to look at him, and he saw she was trembling and his — his girl — again. Her smile was her hand put into his.

The screen door stuck and then gave and she stepped through, holding it open for him. He had a brief impression of many small rooms with uncomfortable furniture as she moved quickly down the hall in the direction of the kitchen at the back.

"Sitting room" — she pointed — "dining room, and pantry. Here." She reached for a flashlight set on the windowsill and handed it to him. "Put that in your pocket. You won't think you need it tonight, and then suddenly it'll be black as sin."

"Right," he said, following her through the pantry, into the kitchen, where a rail-thin woman turned round from the sink, a mound of peeled potatoes humped to the side, paid no attention to him, and frowned at Joan. "I thought there were girls coming to help."

"There are, Jessie," Joan promised. "Mum said they'd be here around four. This is Mr. Levy."

"Might as well not come, then," Jessie grumbled as Len put down the basket full of dishes dutifully beside her. "Everything needs doing will be done."

Beckoning Len, Joan led the way back out of the pantry, through the dining room, and into the front room, where she stopped and turned at last and walked into his arms with a cry. And the world — the hot green summer world outside — vanished in the cave of his chest as she closed her eyes and he kissed her.

After a little, she pulled away and looked up at him.

"It's all over your face." He was smiling.

She let out her breath slowly. "What is?"

He looked at her.

She blushed.

"It's good," he went on softly.

"It's not."

"It's very good."

"A girl like me ought not to look out loud," she observed archly.

"What's that supposed to mean?"

"You know," she murmured, "show the world how she feels."

"Ought not?"

"Yes. Ought not." She drew back into his arms. "My father likes you, you know. He asks questions that you can answer. That you will answer, and he wants to hear your answer. I saw him listening, even when you were talking to somebody else."

Len nodded. "And your mother?"

She hesitated and looked up at him.

"You ought to be careful."

"Careful? Careful how?"

"Not to say too much."

"I am too — talkative?" He couldn't resist.

"That's not fair." She pressed her lips together. "But yes."

"And you?" he asked.

A small smile played at her lips. "I like you fine."

He leaned and kissed her. She kept her face tilted up to him, her eyes serious.

"Why did you come, Len?"

"Moss asked us," Len answered. "Well, asked Reg. And it was hot."

"No." She looked at him. "Tell me. There's something else, isn't there? I know you. You've come with something —"

"Seems like one of the good ones." Mr. Pratt's voice came through the open window, five feet away.

"I'm glad to have him," Ogden answered. They were standing right outside.

"I'll bet you are," Roger said. "He looks like he'll make you some money."

"Roger!" Sarah protested.

"Nothing wrong with being good at making money. And it's damned good of Ogden to bring him in."

Joan looked up at Len. He was rigid, listening.

"As long as the moneymaking is done the right way," Roger said.

She wanted to take his hand but was afraid he'd push her away.

"It doesn't matter," he said quietly beside her.

Joan quivered.

"Only you matter," he whispered as the screen door slammed.

"Oh." Kitty stopped on the threshold of the room they stood in, surprised.

Like water shifting in its bed, Joan reached for the guest book in front of her, as though she'd been in the midst of this already. "I was just getting Mr. Levy to sign this, Mum." She turned toward her mother with a smile. "So we didn't forget."

"What a good idea," said Kitty smoothly. "Have you seen Moss?"

"Did you look up at the barn?"

Her mother nodded and kept going. "I need you in the kitchen," she called.

"I'll be right there, Mum," Joan promised. And opened the book. "Sign it," she whispered beside him.

There was a pen cocooned in the crease of the page. Wordlessly, he took it. "Should I sign Reg's name too?"

"Bad luck," she said, shaking her head, "to do someone else's."

He bent and wrote. And lightly, very quickly, she rested her hand on his back.

He straightened, his pulse racing, the pen still in his hand, her touch electric.

Through the window and down the lawn, he saw Mr. Milton moving inside the boathouse. It couldn't wait any longer. He had to know.

"Len?"

"Joan!" Kitty called from the kitchen.

"Len?" Joan was soft.

"I've just got to ask your father something," he said to her.

With a swift, troubled look on her face, Joan

nodded at him.

"Coming, Mum," she said.

THIRTY-FOUR

"So where should we start?" Min asked after they'd washed and dried the lunch dishes. The counter sponged, a new pot of coffee dripping, the cousins had taken hold of the afternoon, restored by the quiet, the calm of repetition that was the Island's hand on all of them. Here we do this, there we do that, we use these plates, those knives and forks, we sit in these chairs and eat cucumber sandwiches.

Evie turned around. "How about the linen closet?"

Min made a face. "All right."

They climbed the narrow stairs to the long, low room above the kitchen, where boy cousins and single male guests always slept in five twin beds lined up in military precision. The linen closet ranged the entire length of the room's left wall, though calling it a linen closet was stretching the truth. For years now, it had been the catchall closet — one might find in it a copy of *War and Peace* just as easily as one might find a Tampax, a whiskey bottle, or a dead mouse curled in a shoebox upon a taffeta fan. It was where the comic books and *Playboy*s had been stashed during middle school to avoid summer reading, where Harriet hid all her makeup, and where Evie had found a compass from the Second World War tucked in a box of condoms. It became the starting point for her first paper in graduate school: "Lost in History."

"All right," said Min, "let's haul it all out and see what we've got. We'll toss everything awful."

"And keep?"

"As little as we can."

Evie rolled her eyes. "You do realize that you are speaking to a historian."

"Which is nothing but a fancy name for a pack rat, who was the daughter of a pack rat, and" — Min held up four telephone books from Oyster Bay, Long Island, 1947, 1948, 1949, and 1950 — "granddaughter of a pack rat."

"Point taken." Evie grinned.

The first wave was easy. They pulled out sheets and towels, plastic mattress pads for bed-wetting children, a crib bumper, washcloths, hand towels, and five fine linen napkins the color of stained piano keys. A bowl of mildewed wooden fruit. A box of Sanipads, open, nearly empty.

"Toss," Evie said. And the lot went on top

of the pile tossed on the bed assigned to oblivion. It was satisfying to get to the bottom of a shelf, clean it out, get somewhere.

"Look at this." Min turned around with what looked like a rolled-up pennant in her hand. She stepped out of the closet and pulled it wide. Out fell swatches of fabric, one of them the stripe that still remained on one of the chairs downstairs, though it was faded and worn to threads at the elbows. The pennant was a rose-colored canvas, and on it painted in blue lettering, EVELYN.

Evie nodded and bit back a comment about Aunt Evelyn, about territory, not wanting to reopen the hole they had stepped away from downstairs, and turned toward the side shelves, where a row of boxes ranged. None of them were marked.

"Okay, now, here," Evie said, "we need to go slow."

Min snorted.

The first held single socks. Evie passed it to Min, who chucked it. The second was a small sturdy blue box from Merrimade stationers in Boston. Inside were notecards and envelopes with CROCKETT'S ISLAND embossed in blue, and a man's watch, its round face rimmed by gold, the Roman numerals fine. She turned it over and the leather on the band powdered in her hand. Engraved in the back of the face was O.M.M., JR. and the date, 1916. A memory stirred. She pulled herself out of the closet with the box and the watch and sat on the bed. Her grandfather looking down at her sitting beside him in the Herreshoff. She must have been six or seven, because he was smiling down as he nudged the long wooden arm of the tiller over to her.

Go on, he teased, *take it.*

And she had taken it. The boat lurched and spun. *Steady,* he laughed. *Steady on.* His hand closed over hers on the wood and guided the tiller back into wind, and she felt the tension in the water below, the grip of the tide underneath, and his hand warm on hers, the band of this watch cutting against her skin.

"What is it?" Min asked.

Evie held it up.

"Pops's watch? Why was that in the stationery?"

Evie shook her head and fastened it on her wrist. "For safekeeping," she said, glancing at Min.

But Min wasn't looking. She was going along the shelf very quickly and tossing things that weren't in boxes, that had been jammed alongside. More phone books, a couple of *Time* magazines from the late seventies. Several coffee cups. More hand towels. Evie stood up and reached into the shelf to pull out something Min had missed, something rolling away, and emerged with a little yellow car. Some little boy must have jammed it in here and then forgotten. She turned and held it up for Min.

"Nice." Min was unimpressed, and handed her a box. "Why don't you sort through these."

Evie took the box and went to sit on one of the beds, sifting through the jumbled pieces of paper inside. Lists in her grandmother's handwriting, carefully crossed out. Canceled checks from 1957. Nothing was in order, but Evie was used to this. This was how lives silted out. She had spent the past twenty-five years in libraries and archives combing through the stuff of people's lives. There were bills from the forties and seventies, side by side. Two receipts from Foy Brown's boatyard for paint on the *Katherine.* A note from Mrs. Pratt, asking about gardening shears. Lists. More bills. More receipts. Granny K was nowhere and everywhere in these, the spirit of the place.

"Do you remember?" Evie asked. "The oughts?"

Min looked up and nodded. "A woman ought to keep herself slim, upright, fit. Fat is a sign of ill breeding, of having let yourself go. *Liking* food too much bespeaks a weak mind, a flaccid spirit, a lack of ambition. Bad as drinking sweet vermouth —"

"Unless, of course," Evie added, "you were a food critic at *The New York Times* or someplace *reputable* —"

"— in which case, poor man, you suffered," Min finished. "One ought to never burden others with one's sorrows. One ought to keep them to oneself."

"Keep it to yourself." Evie nodded. "That's a little sad, isn't it?"

"She was sad."

"Was she?"

"She was."

Briskly, Min pulled another box from the shelf and opened it, glanced inside, and threw it on the toss bed behind her. Curious, Evie stood up and looked inside. A box of window pulls, a box of candle ends, and a hole punch.

"I wonder what these mean," she mused.

"A hole punch?" Min was skeptical.

"Why did Granny K save it?" Evie countered. "It must have meant something to her."

"Or nothing at all," Min answered. "And how do we know it was Granny K who saved it? It could have been my mother. Or yours."

This was true.

"It looks to me like a completely random assortment of stuff someone didn't know what to do with."

"I do." Evie shook her head. "I spend my life in libraries, looking at artifacts — picking up leftovers from another age and studying them for clues. Without them, whole lives might have vanished. Things *tell.*"

Min leaned against the closet door. "And what do the things tell you? Other than what you put into them, I mean."

"Hang on," Evie said, and bristled, "it's not complete projection."

"But that's just it," Min pushed. "How do you know?"

"How *else* can we know?" Evie answered. "The things that remain matter. Because of them, I can render a plausible life."

"A plausible life," Min said quietly. "Sounds good."

Evie put the lid back on the box and laid it next to the box of stationery on the bed to keep. But Min wasn't finished.

"Listen," she said. "*I* spend my life listening to patients. And the one thing I can tell you, for sure, is that *things* lie."

"Not if you know how to read them," Evie observed.

Min rolled her eyes, went back to the shelves, and reached for another box, opening the lid as she carried it, already walking toward the toss bed. She stopped.

"What is it?"

Min sank down on the bed and pulled a letter out from the box. It was an official letter, the envelope and the paper a thick blue.

"Listen to this." Min held the sheet of paper. " 'Dear Madame, With regards to your inquiry, there is no record of a Wilhelm Hoffman arriving here.' "

"What's that?"

"It's to Granny K."

"From whom?"

" 'Oskar Schmidt, German Jewish Children's Aid,' " Min read.

"When?"

Min checked the date. "In 1960."

"What the hell?" Evie pushed up from the bed and went to stand beside her. The envelopes in the box were uniform in size and shape, and the postage was foreign. There were upward of thirty of them stuffed in the box. She picked through them quickly. They seemed to be from relief agencies all over Europe spanning twenty-five years, from 1960 up until the year she died.

Wordlessly, Min slid open another.

" 'I am sorry, Madame, we are unable to locate Wilhelm Hoffman in our files. You might apply to the Rotes Rathaus, in Berlin.' "

"No, Madame," was written on the third.

No on the fourth, 1985. No, on the fifth, 1977. No. 1980. No. 1986. No.

Evie looked at Min.

Now was as good a time as any to bring the whole thing up.

"I'm sure it's nothing, but I have to tell you something."

"Go on."

"Paul found a photograph of Pops in Berlin in 1935 sitting in a garden surrounded by Nazis at some kind of picnic."

"In 1935?"

570

"Yup." Evie was quiet, watching her cousin thinking it over. "Does that make sense to you?"

"No." Min shook her head. "And knowing Pops, there could be a million reasons for that."

Evie nodded, relieved. "That's what I said."

Telling her cousin, sharing it with her, comforted Evie.

"Still," Min mused. "Why was Granny looking for a Jewish boy named Wilhelm Hoffman after the war?"

They looked at each other. Around them in every direction lay tossed and sorted the stuffing of the past, memory without voices, the dumb language of things. Min stood up from the bed and walked the length of the room, stopping at the window at the end.

"Do you remember that day right before she died, when Granny K told us there were two moments at the gate in every life?"

Evie nodded. "One at the beginning."

"And one in the middle."

It had been her last summer. They had filled the golf cart with pillows from the *Katherine* and driven her up to the house, carrying her through the door into the second parlor, where they had fixed a bed onto which Uncle Dickie had carefully, gently set her down. And she lay there, all the windows open to the air and facing down the lawn — through the foggy mornings, the sunny days, the screen door opening and shutting, all of them calling out around the house, coming in to sit beside her. It had been one of those mornings she had pulled the cousins in, pointed them to the chairs at the foot of the bed, and told them about those gates.

"I've been thinking a lot about that these days. I never had any idea what she was talking about — but Jung believed the Hero was not the young man setting forth with his sword to conquer parts unknown." Min paused. "The true Hero is the man in middle age, who traveled backward in order to be able to return."

"Return to what?"

"His life. The real life."

"And what is that?"

"What I said before, Evie." Min was gentle. "This. Two middle-aged women after lunch cleaning out their family closet, getting ready for a renter."

Evie looked at the room around them, strewn with generations of her family's life. "Hardly heroic."

"No," Min agreed dryly. "But I do know that *all* the chickies come home to roost in middle age."

"Yeah?"

"You can spend your life shooing them away, locking the door, making the roof too shiny for a perch, too slippery; you can chop down all the trees around the house, never come home, keep moving, keep shifting so they don't come, they don't settle; you can sell your house. All the way through your twenties, your thirties, your forties you can do this, and then *whammo,* you hit your fifties, and there they come, their little fluttering, their *hoo-hoo*s, the faint scratching of their claws upon your roof. Settling down, settling in —"

Now Evie was smiling. "And what do you do?"

"Take your slingshot, your arrow, and pick 'em off, one by one." Min squinted at the sky out the attic window. "And then" — Min smiled at her — "you get out of Dodge *or* you build a new house."

"Seriously, Min?" Evie was still smiling.

"The gate at the middle," Min said thoughtfully. "That's where we are."

THIRTY-FIVE

After lunch, Reg had followed the others up the lawn without a clear sense of a plan and continued past the house, to a little graveyard on a hill above it. He could hear Moss on the piano up at the barn. He thought he heard women's voices through the open windows. Up here, at the center of this compass of sound, he was utterly alone.

The most beautiful place on earth, Moss had said to him that night at the Five Spot. And it was. Reg could see the purity of it, the air and the single trees, the sunlit green and that deep, deep blue. But *Jesus,* he thought.

And that morning he was called into the principal's office and told he was going to Harvard, when Harvard was a word that only meant far away, a word that seemed to stick in the mouth of Principal Evans like a morsel he couldn't bear to swallow — that morning returned. He recalled the vast expanse of the Yard and having to cross it by himself, without Len. He remembered the days in the classrooms up there when he had to grab his seat with his hands to keep himself from bolting out of the room. No one knew what to do with him sitting there. Classmate? Roommate? Checkmate.

He had watched as Len pushed out of the front door of the house and made his way, determined, down to the dock. He had seen Mr. Milton turn and catch sight of Len coming through the boathouse and wave as Len walked along to the top of the gangway and down. After a little, the two men left the dock in one of the larger boats, towing a second slowly out into the cove where several boats were on mooring. They worked in tandem, and it occurred to Reg that Len might never ask what he had come for. He had had the curious sensation watching Len on the dock at lunch, expounding, that he was watching someone so firmly in charge of his part that everything he spoke sounded preordained, like lines written by a master. He had hold of every man's attention, and more than that, of Mr. Milton's clear admiration. Len was at the top of a game Reg hadn't understood until that moment. A game Len wanted to win. And Ogden Milton was the player Len wanted to be — one of those men who stood in the world without question. You could hear it in his voice, an ease, a comfort, as though every room he walked into were his own. He talked as though he had all the time in the world. When what Mr. Milton had, Reg knew, was the world.

Sitting beside her on the dock, however, Reg had felt Mrs. Milton recoil as she listened to Len, had felt the chill quiet pulling itself further into the cold. Though she did not mind *him,* Reg felt. He wondered why.

The sun burned with a bright fervor, dismissing the fog and sharpening the afternoon. He could just make out Mr. Milton and Len on the water.

He put his hands in his pockets and started back down the hill.

"Where are you off to, Mr. Pauling?" Mrs. Milton called from the green bench in front of the house, snipping the stems of the roses laid in her basket.

He paused.

"Have a seat," she invited him.

He wandered over and sat down on the bench.

"I'm keeping an eye on Ogden." She nodded toward the dock. "And Mr. Levy."

"Len is good with boats."

She regarded him, the expression on her face unchanging.

"Tell me, how did you and Mr. Levy come to be friends?"

"We've known each other since the third grade," Reg answered. "In Chicago."

Kitty's eye fell on Reg's legs stretched in front of him and crossed tidily at the ankles.

It was peculiar but not uncomfortable to sit here in silence. It would be uncomfortable, she realized, if anyone else were with them. But this man beside her sat as quietly as she sat. This is what could happen, possibly, she thought. We might talk to each other. If no one was watching, a black man and a white woman could talk, after all.

She smiled at him and returned her gaze down the lawn.

"*There's* the heron," she said quietly.

Picking its way down through the thinned trees, the bird appeared, tall and stiff-legged on the flat rock by the boathouse uncovered by the tide. And now it stood. Like a grasshopper on two feet. Looking in that moment like a sentry, or a guard, or something martial. At attention, waiting for an invisible sign to move.

Reg found himself holding his breath.

And then the heron flew. Simply lifted its wings, took a stroke, and off it went. Reg followed it far out in the bay, where lobstermen crossed slowly, toy boats against the low sky. Someone else's world entirely, whose sound came to where he sat next to Kitty, bringing the world out there beyond this island with it.

"Someone once asked me if I thought there was a story for each of us."

He looked over at her. "A single story?"

She nodded.

"And what did you say?"

"No," she said.

He nodded. "And do you think there is one story now?"

"No." She turned to him. "I could never have predicted you, for instance."

His rather serious face broke open into a lovely smile, and he laughed. She smiled back at him. She nodded and turned her head.

"So there," she mused. "Nothing is ever as difficult as it seems."

Ogden and Mr. Levy had put the *Katherine* on the mooring, and Len climbed down off her bow and into the smaller boat beside Ogden.

"Or as simple," she added.

He didn't reply.

They sat together like that, the woman who had been tended and combed all her life, who had dived off those rocks into the frigid sea and emerged laughing, lightly rubbing her limbs down with a thick towel, who had accompanied her husband back and forth to Europe after the war, who turned at dinner tables, like a smooth beam lighting upon her partner — here I am, here you are — and the black man, the slight man whom she had liked right away, who sat easily beside her, restfully, his feet up on the bottom rung of the garden bench.

She felt the thinking in him, she felt the mind beside her pulling out this thought and that, sifting as he sat, silently, and she saw that he had come here without precisely knowing what he had come for, that he stood on the verge of something, and that he was fundamentally, powerfully alone.

She watched as Ogden pulled the runabout neatly into the dock and Mr. Levy jumped out with the rope. Soon they would walk through the boathouse and come to that spot on the lawn, there at the bottom.

"I could have saved a child from the war," she heard herself say out loud. "A Jew."

She could feel him staring.

"His mother asked if I would keep him during the war."

She did not look at him. She could not. She had to finish it now.

"And I said no."

He turned his face away from her and looked down the lawn.

It was possible to say, *Here is what happened,* she thought, but impossible, impossible to explain *how.*

"It *wasn't* because he was Jewish," she said quietly. "It was because he was alive. Do you see? What was *unforgivable* at the time was that he was alive." He sat very still, his hands on the bench.

"And what happened to him?"

She didn't answer for a moment.

"I don't know. I expect I'll never know."

She shifted, turning toward him on the

bench. "And what is one to *do* with that?"

"Do?" He met her eyes. "What is one to do?"

They looked at each other. And then she looked away.

Ogden and Mr. Levy had come to a stop in the doorway of the boathouse. They were talking about something, face-to-face.

Kitty rose from the bench.

"That *man*," she exclaimed, "persists in doing *business.*"

"Jesus," Reg exhaled as Mrs. Milton walked away down the hill toward Len and Mr. Milton. "Jesus Christ."

THIRTY-SIX

Evie and Min sat together on the green bench at the front of the house. They'd worked through every box they'd pulled from the shelves. Emptied of its stuffing, the closet smelled faintly of salt and paint. Mouse droppings dotted the back of the shelves like chocolate jimmies. When they finished, the pile of stuff to toss covered three of the beds. The afternoon stretched across the lawn. Across the Narrows the osprey nest beaconed the chicks, circling farther and farther away and then again, home. The wind had shifted, and the salt air moved toward them on the hill.

A motorboat appeared behind the rim of Darby's Island, coming from the mainland.

"Are they coming in here?"

Its prow settled lower in the flat water of the cove as it slowed, slipping past the empty mooring and taking the last fifty feet with the engine at a low grumble. The driver knew his way around boats, that much was clear.

"Looks like it," Min said.

A child, a girl, emerged onto the bow of the boat and stood along the gunwale, a painter in hand, ready to leap onto the dock and pull the boat in when they landed. Expertly, the man at the wheel cut a smooth circle in the water as he approached the dock, running neatly alongside the edge. From where the cousins stood, they heard the thump as the child's feet hit the wooden float and the brief whine as the boat was thrown into reverse, and then the immediate quiet as he cut the engine.

"We ought to go down."

Evie nodded. Neither of them moved. They waited.

The man emerged into the light patch of green in front of the boathouse, the little girl beside him slipping her hand in his. He raised his hand in greeting.

"Charlie Levy," he called.

"What the hell is he doing here?" Evie muttered.

"I guess he wants to see the place."

"But we're not ready."

"Don't wreck it, Evie. We'll show them around. Then they'll leave."

In spite of it all, Evie smiled. Min's feelings stacked up like plates in a pantry.

"Okay," she said evenly. "Keep your shirt on. I'm not going to wreck anything."

Min sighed and they started forward.

"You must be the Miltons," he said, holding out his hand.

"We are," Evie answered.

"Charlie Levy." His thick brown hair was shot through with gray, and his eyes leveled on her as she shook his hand. He wore himself easily, his windbreaker hanging lightly on his shoulders, his pants loosely belted at his hips.

"Evie Milton," she answered as he turned to Min and greeted her.

"And this is Posy."

"Hello, Posy," Evie said.

The girl glanced up at her and put out her hand. She had a long and narrow face with fine, straight hair that hung low over her eyes and down below her shoulders, and she looked like she had spent her childhood undercover. On a ribbon around her neck hung an electric pink Polaroid OneStep. Evie shook the girl's hand, bemused as Posy sized her up from beneath her bangs.

"I'm sorry to barge in like this," he said. "But Dick Sherman said you were out here, I thought I'd come and see the place. Talk it all over."

Evie crossed her arms.

"We're over at the Stinsons' for the week, over on Vinalhaven," he explained. "Do you know them?"

"That enormous new place on the point?"

"That's right." He nodded.

"No," answered Min. "But we couldn't miss it going up."

They all turned and walked slowly up toward the house.

"You know how to handle a boat," said Evie.

"I've been sailing since I was little. My dad was crazy about it. 'If you want to win at the game,' he told me, 'you've got to know how to sail,' " Charlie said.

"What game?" asked Min, coming to rest in front of the house.

"Well" — Charlie turned to take in the dock, and the boats, and the house on the hill — "this one."

He grinned.

Evie glanced at Min.

"Mrs. Milton?"

Both Evie and Min turned to look at Posy. She was holding her camera up. "Can I?"

The child was breaking every single rule. *No,* Evie was about to say, when Min threaded her arm through hers and said to Posy gently, "Neither one of us is Mrs. Milton, but go on — take us."

"Quick," said Evie.

Posy nodded and held the camera to her eye. "Dad," she commanded.

Min and Evie looked over at Charlie, and he ambled good-naturedly into the picture.

"All right," Min said when it was done. "Come on in." And led the way up the granite steps.

"The sitting room." Min pointed into the tiny room, its four overstuffed chairs, each to a corner framing a round rug. "The woodstove gives off a ton of heat."

"Except if the wood is wet," Evie said.

"Well, yes, obviously." Min raised her eyebrows at Charlie, as if including him in a joke.

"It's not obvious," Evie countered, pricked by what appeared an unexpected alliance, "but one has to know. When the wood is wet," she said, "the room will smoke up immediately, and then you've had it —"

"Okay, Evie, it's not that bad."

Charlie Levy nodded and reached behind him to where his daughter hovered, pulling her under his arm.

"Okay," he said.

"I'm sorry about the wallpaper," Min was saying, behind her. "We didn't have enough time to pick another one and get it up before the season."

"I thought we didn't want to change it." Evie couldn't help herself.

Min opened her mouth to say something else and then thought better of it and glided past her cousin into the pantry, where their grandmother's Wedgwood china was stacked neatly on the open shelves — a complete set of the houses of Harvard. Charlie lifted off a soup bowl from the stack and whistled.

"My grandmother didn't believe in every-day china," said Min.

"Oh no?"

"Because every day is all there is," Evie said archly.

"What's that, *Ladies' Home Journal*?"

"Our grandmother," Min replied. "If you can't take good care of the finest things, you don't deserve to have them."

"Sounds like a challenge."

"I suppose it is," Evie agreed. She glanced at her cousin, but Min was moving the stack of plates farther back on the shelf, needlessly, as if they might somehow blow away.

"Here's the kitchen." Evie pointed through the doorway at the chairs around the table, the guest book lying open on the waxed tablecloth, the sun glinting off the rock through the back window.

The man was insatiable, irresistible, asking question after question, his daughter follow-ing him like an attending shadow. They showed Charlie Levy all over the Big House. They looked in every room, up into the attic, downstairs again, through the living room and the front parlor, out the front door again, where they stood at the top of the lawn. His interest was contagious, and the two cousins grew more and more expansive in their tour. Min was showing off, Evie realized. And found she didn't mind. Min told the story of Granny K and Pops sailing by the dock one day in the thirties and seeing the For Sale sign.

"Probably got it for a song." He whistled.

"Fifteen hundred," Evie answered.

He shook his head appreciatively. "They must have been something, your grandparents."

"That they were." Min was dry, looking at Evie.

They had walked up the hill to the barn and paused there as they came over the threshold and into the big room. Charlie took in the faded curtains, the rotting sills, and the threadbare sofa. A slight breeze came through the great crack in the back wall. Whatever it was he was thinking, he kept to himself.

"We don't, as a rule, like to spend too much money," Evie observed.

He nodded, his arms folded on his chest, gazing up into the enormous reach of the barn roof.

"In any case," he said, following Min out the barn door, "the place is incredible." He turned around, waiting for Evie and Posy to come through the sliding glass door, then pushed it shut behind them, taking care. Posy wandered away, down through the grasses, back toward the house.

"Actually," Min said, "we're in a bit of a crisis. That's why we're renting to you."

Levy swung round to look at her.

"No, we're not," Evie insisted.

"He might as well know, Evie."

"There isn't anything to know," Evie pronounced, "Min."

"Listen, I'd take a piece of this place off your hands in a New York minute." Charlie was earnest.

Min turned to face him.

"I'm dead serious."

"But you'd have to share," Min teased uncertainly, glancing at Evie.

"With one other family?" Charlie laughed. "Not too shabby."

The two cousins were quiet. This was too close to a real conversation.

"Let's not talk business," Evie said to him after a minute.

He nodded.

The three of them remained looking down the hill to the boathouse and the water beyond, and Evie imagined what Charlie saw. The field and the white house, the rocks, the sky above, an uncomplicated kingdom. Unweighted. Ready to own.

For the first time, she saw the place without them in it.

Posy had reached the kitchen door and gone inside. The kitchen door slammed.

Wordlessly, Charlie and Min and Evie started slowly back down the hill toward the Big House.

The screen door clapped again.

"Dad?"

Posy was walking up the path to the barn toward them, clearly excited. She had the guest book in her hand.

"Hey, Dad?"

"What have you got?" her father asked.

"The book," she called. "The book on the table in there. Isn't this Granddad?" She squinted up at him.

Evie and Min stopped where they were.

"Look at that." Charlie bent over the book and whistled, glancing back at Min and Evie. "So he *was* here."

There on the page Posy held up was written *Leonard Levy* in blue ballpoint, the *L*'s quite sharply defined and set off from the smaller letters, and the date, August 25, 1959.

Evie stared at the name, trying to make sense of it. "That's your father?"

The four of them stood there, outside the kitchen door, toward the end of a summer day. The guest book rested in the hands of a girl whose grandfather had written in it sixty years before. The roof of the house defined the sky. The same roof then as now, the arc of history bending toward them.

And she recalled an instant years ago, coming into the living room to switch off the television, Seth looking up at her and asking about the cartoon family on the television, "Do *they* know we are watching?"

She shivered.

"Your grandfather gave my father his first job," Charlie said.

"At Milton Higginson?"

Charlie nodded. "He called it his finishing school."

"So your being here is not a coincidence."

"Coincidence?" Charlie considered Evie. "Not at all. I'm here because I made a promise to my father. I thought Dick Sherman had made that clear."

"But you were surprised to see his name in the guest book."

Charlie was quiet a moment. "Toward the end, my father was saying some crazy things."

"But how did he come out here?" Min asked. "A picnic?"

Charlie shrugged. "No idea. He was a friend of your uncle's."

"Uncle Dickie?"

"No, I don't think that was his name."

"Uncle Moss?"

"That's it."

"But he died years ago," Evie said to him, looking at Min.

"After a party." Charlie nodded. "My father told me. He said a Jew died too."

"A Jew?"

"That's the way Dad said it."

"What Jew?" Evie asked.

"I don't think so." Min shook her head. "Or at least, we've never heard that. Granny K always told us Moss drowned trying to save someone."

"Who?" Charlie asked.

Evie looked at Min. No one had ever gotten an answer from their grandmother on that question, though it would have burnished the shine on the story of their uncle Moss, who otherwise went largely unmentioned. Granny K had always managed to flick off details like bugs, specifics that might prick the smooth surface of a moment.

They walked Charlie Levy and his daughter down to their boat and stood on the dock as Charlie hopped in and turned on the engine, Posy untying the lines.

"Listen," he said. "I have to give you something." He hesitated.

"Go on," Evie prodded.

"Before he died, I told you my father was saying lots of odd things. He told me about an island. And about a point on that island. He made me promise I would find that point —"

Evie raised her eyebrows.

"Find that point," Charlie went on, "find those rocks, he told me, if you can. And when you do, put this there."

Out of his pocket he took an ordinary kitchen spoon.

Evie looked down at it and then back up at him, mystified.

"I know." Charlie was bemused. "It's nuts. But now we know that he was here, I'm pretty sure he meant those rocks off the end there."

Evie looked at Min, who shook her head, puzzled. Evie felt like she was in the grip of a fever, as if something hovered just out of sight, something that she might understand if she didn't look at it straight.

"Could you put it there?" Charlie asked. "It's not my place."

"Sure," said Evie, taking it. "Sure thing."

Charlie nodded at Posy, and she tossed the line into their boat and then hopped after it onto the bow.

Evie leaned and gave them a push off from the dock, out into the Thoroughfare.

"Come back," she said as the boat slowly pulled away. "Tomorrow or the next day. Before you leave."

"Do." Min smiled. "Come for tea. We'll use the china."

Charlie turned to them. "I'd like that."

They nodded at him and waved him off.

The two cousins stood a long while on the dock watching the boat speed toward Vinal-haven, disappearing at last around the point. In the emptied space, a solitary kayaker sliced the water with his paddle like a baton twirler, making headway up the Narrows toward the darkening band of the horizon.

"You'd think we'd have heard the truth about Uncle Moss."

Min snorted. "Our family? You think we ever heard the truth about anything?"

THIRTY-SEVEN

Len leaned on the wooden railing of the pier, looking down onto the empty, sunny dock, trying to make sense of what had just happened. Mr. Milton had left him there, walking away through the boathouse and toward Mrs. Milton when she'd called. He wasn't sure how to feel — he pushed up off his forearms — or even what to feel now. The Pratts were coming in around the end of the cove, the father and son side by side, the two sculls gliding easily forward.

Roger Pratt stroked effortlessly into the dock, leaving Dickie out on the water, rowing in what now looked like laps.

"Need a hand?" Len called out to the father.

"I'll be fine," Mr. Pratt called back. The two men stood in silence as the sculler hugged the one oar tight against him, stirring the water with the other to bring the craft swiftly around and alongside. He sat there, clearly winded, watching Dickie still out on

593

the water.

"What did Mr. Milton say?"

Len looked over his shoulder and saw Reg coming toward him. He shook his head ruefully.

Reg came to stand beside him along the railing.

When Len had come through the boathouse onto the pier, half an hour ago, Ogden Milton was standing down at the edge of the dock handing one of the oars to Dickie, sitting in the scull. On the water, twenty feet or so out from the dock, Roger Pratt was sculling slowly forward against the tide, and though his oars skimmed the surface of the water as he took a stroke, the boat appeared stalled.

"Give it up, Pratt!" Ogden crowed cheerfully. "You'll never make it around the Island in under an hour. This is what separates men from New Yorkers."

He gave Dickie a push off and stood, hands on hips, observing.

"Why then, I'll be fine," Roger Pratt called back, catching water at last, "as I'm from Connecticut," and started stroking cleanly away. Within moments, Dickie had come abreast, and the father and son moved in unison into the break in the fog.

Ogden chuckled and turned around, seeing Len standing at the top of the gangway.

"Levy!" He smiled. "You're just who I need

at the moment. I could use a second pair of hands."

Len hesitated. "Why's that, sir?"

"I want to get the *Katherine* off the dock and out onto the mooring, and those two have deserted me, promising they'll row round the Island in half an hour."

He looked down the Narrows where the two sculls had disappeared. "They'll never make it back in that amount of time." He grinned.

"Where is the mooring?"

Ogden pointed to a spot dead in the middle of the Thoroughfare between Crockett's and Vinalhaven across the way.

There didn't seem to be anything else to do but simply climb onto the *Katherine* with the towline Mr. Milton gave him, cleat it to the bow, and then stand with one of the long oars to fend off any buoys as the runabout slowly pulled away from the dock, towing the *Katherine* through a hole in the fog.

Mr. Milton navigated without slowing down, picking his way through the dank mist unerringly toward the white mooring, which appeared suddenly out of the gray ahead of them. Len reached down and caught the mooring, then tied the *Katherine* on, Milton idling the engine. Within a few minutes it was done.

When they turned back toward the dock, the fog was lifting, and the house and the boathouse stood solid grays against the green. At the top of the hill, Len thought he saw Reg sitting beside Mrs. Milton.

"See that?" Ogden said quietly.

Len glanced at the older man.

"My refuge," Ogden said. "Always has been."

Len turned away, staring forward straight in front of him at the house on its hill. Refuge from what? He swallowed.

They docked and tied up in silence.

"Sir," he said at last, "what are these?"

He pulled out the two contracts from his pocket and handed them to Ogden, who looked at him, unfolded them, and stared down. Then he nodded and looked back up at Len.

"A bad call."

"A bad call." Len's eyes widened. "As investments?"

Mr. Milton shook his head. "The whole damn thing. Though it wasn't about the money." He turned to Len. "It was never about the money, about profit."

"What was it about?"

Ogden frowned, though Levy had landed lightly on that word, *was*. It was so easy to ask from here, so easy to see what this young man must think he saw. As if all of us could see what history will tell, when instead all we see is the present, what's around us. He had seen Elsa, he had seen Walser. He had not

596

looked past them. For that, he could be faulted. But no more.

"Order," he answered squarely. "Stability. Old friends."

Len watched him.

Ogden looked up. "In the end we lost everything. We lost our shirts in 'forty-two."

And until then? Len thought, looking at his boss. All the years *until* then that the money silted solidly up. Money the man before him didn't see, didn't seem to count. Money that was everywhere around them, here in this — refuge.

"But it was a good call until then?"

Ogden held Len's gaze, pocketing the pages. It was clear he understood what Len was asking.

"And?" Reg asked.

Len turned and looked at Reg. "He didn't answer me."

"Ha."

Len looked back out over the water.

"And you let him off with that?"

Beside him, Len was quiet.

Reg saw there was more. "And?"

"He asked me if I loved his daughter."

"Ha," said Reg, more softly. "And do you?"

Out in the Thoroughfare, Dickie turned, making straight toward them, his aim for the dock unswerving.

"Yes." Len nodded. "I do."

Roger Pratt had pulled his own scull up onto the dock and seemed to have fallen asleep down there, in the sun.

"What were you and Mrs. Milton talking about?" Len asked.

Reg shook his head and whistled.

Len looked at Reg. "What?"

Reg glanced at him. "She doesn't like you. She'll never like you."

Len straightened.

"I'm doing fine," he said, though the look Joan's mother had given him there in the front room after lunch had been clear.

"She doesn't like you," Reg repeated.

"In general?" Len refused to take Reg's tone, refused. "Do you think it's general, or more specific?"

Reg didn't answer. In three last strokes, Dickie had come into the dock, pulling the oars in and gliding alongside. In one bound he was out of the boat and pulling the craft straight up and over his head, the water streaming from its wooden flanks. He was remarkably, easily strong, Reg thought, watching him set the boat down.

"What about you? Does she like you?" Len asked.

"Me?" Reg shook his head, smiling up at Len. "I am so far out, I'm in."

Len snorted.

"Let me put it this way," Reg said. "She's suffering you. Isn't that right, Dickie?"

Dickie had come up the gangway and was listening, his hand on the gate to the pier.

Len turned his head. "But you like me, don't you, Dickie?"

"I like you fine." Dickie pushed the gate open and came through.

"See, I told you Dickie was open-minded," Len remarked slowly.

Dickie looked from Len to Reg and flushed. "Listen, you won't find any of that stuff up here."

"What stuff?" Reg was calm.

Dickie looked at him stubbornly.

"You boys ready to dig holes?"

They turned and saw Mr. Milton coming through the boathouse onto the dock and holding two shovels. "I could use you down at the picnic grounds."

"Ready." Dickie came forward. "Ready and waiting."

"Terrific." Ogden smiled as Dickie headed through the boathouse, walking quickly away.

"Come on, boys," Ogden said to Len and Reg.

Len glanced at Reg and fell in behind Ogden without a word.

Having taken all day, when it happened, it seemed like it had happened in an instant. The fog had completely vanished and the day pulled off its hat. Bright blue and lilting, the afternoon greeted them with open arms. The water stretched off the end of the rocks in a still, straight line. A cormorant dove straight down into the water after a fish, coming unseen from the sky. The splash hit the flat calm like a bomb.

There were sixty people expected for dinner and a lobster to boil for each of them, so the two firepits needed deepening and widening to fit the crowd tonight, explained Ogden as he led the way toward the clearing at the picnic grounds.

"And if you two could shore up the rocks around the edges," he instructed Len and Reg, "we'll be done in no time."

Len nodded. "Sure thing."

"The weather's cleared entirely," Ogden said, satisfied.

The farthest row of spruce just at the waterline needed pruning, and Ogden shouldered the clippers and went down through the trees. A caravan of pleasure boats came racing around the point as if released, like arrows shot free by the glorious and sudden afternoon. He reached for the overhanging bough and snapped it, stepping aside as it fell with a thud to the needle-strewn ground.

When Ogden looked up after a little, Moss had appeared in the clearing and had hold of one of the shovels and was pointing out to Dickie how much wider the pit needed to be, taking charge. Beside him Len and Reg pulled the rock borders away from the pits and rebuilt them farther back as the shallow holes extended across the mossy surface. One of them said something, and he heard Moss laugh. There was an ease between the three men, which made Ogden glad. Len Levy and Moss had their backs to him and were bent over their shovels, but just then, Mr. Pauling stood and straightened between them, looking out across the water, his figure black against the blue.

Ogden's gaze returned to Levy. That Len Levy had landed here at the dock, and through *Moss's* auspices, boded well. Perhaps that was what Moss had been trying to get at last night in his inscrutable toast. *Infinite variations.* Rooms of possibility? Yes — Ogden turned and set the clippers on the near joint of the spruce and snapped it — that showed a sense of the future he hadn't suspected Moss had in him. It would carry on. This place would carry on. And though Levy may not understand fully what he held in his hands with the Walser contracts, Ogden felt certain he had defused the man. It was not black or white. He hoped Levy might learn to see that. He set the clippers again. Especially if he loved Joan, precisely because he loved Joan. He snapped the branch. And did she, he wondered, love him? The branch fell away.

When he looked again, Kitty and the girls were moving through the trees toward them, carrying tablecloths in their arms, and buckets of roses.

"Ogden," Kitty called. "Come and take some of these from Joanie, will you?"

Len put down his shovel and turned around.

"Ogden," Kitty repeated.

Len stopped at the tone in her voice.

"We need firewood, Levy, and lots of it," Ogden directed as he passed. "Take these, will you, and finish clearing the branches down at the edge there. Joan, you can go with him and collect what drops."

"Sure," said Len, taking the clippers that Ogden handed him, flashing a tiny grin at Joan, not bothering to hide how he felt. And the straightforwardness, the simplicity of his purpose, his desire, struck Joan. He was too much, too big — he burst over the lines here. He couldn't see it, but there it was. So small she hadn't seen it waiting there for her, the limit of what she could imagine for herself and for him. *Oh god.* He didn't want here. He only wanted her. That girl on the rocks. She moved beside him through the trees, away from the others, struck silent with her longing and her dread.

"Are you all right to tend these?" Ogden said to Reg Pauling as he was rolling newspaper and shoving it in under three enormous logs in the first firepit.

"I am." Reg nodded.

Ogden paused.

"Good man." He clapped Reg on the shoulder. "Thank you.

"And Evelyn." He turned to his daughter. "You are in charge of the tables. Your mother and I will get the rest ready."

And with that, he and Kitty walked back up the path toward the house to meet the six girls due from Vinalhaven to help Jessie in the kitchen — and in the same boat, the gin, the tonic, and the limes.

"How about a swim?" Moss wandered over to Reg. "Come and clean off."

Reg shot a look up at him, standing on the side of the pit. And the promise Reg had caught on Moss's face in his camera — the promise Reg wanted with all his heart to collect on — was clear.

But how could he not tell Moss what his mother had just told him?

"No way." He squinted at Moss. "I put my hand in there at lunch. That water is arctic."

"Even to rinse off?"

Reg shook his head.

"Your funeral," Moss teased. "Come on, Dickie."

And the two men moved off.

Evelyn listened in silence as she unfolded the tablecloths on the long tables, anchoring them with the bricks Joan and she had covered in mattress ticking during the war, used now for doorstops against a banging wind. After a little while, Reg joined her, setting out the knives and forks. She smoothed the cloth down all the way to the end and moved the bucket of roses to the center.

Down on the rocks, Joan and Len stood with their backs to them, facing the water and looking out.

"It won't work, you know," Evelyn said quietly.

Reg set a spoon beside the knife and didn't answer.

"It can't," she went on.

Evelyn glanced across at him. But he wasn't looking at her; he had his eyes on Joan and Len bending together now, gathering wood.

"Have you watched them?" he said. "There isn't an inch of air between them, though they are standing five feet apart."

"She loves him." Evelyn was sad. "I see that. But she can't marry."

Reg shot her a glance. "Isn't that up to her?"

"Yes." Evelyn was soft. "And she's decided. She won't marry, because she'll pass it on. It wouldn't be right. It would be shameful."

"Pass what on?" Reg paused and looked up at her across the table. "There's nothing shameful about your sister."

"Of course not." Evelyn narrowed her eyes and looked at him. "My sister is *everything* — good and great. It's her condition."

"What condition?"

Evelyn pursed her lips and didn't answer. She would protect her sister to the end, Reg saw.

She dropped her eyes. "Even aside from that. It can't work. These things simply don't."

" 'These things'? What are 'these things'?"

"Well," she said, turning to him, "he's a Jew."

She said it so matter-of-factly, so reasonably, it was stunning. Without any embarrassment, without any hiding, any pretense. Surely we could all agree. That's just how things were.

"Yes," Reg answered.

"You don't marry a Jew."

"I'll tell him," said Reg evenly.

She nodded.

And Reg saw that she believed they had settled something. It had been decided. He moved away from the table and back to the fire, released somehow, relieved. He almost wanted to thank the younger sister. Evelyn went on setting the table. After a little while, she turned and walked back up to the house to change for the party.

Joan and Len were moving slowly back toward him, and Len, seeing Reg watching, lifted his hand and waved. Even from here Reg knew that look. The victor. Len couldn't help himself, he was so certain all the time that he had won. He thought because he was here, he was there. He was through. He thought because the girl wanted him — and it was clear she wanted him — that meant she would have him. Watching his friend, Reg felt as old as Time.

THIRTY-EIGHT

The boats rounded the point and came toward them, one after another in the slanting light, the figures standing along the gunwales bursting into motion as they neared. *Hello! Hello!* they called over the diminishing distance. *Hello!*

"They're here." Evelyn ran down the lawn, a brilliant shock of blue, Joan and Anne following. And how Joan loved these first moments when anything at all might happen, the night ahead, and the sun just beginning to sink into the hills, the Island growing dark behind her. "Tie up here," she said to the Fessendens, who'd just maneuvered neatly in alongside the boats tied stern to stem four boats deep from the dock.

They had brought a cousin from the South possessed of a moist beauty, her pale gaze framed loosely by hair, light as wheat, her eyes perpetually wide as if she'd just been goosed. One felt she might wrap around the first upright man she met and never loosen her hold. *For balance,* Joan reflected, smiling at her.

"Hello."

"I've never had such a bumpity ride." Cousin Franny lifted herself from the bench in the cockpit and climbed out of the boat.

Bumpity? Joan caught Moss's eye. But he was the height of good manners, helping the girl over the gunwale and onto the dock beside him.

"I hope there's lots and lots of bad behavior," she whispered to him as she turned to walk up the gangway. He nodded solemnly and winked at Joan.

Peggy, Babs, and Oatsie Matthews sat in the bow of their father Cy Matthews's boat. He had a dirty, irreverent mouth, which her father suffered, Joan knew, because he was an expert around boats and had proven himself useful during the banking crisis of '32, having shown a surprisingly astute grip on when the financial winds would shift, long before others. He cut a wide swath around the gam and backed into the last open spot on the dock.

"My getaway." He smiled conspiratorially and handed Joan the painter. "You look lovely."

Teeni and Bing Lamont were right behind him with their son and new daughter-in-law, née a Ludlow of New York. Blond and sleek and high boned, she stepped onto the dock with the bowline in her hand. Where she walked, one imagined carpets unrolling before her, cloaks of ermine swirling around booted legs. Swords and lashes. Hounds. Having modeled for *Vogue,* she qualified as an out-and-out glamour girl, though she had first been born and bred a Brearley girl, so she was keen minded too. Her name was Constance.

It was generally agreed that of the eligible possibilities, really only Elliot Lamont could have wed her. Joan had heard that Elliot had sat next to her on a transcontinental flight, and as can happen between a very attractive woman and an equally attractive young man, they fell into conversation and a good one.

He asked her how she came to be a model, when was it she first knew that's what she wanted to do, and then, somewhere over the middle of the country, he said, "Listen. What do you think about, standing there waiting for the cameras to click?"

She had turned her lovely eyes and regarded him a minute.

"Tick-tock," she answered.

And the fact that he had asked her, and the fact that she had answered, and then the final fact — that he had known enough to understand the brilliance of that reply — had won him Constance Ludlow.

"Well, hello!" Kitty cried as Rhinelanders, Cabots, and Lowells streamed out of the boathouse. It seemed all of North Haven had arrived in one boat. Kitty kissed them and Ogden laughed and led everyone down the path toward the picnic grounds, where the fires had been started and the corn, soaked for the afternoon in its salt water pool, lay in husks around the embers.

Ten pots full of water had been set to boil on the metal grills laid across the stones of the firepits where the fires had burned furiously upward and had now settled into manageable coals. Ogden loved the challenge set by the ridiculous odds of boiling sixty-odd lobsters for a waiting crew. The kettles would take the better part of an hour to come to a boil, and then keeping them boiling, Ogden instructed, would take a man at each pit. Reg and Len had volunteered for the job and stood a little to the side of the party as Dickie went round with bottles and a stack of paper cups, the Pied Piper of gin. Evelyn and Joan were passing plates of cheese and chutney on Ritz Crackers, and Moss seemed to be everywhere, shaking hands, earnest and warm in a madras jacket and Bermuda shorts, welcoming everyone in, a great smile on his face as he surveyed the shifting tide of people around him.

There were men in sweaters, the sleeves pushed loosely up, tossing horseshoes across the sandy pit, the clang of the iron shoes against the stakes ringing timpanis into the evening. Several of the women had ranged themselves on the rocks around Kitty, their long legs extended from under their skirts.

The Fillmore Baker Juniors arrived with Granny Baker in tow — one of the first to forgo the warmer waters of Long Island Sound and organize Fillmore Sr. to come up here and build an enormous, exuberant folly on the Thoroughfare. Behind them trooped the Cheevers, distant cousins of the Trumbulls, the right Cheevers, no relation to that author.

"God, what a crush of people," Mrs. Cheever drawled, kissing Ogden, and stalled at the edge. "Are they all *our* sort?" She winked at him.

"Of course." He took her elbow and guided her into the clump around Kitty. *Hello,* they cried, *hello.*

A group had taken their drinks and wandered down the paths that stretched away from this spot farther into the Island. Through the trees, the blues and yellows, the linens and silks shimmered as they walked away. The lobster car had been filled with beers and moored to the rock at the end of the ledge, where it bobbed, cold.

Len watched Kitty pull free of the group of women around her and cross over to find Dickie with his bottle, and even here, even in the midst of a crowd, Len saw, what Kitty did drew Ogden Milton's gaze, as though she were the point of perspective, the vanishing point. He flushed and poked at the fire, and then quickly looked up and searched for Joan.

She was moving easily through the clumps of guests, chatting, her sister beside her, the contrast between them plain. Len found himself relishing the difference. Unlike her sister, Joan's flame was banked but glowing all the same. There was the earnest, truthful faith inside her, a charity of soul. Though she seemed smaller to him here. The place defined her, the rituals, the small devotions, tending it, mending it. Defined all of them, he thought. Fine for the academics and poets, men who stayed in one place and spent their lives thinking, tinkering. Fine for Ogden Milton, in whose image the place was. But no good for him. He caught sight of Joan's face in profile, nodding to a woman in a blue cardigan, that little smile upon her lips, that was always on her lips. His chest expanded. He wanted to show her how small this place was — how big she could be, they could be — together. He wanted to tell her all of it, all in a rush.

He looked up and saw Reg standing by his own pit, staring at him, a bottle of beer in his hand and a peculiar expression on his face.

Reg looked at Len, then down at the fire.

"What are you doing?" Len wandered over to Reg.

"What do you think?" Reg answered so

quietly, Len had to lean toward him. Reg turned and looked him in the eye.

"I know you," Len said. "You're about to do something."

Reg shook his head. The two turned back to the party.

Dickie Pratt was wandering around with the gin, and Len held up his cup to be filled. Dickie halted. And for a second it looked to Reg like he'd refuse. But he poured, and then with the other hand, splashed the tonic into the cup.

"Listen." He stalled in front of them a minute, looking from one to the other. He was flushed. "I want to make something clear."

Reg drank, his eyes on him.

"Let's get it straight: I don't dislike the Jews."

Len looked wordlessly back at him.

"You and I work together," Dickie protested. "And I've got a lot of Jewish friends."

Len nodded and looked out into the party. "You know what Otto Kahn said?"

Dickie shook his head.

"A *kike*," said Len, turning to him, "is a Jewish gentleman who has just left the room."

Dickie stiffened.

"Dickie?" Evelyn had appeared at his side, her eyes on Reg. "We need the gin." And she pulled at Dickie, who remained where he stood, speechless.

"Come on," she said quietly to her fiancé.

But Dickie stood there shaking his head, looking from Len to Reg. "What the hell?"

"Dickie."

"What have you two got to be so angry about?" he burst out. "You're at Milton Higginson, Levy, and you —" He stared at Reg. "You went to *Harvard*. You should be on our side. You should be part of the solution."

"The solution?" Reg whistled. "First solution, or final solution?"

"Reg." Len inhaled.

"Oh, come off it." Dickie frowned. "You're at our party."

"That's right." Reg stared back.

"Reg," Len said again.

The moment passed.

Dickie relaxed. "I have nothing to be ashamed of." He wagged his finger. "Nothing at all." He put his arm around Evelyn and steered her off. The fire popped.

"Jesus." Len exhaled.

"There," Reg said. "You heard him."

Len drank. "Dickie is an anomaly."

"Man alive, listen to you —" Reg exclaimed. "It can't hold."

"Why not?" Len said.

Reg didn't answer. Len glanced at him. Reg bent and grabbed a stick off the woodpile and slid it in under the grates.

"You know it can't." Reg frowned. "You know it, Len. A little while ago, you'd have been the first to point that out."

Len's jaw tightened. "None of them matter, Reg. Don't you see? It's just padding around in the dark, hitting wildly. They're silly. All of this" — he took in the horseshoes, the genial melee — "doesn't matter."

"Since when?"

Len shrugged.

"You're bewitched," Reg said to him quietly.

Len glanced at his friend. "What if I am?"

"You don't want all *this*, Len."

"No," Len agreed. "I want her."

Reg looked at Len, then down at his feet. The rip that had started in his heart tearing further. The great dumb ox that was his friend, the *believer.* The rip between them tearing wide. He kicked at the fire.

"Let's get out of here."

"We can't leave, you know we can't."

"Why not?"

"Look, you know why not as well as I do."

"I want to hear what you say," Reg answered.

"Screw you, Reg. Don't be a son of a bitch."

Reg hugged his cup to his chest. "They talk a good game. But it won't matter."

"She's not one of them."

Reg shook his head. "She's just the same. Watch her."

"I am," Len said quietly. "I watch her all the time."

A spark popped out of the fire onto the dry grass. Reg stamped it out.

"You're wrong," said Len. "You think you're right, but you're wrong."

He went to find another beer.

In that moment Reg wanted to be rid of all of them, even Len. Rid of their promises and their hopes and the hand that extended but did not include. He was not in any danger — it was not that simple — but he stood there by the fire, seeing Len's shoulders move through the group, profoundly, intensely alone.

"Reg Pauling?" A surprised voice spoke beside him, and a big woman with wide teeth and merry eyes held out her hand. "I spied you as soon as I got here, and said to Harry, that *must* be him."

Beside her, a beamy man with flyaway hair and a red bow tie nodded.

"Ought we to be offended?" she went on. "You turn us down every year, and yet here you are."

"Yes." Reg found his voice and took her hand. "Here I am. It's good to see you, Mrs. Lowell."

At last, the lobsters were pulled from the pots and set on platters, and the girls brought melted butter in bowls down from the Big House. Hot corn was tossed in baskets and *It's time,* called Ogden, *Come on,* Kitty urged.

Come get a lobster and take a seat at the table.
The enormous single table was made up of
five barn doors set on trestles, and benches
Ogden had had the Rhinelanders' man bang
together for the feast. Down the center were
the vases filled by Kitty with marguerites and
rose hips, and carrying the charm of a summer house — its white beadboard and driftwood, cut glass and steep angles — out here
into the open evening.

"Here," Ogden said to Len, "you'll want
these," and handed him a pair of lobster
crackers, which he took, and a paper plate.

Suddenly, Joan was beside him in line. He
could reach his arm around her shoulders
and draw her in, easily, just like that in the
gathering dusk. If he could have, he'd have
sat her on his lap, wrapped his arms around
her waist, and held her tight. Close wasn't
close enough. Her warm beating body beside
him was a delicious torture. Nothing mattered to him more at that moment than this
girl, this improbable girl on this island.

They moved together, wordlessly, toward
the end of one of the long tables. He set his
two plates down, and the crackers. Then
turned to take hers from her hands.

She slid onto the bench. He slid down next
to her. No one at the table paid them any attention. The lobsters steamed in their red
shells. Around them, the others fell on the
red bodies and pulled them apart, experts at

maneuvering the sharp claws and the edge of the shells. Len considered the lobster on his plate.

"I warn you, it's messy." She took the crackers and began with the tail, giving it a sharp twist to break the tendons and then ripping it off the body. Green bile poured out and streamed onto the plate. Neatly she set the freed tail aside and then tore the claws off with the same quick twist, separating the claw from the shoulder of the body. Her hands were covered in slime and juice.

"Some people like to suck at the legs," she said very seriously, pointing to the fifteen spindles attached to the body. "I don't."

"Is that right?" he answered, equally seriously, and was rewarded by a darting glance at him.

"Pass the lobster crackers, would you please, Joan dear?" Mrs. Gould asked across the table.

"Here you are." Len handed them over the shells heaped in the middle.

"Hello there," said Mrs. Gould. "Who are you?"

"This is Len Levy, Mrs. Gould."

"Ah." The older woman nodded, appraising his plate. "Is this your first lobster, young man?"

"That's right," he answered, grabbing hold of the body and twisting.

Ah, Joan heard the woman's unspoken

remark. But Len didn't seem bothered. He wasn't at all uncomfortable not knowing how to do the thing, or admitting to it. Joan looked down at her plate. That was part of his charm.

He dipped a morsel into the butter between them and put it in his mouth.

Mrs. Gould waited. He swallowed, looked up at her, and grinned.

"Very good." The woman gave a sharp nod of her head and turned to her dinner companion.

Joan and Len ate and said nothing. After a little time, he reached for the bottle of wine at the center of the table and filled her glass, then his. One hand rested on the table, and his head bent to catch the drops of butter falling from the piece of lobster he put in his mouth.

A breeze off the water curled through the grasses, and the picnic on the rocks, the laughter, the familiar group, with Len beside her, filled her. The liquid gold glinting off the water before her echoed the sunburnt gold behind her in the meadow, the swallows racing in and out of the twilight with the gulls. She could close her eyes and draw the place in around her like a hymn.

"I would have made a good nun," she mused, a twinkle in her eye.

"I don't think so."

"But I would like to see all four seasons

here," she said. "I'd like to live here all year round."

"Why?"

"Well — look at it," she said. "It's heaven."

He wiped his hands and looked at the group around the table. "But it's not real. It's not where it all is."

"It's very real." She turned and looked at him. He returned her stare.

"And there isn't a comfortable chair in the place," he said lightly.

Oh god, she thought. She loved him. She looked down at his hand on the table and saw with a twist in her heart that she could love this man, but he did not carry over; it would not do. He looked around with that eye of his, that appraising, impatient eye that did not see — how could it? It belonged to a different world, the one past this — he was, like Mr. Rosset, like Moss even, intent on smashing down the trees in his way and carrying us all forward into some new place. When this place was enough. Was everything. She stood and reached for his plate and hers.

And the sun began dropping into the sea.

People came to the Miltons, thought Sally Lowell, and came away more at ease with things, in love a little more — she turned her brown eyes to her own husband, sitting on the other side of the remarkable Mr. Pauling. She couldn't catch what they were talking

620

about, though by the intent look on each of their faces, she was certain it was political. She was tired of politics. Her eyes roamed over the group again. The Miltons had the knack for throwing a party. Kitty made a man feel proud and a woman understood. Ogden showed you how lucky you were, *damn* lucky to be alive! She put the emphasis where her father always did, cheerfully profane — *damn* fine, *damn* lucky, *damn* hard. He had died years ago, and she still missed him. The party swelled around her.

Wasn't this what it all was for?

So Roger Pratt believed, sitting at the corner of the vast table, getting quietly smashed. Isn't this what it was all for — Groton, St. Paul's, Farmington — all of them had been sown and seeded in the same ground, and here were the blooms, the heads nodding, the laughter and the bright eyes. Nothing was wrong with being like-minded. Everyone here could be trusted to behave as they had been raised. To be good. To be kind. To think of others. And because you expected to be met with what you gave, those qualities grew.

His eye caught on the Jew pushing back from the other end of the table with a glass in his hand and considered him. Maybe he was a good sort. But this was the trouble. One couldn't count on it. One couldn't count on a man like that to do the same as they all did. They agreed on decorum, an *ethos,* damn it, the right point of view. One couldn't rely on him to behave as he ought, or even as was expected. One couldn't prepare.

The party loosened after the lobster, and the candles were lit, though the light in the sky still hovered over the hills at the end of the bay.

"Aldo," Kitty called down the table to Mr. Weld, "let's have a song."

"What'll you have?"

"If He Can Fight. . . ." She sang and trailed off, looking at him.

"Right you are." He nodded. "Come on, men," he called. "Singers, up on your feet."

Men of different ages pulled themselves up from the table, called to the shoe that was forming in front of the fires. Mr. Weld had been the pitch pipe of the Whiffenpoofs at Yale, and he hummed the first note of the song to get it in his head, then walked it round to the men gathered behind him. Dickie stood beside his father, and Ogden and Moss joined them. And on Moss's other side stood Fenno. There was Elliot Lamont, and Cy Matthews, and the youngest Rhinelander boy, who'd sung at Harvard and was a scamp, but who nonetheless was going to try his hand at politics. He had always had the voice of an angel.

The rest of the party stilled and turned

toward the shoe. Joan found herself on one of the benches beside her mother. She had lost sight of Len in the crowd.

The men in the shoe drew close and tipped toward one another, waiting for Aldo Weld to start them off, their eyes on him.

He raised his hand and opened his mouth, and in a light, irrepressible tenor, he led the men forward into the song.

"If he can fight like he can love." And Ogden, Fenno, Dickie, Moss, and Elliot went right along beside him, sending the notes of the song into the air. *"Oh, what a soldier boy he'll be."*

And then Moss stepped forward out of the shoe and toward the guests, swinging into the solo with the light step of a dancer, the words less the enticement than the way the tune climbed up the scale and swung out over the second line. Alone he sang above the notes the men behind him held, sang with the sweet longing of a girl for her lover, and when he stepped back into the shoe, each man knew precisely what he was meant to do, they hardly needed to look at one another, bound and in tune as a chorus followed his solo, and then at last the final lines.

"And if he fights like he can love,
Why, then it's good night Germany . . ."

Their last note rose into the dusk, and from her spot on the long bench at the table, Kitty watched the men stiffen as they held the last note and then relax in the silence that fell, heavy and sudden, over them all. Here were the inheritors of the earth, Kitty thought; the sense of solidity, of granite, of rightness and the force of permanence was everywhere around them. The world had been theirs so long, it was a given. And they would take it and keep it safe, this world, this dream. No one spoke or moved. The sound, for those moments, bound them. Then the men grinned.

Aldo pulled his pitch pipe from his jacket pocket a second time and blew it lightly and looked at Dickie, who nodded, stepped out of the shoe, spread his arms, and directed his rich, warm tenor straight at Evelyn, singing the first line of the song.

"I'll be ready when you are —"

She blushed but held herself very proud and did not look away.

"You can count on me," he sang, *"As ready to go."*

He smiled, stepping back into the shoe. And the song swelled as the seven voices joined Dickie, all of them leaning inward to catch the strain of one another's voice, to catch and to hold it and then to sing.

Standing beside Reg again, Len looked across the fire at the women ranged along the bench. Mrs. Milton stared off toward the water. The Pratts, mother and daughter, leaned together; Evelyn sat rapt. Only Joan had her eyes closed, and her dark head tipped to the side as though she listened for something. More than that: as if she alone heard something in the air. What was it she heard? He stared at her there on her own, and complete somehow. He frowned uneasily. Complete?

He turned back just as Moss stepped into the center of the shoe to sing alone. The men behind him grew softer, letting Moss soar so everyone could hear, there on the rocks, Moss's single treble, again raised to the sky. He was so good, his voice rich and sweet — and light. All light.

Reg watched the glow on Moss's face as he sang. How music filled him, how Moss believed with all the breath in him, in every note he sang, note by note as if the world could be built on air and sound. As if the problems of the world might be solved by men like these, ranged in a tight circle, leaning into the notes sung together, swelling upward into the twilit sky. He knew that this was Moss's dream. And he remembered that night long ago when he'd stumbled on Moss singing just such a song, sending note after note into the air and believing that was enough, and yet Reg's life, Reg's parents' life, were nowhere in those notes, not even buried.

Here on this island in the middle of the Atlantic surrounded by the best and the brightest, the men who ran and who would run this country and who would never lay a hand on him, but who could change the laws, if they could see. And they wouldn't. Reg saw the limit fully in this singing. Moss sang as if the gates of the world could open with him, believing with all his heart that they could. But here on the island, the care with which Reg was being handled, the pronounced attention was merely the opposite face of the face that gave the hard stare, or the push between the ribs, or the whip. Both faces turned to the black man as though to a wall that had to be climbed or knocked down — and always with the infinitesimal moment of wariness that slid immediately into anger or polite regard. As if to say, *Ah, you again.*

This was what he wanted to rip in two. This was why Reg thought he'd come. Why he'd made this trip over in a lobster boat in part for this — to hear what always went unvoiced and to make Moss see that. To make Moss see. But watching Moss singing, the vast uselessness of what he was after caught him there around the fire. Seeing was not enough, speaking was not enough, doing, even, was not enough. He could tear it down for Moss — and for Len, he thought, as Len moved restively beside him — and there'd be satisfaction in it, but little joy.

Joy? The word floated up as Mrs. Milton caught his eye.

He held her gaze a moment, and she nodded at him and looked away.

He shuddered. She was, perhaps, the worst of them all.

Dickie stepped forward once more, holding his arms out again and singing the solo for the last verse right to the end, when he took a breath to sing the last line above the four men behind him, who held the last notes in a single swelling chord.

"I'm ready to go."

And his voice held across the quiet that fell on the group and carried as clearly as the vow he would utter a month later in the white church in Oyster Bay, his promise. I'm ready to go.

Evelyn looked straight back at him. And when the last note vanished, she stood from the bench, ran forward and into his arms. Everyone, delighted by the simple declaration on either side — the big, broad singer and the slight wisp of a girl in blue silk — clapped, and there was a little cheer.

On the tide of this feeling, Ogden stepped out of the shoe and raised his glass. "When you are young," he said, "you dream of what you *want.*"

The party turned to listen.

"And twenty-five years ago, when Dunc and Priss Houghton, and Kitty and I sailed into the cove down there and saw the For Sale sign on the dock, I had never wanted anything more than this rock in the middle of the ocean in my life — except perhaps" — Ogden smiled at Kitty — "for my wife."

Laughter petaled around him. The moon was rising slowly.

"A little further along, in the middle of your life, you find you dream of what you *have.* You look around yourself, your children, your home." He nodded at Evelyn and Joan in front of him and turned back to glance at Moss.

"But the dreams of the old," he said, slowing, "are of what we will lose."

He smiled and then included the whole party in his gaze.

"And tonight I see I will not lose. I cannot. Tonight it seems there will always be a party on these rocks. All of us here, all of us gathered. It's a night to carry forward. And —" He chuckled and turned round again, raising his glass. "Moss will see to it. Moss will carry it on."

Moss turned a dazed smile toward his father and, understanding what was needed from him, bowed — as if to take the crown handed him with his father's words, and set it on his head.

"Now." Ogden turned back to the crowd. "I have had the great good luck of being able to age with my dreams, to want, and then to have, and now not to lose, but to pass along. But it is all because, thirty-one years ago, I chose Kitty.

"Every one of you knows the key to life is in whom you marry. If you set your sights on the right girl, you need never look back. Nothing is more important in a man's life than the girl he chooses.

"So, Dickie." Ogden reached behind him gracefully, drawing his future son-in-law forward. "In all honesty, and with the requisite degree of humility" — he paused and raised his eyebrow, gathering another laugh — "you have chosen well."

He raised his glass.

"To Dickie and Evelyn."

"Hear, hear! Dickie and Evelyn!" The glasses, the cups, and the bottles were all held high.

Joan raised her glass with the others, a fixed smile on her lips. Moss would carry on the Island. Evelyn would marry well. Dickie had chosen right. Her father hadn't meant to set her outside, she was sure. But where was she? Why wouldn't they *all* carry on the Island? Why couldn't she? She looked for Len in the crowd but couldn't find him, and turning back, her eyes caught Moss's. He looked sick, somehow, she realized. Heartsick.

"All right, everybody." Evelyn clapped her hands and pulled out of Dickie's arm. "Up to the barn!"

"Take my arm, Moss Milton." Mrs. Cheever appeared beside Moss. "If I fall, I'm done for," she confided, taking hold of his arm.

"All yours." Moss straightened graciously.

Released by the toast, the party streamed up the hill toward the barn in the dusk, carrying bottles and cans, pulling chairs from inside the dining room in the Big House, even the small sofa from the front room. In honor of the party Ogden had purchased two of the new Coleman coolers lined with plastic, adding to the galvanized coolers they'd had for years, and set them on the rocks outside the barn. Everything had been thought of, and everything was possible. Moss led the way, and Evelyn seemed to be everywhere in the crowd, a lovely flash of blue and white, her wide skirt floating around her legs. And Dickie followed, faultless in form, polite, and gracious, carrying a chair in either hand up the hill.

"Heavenly!" Oatsie Matthews cried, coming over the sill.

They had hung hurricane lamps from the rafters, on nails along the great walls, and Evelyn and the Matthews girls went around lighting them. Moss sat down at the piano, feathering the keys, not wanting to break the silence just yet, hesitating inside the delicious cavern of the moment before the music began.

"Moss!" Evelyn begged.

"Oh, all *right.*" He grinned and started in with a Joplin tune, catapulting notes into the air, fast and furiously, and the mood around him was gay and warm.

Aldo Weld came over the threshold with Ogden and Kitty, followed by the Pratts, and then the Lamonts and Goulds, and the barn began filling. Moss heard the pitch of the room shift slightly as people came in.

"Start us off, Aldo, will you?" Kitty cried. And immediately Aldo began the calling, *"Grab a partner, grab your dancer. Off we go,"* and with a nod at Moss, who shifted straight into "Turkey in the Straw," the room sorted itself into pairs and then into squares and then into the dance itself. Aldo Weld had a great booming voice that skiffed across the top of the music, calling the changes, first to the right, then to the left, now do-si-do, and around you go.

The room was in full swing when Joan and Anne arrived into the throng and felt the heat of the dance on their faces, and the two women stood in the doorway, smiling. "Come on," Mr. Weld called, seeing them pause. "Come on, another square! There's four of you right there." And Joan found Len's arm at her waist guiding her to a spot on the side of the room, and looking over her shoulder, saw Anne being led out by Reg. "Two more couples? Two more?" Fenno Weld and Babs Matthews slid over, as well as Maisie Cunningham and her brother, Bill. There was no time to think. Joan was in the curve of Len's arm, stepping in a round to Moss's piano, her whole being concentrated on the surprise of those thick fingers curled around her ribs, not simply resting there, but holding her. She didn't dare look up at him. The tune went round and round, over and over first one pair, then the next, then the third, then the switch, and Joan was moved from Len's arms into Bill's and from there to Reg, who held her loosely, never pulling her toward him. There was no chance for words, or even a glance at him, and then she twirled from his arms into Fenno's.

Fenno took charge of her in a way the other three hadn't. He had always been a great dancer, lithe and lean, his awkward height made graceful by motion, his hand at her waist rested courteous but firm. They had danced many times together, and his hand reminded her. She flushed.

Then the last change was called, bringing the girls back to their original partners, departure and return, change and change, and come again home. Joan swirled off Fenno's arm and into Len's and this time she did look up at him. The music stopped.

He pulled her close, and she felt him against her chest and thigh. The blood rushed straight up into her face and she looked quickly down.

"May I?" Fenno's hand was on her elbow, but he was speaking to Len.

"Sure," Len said, and released her. She gave herself into Fenno's arms for the Virginia reel. She didn't check to see where Len went, though she caught sight of him above the crowd, at one turn, making his way toward Moss and the piano, where Reg stood leaning, watching the dance. Moss looked up at Reg, as if to make sure he was still there. But they didn't speak to each other. And the music wound and wrapped them all.

At the third dance Kitty came outside beyond the perimeter of light cast by the windows. She walked into the dark and turned around. Through the wide frame of the barn doors, couples dipped and spun, appearing and vanishing. Moss was playing well, and the piano threw music into the cavernous room, the notes tossed high and shivering down between the couples, onto the hair of girls and the shoulders of the men. This was one of those nights everyone would remember, it was clear to her even from here in the dark, one of those nights that spring, glistening and electric, upward through the surface of ordinary days: *We were here.* She and Ogden had made a night for all of them. His toast had been wonderful. He had said exactly what was needed. She looked up into the black dome of the sky, waiting for the pattern to break. We *are* here, she corrected. A star dropped swiftly off to the side.

She followed it down as it vanished below the roof of the barn, and her gaze stuck on the great figure of a man standing in the doorway, not dancing. Leonard Levy. She knew it was him, though she couldn't see his face. It was because he was the biggest man in the room. Bigger and louder than any of the others. Not just tall. Fenno Weld was tall, though spindly, like a bug whose long legs and slight bowed shoulders called to mind a minister, born in a frock coat. No, this man was massive, with his broad chest and thick, solid legs. He was the kind of man one might find chopping wood, or digging coal, or under a sink, not in the world. Not in this world, anyway. She turned away from him, pulling her coat around her shoulders, seeking Ogden.

The Pratts and the Rhinelanders danced into view, grabbing hands and then letting go. She saw them without thinking much about them. She didn't think much of other people's marriages — think, that is, whether or not they were happy. Happy was a word for people who stopped with the small beer of themselves. The idea that life could splay outward, like the five fingers on a hand, and grasp something larger, that was what she aimed for. What Ogden wanted her for. Happiness was small beer indeed compared to moments of glad satisfaction, sharply felt, as she had just then out in the dark, the job well done.

They were so beautiful, these boys and girls. So beautiful, and so utterly unaware of why. All day she had been in the grip of this watchfulness. All day, she had been staring at the children and their friends — though they weren't children, they were in their twenties, she had already had Moss by this age — and been made sad. They would grow old. They would lose their beauty. Because all beauty, in the end, was youth. Evelyn with her heart-shaped face turned toward Dick, turned toward him with the flush of love, her eyes glistening. One looked at Evelyn and one couldn't help thinking *there* is the hope for all of us. That was the reason for beauty like hers in the world. She made the rest of us believe, for a moment, in the very strength of the species. In carrying on.

But there was Joan, she saw, also standing a little apart from it all. Kitty tossed her cigarette and stepped on it, putting it out and watching Joan now, the usual worry unfolding. At the edge of the dance Joan stood without moving a muscle in her body, fanning the mother's alarm. She couldn't see her daughter's face, just the nearly electric rigidity, the staring fixed as a stone. From here it looked like the start of one of her fits. Did anyone else see the girl frozen at the center of the party? Kitty moved slowly back toward the barn, out of the darkness and toward her, wanting somehow to cover her daughter, to make Joan invisible. Wanting to help her slip away so as not to embarrass herself.

Len Levy also moved. And Kitty stopped on the threshold of the barn, dumb with apprehension. He would get to her first. The intensity with which he bore down on her daughter should have soothed her; he wanted her, it was clear even from here. Life with him would mean Joan would always be talked about, she'd enter every room as "the girl who married a Jew." That was too hard. But harder to bear, Kitty thought, harder would be if the Jew gave her up when he found she was not, completely, all there. Kitty stepped inside the barn door and halted. Because Joan's face had opened into a beautiful, heartbreaking smile.

A deliberate smile. Len slowed. A beautiful, deliberate smile, as bright and distant as a star. But it was no good. It was a hiding place. And he tried to think what she could want to hide. He kept going toward her, his eyes on her face. She still smiled as he came, and then he realized she wasn't smiling at him, it was for someone behind him, and turning he caught sight of Mrs. Milton, standing on the threshold of the barn. That was it, then, Joan was smiling this armored smile because of her mother. Len stopped right where he was.

"Come on," Reg said as he came up beside him, "come here to the piano." And he took his elbow and moved him through the crowd, toward Moss, who was playing with a steady abstracted look in his eyes. It had been nearly an hour of music, and he looked to Len like a sleepwalker. But Moss snapped into a smile when he saw the two of them coming, and nodded, playing the chorus again.

"Joanie?" Evelyn was standing right next to her. She had been on the other side of the room and now here she was. Joan's mind unclenched. Her sister was holding her hand. "All right?"

Joan picked herself slowly through the tunnel she imagined in her head when this would begin to happen. When she felt the stop in her brain, when she froze. Inch by inch, she eased back into motion, and squeezed Evelyn's hand once.

"Yes," she was able to say, the word rolling up from inside, slowly up from where it had stuck, like bowling balls coming through the chute back into play.

When Len turned around, he saw Evelyn had come to stand beside her sister and, taking her hand, was very close and whispering in her ear.

Something had happened, Len realized. It hadn't been a fit, but something had stuck.

He reached into his pocket and felt for the spoon he always carried now. Something had happened and he had walked away. He had allowed himself to be walked away by Reg. He started forward, but Moss finished the song with three final chords and then stood up. The room went wild, clapping and shouting for more.

"Taking a break," Moss said, cupping his hands around his mouth. "I need a drink! Joanie —" He called to his sister where she still stood. "Joan!"

Evelyn and Joan looked up at the same time, and Len shivered. Again he had the sense he had had that first time, of the two cats regarding, slowly, the world before them. Joan shook her head at something Evelyn said and then started forward to Moss.

"No, goose," her brother said when she was nearer. "You were standing next to the beers."

"Oh!" She shook her head, trying not to look at Len. "Oh dear."

"I'll go," Len said, moving quickly away. Joan flushed and looked down. Reg leaned against the wall but wasn't listening.

Moss reached for her hand. "Joanie?"

"Shh. I'm okay."

He squeezed. "You've fallen for him, haven't you?"

She didn't answer.

"It's possible," he said.

"Oh, shush, Moss — shut up." She turned

to him. "You're hopeless."

He held her hand. "It's so simple," he said. "I heard it tonight. It's a round — that's the song, 'On the Rocks,' that's what I've got to do. It's one voice joining another, then a third. A fourth —"

She looked at him. There was a dim pain in her head, and the noise around them came from a ways away.

"I've never believed anything more than this. There are no more —"

She heard him searching.

"Walls." He found the word.

The pain was growing, as though someone were knocking far, far in the back of the house and she had only just begun to connect the thudding with the sound. Someone was going to get in. Someone was bursting forward. What did he think he meant? *No more walls.*

"Where's the music? What's happened to the music?" someone yelled.

"Hold your horses," Moss grumbled amiably. He pushed the transistor to the front of the piano and turned the knob. Static crackled out of the box as he played with the tuner, and slowly a station swooned forward from the mainland eight miles away, a clear station. It was Saturday night, and there was dancing over there. Len thrust a beer into his hands, cool, but not cold, sweating the can.

Reg leaned over the piano, and Moss looked

up at him, smiling.

"Let's get some air," Len said, his eye on Joan.

Kitty saw that the danger had passed. She watched her daughter cross in safety over to Moss, and turned away to find Priss Houghton standing alone at the edge of the room, the bright, hard spots of too much drink showing on either cheek.

"Hello, pal." She came to stand beside Priss; Priss looked up at her gratefully.

Kitty glanced again at the four by the piano and saw Reg say something, and saw a softness arrive on her son's face in answer, a wonder she remembered seeing there when he was a boy; and it occurred to her with a start that quite possibly she had been watching, she had been worrying about, the wrong pair.

But that was ridiculous.

"Kitty?" Priss recalled her.

"Yes." Kitty turned back to her.

When she looked again, she couldn't find either Moss or Joan in the crowd. Moss or Joan, Len Levy or Reg Pauling. She stood up, searching over the heads of the party-goers. But they were nowhere to be found.

THIRTY-NINE

Down the hill, past the Big House and toward the moonlit water, the four of them moved farther and farther away from the party, the music from the barn reaching them in pockets, in the dips and hollows of the lawn, bound by the unspoken desire to get deeper into the night. Reg and Moss walked slightly ahead of Joan and Len. The white of Reg's sleeve moved in and out of the tunnel of light cast by the lantern Moss held. He was saying something, but the words passed back on the air didn't amount to a sentence, even a phrase. It didn't matter. Nothing mattered to Joan anymore but being in the arms of the man beside her in the dark.

They walked through the boathouse toward the water, where the stars bounced on the calm surface offering them light up ahead. It was low tide and the sea unmoving. If she put her hand out right then, she would hold the fabric of his shirt in her fist. Moss reached and pulled open the gate at the top of the gangway. "Come on," he called over his shoulder. "Let's turn the lights on."

"Moss," Joan laughed.

"Why not?" He was down the gangway and had walked to the edge of the dock, turning his back to them. Moss perched himself on the tip of the dock, fumbling with his pants, then he thrust his hips forward and a circle of light appeared in the water just beyond him. A circle of light that moved and unrolled like a ribbon up and down and around and disappeared in a flash of tiny sparks.

"Phosphor?" Reg asked.

"And piss," Moss answered cheerfully over his shoulder. "Poor man's paint."

"Anyone else?" Moss zipped his fly and turned round to face the three of them ranged in a line on the gangway.

Len cupped his hand around the flame on his lighter and drew it to the tip of the cigarette in his mouth. The *puff puff puff* as he drew in was the sound of bird wings. Reg pushed the gate open and walked down to join Moss standing at the end of the dock, the last of the phosphor on the dark water fading. There was no breeze. The squares of yellow light from windows across the Narrows shone steady and solid in the black.

She waited for him to turn toward her, willing him to look at her. They stood together without touching.

"Let's get out on the water," they heard

Moss say to Reg, standing on the dock. "Let's take a row."

"Let's go," Len said at last. They turned around and walked back through the boathouse and onto the lawn.

At the turnoff to the picnic grounds, Len reached for Joan's hand, still saying nothing. Now, away from Reg and Moss, they walked hand in hand through the grass to the trees that marked the beginning of the climb down to the picnic grounds. He dropped her hand for a moment, reached and drew the flashlight from his pocket and switched it on. Then he led the way forward, heading for the twin eyes of the bonfires, now burned to dull red spots in the dark. When they reached the open clearing of the picnic grounds, he turned and took her hand again, moving them past the table cleared of bottles and silverware, the vases of flowers standing guard above the bare wood. There was a bench at the end, right on the water, near the rocks, and they sat down.

Across the cove in front of them the lantern on the boathouse lit up the bows of three boats, all tied to one ring on the dock. And the half-seen hulls of other boats bobbed like white shadows behind these nearer ones. The night was perfectly clear, and the stars bent over them in the sky, making patterns of light on the water that shivered and withdrew with the turn of the tide. She thought she saw the shadow of Moss and Reg sitting at the end of the dock.

Her hand was warm in his. Warm and firm, and stirring.

"Joan."

She turned her face, and he tipped her chin toward him and bent to find her in the dark. Her lips were as warm and firm as her hand, and wet. In one motion, he lifted her onto his lap, tucking her legs sideways, her chest turned against his, sidesaddle. A groan started deep in his chest and pushed up through his lips and into hers. The sound joined them. She kissed him back, not carefully anymore, harder, and her arms went around his neck so he could pull her in tight. He kissed her throat and down to the cleft of her blouse, and a little gasp escaped her and she put her hands around his head. The first button slid easily out, and very slowly, his lips traced the middle line, button after button opening until he had reached the top of her skirt and her skin gleamed around him. She reached and unhooked herself and then pushed herself off him and stood to undo her skirt.

They left their clothes and walked down to a softer, mossy place at the edge of the water. The tide was dead low and the drop was steep. In the moonlight, the wide white granite humps looked soft and the black water, hard. The breeze that had blown the fog out to sea earlier had dropped and the night was humid and still. It had been hot in the barn, and down here it was simply still. A cage of air.

He cupped her breasts in his hands and held them, then leaned down and kissed each one, as she reached and put her arms around his neck. And sighing, she pulled him down with her, gathering him, rocking with him, and he came in quick and so hard she opened her eyes and saw a face she'd never seen, saw then how much he wanted as they rode all the way to the end together, alive to the very core.

And afterward, as the tumult inside quieted to a hum, she lay there, drowsing. She couldn't have moved if she tried.

"Look at me," he whispered, still inside her.

His face was the moon. And she stared up into him and smiled.

His finger landed on her neck and traced the line down to the hollow.

"This is the picnic grounds," she said dreamily.

He didn't answer. She tried to sort out what she wanted to say.

"But from now on," she said, looking at him, "it's our spot and —"

"The spot that marks us," he broke in tenderly. "Where we began."

"Began?" Her voice caught.

He nodded. He was serious. "Here is where

645

it happened."

He rolled onto his side, lifting up on his elbow, and folded her hand into his, mooring it on his chest. She lay on her back on the moss looking up through the spruce boughs to the starlit sky, her hand in the thicket of his chest as it rose and fell.

"We've made love before."

"Not like that." He stroked her arm. "Not like this. You came away with me tonight. You left the party."

She looked up at him uneasily. The confidence, the vital assurance, kin to triumph, was unmistakable.

"Accident is not accidental," he said quietly. "We were meant to meet that day in the station. You were meant to be mine, to come with me. You are meant to —"

"You believe that?"

He nodded.

"We have something big and real. You see it. You love me," he whispered in her ear. "I thought I had lost you up there, but you love me. You do." His mouth found hers again, and she felt herself give up, she felt herself give as he whispered above her, kissing her, whispering into her ear. And she listened. She listened to him conjure a life out of words and lips and air. He would dress her and keep her, and never let her go. There was the whole world to see. There was so much. So much more than here, and they would see it together.

But she also heard for the first time something she hadn't yet understood — the image came flooding in — that after her own apartment, perhaps there'd be another, but there was always this room afterward, the one that men held the door open onto. Len was about to offer the door to this room. She had a sudden exhausted vision of them all, each with a door and a woman just about to enter. Men build the walls of the room and the women step inside them, and then they close the doors on the woman inside. There was sex, there was this flood that burst through the rooms, but here it was, nonetheless.

She uttered a soft little moan. And even as he boxed her in, here was not enough He wanted more, more than this place could offer. He could not see how the Island held everything and more — how it could hold everything not yet made or thought or spoken between them. The Island held the unseen world bending and opening around the two of them, the world she felt when they made love, a beckoning, a calling from something more than each of them. The Island held them.

He could not hear the Island's call. She could see he thought he was bigger. And he *was* bigger, and a little blind. That too she could see.

She could not go with him. And it would

hurt. She loved him with every atom, every brush of his fingers on her skin, she loved him. And she loved past him, here. But she would not go with him.

"Stop." She pulled her hand free gently and sat up, a little dizzy. "Stop talking."

She rose from him, naked, and made her way across the smooth granite to the water. After a little, he followed.

There were twenty-odd boats tied up, and boats tied off of other boats, and at the very end, the dinghy that belonged to Crockett's swung on the tide. Moss and Reg picked their way across cushions and along wooden decks made slick by the night's dewfall and landed in the rowboat, winded. All the drink had cleared from Moss's head, and he felt alert and alive. Reg climbed into the stern, and Moss climbed in after him, untied the bow, and pushed them off.

A fish splashed off to the right. The water hiccupped around the prow, and Moss shoved out the oars and took a stroke to pull free of the nest of boats and glide out into the Thoroughfare. Out into the middle of the channel. Moss rowed for several minutes and then stopped, crossing his oars and letting them skim the surface, the boat gliding under its own momentum. The moon spilled light onto the water. The air was humid and still.

Moss pulled and then leaned away, and the

boat sprang easily forward. Closing his eyes, he pulled again, and the water closed over the oar and released as he pulled up on the catch. The boat moved, and when he opened his eyes, Reg was looking to the side, his eyes on the dark hump of the island sliding by. Behind Reg's head the water shimmered away, a carpet unrolled between them and the mainland where the Camden Hills climbed, lodged in Moss's mind's eye. He pulled and pulled and he felt he could row right out of the bay into the sea, with this man in front of him. He kept on, and then out in the middle, he stopped. The boat bobbed in the sudden arrest.

And the feeling that had floated under him all night long, through the music and the dancing, everyone gathered in one enormous room, buoyed his spirit. He imagined Joanie in Len's arms somewhere in the woods, and it underscored the song. This was the new song, a song without — *walls.* The voices adding one to the other, voices *adding,* joining the strain. There was the bass. There was the melody. The future seemed to him just then to spin on the point of the world and find itself here on the water between islands, in the dark, on a boat with this man.

He paused and leaned on the oars and looked at Reg, complete.

"Look at that." Moss pointed.

Reg turned and saw the lantern on the dock

and the lights shining from the front of the house, and then, higher in the dark, he could just make out the lights from the barn. "How many tanks of gas do you suppose it takes to light all that up?"

Moss couldn't read the expression on his face. "I don't know." He took a stroke with his starboard oar to keep the boat facing the hill. "Two?"

"Light into the darkness." Reg paused. "Tennessee Valley Authority. Remember their slogan, 'The great light hope. Bringing light to the Negroes'?"

Moss shook his head. "Window dressing."

They were quiet. Water dripped off the blades of the oars into the sea. Reg's mood was hard to fathom.

"There was a place I used to go to in Berlin," he said slowly, "in the old American sector. All the time. It was one of those hidden cafés at the bottom of town halls, what they call rathskellers."

Moss took a stroke.

"There was an American who came in every so often, a soldier."

"A soldier?"

Reg nodded. "A soldier who never came home."

"He stayed in Germany."

Reg exhaled. "Yup."

"The soldier had liberated the camps. He'd been on one of the first jeeps into Buchenwald, and was there for ten days."

"Jesus."

"He told me about those first days, about marching the villagers through the camp, about turning off the ovens, and then he told me about a guard that had run away but that had been captured by the survivors and brought back.

"They brought him into one of the store-rooms and handed him a rope. They told him to make a noose. 'I do not know how,' he said. They showed him. They told him to put it around his neck, climb onto the table shoved into the center of the room, and hold the end of the rope up to the ceiling."

Reg was not looking at Moss. He was far away.

"And he did that. The guard stood on the table and held up the rope so it touched the ceiling, and looked down at the survivors, and waited.

" 'And we all knew what we were doing,' said the soldier. 'I was standing at the back of the room.'

"Then they told the guard to get down off the table."

Reg stopped.

"He pissed his pants with relief. He got down off the table, shaking, weeping, and sank to the ground.

"The survivor giving the orders nodded at him. And gently took the noose off the guard's neck."

Moss sighed. "And?"

Reg looked at him.

"And climbed onto the table himself and fastened the end of the rope to the hook in the ceiling, tested the knot, and climbed back down."

" 'Go on, now,' he said to the guard."

Moss shuddered.

Reg nodded, looking at him. " 'And why should that death be the one I can't shake?' said the American soldier to me."

"The guard's?"

Reg nodded. "The guard's."

Moss went cold inside.

"Why are you telling me this?"

"Do you know what your sister said to me today?" Reg looked at Moss for the first time.

"Joan?" Moss took a stroke with the left oar.

Reg nodded. "We were talking about this place, and she said, very sweetly, almost reverently —'Nothing will ever change. Sunlight. Starlight. Drinks on the dock. A single sail out in the bay. It will never change. It seems to promise, "You will not die." On and on. Like a painting,' she said. 'Here you are. As long as the Island stands, we stand. Time never minds.' "

Moss took another stroke.

"She said all that with a deep joy, as though she had in her hand one of the Verities, and I thought to myself, *There is the trouble.* That verity — nothing will ever change — does not include me. She means well, I know she does. But I cannot hear that nothing will ever change."

There was a bitterness in Reg's voice Moss had never heard. He dipped both oars in, leaned forward, and pulled hard. The boat soared. He pulled again.

"But of course it will," said Moss. "It has to. That's just Joan speaking. And she's out there right now with Len."

"Everyone up there" — Reg pointed up the hill toward the barn — "is so unfailingly *polite.* Earnest. Good-spirited."

"So?"

"They are holding their breath. We are," he said tiredly, "ruining the party."

"No," Moss said.

"No?" Reg searched his face. "Look at me honestly and tell me that you aren't proud to have me here."

"Proud? Of course I'm proud." Moss was mystified.

Reg put his hand in the water and drew it sharply back. It was bone cold.

"I don't want to be a badge of honor worn on the outside," he said. "I don't want to be taken up, like knitting, like a dog, *un chien de salon,* the whole race problem tamed. Because that's what I imagine them all thinking up there. At the party. A black man can be taken in stride, even taken in *hand,* because we were all standing there, drinks in our hands, looking at sunsets, singing. We were all standing together." He shook his head. "I want to be inside; I want to be *alongside.*"

"You are." Moss was fervent. "You are. You are the whole —" *Thing,* he wanted to say. *You are more than that.*

"Reg," he went on, "this afternoon I saw it, I saw how you were at the center of it all, and I wrote it. I got it down. The song — the song about all this, about the black man, how you are the new note and the —"

"Listen to me, Moss. *We* have *always* been here at the center. Always. It's only that you've just decided to take a look."

Moss shook his head. "But —"

"And I'm not a goddamned bell. I'm a man."

Moss gave a laugh that was half a groan. "Damn it, I know that."

Reg shook his head. "You can't slip your history, man. That's what I'm telling you. That's the story I keep getting, again and again. Those people," he said, pointing at the island, "your parents — whatever they did, whatever they didn't do in their lives — that's what's in you. No matter what you say, or do —"

Moss shook his head. "Listen to me, Reg. You're right with me, we're here. We can make it all happen, we can show people the change that's coming, that's possible —"

"Change?" Reg repeated.

The ferocity of his bitterness surprised him. All that he had held back, all that he hadn't said was directed at the man across from him in the boat.

"You think change comes without *change*? You think you can open the door and then keep the rooms on the other side exactly the same? *Come in, come in, sure — but don't touch, don't sit on the furniture. Watch where you're stepping.* That's not change, man — that's a dinner party. All the guests come and then all the guests go home."

Reg saw the expression on Moss's face and was so weary just then, so tired. He was tired of being the man at the center banging the gong. He wanted — was it too much to ask? He wanted Joan to choose Len. He wanted to ride in this boat, he wanted to walk with Moss arm in arm through the door Moss imagined was open. He wanted — was it always too much? — a happy ending.

"Do you want to know what your other sister said to me?"

Moss shook his head.

" 'You don't marry a Jew,' she said to me. Change would be your sister marrying Len and your mother rejoicing at the wedding. Change would be the white boys and the black boys going to school together, the same school, and two years later all those boys in jobs, instead of those black boys cleaning the toilets of the girls and boys they walked off the graduation stage with —"

"Then that's what we have to tell people."

"People? What people?" Reg thrust. "Black people already know the news, Moss. White people have to face it. And it is a rare man who points to it and says, *Look there. Look there at what is between us.* Who calls it into the open. Who *admits* there is a fight and says, *Now what?*"

Moss sat listening, sick at heart. "But when you say it like that — black people this, white people that — you separate, you draw attention to it, you make it worse."

"It was already *worse,*" Reg answered slowly, "before I arrived. America rose out of that handshake in Philadelphia, 1776. That single, simple deal. You give us your signatures to fight the British, we'll give you your slaves. *That* is what's at the bottom of the jar. And some want to remember and some want to forget, but you can't take a sip and not take it in."

"But —"

"Black people can't forget what's at the bottom, we will never forget what's at the bottom. But if this country could just say it — say it, say — *all right, yes, it's there* — then we can fill the jar, Moss. *Then* we can start — singing."

A spasm of pain crossed Moss's face.

"So help me god, you are a good man." Reg leaned toward him. "And you mean well. But when you look at me and talk of change, of hope — from on top of an island in Maine — I think, I can't help but think, *He can't possibly mean me.*"

Moss shook his head. "You are wrong."

"Am I?" And though he could see Moss's face collapsing, Reg kept going, striking word upon word. "You wanted me to come and see you, warts and all, you said. You wanted me to come and see — you wanted me to absolve you, Moss. I can't absolve you."

Moss had gone white in the face of this tirade, the scorn which Reg himself had not felt rising, which lurched now from his chest. But the weight, the intolerable weight of the monster was gone. "I can't absolve you. I can't prove that you are good. Do you hear?"

Moss reached for him and put his hands on his shoulders. The fear in his eyes equal to the need.

"Why did you come?"

"Because," Reg choked. "Because you asked," he cried. "And because I like you —" He looked at Moss directly. He couldn't lie. "And because I wanted you to see what I see. And I wanted to see if you could."

"Is that all this was?" Moss dropped his hands. "Is that what I am to you? Some kind of test?"

Reg hugged himself, wordless in the face of

657

the man in front of him.

Moss set his oar and took a long, violent stroke.

Then again, once, twice. The boat surged forward, gliding silent across the black night. Reg closed his eyes.

"*Damn it,* Reg." Moss jammed the oars into the water, jerking the boat to such a sudden stop, Reg had to grab the gunwales. Then Moss stood, throwing his weight in the boat to the left, to the right wanting to shake it, tip it, his eyes on Reg.

"How about seeing what *I* see? How about that? Look *here.* Look at us. Damn it, look at me. In *this* boat."

"Stop it, man." Reg clung to the wooden rim. "Stop —"

Moss sat down so suddenly, the boat lurched to the left and then, righting, calmed. The two friends looked at each other, their breath ragged in the night air.

And then they heard shouting.

"Reg!"

It sounded like Len.

"Moss!"

"Mother of god," Reg breathed, catching sight of Len standing, naked, it looked like, on the rocks.

Moss turned in his seat.

"Moss!" The panic in Len's voice came clear and loud across the water.

It looked like Len dove in after something

in the water, something thrashing and struggling, and then Moss saw it was Joan he was going for, Joan pushing against him and going under, Joan struggling. *God* damn *him,* Moss thought. Len had taken her swimming.

"I'm coming, Joanie!" Moss dropped to his seat and started rowing as fast as he could, the scene on the rocks hidden by the bow of the boat.

"Get off." He pulled on the oars as hard as he could. "Get off her, asshole."

Joan couldn't breathe. Someone was knocking in her head. Was that Moss out there in the boat? *Moss,* she thought. Moss, and someone else? The boat hovered above the surface of the water like a white ghost floating. She needed Moss. Someone was going to get in. Someone was bursting forward, hurling himself — *Moss.* She got out, just before the door crashed open, and she fell into the water, in the grip of the seizure. The light in the doorway shone in her eyes and she tried to put her hand in front of them, she tried to cover her eyes, but her hand wasn't working and it hit against her cheek instead. Hands were lifting her up, no no no, holding her up. *Moss! Moss!* She tried to call her brother, but the shaking had started and she had to concentrate as her knees gave way, and the water opened and took her.

Len dove again under the frigid black water

and grabbed at Joan, writhing just beneath the surface, clawing at the water, her eyes wide open. She heaved and clutched, and jerked away from him just when he'd gotten hold, and slid free as the fit took her body backward. *Joan* — he reached again — goddamn it, *Joan,* he was crying, and grabbed her hand this time, and held it fast and yanked her toward him, his lungs exploding, dragging her with him up to the surface as she kicked and flailed against him. He held on to her, struggling to get them onto the rocks, so he could grab her entirely and carry her up. He thought he heard the boat behind him, but he didn't dare turn around, concentrating on making it to the rocks. It seemed Joan was struggling less, and he risked a look backward and saw her eyes had closed.

"Joan," he said, coughing. "They're coming."

His foot hit on the edge of a rock and he pulled them forward as the other foot caught and he paused and pulled her closer in now that he had something to stand on. She was going limp, as if she were falling asleep. "They're coming," he said again, trying to keep his voice calm, as he reached for the rocks and pulled her in, climbing backward, the barnacles cutting his hands and knees. He could see Moss rowing toward them and with an enormous effort, succeeded in getting them both up and out of the water and onto the rocks just at the edge. Moss and Reg were coming. He stood up, thinking to get Joan's clothes, something to cover her, and turning from the water saw Evelyn standing there. She wore Dickie's coat, holding it closed at the neck with one hand, and she looked for a minute like a dangerous child, the danger in the single-minded expression on her small features. Carrying one of the boathouse lanterns, she looked ancient to him, the incarnation of all the watchdogs at the gate. Coming fast behind her were Mr. and Mrs. Milton.

He covered himself with his hands and turned back toward Joan to protect her from all those faces.

So he did not see Evelyn coming for him, did not see how she hurled herself at him, giving him a sudden, hard shove, so hard, he lost his balance and tripped, plunging the ten feet straight down and back into the freezing cold. His face slammed into the slope of granite below the water, and his nose snapped, the water pouring into his throat, choking him. He fought against the water, but he couldn't breathe, he couldn't pull up; the blood rushed down his throat with the water. He kicked and fought to get back up to the top, panicked at the water pouring down his throat.

Someone grabbed him by the elbow and tugged. He kicked against the hand. Both his arms were seized, and someone swam behind him and was pulling him up. There were arms around him, but his head was pounding and he couldn't breathe. There were arms around him, yanking him up, back up.

He gasped in the air. He choked and gasped, his chest heaving air, the taste of blood in his mouth. "You're all right," Ogden Milton said to him, his arms around Len. "You're all right."

Moss leaned all his weight into the oars, pulling and pulling toward the sound of the splashing, pulling with all his strength to get there, sound fallen away, everything fallen except the adrenaline pumping his arms for him. He had to get to Joanie. He had to save her. Nothing else mattered.

"Stop!" Reg was shouting at him, pointing, and then Reg leaped at him to grab the oars.

"Stop, Moss," he heard his mother shout. "Stop it!"

Moss understood the danger in time and jammed the oars down to stall the boat. His father had Len under the arms and was pulling him onto the rocks, both of them panting and the blood pouring down Len's face.

"Jesus," cried Moss.

His mother was kneeling over Joan, her arms on either shoulder, holding her steady and talking to her quietly, trying to cover her daughter's shivering body with her cardigan.

He pulled in and grabbed hold of the rocks, and he and Reg climbed out.

"What happened?" Moss asked. "What the hell happened?"

"Are you all right?" Reg said to Len.

"Nothing happened," Ogden answered swiftly, the water streaming down his face. "I'm so sorry."

He looked at Evelyn. Shaking, standing off to the side, she looked back at him and lifted her chin.

"Get Joanie's clothes," Kitty instructed Moss without taking her eyes off Joan's face.

Moss walked back to the edge of the rock, picked up Joan's shirt and her skirt and brought them all over, looking away from his sister's nakedness.

Then he went and got Len's shirt and handed it to him.

Reg put his hand on Len's shoulder. "Are you okay?"

Len nodded, his eyes on Joan. The fit had passed. No one spoke. Len pulled his shirt over his wet head and shoulders and went for his trousers. Joan's eyes opened and shut. Slowly, Kitty turned on Len.

"You were a guest."

Dripping wet and bleeding, Len stared at her.

"You came as a guest here," Kitty said to Len again, her breath catching in her throat.

"You were *invited.* And you took advantage
—"

Len pulled his trousers swiftly on and stood
up, blood streaming from his nose.

"Come on, Len," Reg said. "Come on.
Let's get out of here. They don't want us.
They don't —"

"Shut up, Reg," Moss pleaded quietly.
"You'll only make it worse —"

Reg wheeled around. "*I'll* make it worse?"

"Don't you dare call us 'they,' " Evelyn
spat. "Don't you dare. Who the hell do you
think you are, coming here, stirring things up
—"

"Evelyn!" Moss cried.

"And you." She turned on her brother.
"You can ride your high horse straight to hell,
I don't care. This isn't some experiment. This
is life, Moss. And Joanie almost died. This
—"

"Evelyn," Joan said weakly. "Stop."

Her sister turned around.

"Stop it." Joan put her hand up to her
forehead and, holding her shirt to her chest,
she pushed herself up to sitting. Kitty sank
down beside her, and Joan looked first at her
mother, then at her father.

Her eyes rested at last on Len standing
above her, and she simply started to cry.

He crouched down beside her. "Let's go,"
he said softly, as if they were entirely alone.

Her tears slid down her cheeks.

"None of this matters."

"Len."

"Remember that. What happened is the only thing that matters."

"Len," she whispered.

He stopped.

She knew that he had heard her. He had heard her, and refused to hear.

"Joan," he said. "It's so simple."

His voice on her name brought back the dark and his lips on her lips, and she shuddered. Her name, the single syllable of her name uttered with such precision, such care, was his proposal. She looked at him and tried to memorize it all. The man in the moonlight, the water, Moss and her mother beside her. It wasn't simple at all.

"I can't," she whispered. "I can't give you what you ought to have —"

"You love me." He spoke low.

She nodded, looking up at him. "I do, Len. I do. God, I do — but you need more than this. More than me. It's so clear —"

The expression on his face stopped her.

"I'm a Jew," he said slowly. "That's it."

Her eyes widened. "A Jew? No. It's because of me. Look at you, Len — you are big and wide and —"

He gave a short amazed laugh. "Reg was right."

They stared at each other.

"Len." Her voice broke.

"Come on." Reg gave Len's arm a tug.

Len couldn't move.

"Get in, man. Get in the boat."

"This isn't what I meant to happen." Moss was urgent. "Go on."

Reg looked at him in disbelief.

"Go to the Welds' dock," Moss said to Reg. "It's straight across. I'll meet you there."

"Meant to happen?" Reg repeated.

Moss straightened.

"Do you know what you said back there in the boat —"

Moss looked at him.

"The first thing you said?"

Moss frowned, trying to remember.

" 'Get *off,* ' you said," Reg whispered. " 'Get off her, asshole.' "

Moss went white.

Reg shook his head. "You're just like the rest — when push comes to shove, you see just what you want to see, like all of them. Just like them — only kind."

"Reg!" Moss cried.

"Enough." Kitty rose from Joan's side and moved toward Reg. "How dare you? How dare you paint us blacker, meaner than we are!"

"Blacker? Meaner?" Reg stood his ground. "How *dare* I? Tell them, Mrs. Milton. Tell them what you told me."

She froze.

"Go on," Reg said, his heart pounding so

hard he wanted to shake it free. "Go on. Tell them what you told me up there on that bench —"

Ogden wheeled around to look at Kitty.

" 'The bill is due,' " Reg pushed. "It is not *coming* due. It is due. And it must be paid — or this shit will go on and on and on."

No one moved. Shaking, Reg heard himself and saw the stunned white faces as he unleashed the words that anywhere else would have gotten him shoved, knocked down, knocked out — killed. But they wouldn't say a word. These wouldn't. Years and years of the leash, he got it. He got it now. They wouldn't, they couldn't, they were too *good.* So good.

"And why did you tell me, Mrs. Milton? Why me?" He leveled his gaze at her.

"Reg," Len said.

"You thought you'd bury your memory in a deep, dark place? Bury it in *me?*"

Kitty took the three remaining steps and slapped Reg hard across the face.

"Mum!" Moss cried.

And the slap rose up in Reg like a smile given to a chuckle, and he simply started to laugh. A great laugh that began in his chest and erupted from him, and he found he couldn't stop. He laughed and laughed into the stunned silence. He laughed. Goodness. Kindness. What a tribe. They were already dead. Already ghosts.

"Come on," he said to Len, and turned his back on all of them and climbed down into the boat.

Len stood a moment longer, his eyes on Joan. And very slightly, but clearly, she shook her head.

With one sudden violent motion, Len turned and threw himself into the bow of the dinghy, pushing off from the rocks, and moved to the middle seat, grabbing hold of the oars and shoving them out and into the water. Reg had to grip the gunwales in the stern so as not to fall out as Len stroked, the wooden shafts solid in both hands.

Without a word or a glance, Len reached and felt the water under his oars pull against him, tense and dark, and took another stroke against the Miltons on the rocks. A stroke away from Joan. And then another and another, and a fury washed over him in waves. The idea he had had, that there could be clear sailing, that you could set your sights on a point and simply go toward it, and get there just like anyone else — what had he thought? *Think Yiddish, dress British.* It was a game, wasn't it, after all. Come and visit. If you're up there anyway, come and see us. Visit. You went to Columbia, you went to Wall Street, but you were a visitor. How could he have missed it? He was a *guest.* He had wanted to keep the rules and best them, not break them. *Well, fuck them,* he thought. *And fuck that house.* He was done. He would never pull his punches again. He took furious, heartbroken strokes across the smooth water and felt his heart would burst. He rowed and rowed until at last, in the middle of the Narrows, the sob beneath the fury pushed up and burst free at last, and he cried. He cried for Joan, he cried for himself, and for the dream he had had. But the Jew was dead. Long live the Jew.

FORTY

The rowboat pulled into a shaft of moonlight on the water, just for a minute. And Joan saw Len bearing down on his oars, reaching forward and pulling back, easily sliding across the surface. Then gone into the dark. The oarlocks sang across the water. She knew she would never see him again. His lips and his mouth and the weight of his body were gone. And she had sent him off. She turned her head and closed her eyes.

Moss watched the boat disappear. *You're just like the rest, only kind.* Reg had damned him far more than he could know. Water splashed in uneven drops on the rocks in the single beam of Ogden's flashlight, and Moss found himself counting them. The sound of the oars turning in the metal locks kept time. Away, they turned. Away. Reg was going. Everything Moss thought he had been listening to, all he had been listening for, was rowing away in the dark.

In the distance they could hear the party

breaking up, the sound of the guests coming down the hill, singing. Lanterns began emerging from the boathouse and moving toward the dock. The stars were out; it was time to leave. Lights on the boats wobbled in a long line speeding away over the water. Everyone would have a smooth ride home.

The boat carrying Len and Reg had vanished around the point across the way and into the Welds' dock on Vinalhaven's cove.

"Come on." Moss tenderly gathered Joan in his arms and carried her up the path through the trees and out onto the broad path up the hill to the house. She was still dazed, and she leaned her head against her brother's shoulder.

"Are you all right?" he whispered to her.

She reached up and touched the bottom of his chin.

He walked forward.

"They've gone," she said.

He nodded.

A tear escaped and slipped sideways into her hair.

"What happened!" Anne cried as the little group made its slow way up the lawn in the dark. "Where have you been? Dickie and I have been looking all over for you."

"There was an accident," Ogden said quietly.

"What accident? Where? Where have you

all been?" Dickie went to Evelyn's side.

"It's all right, Dickie." Evelyn looked up at him wearily as he put his arms around her. "I'm all right."

Kitty took charge. "We need to get Joan into bed. She's had one of her spells."

Moss helped Joan up the stairs. The lights were put out at the barn. Downstairs, the front door slammed, and the sound of voices drifted up.

The party was over. Joan lay on her bed in the pink room. Her eyes followed her mother pulling down the shades. *I loved him,* she wanted to say. *I love him.* But her mother was the last person who could understand.

For Len had been right. Something happened. Something had happened that could never be dislodged. *Ask me,* she wanted to say to her mother's silent, tending form. Ask me something, anything about him. But she knew that nothing would be said, because what good could come of flushing everything up to the top. Then there it would be, floating between them, requiring attention. Requiring address. Hurtful to draw attention to what could not be fixed. Better not to mention it. For the heart, that way, could heal. It was best for all of them to put one foot after the other and go on.

And she wanted to go on, she realized. She badly wanted to go on in this room in the place where she knew precisely who she was, the edges firm, the corners strong.

"Mum," she whispered.

"Try to sleep." Kitty turned to her, leaned forward, and touched her cheek. "You've had a shock."

"Where is Evelyn?" Joan asked. "What about Evelyn?"

"I imagine she's with Dickie." Kitty was even.

"And Moss?"

"Moss is downstairs with Dad," Kitty soothed. "I can hear them both."

Joan nodded, closing her eyes.

Kitty waited for Joan to fall asleep under the pink coverlet, sitting in the chair at the end of the bed, her exhausted mind crouched and waiting. All of them there, all of them waiting, brought back by that black man's words: Elsa's face on that porch, and Willy shaking her hand, and Neddy turning in the moment he fell, and —

"Joanie?" Anne Pratt poked her head in the door and Kitty put her finger to her lips and shook her head. Anne disappeared round the corner. A few minutes later, Kitty heard her passing with Evelyn down the hall to Evelyn's room. Then the door closed.

When Joan's breathing began to slow and steady itself, Kitty rose and went into her own bedroom. The room was just as she had left it before the party, the bed tucked tight.

She walked to her bureau to look at her face in the mirror. She could hear Moss and Ogden talking in the room below. Her girls lay in the rooms on either side of her. Everyone was safe. No one was hurt.

She went slowly down the stairs toward Ogden's voice, urgent and low, though she couldn't make out the words and stood a moment in the dark hall outside the door to the front room adjusting her eyes.

"No, Dad," she heard Moss answer as she put her hand on the knob, listening.

"You passed the baton to me tonight, Dad," Moss was saying. "But I'm not the man to take it. It's a lie. This idea of the Miltons, better than anyone, righter than anyone, the Island as the sign of having gotten it *right*. We can't pretend. We're not better because we own a place like this."

"No one thinks —"

Kitty opened the door and stood on the threshold. Ogden's face was drawn but resolute. Moss was on his feet and standing in the middle of the room, his madras jacket crumpled in one hand. He seemed broken, as if something inside had snapped. And he was still wet from having carried Joan.

"Moss." Her worry made her sharp. "What is going on?"

Ogden didn't look at his son and didn't move from where he sat.

Wordless, Moss turned, walking past her

and making for the front door.

"Wait." Kitty put her hand out to catch him, following him into the hall. "Moss."

He pushed through the screen door into the dark outside, where he turned and stood on the granite stoop, looking back at her.

"It's poison, you know, Mum. This place."

"Shush," she pleaded. "You are soaking wet. Come back inside."

"Mum, listen."

"Stop it, Moss. You are drunk."

"I'm not."

She quieted.

He studied her, then looked down the hill a minute, as if gathering strength from the dark, before facing her again.

"Somehow, Mum," he began softly, "no matter how old I get, no matter how far I go from here, there is always this image in my head — of a boy following after his father, knowing he can't catch him, the father carrying a girl he's just pulled choking from the water. That day Joanie had her first fit down there by the dock, I couldn't do anything. I couldn't do anything but watch."

"Moss," she protested.

"And it comes to me swiftly and from nowhere, and it is an image of immense loneliness, of futility. No matter how fast I trot behind Dad, no matter how fast I swim toward her, I will not catch up. I will not get her, and there the helplessness is run through with fascination." He paused. "I can't simply watch anymore. I've got to go do something. Somewhere else."

She came through the door and stood beside him on the stoop, putting her hand on his arm.

He looked down at her hand.

"No matter what I do, Mum," he said quietly. "I can't change it. This place is a pile of lies. If we are not good or right, we are wrong. And that — down there on the rocks" — he paused — "was wrong. And you know it. You must know it."

Kitty could not bear the look on Moss's face. She couldn't bear it. Even as he denounced them all, she saw how badly he wanted her to comfort him, prove him wrong, save him from some wide-open idea he had — and his broken voice made it easy.

"Nonsense," she said to him.

And standing there in the threshold looking back at her, Moss remembered her standing in a doorway, long ago. He didn't know where it was, but he was very small, and was sitting on a chair, he thought, and she was standing in the doorway looking at him. At him and not him. At a place beside him. And she was tall and green. And staring at him. Something had happened. And then, he remembered, she had simply shut her eyes.

A sound like a sob rose in him, and he shook his head against it. "Make it right," he said softly. "Write to Reg, to Len, and make what happened down there right. Do something that shows the good."

She held out her hand, as much to grab hold of him, to draw him toward her, as to stop him from saying anything more.

"Promise me," Moss said. "Otherwise all the rest is just words."

"Of course it's not just words," she said.

He held her gaze a long moment and then finally nodded, turned from her, and walked away. She watched his figure down the lawn, his white shirt vanishing to gray, and just at the edge of the perimeter of light cast by the house, she caught the lift of his arm in a backward wave, the jacket hanging from his fist like a flag.

And even up to the morning she died, years later, she'd wake from the usual nightmare, thinking she held Moss's hand in hers. Thinking he had taken her hand, instead of walking away in the night. Thinking that she had stood on the step of the Big House and called her son, her only son, back.

She drew back into the front room and sank down into the chair under the window, sitting with Ogden in quiet by the light of a kerosene lamp on the table between them. The generator had stopped, and the only sound was the foghorn in the bay. Ogden raised his eyes and finally looked at her.

"What was Pauling talking about out there

on the rocks?" Ogden asked slowly. "*What did you tell him?*"

Kitty returned his gaze. *All right, then,* she thought.

And so at last she told him. She told Ogden about Willy and about Elsa and how he had seemed so set against the woman on that afternoon long ago. How it seemed to her that Elsa had pushed and pushed, and Kitty had stepped in to help. She had thought she was helping him. In the quiet house, her voice threaded back and forth between them, between the time past and the present, trying to make some kind of sense. And when she had finished, Ogden was silent for a long while.

"We couldn't take him," she pleaded. "How could we have taken him, Ogden?"

He sat forward in the chair and reached for her hand. She looked at him, uncertainly at first. And then, when he kept his gaze steady on her, she gave him her hand, and he held it.

"I thought I was helping," she said again.

He nodded.

She looked down at their clasped hands.

"We won't speak of this," he said to her. "We needn't speak of this, ever again."

"But Moss thinks —"

"Moss is young." Ogden paused. Moss had not yet run into the wall inside that waits for all men, no matter the era, the wall inside where a man runs into his own aging face. The wall Dunc was hurling himself against, the wall Ogden recognized himself. He looked back at Kitty.

"He thinks he can change the world —" He sighed. "But the world does not change. Only you do —"

There was such a deep, abiding sorrow in his face, she couldn't bear to see.

"And those friends? Mr. Pauling? Mr. Levy?"

He took a long while before he answered her. "They are good men."

"Who didn't understand what's what."

He raised his face and studied her. "What *is* what?" he asked.

She rose and stood before him.

"Come," she said quietly. "It's very late."

He looked up at her. She nodded.

"Come," she said again.

Out on the moonless water, Moss was rowing toward the Welds' dock. He could hear Reg and Len talking long before he could see them. Talking and smoking. Sitting close at the end of the dock, the light of their cigarettes moving up and down against their dark shapes. Moss shipped his oars and watched them, the water around him flat and quiet and calm.

He could not hear what they said, but the ease and the comfort between the men, the

679

long steady years between them, made it clear. He could never join them. Reg had been right. There were tribes. In that instant, all of what he had been after, all that he had imagined for himself, rose up and fell to dust. What had he thought? That he could write something that would change the world? The song was no more than a schoolboy's wish — worse, it was a joke — the song leaped its borders; he had been a fool to imagine anything so tidy. He had been nothing but a fool, all along. It was bigger than him. It couldn't be contained. There was no form for it. He could watch. He would watch. He felt sick. He would watch from a desk in his father's office.

And Reg would walk away.

He shoved the oars back out, took one deep stroke to turn the boat around, and then started to row, hard, down the Narrows between the islands. He rowed his sorrow and his helplessness, pulling through the still water. He rowed Joanie's white, exhausted face and Evelyn's protective fury on the rocks. He rowed his mother on the threshold and his father's doubt. He rowed the thing inside him that he didn't feel, but had risen to his lips despite it all. *Asshole.* He rowed, rowing away from what he loved with every stroke, rowing so hard he was upon the rock ledge before he saw it, his oar catching so hard it lifted him out of the boat in one swift instant, his head slamming down on the wood as he fell, fell so hard and so clear into the water, so clear in his last terrified instant.

FORTY-ONE

The morning dawned bright and blue. Silently, Kitty raised the covers and slid her legs out and stood up. Her bathing suit lay in the top drawer next to her bathing cap, and she slipped out of her nightgown and pulled it on, and then wrapped her towel around her waist for warmth.

There was no one in the upstairs hall, and no one she could hear stirring below. She walked down the stairs, slipping out into the day. The lawn was a little battered, and the big coolers sat upended by the flagpole. She wandered down the hill into the woods in the direction of the picnic grounds, the dew thick on her sneakers.

The same disheveled, slightly beaten air greeted her as she moved past the tables, the vases, someone's slipper left in the grass, to the rocks, to stand and look out at the water.

Something was caught in the lobster car that had held the beers the night before, some fabric, no — she stopped where she was on the rock — a jacket. Someone's jacket sleeve was wrapped in the netting. Her legs moved heavily forward. She tried to move forward but felt she was having to lift them over the rocks toward the water's edge where the thing had washed up. It was a madras jacket.

"No," she heard what must have been her voice cry low and thick in her own throat.

Quick. Quick. He might be down there, caught under there, under the water. She must get him. Quick. Now she was able to move, as if a spring had been released and she had been let fly. She scrambled down the rocks to the open lobster trap, her legs giving way beneath her, and sat heavily down on the granite. The sleeve was empty, she saw. How could she have missed it. So he must have swum free, he must have gotten out of the trap and swum free. She gave a little moan of relief, her breath coming out ragged and hard. Thank god. She sat catching her breath.

The foghorn on the buoy in the Narrows sounded, and right away after the single note, the long sustained answer from the Vinal-haven ferry passing the end of Crockett's Island, bound for Rockland. The two worked for her like voices of the place, calming, comforting, the notes of safety. She turned toward the comfort, toward the buoy and the ferry, and saw something broken on the rocks. Something white and thick, the size of a child's mattress, thrown up on the wide

683

granite face and soaking wet. It was a man in his undershirt, the two arms splayed on either side, but at impossible angles, as if they had been broken off and reattached.

FORTY-TWO

They buried Moss in the graveyard on the hill behind the house, next to the Crockett stones. A month later, Ogden walked Evelyn down the aisle and gave her away to Dickie Pratt.

And *nothing,* Joan realized, looking in the mirror at the doctor's office after he had given her the news, is as you had thought. She studied her face. Nevertheless, you take the cards you are dealt and you play your best hand. Very well. She turned and pulled the door open, nodding goodbye to the girl at the typewriter in the doctor's office, so pleased to be pushing the carriage along, typing fast and cleanly upon the blank pages. Very well. Joan pushed out into the autumn afternoon, making her way to meet Fenno Weld in the park where he was waiting, Fenno with his dear deep laugh, his devotion. *Joanie.* He rose from the bench as she came toward him. She dipped her chin. *Let's not wait,* she said.

Joan married Fenno. They had a baby girl and named her Evelyn, after Evelyn, who kissed her sister with her own new baby, Henry, in her arms. Evelyn, after Evelyn, after Evelyn, after Evelyn, Evelyn murmured, delighted. Fifth in a row.

In the house on Crockett's Island, new children grew. Passing through the Thoroughfare, one might catch sight of the Miltons up on the lawn, the children running down the hill, or in the woods through the spruce, clipping branches, or simply walking. There had been that terrible accident after a party, someone slipped and it was said the son had tried to help — and drowned in the doing of it.

Still, there they were out in their boats, the sisters and their children, at the picnics on the rocks, and in the market in their cutoff shorts and Fair Isle sweaters, old Mrs. Milton with her basket and Mr. Milton in his long-brimmed cap, tacking round the coves.

There were cocktails on North Haven, or suppers across the way, and as the Miltons returned home in the *Katherine* through the near dark, skimming over the black water under the open sky, the grandchildren packed in the bow of the boat facing forward, the grown-ups ranged in the stern behind them, there was such calm, such surety. *And here it is,* Evie thought one night, a teenager beside her cousins, *here it is,* everything. This moment. She turned her head and found her mother's eyes upon her and, reassured, turned back around.

She would never tell her daughter, Joan realized then, her hip resting on the transom, aware of her mother and Fenno sitting in the stern with Evelyn. She couldn't. It would be hurtful to them all — to her mother, to her father, and to Fenno, who had been so good — most of all.

Joan stared out across the heads of the children in the bow as the island grew closer. But Evie would have this place. Joan crossed her arms in the wind. Evie would have all this.

At the end of the seventies, Milton Higginson was sold to Merrill Lynch, its offices closed at 30 Broad Street, the building Ogden Milton's great-grandfather had built in 1855. Ogden moved his father's desk into his new office in the high-rise in the middle of the city, rode the elevator up in the mornings, and settled in behind it. There was no one to pass the desk along to. There was no water, no boats, and nothing to see but the city out of the new windows.

They buried Ogden the following summer, next to Moss.

Henry, Evelyn's oldest, took to wearing Ogden's sailing cap that year. He was twenty. The old brim had long ago cracked and collapsed, and the khaki faded to dun. But it suited him, Kitty thought, watching as he pushed the wheelbarrow down the lawn to collect the groceries, proud of being the eldest, proud of knowing what to do.

Ogden. Kitty shifted on the bench. That *hat.* It used to hang on the hook in the back hall. That summer every chair held him in it, every boat had him on it, every shout from across the field crossed in his voice. He had held his seat opposite her so long, the dining room table seemed to list without him, though they set a knife and a fork every night at his place and someone else would sit there.

Across the way she could just make out Aldo Weld appearing on the dock. He had grown smaller as he aged, though his step was spry. Fanny had died long ago. The old man stood there waiting as Fenno rowed forward in a dinghy toward him. Fenno was a good son, she thought, watching the son ship his oars as Aldo bent and caught the bow. Poor Fenno.

And when Fenno died very suddenly in the middle of the night eight years later, *poor Fenno* was what Kitty thought again, putting down the telephone.

It was 1988.

They arrived late in the evening that first summer without him. It was the first time they'd had to ask Jimmy Ames to ferry them out to the Island from Rockland in the boat.

Ogden had always done it. Then Fenno had. Now Dickie ought, but Dickie couldn't leave work.

Kitty had stood at the bottom of the hill looking up at the house in the twilight and stalled. She could see them all — Priss in the circle of Dunc's arm, Elsa, Willy, and — Ogden. *Oh.*

"Come on, Mum," Joan said, slipping her arm under Kitty's.

After breakfast, after the dishes and the putting away, Kitty took up her seat on the green bench, her bad leg raised on a tower of pillows brought up from the boathouse. Beside her she had her binoculars and her book. Evelyn sat in one of the big white chairs on either side of the bench, some needlepoint spread across her lap. Joan stood a few feet away with the garden clippers in her hand, eyeing the lilac.

There were no boats for the time being. It was quiet in the Narrows. Kitty stared at the water. The day had begun.

Most of the grandchildren were down on the dock, though Minerva was lying on the lawn, her hair fanned out in the sun. Evie sat beside Kitty on the bench, her knees up like a boy, her arms wrapped around them. Minerva's legs raised slowly up from the ground in tandem, and back down again, performing some type of exercise.

What did one do with these two? Kitty

wondered. They made no sense to her at all. It was fine for them to go to their fathers' colleges — but it was gilding on the lily. They were girls. Their place was to adorn, to protect — to guide, by example. Though neither one of them appeared in the least interested in that; both of them were in *graduate* school.

"What are you working on, Evie?" Evelyn was threading her needle.

Evie straightened, sitting forward a little, and started in.

How she talks, that one, thought Kitty, half listening to her granddaughter, following the dip of a gull over her words. *Lacuna in the documentary record* — Kitty kept a straight face. *Oh, indeed.*

"For instance, this moment," Evie was saying. "What is this moment? Right *now.* Something is happening. It's history in the making, but we can't see it, do you see? We're alive and dead all at the same time."

She was very pleased with herself, Kitty observed.

"History?" Kitty broke in. "Never mind history; let that happen to others. These are the best years of your lives, you two. You don't know it, but it's true."

Someone had said that once. Who? Kitty shook her head.

"God, Granny," Min said, speaking up to

the sky from her spot flat on the grass. "I hope not."

"They are, Minerva." Their grandmother was firm. "Nothing has happened to you yet."

"I know," groaned Min, flinging her arms wide. "It's horrible."

"It's the simple truth," Kitty said swiftly, an unexpected heat rising against her grand-daughters. "What's done — once done — cannot be undone."

"But it can be *revised,* Granny," Evie said squarely. "It can be revisited."

"Revised?" Kitty frowned. "What on earth does that mean?"

"Freedom," Evie offered, "to see it in a new way."

No one spoke for a minute.

"Don't be absurd, Evie," Joan said quietly.

Evie turned to her mother, startled.

"You can't revise what's happened. Nor should you. A life can change in a single mo-ment, and from there you simply move for-ward."

"But can't you redo, Mum?" Evie asked her mother. "Can't there be many moments? Can't a life turn and re-turn and turn again?"

Kitty and Evelyn and Joan all turned their heads and looked at her.

Evie froze as if she had been caught steal-ing. She had spoken without thinking, but it was exactly what she had been thinking, what she was working on. It was the first time, she realized, looking back at them, that she felt different, *was* different from these three.

"Nothing can be redone," Evelyn observed at last, pulling the thread through. "Because no one ever forgets."

Joan turned around and stared at her sister.

"Or *forgives,*" Evelyn continued, looking back at Joan.

Evie sat very still.

Kitty rapped on the bench with her knuckle. *"Girls."*

Min turned over and pushed herself up onto her elbows. This was interesting.

Joan turned slowly away from her sister and stared back at the lilac.

Evie caught Min's eye.

"Girls," Kitty said, "go on down to the dock and get Henry and Shep and Harriet to help you. We need the mussels. The tide is right."

Reluctantly, Evie and Min picked themselves up and started slowly down the lawn, aware of their mothers and their grandmother watching them go.

"I only —" Evelyn began.

"Evelyn, leave it alone."

Evelyn wove the needle into the canvas and set it down on the grass. Joan put down the clippers.

Halfway down the lawn, Evie looked back at them and Kitty drew in her breath sharply. There was Len Levy, again. There he was just then, glancing back to find Joan, making sure of her that day. Kitty shook her head. She could go years and forget until her granddaughter would come striding up the lawn, with that same air about her — *the world, the world is all mine* — a decisiveness that couldn't be smoothed away, a surety that barreled into every room. And there he'd be again, right here, Len Levy. And that Mr. Pauling.

And then, with him . . . Moss.

Oh. She pushed up from the bench, walking blindly away from her daughters. *Dear god, what does it matter?* Everything gets through in the end, doesn't it, nothing can protect us — close all the windows, shut all the doors, pull down the curtains, lock it all out — for here they came nonetheless.

Moss. Moss at the piano, Moss on the trails. Moss at a dinner party. Moss in short pants. Moss, she thought, and closed her eyes, Moss's little face looking at her, trusting her as he turned from that open window so many years ago. *Where was Neddy? What happened to Neddy?* A little moan escaped. She had *saved* him. She had pulled him back. And then, Moss in the doorway that last night, turning to look at her through the screen. *Let me go,* he had pleaded, walking down the hill and into the dark. And there he was, in the dark rowing —

Toward what?

She stopped in the middle of the lawn, her heart struck dumb with sorrow.

"Granny?"

Evie and Min had reached the bottom of the lawn and turned around. Their grandmother was standing halfway down the hill, motionless. Their mothers stood frozen in front of the house. The three women marked a triangle of quiet.

What had happened?

The old woman in the middle swayed unsteadily.

"Granny K?" Evie called, the worry clear in her face.

Kitty blinked, startled by her name.

"Granny?" Evie started walking toward her.

Kitty gazed at Evie thoughtfully.

Revise?

■ ■ ■ ■

HERE

■ ■ ■ ■

FORTY-THREE

Evie.

Joan stood at the foot of the bed, waiting. There was light in the room. There were birds. *Evie,* she said, her hand on the bedpost. *Evie,* she said looking down.

Stop, Evie moaned, way down in her sleep.

Evie.

Stop, Mum. Stop. I am sleeping.

Evie, she said, her voice pulling Evie out of the bed at last, pulling her out again, pulling her out of the room and down the stairs and through the door into the morning, out into the morning, out into the dew, their feet wet, their feet moving quickly, quick quick, up the hill, up we go —

Evie sat bolt upright, her throat raw, as if she'd been crying, her mother's face receding. The room around her was still.

It was morning. She turned her head. It was morning on the Island. In the pink room. She was here. She slid her legs over the side of the bed and stood.

When would it end, this dream? She splashed water on her face in the bathroom sink. When would she be free of it?

In the kitchen, the coffee had been made and a mug put out. The English muffins sat beside the toaster with a knife and the butter. The windows shone. There was a new oilcloth on the battered table. Since the first day in the linen closet, the cousins had worked through the house, touching every surface, pulling out every drawer. The laying on of hands, Min joked. Every dish had been taken from the shelf and washed, every shelf wiped and repapered. Yesterday, they had painted the trim in the dining room and front room, and though there was nothing to be done about the wallpaper, they had glued some of the hanging strips. Jimmy had repaired the torn screens and replaced the warped jambs. There were sheets and towels to be gone through. Mattresses to assess. There were the sails for the catboat to be pulled down from the attic and aired on the lawn. The house was nearly ready for Charlie Levy, for the swims, the sails, and the naps.

"Min?" she called.

"Out here."

Min was sitting on the green bench, her coffee resting at her side.

"What are you doing?"

Min turned to look at her. "Sitting."

Evie pushed out the front door.

"Did you have a nightmare?" Min asked.

"Why?"

"You were shouting."

Evie exhaled. "Just a dream."

Min nodded.

Evie stood a minute longer, her hand on the lilac bough. Min had been right, she thought irrelevantly, looking up into the leaves, the lilac was in glorious bloom. She came down the steps and sat beside Min on the bench. The Polaroid of their mothers and their uncle was lying on the wood in the sun.

Evie bent and picked it up.

"They were happy," Min remarked.

Evie nodded. "They were girls. They were half our age."

Min sipped her coffee. "I loved your mum. I became a shrink because of your mum."

"You're joking."

" 'It's not enough to see the truth. You have to *do* something about it,' she said to me one night drying dishes. I was just thinking about that out here."

Evie shook her head, mystified. "But what did my mother ever *do*?"

Min looked back at her and didn't answer.

"Honestly." Evie reached and picked up the Polaroid again. "Look at these two. We've spent days and days up here, and I realize I don't know anything more about her at all. I remember her up here. But the facts, what she was thinking, what she did and laughed at —" Her voice caught. "It's obvious, absurdly obvious, but I have spent my life in the archives, with records and diaries, births and marriages, deaths — receipts, bills of sale. Travel documents. Life caught in fistfuls of paper, in scraps."

"And you make a plausible life," Min teased her gently. "Remember?"

Evie nodded and crossed her arms. "But I can't seem to make one for her," she said softly.

Min didn't answer.

"That dream I had this morning," Evie said. "It's not the first time, you know. Mum keeps coming to me. And she's angry at me. She never got angry about anything."

"What had you done?" Min turned to look at her.

"I buried her in the graveyard. Instead of out on the rocks."

Min considered this.

"Why there, do you think?"

"I don't know," Evie said. "But she said she told me why."

"And you don't remember?"

Evie turned to Min. "No. I don't."

Min looked at her and stood up from the bench. "Let's walk," she said. "Let's get into the woods. I've got to stretch my old bones."

The forest path plunged away from the

house, veering from the water and deeper into the woods. In here the light cataracted through the tree trunks and hanging branches, dimmed, the sharp pine mixing with the slow creak of the trees, swaying like the masts of ships they would never become. Their roots grew above the pine floor in long, thin shafts like the bones in an old lady's hand.

The two of them walked without speaking, following the blazes cut by their grandfather in the thirties, stopping to clip branches threatening to block the path, inscribing the way forward as they had been taught to do every summer, clearing and cutting for everyone to come. It was close in the woods, and the air was heavy, and Evie started to sweat, her body loosening in the heat as she cleared the brush and walked. A woodpecker worked hard above them, punching the clock, over and over and over, the knock in the air.

The path wound along the backside of the Island and then hugged the water, sticking to the granite coastline all the way back in the direction of the house, ending at a cleared area, now long overgrown, that had been the picnic grounds once, whose meadow ran down to a rim of granite boulders, a cliff at low tide, and a ledge when the water was high facing the Narrows. As children, they had always slowed down right here, wanting to stop, but none of the grandchildren had been allowed to swim off these rocks, though it was a perfect pool below at the right tide. Naturally, this meant that as teenagers every single one of them had gone and dove from the top. The image of her grandmother on these walks moving quickly past these rocks, not looking at the spot, not turning her head, deliberate and intent, rose fully now in Evie's mind.

Evie and Min looked at the spot before them, the picnic tables given to lichen and rot. One big firepit remained, though the rock walls had crumbled. It was high tide. The water sucked gently at the shore. From here they could see the blue ridge of the Camden Hills on the mainland in one direction, and then in the other, the vast empty line of the sea. The tide was turning and the water swelled slowly beneath them, slapping the rock.

"Do you think it's true what Charlie Levy said?" Min asked.

"What part?"

"That this is where Uncle Moss died?"

Evie shook her head. From here she could see through the trees to her grandparents' old dock. Her father had sold the place after his father died. Her grandfather Weld used to stage treasure hunts for all of them in those trees.

Someone across the way was raising the sails of a dinghy.

"The last time Aunt Joan came to see Mum, they fought, you know," Min said softly.

Evie turned. "Is that why you wouldn't let Mum come say goodbye at the end, when Aunt E was dying?"

"Dad wouldn't. He said your mum was too upsetting."

Evie sighed. "She was so hurt not to say goodbye."

They were quiet.

"What was that fight about?"

"This stone she wanted. Mum thought Joan wanted to punish her."

"Punish her?"

"That's what she said," Min answered, slowly, remembering. " 'You want to rub my nose in it, you want to make me pay.' "

"Pay for what?" Evie frowned.

Min shook her head. "I don't know, but your mum was so —"

"What?"

"Fierce." Min shook her head, trying to bring the conversation back. "Fierce, and furious."

"Go on," Evie prodded.

"I think Mum asked why should they be reminded all the time."

"And?"

Min looked at her straight.

" 'Because it happened,' your mother said.

'It happened there. Right there. And I was alive.' "

"What?" Evie's eyes widened.

Min nodded.

Evie looked away, her eyes filling.

Min was quiet.

The dinghy across the Thoroughfare slowly glided from its mooring.

"And it doesn't bother you that we'll never know why?" Evie asked after a little while.

"Honestly?" Min turned to her. "It doesn't. There is never any bottom to a why."

Evie smiled and sniffed, shaking her head. "I'm so tired of it, though. All the quiet and the half-saids, the unsaids. And I used to love uncertainty, the fact that the past was a mystery that could be turned and turned again, that that might lead you to some kind of truth that you hadn't seen, just over the ridge of a hill, just to the side of a page —

"Now I just want an answer, a direction. I want sunlight and words, because I'm stuck in the woods. I wish there was a hand in the sky, a finger pointing, saying, *There. That was the moment. There was the turn. Here is the reason — go back,*" she went on. *"Or go forward.* Right now, everywhere I look I just see the end, the end, the end, and I can't figure how to get past it, how to get *out* of these woods. I can't see what I'm supposed to do *now.*"

"Now, you bury your mum," Min said gently.

Evie's throat closed.

"Bury her in an unmarked grave?"

"It's not unmarked, it just doesn't say her name."

"Here?"

"It's what she wanted."

"One word for a whole life?"

"I thought that was your specialty," Min said quietly.

Evie nodded. The dinghy's sails luffed and stalled as the man at the tiller came about to find the better tack.

"Fuck." She cleared her throat after a moment. "It's all so lonely."

Min glanced over at her. "What is?"

"The past," Evie said.

Min snorted.

"I mean," Evie went on, "do we all mostly just rise up, wave a little, and vanish without anyone seeing?"

"Jesus," Min said. "What did you eat this morning?"

Evie smiled and straightened. "Gruel."

Beside her, Min shook her head. "You miss your mother, Evie, that's all."

The sails had filled and caught, and now the dinghy ran before the wind on a straight tack, free as an arrow shot from its bow. The cousins watched it all the way down the reach in quiet.

"What about Henry?"

"Fuck Henry," said his sister with a wide grin.

"Min."

"Don't worry. I'll talk to Henry."

Evie nodded, and the cousins turned from the picnic grounds and started back through the trees to the house.

When they emerged from the woods Min and Evie stood a minute on the rise, looking across the field to the boathouse and the water beyond. The flag waved from the flagpole, and Jimmy Ames was mowing down at the bottom of the lawn. The wind had shifted and the salt air moved toward them on the hill.

And Charlie Levy was just coming out of the boathouse. Behind him, walking slowly, was Posy, and leaning on her arm was a slight black man.

FORTY-FOUR

"There they are," Charlie said. "See them? Up on the hill."

Reg lifted his hand to shade his eyes. The two women had started toward them.

"Hello," Charlie shouted, walking forward. "Have we missed tea?"

The blond one lifted her hand and waved.

After Len died, when Charlie had told Reg of his father's irrational request and of Charlie's equally irrational promise, Reg had said nothing. When Charlie came back from a weekend in the spring and said he thought he had found the Milton island, had seen the rocks, he didn't say *Yes, of course that's the place, of course those are the people,* he'd only listened. When Charlie called him and said he was going to rent the island at the end of the summer, and would he like to come, Reg hadn't answered.

But when Posy and Charlie had come back from their little impromptu visit the other day and Posy showed him the picture she had taken of the two women standing in front of the house, his breath stopped.

Now, as Len's child walked down the hill toward him, he hadn't any idea why he'd agreed to come. He wanted to see her. And he wanted to turn around. All these years Len had never known. Reg crossed his arms against the angry tangle in his heart. But Len had been happy, Len had shoved off from here and made his own tremendous life, as big as his broad shoulders, his hands.

Oh god, Reg thought. *I am old.*

And this place still hurts.

"Hello, hello again." Charlie closed the distance between the women and themselves.

"Evie," he said. "Min."

The women smiled back at him. The blond one looked over Charlie's shoulder at Reg, and Charlie turned.

"Yes," he said. "I brought my godfather —"

Reg stepped toward them.

"Reg Pauling." He put out his hand to greet the blond one.

Her eyes widened. "Pauling?"

The two women halted, though only for an instant, before the blonde recovered herself and shook Reg's hand.

"You must be Evelyn's," he said politely.

"Her eldest daughter." Min nodded, adding, "And this is my cousin Eve Milton."

Reg looked at her at last. And there was Len staring down at him, a silver-haired woman with his straight-ahead eyes, that upright body, honest and true. But her smile was her mother's.

"Reg Pauling" was all he could manage.

"Mr. Pauling." She smiled and took his hand. "You knew our uncle Moss."

It wasn't a question. He shook her hand. She was studying him.

"I showed him the picture I took of you the other day." Posy squinted up through her hair at Evie and Min proudly. "He wanted to meet you —"

"That's true." Reg nodded at the girl. "Without Posy, I wouldn't have come." His gaze wandered up the hill to the Big House. "I never imagined I'd be here again."

"You've been here before?" Charlie asked, surprised.

"Yes."

"With Dad?" Charlie asked.

"Yes."

"But you didn't sign the guest book," Posy prodded. "You weren't with Granddad."

"No." Reg folded his arms. "No. I'm not in there."

They all stood looking up at the house.

"So?" Min asked into the little quiet. "Tea?"

"Yes," Charlie answered. "Great."

"But Dad."

"Oh, right." Charlie looked at his daughter and nodded. "Actually, Posy was wondering if she could go for a swim first —"

"On the big rocky beach," the girl said to Min. "Around the cove. We sail by it all the time."

Min looked over at Evie. "Gravelly Beach, we call it."

Evie nodded at the girl. "The tide should be good for a swim."

"Uncle Reg?" Posy asked him.

"You go on." Reg shook his head. "I'll wait for you, right up there." He pointed to the green bench.

"Keep inside the line of the beach," Charlie said to his daughter. "And no farther than where you can still touch the bottom."

"Okay." She grinned and started down the hill to find the path.

"Shouldn't someone go with her?" Evie asked.

"She'll be all right. She's on the swim team at home." Charlie took hold of Reg's arm again and they climbed the rest of the lawn up to the house, the others following slowly after.

"Would you keep me company out here?" Reg looked up at Evie as he sank down onto the wooden seat.

"Sure," she said, glancing at Min.

"I'll make the tea," Min offered.

"I'll help," Charlie said.

The screen door slapped behind them. Evie went to sit beside Reg. He leaned back against the bench. The two of them watched

Posy disappear into the trees, her red shirt slipping in and out of the patches of late-afternoon sunlight and shade. The line slapped against the flagpole. The tops of the grasses ruffled. Reg shifted his weight on the hard seat.

"I've tried to write about this place, you know. For years."

"I'd imagine that's true." Evie nodded appreciatively. "Everyone who comes here feels it's heaven."

That breezy comfort. He had almost forgotten.

"You sound like your grandmother."

Evie looked at him, puzzled. "That doesn't entirely sound like a good thing."

"No." He looked away.

"The good thing here," he said after a little, "was your uncle Moss."

Moss, whom he had loved, and hated that he loved, with the blind fervor of the young. Moss, whom he had wanted to punish and wanted the sweetness that would come in forgiving, not taking back what he had said, but taking Moss's hand. Moss, whom Reg had left that night at the beginning of an argument — not the end, never meaning it to be the end.

And why had Moss been out that night? What was he doing, rowing out there in the dark? What could have taken him out onto the water?

"Your uncle," Reg said softly, "was an extraordinary man. And we broke his heart."

"Who did?" Her eyes didn't leave his face. "How?"

He studied the woman beside him, who was staring at him now with the same open need as Mrs. Milton long ago, needing him to tell her who she was — this woman who was mixed and didn't know it, had been protected from that simple single truth all her life. The Milton quiet went on and on and on.

"He couldn't hold all the pieces together."

"All what pieces?"

So, Reg thought. *Begin.*

"Moss had been trying to write a song," he heard himself tell her, "a song — an impossible song about this country that no one could hear yet, a song with new notes, as he called them, and he said to Len and me, 'Come and see, come and see it's possible, come up, come out and ring the bell on that dock down there and stay.' And so we came, Len and I, though I found myself all tangled up and blue from the moment we set foot on that dock down there."

He didn't look at her. He could feel her listening beside him and he went on talking.

He told her about Moss and Evelyn and Dickie, about the fog and the piano. He told her about the morning and the lunch, about the afternoon, and the twilight, and the party and the barn at night. He told her all of that and knew he hadn't told her anything, but saw how she was listening, really listening to his voice, and so he went right on. He told her what her grandmother had told him. Right here on this bench, he said, right *here,* she told me what she had done. What she had said to the Jewish woman. He told her about the boy.

And then he kept telling Evie past her shock, kept right on telling her what her grandfather had also done, and what he'd said to Len when Len had asked him, and how the two of them had carried right on into the party as if they had said nothing to anyone, as if nothing had happened. As if they had done nothing. The two of them had sung songs and cracked lobsters, and the party went on and on, until some of them left. He paused — not telling her, he wouldn't tell her that.

"Some of us went rowing. And by that time I had had enough. That's when I took Moss's song and I tore it in two — there was no such thing as new notes, no matter how much you might wish them — showed it had been nothing but a paper dream. I ripped it. I wanted to punish the dreamer for dreaming he was different — hell, I wanted to punish them *all.* All those people."

He shook his head.

"And by then, we were down there on those rocks at the picnic grounds, and your grandmother, so noble, queenly even still, tried to cast us — Len and me — away, and so I reminded her of what she had told me about that little boy, I had the gall to dare her to say out loud to them what she had said to me, say it in front of them all, so they all knew what she had done, and instead she looked right at me and slapped me across the face."

Evie couldn't move.

"And Len and I got in a boat and rowed away."

Evie drew out her breath.

"And later, that's where they found Moss," he finished.

"At the end of the Island?"

He nodded.

Evie turned away.

Reg stared straight ahead, his arms clasped around his chest, his feet up on the bench, seeing nothing in that moment. Nothing but Moss.

"Why would it be there, then, that my mother wants her ashes buried?"

Slowly, Reg looked at her.

"What do you mean?"

"She wants her ashes put under a stone out there. A stone that says 'Here.' "

Dear God. Reg stared at Joan and Len's child. *My heart. There is no end, is there?* Below the one story, there was this other. A plank dropped down another floor, and there he was. This was why he had come. And something Jimmy had said to him long, long ago, something he'd thought he'd understood, he understood again. *Love does not begin and end the way we seem to think it does. Love is a battle, love is a war; love is a growing up.*

"Just say it," Evie said softly, looking at him. Directly at him. Ready. "I'm so tired of the quiet."

"Do you know, it's yours," she said, after he told her that second story. "Uncle Moss's share of this place — my grandmother has asked us to give to you."

He straightened. "*Moss's* share?"

"She left it up to us," Evie went on, wanting to be truthful, not wanting to let themselves off the hook, "to decide."

"Ha," he said softly. "What would I do with a share in this much sorrow? I have enough of my own."

"I'm sorry we didn't tell you."

"But you have."

"Not right away." She shook her head and gave him a slight, sad smile. "It was the one thing we all could agree on."

"Not telling me?"

"Not even wanting to find you. As if somehow maybe you'd just go away if we didn't do anything."

"Ha," Reg said again. "The old story."

"It wasn't meant to be hurtful. We just didn't want to have to decide."

He raised his eyebrow.

She held his gaze.

"It doesn't matter," he said after a moment. "I don't want any part of it. Not the Island, nor the gesture. Your grandmother's guilty conscience has tangled me up with all the dead."

"But must it only be guilt?" Evie crossed her arms, looking at him. "Couldn't she also mean it clean? Couldn't she have wanted to recognize your friendship? Couldn't she have wanted to do something good?"

"Good," he repeated flatly.

She nodded, frowning. "Isn't it possible? Now, and here?"

He looked at her. "Even if it were possible, why would I want it? Any part of it? You heard what it all is — why would anyone want to hold on to it? Why would you?"

She looked down the lawn. There were no boats on the water. The weather vane on the boathouse roof swung lazily round.

"Because it's mine," she said. "They are mine."

He studied her. "All of it? *All* of them?"

She faced him.

"Yes," she said, understanding. "All of it."

Reg looked at her a moment, and then an enormous open smile broke upon his face. "Well, you can keep your share and have mine, too. I give it right back to you."

She stared back at him and then, caught up in the breeze of his smile, started shaking her head, and finally laughing out loud.

"Who's talking about shares?" Charlie came around the corner of the house, the tea tray in his hands.

FORTY-FIVE

They walked Charlie and Reg and Posy down to the boat, and after they'd waved goodbye, as the boat turned from the dock in a wide circle and sped away toward the mainland, Evie pulled on her mother's thick black boots and picked her way down to the cove for mussels. She hoisted the bucket onto the granite rock covered in barnacles and waded in. The water poured through the hole in the front toe of her boot, making her gasp as she walked deeper, toward the spot where the clumps of mussels lay just below the clear surface.

The water was icy cold around her wrist as she grabbed for the nearest bunch, pulling it straight up, tearing each mussel off the clump, testing it, and turning to toss it into the bucket, where it fell with a clatter. The tide sucked slowly backward as she worked. The lobstermen slowed through the Narrows, the day done, heading with their hauls into town. When she looked up, one of them waved. She lifted her arm in greeting, pushed her hat back off her forehead, and bent again into the water.

"What will you do now?" Reg Pauling had asked her as they shook hands goodbye. "With all of this."

"I don't know," she answered truthfully, looking at him.

He studied her a minute.

"That's a start," he answered. And smiled, releasing her hand.

"I hope you'll consider my offer," Charlie had said. "Pass it along to your cousins."

Min nodded. "It's very generous."

"It would be a way for you to keep all of this." He nodded. "Think about it."

All of this. Evie thought, hearing the echo. Her mother. Her father. Her grandfather. All of them. And a brother. She shook her head. All of them here in this place now. What they had done. And not done. All of it.

We repeat what we don't know, Paul had said that night with Daryl. The night he had shown her the photograph.

And standing in the frigid water, Evie was suddenly and completely filled with a great unreasoning joy that shot through her like a shaft of light. She was here. She knew it now. A Milton. And not. Solid and alive. No more than that.

The empty water before her stretched wide and silent to the sea. She bent again, searching for the mussels with her hands, pulling them from the rocks below the surface and walking them to the big black bucket to drop them in.

When she looked up, a lobster boat coming from the mainland had started to slow as it entered the Narrows. She bent down again.

When she looked up the next time, there he was.

"Paul?" she cried. Seth!" She caught sight of his head moving along the railing. "You're here early!"

"Hi, Mom." He leaned over.

"It's you." Evie put her hand up to shield her eyes, loving the sight of the two of them.

"Hey," Paul said, grinning. "Get out of the water."

Dazed, Evie pulled herself out of the muck and carted the bucket of mussels up the beach to the boathouse. Seth had already started up the lawn to the Big House. Paul was waiting in the grass.

"Hey." Paul pulled her into his arms.

He felt so good against her. She had forgotten how good it felt to be held. She closed her eyes and drank in his smell.

"Hey," he said quietly.

She caught hold of his belt loops but didn't answer.

She had walked all the way to the end, past the end. And she wanted to turn around and come home. She wanted to feel the tug again homeward, the invisible ties. She wanted this man. She wanted Paul. Her mother was dead. Her father was dead. And Len Levy. Dead too. There was no more to know. She was free. She looked up into Paul's face.

There was so much to say to him.

Seth came out of the front door and stood under the lilac, waiting for them to walk up the hill.

"Glad to be here?" she called.

He nodded happily. "My rock collection is still here."

"Of course it's here," Min remarked, coming around the side of the house. "Nothing changes."

She hugged Seth and kissed Paul on the cheek.

"Not exactly," teased Paul, pulling back and looking up at the house. "The place looks terrible."

"Thank you very much," said Evie dryly. "We've been working all week."

"I can see that." He arched his eyebrow.

"Okay, it's a little tired," Evie agreed. "But freshened."

He pulled open the screen door.

"And there *still* isn't one comfortable place to sit," he observed, carrying the bucket of mussels into the kitchen, where he dumped them into the pantry sink.

After dinner, she and Paul walked down to

the dock and stood at the end, holding hands.

"You were right, you know," she said quietly, "about the photograph."

"Evie." He was wary.

She nodded. "And about Pops's business. All of it."

He didn't say anything for a long while.

"I met Reg Pauling today," she began. With him listening beside her, all that she had heard that afternoon, all that had happened, circled round and landed fully. Telling Paul made the full history real. There could be no more quiet.

When she had finished, Paul took her by her shoulders and turned her toward him, pulling her against him.

"What do you want to do?" he asked into her hair.

She shook her head and let herself be held.

"It's not just them here, Paul," she said after a little. "We're all here, you realize. It's my past." She looked up at him. "And yours. Ours. Seth's. This is his, too. This place holds all the pieces."

"Ours?"

"Yes," she said. "Whether we have it or not."

They took Joan's ashes down to the picnic grounds to bury her the following evening. Seth carried the wicker basket with the Scotch and the Dubonnet and the stackable plastic cups from the eighties that had cracked but still held the cold. Anne and Eddie Fenwick had come across, and Paul dug a hole deep enough and wide enough to set Joan's ashes in. Carefully, Evie leaned over and placed the box in the spot, sat back on her heels, and threw a handful of dirt on top. No one spoke. Not even Aunt Anne. Then Seth squatted down beside his mother and slid some dirt on top. Then Paul. And Min. And slowly, very slowly, Anne.

When the hole was halfway filled, Evie set the stone on top. And then she filled in around it with more dirt.

Here.

She stood up.

"I feel like we ought to water it." She smiled at Min, standing across from her.

Paul found Evie's hand and took it in his and slid it into his pocket as they all turned around to lay out cocktails. They had decided to steam the mussels down there, and Evie realized they'd forgotten matches and ran back up to the house to get them, and saw on the windowsill beside them Charlie's spoon where she'd tossed it yesterday. She slid it into her pocket.

When she arrived back down at the picnic grounds, she caught sight of Seth standing apart from the others, facing the water, his hands in his back pockets. Alone.

There had been a day in the winter, an

ordinary school day when she was walking with him after school. She had asked about his day and he had answered. She had tucked her hand in his elbow and they walked loosely in their coats. It hadn't been too cold. They fell into the sturdy silence that always lay between them. And why just then, why that moment was the moment in which she understood quite suddenly her own death, she couldn't say. Simply, she saw how he would miss her. She saw the middle-aged man he would become, struck dumb by the memory of this moment, of her beside him, his mother, asking him about his day. She could see it almost as clearly as if the future were her memory. And her heart pealed for her son, for what was coming that she could not put out her hand and protect him from. She would have done anything to keep him from the hole where there used to be her face turned to his, listening.

And she saw now, though he would miss her, that he could not know her completely, standing behind him on the picnic grounds watching. If he turned to look at her, he wouldn't see *her*. This unknowing would go on and on.

Beyond him stretched the waters of the Narrows, blackening as the sun settled down. Blackening and moving always toward the sea. It was the cocktail hour and the grown-ups were drinking. The tall boy stood with his back to the grown-ups, looking out.

Evie had stood this way countless times. Waiting for the grown-ups to finish their drinks, their talk. Waiting for this part to be over so the next could start. She had a sharp, sudden memory of her mother standing behind her when she was a child, just there, and watching her, leaning against one of the old picnic tables, still well, still young, her low contralto laugh escaping. *Mum.*

And Evie was the grown-up now. She was in the line of grown-ups behind the child. Her eye rested on Joan's stone there at the edge of the clearing. She walked to it and then walked out past it and onto the rocks that stretched beyond.

And there, almost at the end, she leaned and carefully set down Len Levy's spoon.

Slowly, she rose, still facing the water. The evening sun was warm on her skin, and a tern raced the thread of gold stretching across the reach of the sky. The grasses whispered in the small breeze. As they would in fifty years. And she would not be there to hear them. She turned around. Aunt Anne and Uncle Eddie sat on the bench, deep in conversation with Paul. Min had her hands on both hips, her head bent listening. And past them, down the way, Seth crouched and picked up a stone, then stood and hurled it in one long, fluid arc to the sea.

"We vanish," Evie whispered.

ACKNOWLEDGMENTS

I spent most of the years of writing this book writing in the dark, writing my way toward something I wasn't quite sure was possible to see, let alone say. Throughout those years, the guidewire, the voice in that dark — challenging, loving, sustaining — was that of the poet Claudia Rankine. This book would simply not have come to be without our conversations. For her nearly thirty years of friendship, I remain in gratitude, alongside.

Readers give a writer eyes to see. And I am lucky enough to have had great readers through the many stages of this book's becoming: my sister Elinor Blake, Venetia Butterfield, Maud Casey, Katherine Dunbar, Ivan Held, Howard Norman, Linda Parshall, Diana Phillips, Claudia Rankine, Deb Schecter, Shields Sundberg — and Joshua Weiner, my more than reader.

I was inspired by the work of several writers and artists as I wrote this book. Professor Sarah McNamer opened the window on the world of medieval anchoresses for me. Her theory of ancrene marriage underlies Hazel Graves's. The stumble stones that Paul photographs refer to the Stolpersteine project, conceived and carried out by the German artist Gunter Demnig, beginning in 1992 and continuing to this day. A. O. Scott's pitch-perfect phrase "everyday wickedness," describing nineteenth-century slavery, is from his October 6, 2016, review of Nate Parker's movie *The Birth of a Nation* in *The New York Times.* On their first date, Joan quotes two lines of Edna St. Vincent Millay's poem "Recuerdo."

I am so grateful to have been given both time and place by the Virginia Center for the Creative Arts and the Corporation of Yaddo while I was at work on this book, and I will be forever grateful to my cousins Harold Janeway and George Montgomery for their tenacity in finding a way to hold on to the island, and for their continued stewardship, carrying it forward.

Anna Worrall and Ellen Coughtrey at the Gernert Company have been always at the ready with answers and perspective, for which I am so appreciative. Caroline Bleeke, Bethany Reis, and Conor Mintzer at Flatiron Books prove that one can mix editorial rigor with great good humor, and I thank them from the bottom of my heart for all their attention.

And finally, for the two without whom my books would never be made — Stephanie Cabot, agent, warrior, friend, who listens deeply, and exhorts fiercely, and Amy Einhorn, who never once shies from asking every possible question of a scene or a sentence, but whose patient faith in the work girds me and spurs me on — there are not thanks enough.

ABOUT THE AUTHOR

Sarah Blake is the author of the novels *Grange House* and the *New York Times* bestseller *The Postmistress*. She lives in Washington, D.C., with her husband and two sons.